DARK INSTINCTS

DARK INSTINCTS

THE PHOENIX PACK SERIES

SUZANNE WRIGHT

Published by Montlake Romance, Seattle

www.apub.com

Amazon, the Amazon logo, and Montlake Romance are trademarks of Amazon.com, Inc., or its affiliates.

ISBN-13: 9781477828748
ISBN-10: 1477828745

Cover design by Jason Blackburn

Library of Congress Control Number: 2014955194

Printed in the United States of America

For: _____

(Please sign your name)

Thanks so much for buying this book.

Seriously, you're amazing.

CHAPTER OИE

Opening your eyes to find that you're upside down can't be good, can it?

Through the cobwebs clouding her mind, Roni Axton realized that it wasn't just *she* who was upside down. The car had toppled over.

Well, that sucked. Clearly the fuck-up fairy had made an appearance.

Strangely, Roni felt no rush of panic, no fear. And despite that she was pretty sure her head was bleeding, there was no pain. There was only a feeling of weightlessness. Even the fact that her wolf was frantic didn't disturb Roni in this dreamlike moment.

Her brain distantly registered that the car kept leaning sideways, as if something was repeatedly pulling at it. But it was the various sounds that penetrated her mental fog: low moans, a phone ringing, a child crying, and strange voices arguing.

Sensing that the ringtone and the moans were coming from her left, Roni turned her head to find a male wolf shifter in the driver's seat, eyes closed. *Tao.* Huh. Odd that the Phoenix Pack's Head Enforcer was with her. She rarely hung out with anyone outside her pack. In truth, Roni counted very few people as friends.

Sadly, she was very like her brother, Alpha of their recently formed Mercury Pack, in that she found social situations uncomfortable. In Nick's case, it was because he didn't like most people. In Roni's case, it was because most people didn't like her. Even when she was a kid, she'd found making friends difficult, especially at school. It was kind of hard to fit in when you were a tomboy with a higher IQ than that of your teachers.

It probably made things worse that she didn't "get" her own gender. But she just didn't see the appeal behind constantly gossiping, shopping endlessly, asking deep personal questions, or having different lotions for different body parts.

Roni was more comfortable around guys, particularly her two brothers and her Beta male, Derren. Men didn't care that she wasn't a people pleaser, or that she didn't know how to satisfy social niceties, or that she preferred chocolate to living beings of any species. The only female she thought of as a friend was her Alpha female, Shaya, who—

A succession of memories suddenly hit Roni hard: Shaya singing to a toddler in the backseat, Tao playfully grumbling about the noise, the sound of tires screeching, an unexpected impact to the side of the vehicle, a blow to her head that made everything go black.

Grasping onto those threads of memory, Roni remembered how she had escorted Shaya—who was two months pregnant—on a daytrip to the zoo with Shaya's godson, Kye, and his bodyguard, Tao. The Alpha female had wanted a break from Nick and his extreme overprotectiveness. It was during the drive back to Phoenix Pack territory when a car had slammed into theirs.

And then she'd gone and passed out like a girl. How embarrassing.

Blinking rapidly, she swiveled her head as much as she could. She might have winced at the sharp pain that lanced through her neck if she hadn't been distracted by the fact that Shaya wasn't in the backseat beside a still crying Kye. That was when Roni noticed the female body sprawled like a ragdoll on the grass a few feet away from the vehicle. *Fuck.*

The dreamy quality of the moment disappeared as reality crashed into Roni, and her wolf howled in fear and rage. One word dominated Roni's thoughts: out. She had to get out.

Forcing a reassuring smile for Kye, who was squirming in his safety seat and reaching for her, she crooned, "It's okay, little man. Give me a second and I'll—"

The car wobbled sideways again. "This crowbar is a piece of shit!" griped an unfamiliar voice.

"Hurry up!" ordered an equally unfamiliar voice. "We don't have much time before someone shows up. Coleman and Axton will sense through their pack links that something's wrong with their wolves."

The stranger was right about that: she could sense Nick's rage and anxiety. She could also sense Shaya through the pack link; she was alive, but unconscious.

"I can't open the door, it's jammed."

A growl. "Move. I'll do it." The car swayed again. That was when Roni understood what was happening. Someone was yanking at one of the rear door handles, trying desperately to get inside . . . trying to get to . . . Kye. *Oh, the fuck no.*

Roni awkwardly fought to unclip her seatbelt. It eventually snapped open, and she cried out at the sensation of falling onto a bed of glass. She shelved the pain as she righted herself and began to slide toward the backseat on her stomach. "Tao, wake up! Get to Shaya!" All she received was another moan.

"Shit! One of them is awake!" Rather than flee, the strangers redoubled their efforts to open the door.

Their efforts paid off.

Just as the top half of Roni's body wriggled through the gap between the seats, the door was yanked open, and a tanned arm reached for Kye.

Roni unsheathed her claws and sliced at the limb, causing it to flinch away. Her wolf growled her approval. "I swear to God, if any part of your body tries to touch him again, you won't get it back intact!"

"You bitch!" Two arms reached inside this time, both sporting claws of their own. One set of claws acted as a barricade between her and Kye while the other set cut through the belt that secured Kye's safety seat to the car. In a lightning fast motion, the arms caught him before he and his seat could crash to the floor.

Roni stabbed her claws through one long, muscled arm, past bone, and all the way into the rear seat, pinning the arm in place. He howled in pain, hurling obscenities at her. Well, she *had* warned him; he'd chosen to ignore her, so there was really no need for that kind of language.

With her free hand, Roni worked Kye's belt open. His little body toppled out of the safety seat and onto her outstretched arm. If her wolf could have sighed in relief, she would have. Curling her arm around him, Roni pulled him tight against her body. Only then did she release the would-be-kidnapper from the grip of her claws.

She was feeling a hint of victory when someone grabbed a fistful of her hair from behind. Turning her head as much as the strong grip would allow, she realized that the second male had come at her from the other side of the car. He held her in place by her hair while the other shifter frantically struggled to drag Kye from her grasp. The toddler was wailing and clinging tightly to her, absolutely terrified. When two large hands got a firm grip on his little waist, panic bit into her. No, no, she wouldn't let—

Her hair was suddenly released, and a scream mingled with a familiar animal growl that meant Shaya had shifted into her wolf form. While Roni was relieved that she was conscious again, Roni did not want the pregnant female, ruthless or not, fighting a male shifter.

"Don't shift!" the other male yelled. "A car's coming!"

Footsteps thudded along the ground as the two males disappeared from view. Seconds later, there was the sound of a car speeding away, and a heavy sense of relief surged through Roni.

Hearing Shaya's wolf pawing at the vehicle, whining, Roni assured her, "We're fine." But, really, Roni wasn't fine. Her head was now throbbing, her body ached in several places, and her vision was starting to blur and darken. If she passed out again, she would be seriously unhappy. Dominant females did *not* pass out, dammit.

"Roni, how badly are you guys hurt?" Shaya asked, back in her human form.

Roni wanted to answer her Alpha female; wanted to ask Shaya how injured she was and reassure her that everything would be fine. But Roni's mouth suddenly felt stuffed with cotton, her chest felt tight, and black spots were dancing before her eyes. Worse, there was a horrible ringing sound that made her head pound even more.

She opened her mouth to speak, but nothing came out. Her wolf began to panic once more as the ringing became deafening and a dark veil fell over Roni's vision.

Then there was only blackness.

CHAPTER TWO⊙

Sitting on an infirmary bed at Phoenix Pack territory half an hour later, Roni flinched as Grace used tweezers to pluck yet another piece of glass from Roni's palms. Silently, she seethed, annoyed with herself. She—a dominant female who could outrun both her brothers, who could defeat a wolf while in her human form, and who had once almost made an Alpha male sob when she beat him at an arm wrestle—had passed out. Twice.

What was wrong with the world?

"Done," announced Grace. "I have to thank you again for what you did. I dread to think what could have happened to Kye if you hadn't kept him safe."

Roni took her strawberry-flavored lollipop out of her mouth only long enough to respond with: "It's what anyone would have done."

"Don't try to play it down. Protecting another with your life is never a small thing." The brunette squinted as she studied the cut on Roni's forehead. "That's looking better." It was the benefit of having a shifter's accelerated healing rate. "What about the rest of you?"

"Healing." Shifters weren't easy to hurt, which was largely why Roni had escaped the incident with just cuts, bruising, and a cracked rib. Thankfully, Tao and Kye had walked away with only a few scrapes and bruises. As Roni was almost fully healed, she'd turned down the Phoenix Alpha female's offer to heal her. Shaya, however, had needed Taryn's healing skills since she'd had a broken leg and a fractured wrist. Shaya had been fine by the time Nick and Derren arrived. Even so, Nick had freaked out—Roni had been able to hear him from the infirmary yelling and growling in the kitchen while Shaya desperately tried to calm him.

The sound of heavy footsteps striding through the network of tunnels pulled Roni from her thoughts. Seconds later, a tall, dark, broad-shouldered vow of sexual satisfaction entered the room. Two pools of electric blue locked on Roni, and the atmosphere snapped taut as awareness throbbed between them—it was always the same.

Marcus Fuller exuded sex, confidence, and a raw compelling charisma that commanded the attention of those around him . . . which was why the Phoenix Pack enforcer was the star of her every X-rated fantasy. He deserved an Oscar for his performances.

Anger and concern radiating from him, he demanded, "How badly are you hurt?"

As if he had every right, he ate up her personal space, skimming his gaze over her body. His dark scent slammed into her, and Roni once again found herself wishing she could bottle it. Earthy, spicy, and with a hint of leather, it never failed to tantalize both her and her wolf.

Determined not to let him see the effect he had on her, Roni shrugged nonchalantly at the six feet of pure male power staring down at her. "I'm fine."

Clearly unconvinced, he turned to Grace for an answer. The traitor sang like a canary before reassuring him, "She should be fully healed within the hour. Now I have to get back to my daughter. She'll wake up any minute now."

Once Grace was gone, Marcus's gaze again locked on Roni. Anger no longer spilled from him, but she knew it was still there, simmering beneath the surface. Maybe everyone else was fooled by his laid-back manner, but Roni knew this wolf was as dark and dangerous as any predator.

The minute she'd met the enforcer, her wolf had sensed the danger in him, the intensity, and the power . . . and then she'd practically rolled over, panting, totally in lust. It was just so . . . undignified.

"How are you feeling, gorgeous?"

Honestly? Like she wanted to gouge out those piercing eyes that took in her every move and expression. It was the stare of a hunter, and Roni very much felt like prey when he focused his full attention on her. It was something he did a lot, which only intensified the sexual tension that pulsed between them—a tension that was unexpected considering she was nothing like the foo-foo attention-whores he dated.

In the beginning, his flirtatious nature had irritated Roni, despite her powerful elemental attraction to him. Sublimely gorgeous people intimidated her, particularly the typical "smooth talkers"—guys who had mastered the art of making females part from their clothes using speech alone. Roni liked a male with substance, not a player who was incapable of loyalty and relied on his looks to get him what he wanted in life.

However, her irritation had soon given way to curiosity, because the more time she'd spent around Marcus Fuller, the more she'd come to realize that the whole "smooth talker" act was nothing but that—an act. He hid behind the charm and the carefree attitude he projected to the world.

This guy cared very deeply about *something*. There was so much anger there, packed in ice . . . yet no one seemed to see it. No one seemed to see that this was a wolf with secrets.

He was also a wolf who was annoyingly impossible to dislike. She envied how he could so easily put people at ease. Envied his ability to mix well with others and be instantly accepted into any social circle. Roni, by contrast, had a tendency to make people feel uncomfortable with how out of tune she was with others' feelings and their social expectations.

At his impatient expression, she removed the lollipop from her mouth. "I told you, I'm fine." She slid off the bed, and he cupped her elbow to support her as she stood upright. The simple skin-to-skin contact caused her nerve endings to spark to life. She pulled her arm free from his grasp. "I can walk perfectly fine without help."

He flashed her that infamous smile designed to make any female blush and trip over herself to get to him. "You should know that prim, schoolteacher tone totally turns me on."

Roni would have been immune to that smile if it were sleazy. But no. It was a confident, mischievous, "I could make you come all night long" smile. She would bet that he damn well could. Not that she'd ever find out. Marcus flirted with her, sure, but only because he didn't know any other form of communication. And besides, tomboys weren't his type.

Her wolf loved having all that raw sexuality and seductive charm directed at her, and she constantly pushed at Roni to act on her desire for him. It was taxing, since she and her wolf were so extremely close that the line that existed between her human side and animal side was blurred. It didn't mean she didn't have full control of her wolf, but it did mean that her wolf's emotions could intrude on Roni's human responses, and vice versa. As such, her wolf's desire for him fed her own, making it even more difficult to resist him.

Frustrated with him, herself, and her wolf, Roni stuffed her lollipop back into her mouth and offered him a blank look, refusing to let him see that she was no more resistant to his charm than every other female.

Nothing. The female in front of him didn't give him the slightest reaction, which only made Marcus smile wider.

He had been on his way home from visiting his sister when he'd received a call from his Beta male, Dante, to let him know about the crash. He'd broken all kinds of laws as he drove like a maniac to get home and see for himself that everyone was fine, that Roni was fine. And now here she was, doing that aloof act again. And he was nothing short of amused.

Initially, Roni's apparent indifference had galled him. He hadn't liked that he seemed to be the only one feeling this intense attraction that bordered on magnetism. Every time they were in close proximity, the air crackled with sexual energy, and he hadn't believed that could possibly be a one-way street. Yet, while the idea of skimming his hands over that seductively lithe body and having those supple legs wrapped around his waist often consumed his thoughts, Roni always appeared totally unmoved. It made no sense.

Rather than push, Marcus had backed off. He'd watched her closely, studied her every reaction to him, and soon come to realize that she wasn't so indifferent to him after all. Why she was fighting their attraction, he didn't know. He wanted to find out, to figure *her* out, so he could find a chink in her armor. Roni was incredibly intelligent; in order to seduce her physically, he'd need to first seduce her mentally.

The problem was that Roni was a difficult person to get to know. She held back from everyone outside her own tiny circle of people: her brothers, her Beta, and Shaya. But his old Alpha hadn't labeled Marcus "that stubborn little shit" for nothing.

When Marcus wanted something, he would hunt it down until it was his. And he wanted Roni Axton in his bed; he wanted to explore this thing between them until all that sexual tension had burned out, until she no longer dominated his thoughts and fantasies.

There was just something about her . . .

Maybe it was that she was so very different from the females he usually dated. Maybe it was that she didn't stroke his ego, didn't fawn all over him in that way he'd come to find distasteful. Or maybe it was just that she had the most luscious ass he'd ever seen.

It was probably all three.

Of course, it could also be that in addition to being truly delectable and exceptionally capable, Roni Axton was downright lethal. He'd seen her fight when a large number of prejudiced humans had invaded his territory; she'd been sharp, fast, and merciless. And it had been damn hot.

His wolf liked Roni too—particularly her vicious streak. Just like Marcus, he craved this dominant female to the extent that she was quickly becoming an obsession. Her indifferent, elusive air was a challenge that drew both man and wolf.

Ordinarily, Marcus would avoid pursuing a female so hard for fear that it would give them the impression he wanted more than casual sex. But he had no worry that Roni would become attached. She didn't seem any better at emotional intimacy than he was. She wouldn't be clingy or needy or play the kind of games he'd tired of long ago.

Considering he didn't have the best reputation, he'd expected her Alpha female to warn him away from Roni. Shaya had seen the way he looked at her mate's sister, knew exactly how much he wanted her. Although Shaya was a close friend of his, she was also very protective of Roni. But surprisingly enough, Shaya appeared to be trying to set them up. And Taryn appeared to be helping.

It was a good thing, really, since he doubted any warnings would have kept him away—particularly since an element of possessiveness had been there from the very beginning. The new feeling had come as a surprise, had even spooked Marcus slightly. But really, could he expect to be this determined to have someone and *not* be possessive on some level? Once the sexual tension was alleviated, he figured the possessiveness would surely fade.

Ignoring Roni's cautioning look, he placed his hand on her lower back and guided her forward. "Sweetheart, you heard Grace; there's a chance you could have a concussion. There's nothing wrong with taking it easy and accepting a little help." She sniffed haughtily at him. Not that he'd expect anything different from a dominant female shifter. Their independent streak was a mile long. Still, he forced a put-upon sigh just to needle her.

She dumped her lollipop stick in the trash can. "Did you know that a sigh actually acts as a physiological reset button?"

Marcus had noticed that Roni did that a lot—abruptly blurted out a completely useless fact. At first, he'd thought she did it in an awkward effort to be friendly and make conversation. But he'd quickly come to realize that she did it to make people go away. It worked. They immediately pegged her as someone weird and boring, or they would feel as uncomfortable as she did.

Marcus wasn't going to fall for that. Besides, all that intelligence was kind of hot, especially when she slapped him down with it. "Really?" He fingered the ends of her long ash-blonde hair, admiring the natural, loose curls. "Your brain is like a sponge. I like that."

Roni cast him an odd look. Why was he looking at her like she was . . . interesting? Roni wasn't interesting. And now he was smiling at her again. Her wolf wanted to lick every inch of him, which was just downright annoying and pathetic. Okay, Roni could agree with the animal that this male who had fought at her side was strong, solid, and deliciously dominant. But allow Marcus to sense that? Not a chance.

She straightened her spine and gave him a dismissive wave of the hand. "Why don't you go play with Betty Boop?"

"Betty Boop?" he chuckled. "If you're talking about Zara—"

Oh, yeah, she was talking about Zara. Curvaceous, elegant, graceful, she was everything that Roni wasn't.

"—that's very much over." There was only one female he wanted.

"Well, then . . . go play with the treat you're presently sampling and—"

"You have the cutest nose." He lightly tapped it with his finger.

Unbalanced by his unexpected compliment, Roni shrugged past him and marched off. And her nose was *not* cute. Marcus easily caught up to her and stayed at her side as they advanced through the network of tunnels that made up Phoenix Pack territory. The ancient cave dwelling had been modernized beautifully, and the Alpha female had long ago branded it "Bedrock." For that reason, Taryn often referred to her mate as "Flintstone."

Roni had only taken a single step into the crowded living area when suddenly a dainty body wrapped itself around her. Roni puffed various streaks of blonde hair out of her mouth.

"You stopped them from taking my son," sniffled Taryn. "Thank you." It was the third time she'd thanked her.

Trey stood behind Taryn. His arctic-blue eyes were wild, manic, and his large form was fairly vibrating with anger. "If you ever need anything—*anything*—it's yours." The rest of the Phoenix Pack nodded their agreement.

"We're in your debt," said Greta, though she didn't look happy about it. In fact, her gaze narrowed dangerously as it took in how closely Marcus stood to Roni.

Trey's somewhat neurotic grandmother was very possessive of "her boys"—those being Trey, Tao, Dante, and the four enforcers, Marcus, Trick, Ryan, and Dominic. As she was convinced that every unmated female was determined to claim one of them, she made a distinct effort to frighten them away. Of course it hadn't worked with Taryn or the Beta female, Jaime, but Greta persisted in trying to make their lives difficult.

Not sure what to do with all the attention or the body still curled around her, Roni threw Marcus a pleading look.

Smiling, Marcus took pity on Roni, satisfied that she had looked to *him* for help. "Taryn, why don't you find Roni a place to sit? She could have a concussion."

"Of course." Taryn led Roni over to the armchair on which Dominic sat. "Move it."

"I'm hurt too, remember," he griped. "None of you even praised me for intervening between two fighting wolves."

Taryn rolled her eyes. "It's not exactly uncommon for Trick and Ryan to get carried away when sparring. You only had a few bruises. Most of them had healed by the time you walked through the door."

"A few bruises?" Dominic rose from the chair. "My chest had so many black patches, I looked like a Holstein cow. And I don't care what you say, I had internal bleeding."

Trick shook his head at Dominic. "Could you be any more dramatic?" When he noticed that Marcus had perched himself on the arm of Roni's chair, Trick arched a brow. Then a taunting smirk surfaced, deepening the claw marks on Trick's cheek. For as long as Marcus could remember, Trick's favorite pastime was tormenting people. He thoroughly enjoyed teasing Marcus about Roni's apparent indifference to him. Asshole.

Roni stiffened as Shaya, Nick, and Derren entered the room. She suspected a lecture from her brother. Within seconds, Nick's nostrils flared as he scented her. Then his eyes fixed on Roni and darkened. Yep, a lecture was coming.

Nick strode toward Roni, his face like thunder. "I can't believe you put Shaya in danger like that!" Rage seeped from him—a rage so acute that it seemed to thicken the air. It made Roni jump to her feet and put her wolf on high alert. The Phoenix wolves immediately gathered behind her, and Marcus pressed up against her side. *What was that all about?*

Shaya, ever the peacemaker, smoothly slipped in front of her mate. "Now, Nick . . ."

He glared at Roni over Shaya's shoulder. "Do you think I give out orders purely for fun, is that it?"

"No, I don't," replied Roni calmly. Her cool demeanor seemed to further anger him.

"Shaya's your Alpha female, she's pregnant with your niece or nephew, and you put them in danger!"

"That's not fair, Nick," reprimanded Shaya. "She had no way of knowing what would happen. I asked her to get me out of there; I needed to *breathe*. You're so overprotective, it's suffocating!"

Roni knew exactly how that felt, as she dealt with it daily from her mother and Nick. She loved and respected her brother, trusted him more than anyone. But his level of overprotectiveness made her feel hurt, offended, and stifled. There was nothing more insulting or disrespectful to a dominant female than treating her like she couldn't take care of herself.

"I'm just trying to keep you and our baby safe. And you *would* have been safe if Roni hadn't disobeyed me!"

"And what makes your word have more weight than Shaya's?" Roni felt compelled to ask.

"Excuse me?" Nick's voice was quiet, menacing. Derren winced.

"You can't call her Alpha female and then undermine her by dishing out orders to everyone that effectively give her no say in her own life."

"That isn't what I'm doing!"

"It is." Shaya's voice was gentle but firm. "I was ready to explode; that's not good for either me or the baby."

"It's better than you being in a car accident!"

Roni barely refrained from growling in irritation. "You're not listening to a word either me or Shaya is saying." Nick advanced on her, teeth bared.

Marcus blocked the Alpha's path. *"Don't* touch her."

Nick drew back, glowering. "What does this have to do with you? With *any* of you?"

"Roni protected my son," said Trey. "She now has the loyalty of everyone in this pack. They'll protect her from anything, including you."

"I'd never hurt her! She's my sister!"

Roni sighed. Shifter male posturing was boring as shit. "I can speak for myself."

Mouth curved into a small smile, Marcus very briefly glanced at Roni over his shoulder. "Yes you can, sweetheart, but your brother's not interested in listening to you right now. Blaming Roni isn't fair, Axton, and you know it."

Nick's eyes flared with anger. "If she hadn't—"

"Do you really want to play the 'if' game?" Marcus tilted his head. "Okay, if you hadn't ignored your mate's anxiety—and don't tell me you didn't know exactly how she was feeling through your mating link—Shaya wouldn't have needed a break. The shifters who crashed into her car are the ones who deserve your anger."

That seemed to take some of the hot air out of Nick. Shaya slipped her arms around him, whispering soothingly into his ear.

When he focused on Roni again, his breathing had regulated and his rage was under control. But she knew that it was only the feel and scent of his mate that was keeping him composed.

"Roni was hurt too," Shaya gently pointed out.

"What?" Nick studied Roni intently. When his eyes settled on the cut on her forehead, a low growl escaped him. Great, he was back to being overprotective. She preferred his anger.

"But thankfully," Taryn quickly injected, "everyone is fine. So how about we all sit?"

It was as Roni returned to her seat and Marcus again settled on the arm of the chair that she noticed someone was missing. "Where's Tao?"

Marcus bent his head, putting his mouth to her ear, and almost groaned as her scent furled around him. God help him, she smelled like warm cinnamon rolls and pumpkin pie. "He's off somewhere, feeling sorry for himself. It nicked his pride that he blacked out and couldn't help."

Roni could understand that. "Why are you hovering over me?" And why, exactly, had he shielded her from Nick? Standing at her side or her back was one thing, but shielding her was a whole other thing. She shooed him away, but he simply smiled.

"Do I make you nervous or something?"

Yes. "Of course not."

"Then you won't have a problem with me staying right here." He smiled when she narrowed her eyes and shrugged.

"Grace said you had some pretty bad cuts." Derren came over and lifted Roni's hands to examine them. Instinctively, Marcus draped his arm over the back of the chair and laid a possessive hand on her shoulder. Noting the move, the Beta smiled in amusement.

Roni pulled free of Derren's grip. "Really, I'm fine."

"You sure *look* fine." Dominic smiled flirtatiously. "I swear, I could fall madly in bed with you." Jaime laughed while everyone else groaned. The unfairly hot blond had a habit of dishing out cheesy chat-up lines that should act more as repellents than seductive techniques. Yet, they somehow worked for him.

Roni believed in giving as good as she got, so she did what she always did: she hit him with another line. "Are you a water fountain, Dominic? Because you're getting me wet."

He scowled petulantly. "Stop that! Saying cheesy lines is my thing!"

Marcus sighed. "You have issues, Dom." The jerk would also have a black eye if he kept that shit up with Roni.

A cute giggle was followed by the entrance of Kye and Lydia, one of the mated females. "Ro!"

Roni smiled as Kye dashed toward her, holding out a small truck. Kye Coleman was the cutest thing ever and, shockingly, seemed to like her. Ordinarily, Roni wasn't good with anything that breathed. "Wow, is this yours?"

He nodded proudly, but when she went to touch the toy, he frowned. "Mine." He'd obviously inherited his dad's possessive streak. With his other hand, he held out a second truck. But when she moved to grab it, he frowned again. "Mine."

Oooookay.

"It's his new favorite word," said Jaime, stroking the chubby ginger cat that was batting at her long sable braid. "That and 'no.' Aren't you going to share with Roni?"

"No."

Jaime sighed. "See what I mean?"

Marcus smiled as Kye babbled to Roni, who nodded along and babbled back. She always softened with Kye and gave him her full attention. Marcus had noticed her occasionally sneak him little treats when she thought no one was looking.

Trey, a statue of barely contained rage, took position in the center of the room with Taryn at his side. She placed a comforting hand on his arm, and some of the tension left him. "I'd like to talk about what happened, Roni. We've already heard Shaya and Tao's versions. We need to piece everything together."

Everyone turned to Roni expectantly, and the massive amount of attention made her tense. To her surprise, Marcus gave her shoulder a supportive squeeze. "The car seemed to come out of nowhere, but it was no accident. I blacked out"—she said through her teeth—"and when I woke up, two males were struggling to open the door to get to Kye. I didn't get a good look at them."

"That's okay," Taryn assured her. "Shaya was able to give us detailed descriptions."

Dante leaned forward. "Did they say what they wanted with him?"

Roni shook her head. "They didn't use names or mention any packs. But I know they weren't wolves."

"They were jackals." It was always a jolt to hear the mostly mute and grumpy-looking Ryan speak. "I smelled their blood in the car."

"Jackals?" Greta sneered. "Sly little things."

"I've never met a jackal that I liked," said Gabe, Jaime's brother. His mate, Hope, made a sound of agreement. "They're into just about every illegal activity there is and live by their own set of rules. Those rules are basically: One, don't get caught. And two, if caught, deny everything."

Lydia's baby-faced mate, Cam, spoke. "I think the nearest jackal pack is at least three hours away."

"Yes, and we need to talk to them." Trey made "talk" sound more like "destroy."

Grace stood with baby Lilah in her arms. "How about I take the kids into the kitchen? I know they won't understand what's being said, but . . ."

"I was just about to suggest that." Taryn shot Grace a grateful smile.

"I'll come too." Taking Kye's hand, Lydia led him out of the room with promises of cookies.

Once they were gone, Marcus looked at Trey. "We don't know for sure that the jackals in question are from their pack."

Trey shrugged carelessly. "We won't know until we ask." What worried Marcus was that Trey might be too livid to bother "asking" anyone and would simply attack. He knew how temperamental his Alpha could be. If it hadn't been for Taryn's ability to keep him calm, Trey would have already exploded by now. His wolf, who had a tendency to turn feral when enraged, had to be going insane.

"Have any of you ever had problems with jackals?" asked Jaime. "We know from Popeye's experience that even a jilted girlfriend can bring problems."

Dante frowned at his nickname, though it suited him due to his muscular frame. "Glory wasn't my girlfriend; she was a one-night stand."

"A one-night stand who tried to kill me, so I think we can agree that I have a point."

Trey ran his gaze around the room, one brow raised questioningly. Everybody shook their heads.

Dominic spoke from where he was leaning against the wall. "All right, so what are the usual reasons for abducting someone?"

Dante puffed out a long breath. "Ransom, extortion, or blackmail. Other times, the reason is much darker, like traffick—" When Taryn held up her hand, he gently said, "We have to consider everything. The jackals had a motive, and we need to find it."

Trey turned to Rhett, Grace's mate and the resident computer geek. "I want you to find everything you can on the nearest jackal pack."

Rhett nodded. "I'll have the info by morning."

Nick spoke to Trey. "I'll be joining you on the hunt."

"Me too." Shaya shot Nick a cautioning glare that told him he wasn't going to stop her.

Nick chuckled humorlessly. "No fucking way."

His mate sat upright, glowering. "Those bastards put our pup in danger and tried to snatch my godson!"

"Exactly. The jackals will have known who you are, Shay—they thought nothing of risking my pregnant mate's life, just as they thought nothing of trying to kidnap Taryn and Trey's son. That speaks of some seriously unbalanced individuals."

Taryn gave a flat smile. "We're not exactly known as warm, fuzzy people."

Shaya gawked at her best friend. "I do hope you're not siding with him on this, because I'd hate to have to cut off your beautiful hair. There's no chance I'm staying behind." A chorus of "Nor am I" quickly followed.

"There's something we need to consider," Dante interrupted. "Unbalanced or not, the jackals will have known that the instincts of both Alpha pairs would be to group together their Betas and enforcers and track them down as one unit, thus leaving the rest of the two packs—particularly the pups—vulnerable. Maybe that's part of whatever neurotic plan they have, maybe it isn't. But leaving either of the packs vulnerable isn't a good idea in any case."

Taryn nodded. "He's right. We need to be smart about this."

Trey swept his gaze around the room. "Dante, Marcus, Ryan—I want you three to join us on the hunt."

Jaime opened her mouth to argue, but Trey silenced her with a raised hand. "I'm not leaving you behind because you're not useful, Jaime. I need you to stay behind *because* you're useful. You're our Beta female, you've passed the exact same training that all of the enforcers went through, and there isn't a person in this world who could sneak up on you. Tao, Trick, and Dominic are tough fuckers. I need to know my son and my pack are surrounded by tough fuckers when I'm not here."

Mollified, Jaime nodded. Dante clasped her hand in his, earning himself a hiss from the ginger cat.

Seeing that her mate was about to speak, Shaya piped up, "Don't order me to stay—"

"I'm not."

She searched Nick's face, her expression suspicious. "You're not?"

"Not if you feel you need to do this." He exchanged an odd look with Derren, who responded with an almost imperceptible nod.

Derren's dark eyes found Shaya. "What about the meeting you have tomorrow?" As the shifter mediator for the California packs, Shaya helped packs solve disputes in the hope that wars could be avoided. Nick had been pressuring her to temporarily give up the position while she was pregnant, and she had agreed to do so after this particular situation had been resolved.

Shaya cursed under her breath. "I'll see if another mediator can cover for me."

"With such short notice?" Derren's look said "doubtful."

Nick tucked her red curls behind her ear. "Do the two parties still seem close to war?" If Shaya's worried expression was anything to go by, the answer was yes. "Don't worry, baby. If you can't come along, it doesn't mean you're neglecting the people you love. We understand you're needed elsewhere."

Clearly feeling guilty at the idea of trying to escape the meeting, finally, Shaya sighed. "Fine. I'll go to the meeting." Nick and Derren exchanged discreetly smug smiles. "But don't think I don't know that you guys just played me, *or* that you won't pay for it later." Their smug looks vanished.

"So who *are* you involving in the hunt?" Taryn asked Nick.

"I can't afford to involve many of my wolves; I want Shay to be well protected. I'll take Derren and Eli. That way, Roni, Jesse, Bracken, and Zander can—"

"Wait a cocking, fucking second," snapped Roni, shuffling forward in her seat. "You can't shove me in the backseat."

"I need to be sure that Shay and our pack is safe, and I trust you to ensure that."

"Bullshit. You're trying to protect me."

"Come on, Roni, you have to admit you don't work well with others."

"What's that supposed to mean?" She knew her eyes had briefly flashed wolf. The animal had no more tolerance for this crap than she did.

"Although you're unfailingly loyal, you don't have any interest in leading or following anyone. You do 'Roni's thing,' and you reject anything that interferes with it. On the one hand, it's what makes you a good enforcer—you don't follow me blindly, you think for yourself. But it means you're awful at working with people.

"Taking part in a hunt is serious. The tracking, the chase, the capture—all of it takes skill, patience, perseverance, and teamwork. We need to be able to rely on each other. It's likely that we'll be splitting up several times to stretch our resources. Four times you've left Bracken in the dust when I partnered you with him on something."

"Because he drags his heels. Assign me a better partner and we won't have a problem."

"You could team up with Marcus." At Taryn's suggestion, everyone looked at her curiously.

Roni had to have misheard her. "What's that now?"

Taryn shrugged casually . . . a little *too* casually. "You'll do better working alongside someone who's of equal status. Anyone with a higher position will rub you the wrong way. You won't have that problem with Marcus." She shot a meaningful glance at the male hand resting possessively on Roni's shoulder—a move that her wolf hadn't bristled at, which spoke volumes about her comfort level around him.

"She's *not* working with the man-slut," spat Nick.

"Personally, I think it's a good idea." Shaya wasn't affected by Nick's glower. "If she has a partner who matches her well, you won't have to worry that she'll wander off. Marcus won't smother her, but he won't let her walk all over him either."

"Roni isn't going!" Nick growled warningly when Roni opened her mouth to argue. "No. As your Alpha, the decision is ultimately mine."

Not liking Nick's high-handedness, Marcus decided it was well past time he intervened. He could respect that Nick was Roni's Alpha and that it was only natural that he would want to protect his sister, but stifling someone as dominant as Roni would be a huge mistake. "You must understand why he's asking you to stay behind, Roni."

She rounded on Marcus. "Who the fuck asked for your opinion?"

"I'm just saying, his decision makes sense."

She might have clawed his face off, but then she saw the calculating glint in his eyes. Deciding to play along, she asked, "How did you reach that messed-up conclusion?"

"He's taking Derren and Eli with him—his Beta *and* his Head Enforcer. That will mean the three most dominant males in the pack are concentrating on something other than Shaya's well-being." Marcus let that sink in for a minute and watched in satisfaction as Nick frowned thoughtfully. If anything would have the Alpha rethinking his decision, it was the idea of how that decision would affect his pregnant mate.

"Although you didn't follow his order today and things sort of went tits-up," continued Marcus, "I'm guessing you'll be sure not to do it again." Nick's frown deepened, and Marcus knew the guy was considering how she did "Roni's thing" and would in fact disobey his orders if she felt it was in Shaya's best interests. "You should be flattered he's placed that trust in you."

Roni liked how this wolf's mind worked. She stifled a smile as she watched an array of emotions flash across Nick's face. He was clearly struggling with this.

Finally Nick released a heavy breath. "All right, Roni, you can come. I'll have Eli stay behind. Maybe you and Marcus *would* make a good team, considering he can be just as cunning as you."

Trey gave him a mockingly sympathetic look. "You might be an Alpha, but your family will always find a way to play you."

Nick just scowled at him. "I'm glad you find this amusing, Sailor Joe."

It seemed to take a few seconds for the words to sink in, but when they did, Trey spun to snarl at Taryn, *"You told him?"*

She laughed awkwardly. "Of course I didn't tell him." In a low voice, she added, "I told Shaya."

While everyone else was doing their best to hide their amusement, Dante was outright laughing his ass off. "A sailor, huh? Didn't think that role-play was your thing."

Trey glowered at him. "Something funny, Fireman Sam?"

The laughing abruptly stopped, and Dante rounded on his mate. *"You told him?"*

Jaime spluttered. "No!" She cleared her throat. "Although I did tell Taryn. And Shaya. And Roni. But I didn't tell them about the time you—" A large hand clapped over her mouth.

"About the time you . . . ?" prodded Nick, grinning.

Wincing as Jaime bit into his palm, Dante shook his head. "Nothing."

Shaya snorted at Nick. "You're not really one to judge, considering you—" Her words were cut off as he kissed her hard.

Squirming under Trey's glower, Taryn obviously felt it was time to change the subject because she turned to Nick, Roni, and Derren. "Good to have you along for the ride. We'll expect to see you all here tomorrow, bright and early."

CHAPTER THREE

B right and early the next day, Roni strolled into her pack's main lodge to have breakfast. The huge hunting lodge had been revamped to Nick's specifications and was absolutely amazing: the luxurious furniture and the spacious open-plan living area, dining room, and kitchen were all done in a rustic tone. Each of the lodges scattered around their territory was similar but on a much smaller scale. Roni loved her lodge, loved the homey feel to it, and loved that it was the most isolated of all the lodges on the land.

What she *didn't* love was that her maternal aunt was seated at the long table. Petite with caramel-blonde hair and devious eyes, Janice refused to age gracefully and insisted on short skirts, high heels, heaps of makeup, and thin vests that broadcasted her cleavage . . . as if dressing up like a twenty-year-old fought the aging process or something. Hey, that was fine—to each their own. What wasn't fine was that Janice liked to demean others to make herself feel better, and Roni was her favorite target.

"Good morning, Roni," said her aunt with forced affection.

Roni's greeting was just as falsely sweet. "Hope you slept well, Janice."

Kathy placed a plate piled with pancakes on the table, which her brother Eli practically attacked. "Roni, eat. You need to build up your strength." Kathy talked as if Roni was an undernourished eight-year-old. They had one of those mother-daughter relationships where they loved each other but got along better when they had plenty of space between them. Like oceans, for example.

Roni took a seat between Derren and Eli and loaded her plate with food. Nick's dog, Bruce, appeared at her side, panting and licking his muzzle. As Roni did every morning, she threw him a slice of bacon.

"When are you going to play a proper role within the pack, Roni? It's not usual for females to have the position of enforcer." Janice didn't hide her disapproval.

"It's more common than you'd think." Shaya shot Roni a supportive smile. "And Roni's excellent at her job."

"Hmm. I suppose I shouldn't be surprised that you have a masculine role. You never grew out of the tomboy phase. It just supports my theory that you want a sex change."

A shocked laugh burst out of Zander, almost causing the hot, sharp-witted blond to choke on his coffee. An equally stunned Kent patted his back while Caleb gawped at Janice.

"Some people just don't like skirts or dresses." Shaya's agitation had leaked into her voice.

"Hmm." Janice sniffed. "Maybe it's for the best, since you can't flaunt what you don't have."

Roni shoved a forkful of scrambled eggs into her mouth to stop herself from cursing at her aunt. Roni was happy with who she was, with her style, with how she lived her life. She wasn't going to defend any of that to anyone.

Kathy had always tried to change her, like Roni needed "fixing" or something. When she was younger, Kathy had forced her to spend time with Janice's daughters, hoping their girly ways would rub off on Roni. The bitches had teased and taunted her rather than played with her. So she'd pulled all the heads off their Barbie dolls. As such, her aunt thought of her as a lost cause.

"She makes an effort for special occasions." Kathy was defending her? That was new. "When it was Nick and Shaya's mating ceremony, she even wore a little makeup. She looked so different. So pretty." Ah, a backhanded compliment.

At that moment, Jesse entered the kitchen with his on-and-off girlfriend, Eliza. She was an attorney who represented shifters, which might have made her likeable if she wasn't so shallow and superficial. Seriously, the female was like a coin—two-faced, mostly without value, and regularly handled by different people. She had even slept with a few of the Phoenix wolves, including Marcus. Roni refused to believe that the feeling in the pit of her stomach was jealousy.

According to Jaime, Eliza had originally tried befriending the Beta female, Jaime, and Taryn, dropping hints about moving to their pack. When Taryn had made it crystal clear that it wouldn't happen, Eliza had moved on to Jesse. Roni suspected the female was now trying to get herself a place in the Mercury Pack.

Sitting at the table, Eliza pleasantly smiled at everyone . . . except Roni, who received a snarl. Yeah, the dislike was mutual, since Eliza was threatened by Roni's level of dominance. In addition, she believed Roni took no pride in her appearance—unlike Eliza, who was primped from head to toe—and was also whimsical and easily distracted. In actuality, Roni was an extremely focused person . . . when she found the subject stimulating. If she didn't, she had a tendency to either zone out or walk away.

"I'm guessing by your good mood that you won the case yesterday," said Kathy.

Eliza smiled cockily. "Of course."

"Do you get many cases?" asked Janice.

"Unfortunately, more and more shifters are needing representation against humans. The anti-shifter groups continue to make false accusations that are so far-fetched and unfounded that they're thrown out of court. But it always has the desired effect—causing upset to the shifter community."

Janice shook her head. "After what happened not so long ago, you'd think the extremists would keep a low profile."

The extremists had previously appealed to have restrictive laws put into place that would confine shifters to their territories, place them on a register like child molesters, and prevent them from mating with humans—claiming they were too violent and dangerous. The extremists' opinions, however, were discredited and dismissed when evidence came to light that these supposedly nonviolent groups were part of a hunting preserve that allowed humans to hunt, torture, and kill shifters.

"They've begun a campaign to restrict shifter couples to having only one child in order to stop the population from becoming too widespread." Eliza turned to Nick. "You had a major run-in with extremists in Arizona, didn't you?"

Nick tensed. He'd been targeted by the leader of the group, who had been a guard in the shifter juvenile prison where Nick had been incarcerated. The guard had had a grudge against Nick for badly injuring him when he'd fought off the bastard's attempts to abuse him, and he'd wanted to make him pay.

It was no secret that the extremists had targeted Nick, but there was still speculation on how it had ended, considering those particular extremists had mysteriously "disappeared." That speculation was what kept other extremists at bay. Openly admitting that they had in fact destroyed the humans when they invaded Phoenix Pack territory would be dumb. "Yes. That's why we moved here. Thankfully, that was the end of it." It wasn't a lie, but neither was it the full truth.

Noticing Shaya massaging her stomach, Janice patted her hand. "I really hope you'll reconsider letting me deliver your baby."

Shaya cleared her throat. "Thanks again for the offer, but I really want Grace to be there."

"Wouldn't you rather have family helping? I know we don't

know each other well, but we have plenty of time to fix that before the birth."

Kathy nodded in agreement. "Janice is very good at what she does, Shaya."

"I'm sure she is. But I want Grace."

Kathy smiled sweetly. "If that's your decision, honey, I'll respect it."

Roni almost snorted at the barefaced lie. Irritatingly, Kathy believed she had the right to interfere in her children's lives for no other reason than that she was their mother—and that extended to her son's mate. The amazingly stubborn woman was extremely good at getting her own way, and she never gave up without a fight.

"You know, Shaya, I was thinking," began Kathy, still smiling sweetly, "you should come shopping with Janice and me later on today. It would be lovely for us all to spend some time together."

Nick went to object, but Shaya beat him to it. "Thanks, but I have things to do."

"What a shame." Janice looked at Roni. "What about you, Roni?"

Eliza's smile was a little hateful. "You could certainly do with a makeover."

Roni's wolf growled, but it wasn't because of Eliza's comment—the female was so insignificant, she wasn't even a blip on her radar. No, her wolf was alert and watchful because she had picked up a very familiar, very yummy scent. Startled, Roni swerved to find Marcus entering the kitchen with Bracken.

Instantly, every female in the room perked up.

First, Shaya got to her feet and gave Marcus a friendly kiss on the cheek, which made Nick growl. Then Kathy urged Marcus into a chair opposite Roni, and placed a huge plate of bacon and eggs in front of him. Eliza vainly adjusted her hair and clothes. To Roni's horror, her *mated* aunt plastered a flirtatious smile on her face.

Marcus gave Roni a wide smile—and that strange, almost electric connection between them instantly snapped into place, making his wolf growl in satisfaction. "Hey there, gorgeous." He almost laughed at the "Quiet, you're boring me" logo on her camo-green T-shirt. Her wardrobe seemed to consist mostly of clothing that was branded with antisocial wording.

Roni scowled at the endearment. "What are you doing here?"

Refraining from laughing—Marcus wouldn't have thought it was possible for a scowl to be cute—he took a moment to greet the males . . . even Zander, who he didn't like for the simple reason that he suspected Zander had a thing for *his* pretty little wolf.

Leaning toward Marcus, the unfamiliar female said, "I'm Janice, Kathy's sister."

Marcus smiled. "Good to meet you. I'm Marcus."

"I take it you're a friend of Nick's?"

"No." Nick's expression screamed "outsider." "He's a Phoenix Pack enforcer."

"Nice to see you again, Marcus," purred Eliza.

Roni would have expected Jesse to be annoyed by his girl-friend's flirtatious tone, but he didn't appear to care. Then again, it was hard to tell, really, since the surly enforcer was mostly expressionless. Eliza and Janice blushed at the greeting smile that Marcus gave them. It seemed he had a way with all females, no matter their age.

"You didn't answer Roni's question: Why are you here?" grumbled Nick. He stabbed his fork hard into his bacon, and Roni had the feeling he wished it was Marcus. Shaya rolled her eyes, well accustomed to her mate's antisocial ways. His body was practically fused to hers in an extremely possessive gesture. Roni would have expected it to make the Alpha female bristle, but Shaya seemed to like it, as if it made her feel safe and treasured. Roni couldn't imagine her own mate treasuring her. The poor guy would most likely feel he'd drawn the short straw.

"I was returning something to Bracken." In truth, Marcus wanted to get an early start on his "breakdown Roni's defenses" plan.

"If you mean his newest Call of Duty game, it's about time." Roni refilled her coffee mug. "I had it completed within a week."

Bracken nodded, his playful eyes twinkling. "She's freakishly good. Plays like a guy."

"Fights like a guy too," chuckled Eli. Although he wasn't as broad or tall as Nick, her little brother was still powerfully built. He was also totally ruthless.

"You should know, since all you two ever do is use each other as punching bags," muttered Kathy.

Eliza snorted in disgust. "Maybe she should have *been* a guy."

"She's always been a tomboy," Kathy told Marcus. "Hated pink, dolls, and ballet. She liked blue, cars, and playing football with the boys. And she's always been so competitive, *hates* to lose."

Nick pushed his empty plate aside. "Dad taught us that second best didn't count."

"Yes, and he was very proud that his little girl was so 'tough.' Had he been alive at the time, I'm sure he would have laughed when the school called me in because she'd beat up an older boy who'd tried picking on Eli—that was when she was nine." Kathy shook her head. "To add to that, Eli had then beat up the kid's friend when he moved to intervene. And that wasn't the last incident of that nature."

Eli shared a conspiratorial smile with his sister. "Ah, the good old days."

"They both fought all the time," continued Kathy. "And I don't just mean physically. Always played pranks on each other merely for their own entertainment. But Roni would never let anyone else hurt him, just as Eli would never let anyone else give her trouble. I'd like to say they're much more mature nowadays, but the fights and the pranks are still ongoing."

"Yeah, we do find unbelievable joy in irritating each other," admitted Eli with a grin.

Kathy glanced briefly at Roni. "I know she doesn't look it, Marcus, but she's so intelligent it's intimidating." Yet another backhanded compliment—her mother was on a roll. "She never cared that she was smart, though. She was never interested in anything academic. She wanted to play sports, learn combat, and speed around town in cars that didn't belong to her."

"Okay, can we stop talking about me now?" Roni really didn't need to be reminded that she wasn't the daughter her mother had ordered. So she liked physical activities and could be competitive, so what? Roni thought it was unfair that smart people were stereotyped as nerdy, obsessive, socially awkward people— although, to be honest, she did have the socially awkward thing down.

Eliza seemed pleased by Roni's discomfort. "You sure you're not a guy trapped in a female body?"

Roni cocked her head. "Did you know that an ingredient of many lipsticks is crushed parasitic beetles?" At once, Eliza and Janice brought their fingers to their lipstick-covered mouths, looking queasy. What fun. Noticing that Marcus's gaze was intensely focused on her, she frowned. "What?"

Marcus shrugged. "I like looking at you."

Roni knew her cheeks were burning. "Eat shit, Fuller." He actually chuckled. Nick, however, went ramrod straight in his seat and growled warningly, clearly intent on protecting his sister's virtue—not that Roni had any virtue to protect. A dark look from Shaya made him return his attention to his breakfast.

Satisfied that he'd knocked Roni off balance, Marcus smiled inwardly. He liked seeing her flustered, just as he liked learning more about her. She interested him with the many different facets of her personality. What he didn't like was that Kathy, Janice, and Eliza seemed to enjoy putting her down.

Rather amusingly, she did her best to ignore him as they continued eating. But Marcus knew just how to get her attention. "Since we're teamed up for the hunting party, you might as well ride to my territory with me."

That made Roni pause with her mug halfway to her mouth. "Ride with you?" Be alone with the guy who had fucked her within an inch of her life during her dream last night? Nah.

Marcus barely refrained from laughing at the panic on her face. She could deny it all she wanted, but he made her nervous. "Yeah, ride with me."

Again Nick went rigid. But then he jerked, wincing. "Ow! What was that for?" he growled at Shaya.

She sniffed. "I'm hormonal, I don't need a reason."

"There's really no need," Roni assured Marcus. "I can ride with Nick and Derren."

Marcus cocked his head. "You *could*, but it makes sense for us to ride together." He arched a brow. "Unless, of course, you don't think you can work with a partner after all . . . ?"

Well, he had her there, didn't he? She was determined to prove her brother's "Roni can't work with anyone" theory wrong. She didn't like to lose or to lack at anything.

"Think of it as spending the day with an insanely hot wolf." Kent was eyeing Marcus appreciatively. Caleb gave his boyfriend a mock scowl and then flicked scrambled egg at him. Kent wiped it away, sending him a look that promised retribution.

Over the rim of his coffee mug, Marcus's gaze locked on Roni. "You know, if I didn't know any better, I'd think you find it hard to be around me." His smile turned teasing. "Maybe you're not so indifferent to me after all."

Derren—who had long ago guessed at Roni's attraction to Marcus—began choking on his food, clearly amused at her expense. So she let him choke. Sadly, Caleb came to his rescue, patting his back hard.

Shaya gave Marcus a pitying look. "Sorry to break it to you, but Roni is totally immune to you." Supportive words, but there was a strange glint in Shaya's eyes that made Roni wary. "She'll be absolutely fine in your company. Won't you, Roni?"

And what else could she say but . . . "Of course."

"I have to wonder if the girl's a lesbian." Janice's words had everyone gaping at her. "If she doesn't respond to a male as gorgeous as Marcus, she's not going to respond to any male."

"I hope you're wrong, Janice," said Marcus, "because it would be a bummer for the male population." When Roni shot him another scowl, he held up his hands in a placatory gesture. The entire time Roni ate, she kept that scowl focused on him, and it took everything he had not to laugh. Ten minutes later, they were ready to leave, and she was still scowling.

"Are you sure you won't come shopping with us later, Roni, and get yourself a makeover?" asked Janice.

Pissed, Marcus stated, "Roni's fine as she is. Come on, gorgeous, let's go."

Taken aback that Marcus had defended her—again—Roni proceeded to leave the room, not pausing when she heard Eli yelling her name, coughing and balking.

Then there was her mother's voice. "Oh, Roni, tell me you didn't put salt in his coffee again!"

"He deserved it!" shouted Roni. The bastard had put whipped cream in her brand-new trainers. She knew he'd expected her to massively retaliate, which was why she'd gone for one of her many simple pranks. He wouldn't have been on guard for something small.

Smiling in amusement, Marcus followed Roni as she left the kitchen, watching that pert little ass swaying, unintentionally provocative. Shaya stopped him at the front door, but she didn't speak until Roni was out of hearing range.

"People look at Roni and see how self-reliant and reserved she is, and they automatically think she's cold and detached. The truth is that girl has a real depth of emotion, and she's a total softie for those she loves, even if she doesn't seem it . . . Admittedly, she's pretty ambivalent toward the rest of the population. She's been through a lot. Be careful with her."

He had been since the beginning, because he'd sensed the vulnerability behind that core of steel. Roni was unbelievably tough in some ways, yet soft and unsure in others. She reminded him of a solitary wild animal—she liked freedom and space, was distrustful and wary of strangers, and took time and patience to get close to. Good thing he was patient. "I won't hurt her, Shaya."

The redhead studied him for a minute. "Good, because I'd hate to have to mess up that pretty face."

He chuckled. "Roni could do that herself." Reaching his pack's Toyota Highlander, Marcus noticed Derren and Nick heading to their SUV, intending to follow. Inside the Toyota, Marcus smiled at the sight of Roni buckled into the passenger seat, *still* scowling. "It has to be said, you're a constant ray of sunshine, Roni."

She narrowed her eyes. "Bite me, Fuller."

He laughed, switching on the engine and reversing out of the parking space. "It's tempting, sweetheart, it's tempting."

As they journeyed to Phoenix Pack territory, Roni couldn't help but repeatedly glance at the wolf beside her. Marcus drove the way he did everything else—smoothly, confidently, in total control. He'd certainly been that way during her X-rated dream. She almost blushed as snippets of it sailed through her mind: his tongue curling around her nipple, his teeth nipping the curve of her breast, his hand sliding into her—

"Do you like being an enforcer?"

The question yanked her out of her fantasy—dammit. "Yes." In truth, no. As Nick had pointed out, Roni had no interest in leading or following. She was a very individualistic person; she was happy to just *be*, and liked to do what she wanted without confining commitments.

"Lying's a sin, sweetheart."

Her head whipped around to face him. "Why do you think I'm lying?"

"You have a tell."

She'd have to be careful with this one; he was incredibly perceptive. "What's my tell?"

"If I told you that, it would help you lie better. So tell me, why be an enforcer if you don't like it?"

Because she owed Nick. He was just thirteen when he'd been sent to a juvenile prison for not only killing a human who had attempted to rape her but also for badly maiming two others who had tried holding Nick back. Most of his teenage life had been spent in a place where torturing, raping, and killing shifters was considered the norm for the human guards.

Of course, on an intellectual level she acknowledged that she wasn't directly responsible for any of that, but it didn't erase the guilt. It didn't erase the fact that, at just thirteen years old, Nick had killed for her and spent much of his young life in prison. Killing someone left its mark, and it had marked him; she'd seen it every time she visited him at that fucked-up place.

How did a person repay something like that? All he'd asked of her was that she be an enforcer within his pack. How could she refuse?

Shortly after the incident that led to Nick's imprisonment, she had started disappearing in her wolf form for long periods of time. People had mistaken it for trauma, thought she couldn't face what had happened to her and that she was left fragile and scarred. It was that very reason why Nick had offered her the position of enforcer: he thought giving her a sense of purpose would stop her from doing it. He was trying to get her "settled."

What he didn't understand was that she wasn't fragile or traumatized at all. Oh, sure, she carried emotional scars, but who didn't? One thing Roni had never done was feel sorry for herself. No. What right would she have to do that when, although the attack had been horrible, others had been through far worse?

How could she make it all about her when her family had also been badly affected by what happened? No, Roni had come to accept the attack—she was nobody's victim. But dealing with the aftermath . . . that had been a different story.

Remaining in her wolf form had been her escape from the oppressing guilt, the pitying looks, the shame, the sense of powerlessness, and the backlash of the attack. She'd battled against rumors, false versions of the incident, and utter hatred from those in her pack who blamed her for Nick being incarcerated.

The Alpha's son, Nolan, had caused her the most trouble—pissed that the incident had drawn the attention of the anti-shifter extremists. The extremists had dug into his father's background, searching for dirt . . . and they'd found some.

Apparently the Alpha, Mitchell, hadn't left his old pack voluntarily; he'd been banished from it after being "under suspicion" of laundering drug money. In shifter-speak, that meant the rumor was true but the pack hadn't wanted to make a fuss or it would have brought attention to them, so they'd banished him instead. This hadn't washed down well with the pack he was currently acting as Alpha for, and dissention had quickly spread.

Shortly after Roni and her family had left the pack, Mitchell had been challenged and lost his position. It was rumored that the new Alpha had driven him, his mate, and Nolan out.

At that time in her life, it had felt like everything was falling apart around her. Even that, however, wouldn't have led her to escape in her wolf form so much. No, what she had really needed an escape from was her family. The worst part of the aftermath was that they'd wanted to coddle and cocoon her. Her mother had become even more overbearing than ever before, literally monitoring every step Roni made. That overprotectiveness had never been good for her. It hadn't helped her move on; it had prolonged that sense of helplessness she'd felt during the attack—a feeling no dominant female dealt with well. It had stifled Roni and driven her wolf insane.

She'd wanted to move away, make a fresh start, but how could she leave them? How could she leave a brother who'd killed for her, a mother who'd already been through so much—including losing her mate—and a brother who'd been forced to fight in an illegal fighting ring as a direct result of their family transferring to another pack? A transfer they had made *for her.* She couldn't leave; she owed them all.

There had been only one other way to escape: remain in her wolf form. So whenever it got to be too much, that was what she did. Still, baring her soul wasn't on her list of things to do, so she simply responded to Marcus's question with: "I get bored easily; this job keeps me occupied."

Marcus wasn't buying that for a minute. But he decided not to push. Too much pressure would make Roni shut down rather than open up. "What else do you do to fight boredom?"

She sighed. "Look, I'm not good at this, okay."

He flicked her a confused glance. "Good at what?"

"Small talk. Useless chatting." To punctuate that, she shoved a lollipop into her mouth.

"I'm not making small talk. I want to know you."

The lollipop was suddenly yanked from her mouth. "Hey!"

"You don't get to do that with me, sweetheart." His voice had been gentle, but it was also pure steel.

"Do what?"

"Evade conversation." The female was almost constantly sucking on lollipops, and the sight was erotic enough to risk him coming in his jeans. He'd noticed that she did it when she was uncomfortable or anxious. He'd also seen her do it before battle, as if it helped her focus and think better. But she also did it when she didn't want to talk. "It's hard to get to know someone when the conversation is one-sided."

"Why do you want to know me?"

He almost laughed at the confusion on her face. "You . . . intrigue me."

He constantly surprised her, and she wasn't sure if she liked it or not. Her wolf liked it a lot, liked his impish streak and wanted to play. "But . . . why?"

"I've watched you closely enough to learn things about you. You're tough, smart, capable, and loyal—all qualities I like and admire. But for a very confident person, you hold back a lot and can be pretty uncomfortable in social situations. You can also be very self-conscious at times." It was sort of cute.

She couldn't help feeling a little defensive. Faking a delighted smile, she said, "Ooh, are we reeling off flaws today? If that's the case, I've got some for you, Romeo."

"Yeah?" He wondered if she even realized she was playing with him. Unlike her wolf, Roni was often too serious to play. "Hit me with them."

"You come across as a smooth, easygoing flirt who's all soft and cuddly. But in reality, you're a dangerous fucker who's simply very prettily dressed in charm."

"Flattery won't get you anywhere, Roni. Except, of course, if it's accompanied by a kiss."

"You hide behind the charm, flirt constantly, flash that bad-boy smile at everyone, and live by the 'no strings attached' rule. But in doing that, you've reduced yourself to a sex toy." It made her wonder why and what he wanted to hide. Pain? Guilt? Shame? Loss? The guy was a puzzle, and that appealed to the curious side of her nature.

Her disappointment in him sat heavy in the air, and Marcus didn't like it. "Well, if your opinion of me is really that low, it's going to make my goal to seduce you even harder."

She did a double take. "What's that now?"

"Come on, Roni, are you really going to pretend you didn't sense me circling you the past few months?"

She spluttered. "That was just you being your usual flirtatious self. I'm not your type. You like foo-foo females."

"Foo-foo?" he chuckled.

"High maintenance, perfect appearance, devoted to spas, needs constant reinforcement, and—*oh my God*—do they ever shut up?" She'd expected him to be offended, but he laughed. "You lay on all that charm, give them your attention, but you don't commit to them. You just kind of . . . float around them."

He couldn't argue with that. All of Marcus's past relationships could be described as short, simple, and sweet. But he wasn't equipped to cope with serious relationships or to meet the emotional needs of others. How could he be, when the only example of love he'd ever known was warped and twisted?

Roni shrugged. "But maybe you're just saving your commitment for your true mate."

In truth, the thought of mating absolutely terrified Marcus; his upbringing had showed him that a mating could be more of a trap than a blessing. Having watched as Trey, Dante, and Shaya found their mates, he'd seen how the bond could be something worth protecting. It might have given him hope if it weren't for the conversation he'd had many years ago with the Seer within his sister's pack.

She'd told him that he would find his mate, had even described her to him—small, slim, strawberry-blonde hair, and huge baby blue eyes. But the Seer had also told him other things about her, about what lay ahead for them, and the thought of having a future like that scared the shit out of him.

Returning his focus to the conversation, he said, "My problem is that I seem to attract clingy females." He wasn't lying; it was indeed one of his problems, just not the main one. "I'm not just talking physically clingy, I mean—"

"Females who need constant attention, get extremely jealous, take everything personally, and don't accept responsibility for their own feelings—their unhappiness, rage, and envy are all your fault?"

So damn astute. "Yeah."

"Zara was a classic example. It's not all that shocking that you attract them, since they tend to go for strong, competent people. You know, their needy behavior can be a form of control and manipulation in some situations; it forces their partner to be their caretaker and address their every need."

He really liked that brain. "You think I'm strong and competent?" She simply rolled her eyes. "So, we've established why I keep things casual. What about you?" She didn't respond to his prodding. Pulling up outside Phoenix Pack territory, he turned his gaze on her as he waited for whoever was on security duty to open the gates. "Talk to me, Roni. It's not so bad to 'share.' Try it. You might like it."

It was the dare in his eyes that made her elaborate. "I'm not good at relationships because I don't know how to be an 'us.' I'm not touchy-feely, and I'm not the type to feed a male ego by lavishing it with affection." Male shifters liked to feel needed, and Roni didn't like to need anyone. "When a guy senses how dominant I am, his instinct is to try to control me in order to firmly establish that he's 'the boss.' Let's just hope my mate won't do that."

What Roni didn't say was that she was probably too messed up to even sense her mate. Jaime had once said her mother had compared the mating bond to a frequency. If it were jammed by things such as doubts or fears, it couldn't be picked up. Roni knew she was guarded, knew she found it extremely difficult to let people in. How could someone who struggled to allow new people into their life sense their mate?

"It stands to reason that your mate can accept you as you are," Marcus assured her as he drove through the now open gates, nodding at Cam in greeting. "That he'll want you any way he can have you." Although that wasn't always a good thing; his parents' mating was proof of that. But he wasn't interested in darkening the mood, so he flashed her another smile. "And that delectable ass of yours totally makes up for your flaws."

She didn't know whether to scowl or thank him for the compliment. She went with scowling, which only made him laugh again. She was sure she'd never met anyone who liked to laugh as much as Marcus did. Yet despite that playfulness, there was an intensity about him that even her extremely dominant brothers couldn't match.

"My wolf wants to take a bite out of it. I can't say I'm opposed to the idea."

"I'm not your type," she again insisted.

He didn't deny it, since it would only insult her intelligence. "And yet, I want nothing more than to strip you naked and have my wicked way with you." She said nothing. "You want me as much as I want you, Roni." Pulling up inside the concealed parking area, he leaned toward her. Raw need pulsed between them, drawing him closer. "Admit it. I dare you."

Roni was no coward. Had he been anyone else, she would have admitted the truth. But with Marcus, she couldn't be sure that this wasn't just harmless flirting. Uncomfortable with the way he was staring at her, she dropped her gaze . . . and it fell on his mouth. That sinful, erotic mouth that was most likely very talented.

When she didn't answer, Marcus persisted. "Roni?"

"Sorry, I was just imagining putting a moth in your mouth. I saw it in a movie once."

He had to smile. "I'll let you live in denial a little longer," he told her as they exited the car—though if her brother and Beta weren't due to enter the lot any second, he might not have been so well behaved. "But we both know that's exactly what you're doing."

She huffed as she followed him up the steps that were carved into the cliff face. "You're very sure of yourself, aren't you?"

Opening the door wide, he smiled at her. "You like that."

He was right, she did.

CHAPTER FOUR

---◈---

Once the entire hunting party was seated at the kitchen table, Rhett began to talk as he flicked through a pile of papers.

"Okay, the name of the jackal pack in question is Glacier, consisting of only ten jackals. The Alpha is Sergio Milano and, according to the proverbial paper trail, he's thirty-five years old, lives above the successful Italian restaurant he owns—which is basically the only territory his pack has—and drives a silver Lexus. He's also unmated, very powerful, and the most respected of the jackal shifters. Dig deeper, and you'll find that he also enjoys smuggling weapons for humans in his free time."

"Sounds delightful," commented Taryn dryly, glancing at the photo of said Alpha that was being passed around. "Do you recognize him?" she asked Trey.

He studied it closely. "Never seen him before." He was surprisingly composed, but Roni had to wonder if it was more of a case of "the calm before the storm."

"Any indication that he's into human trafficking?" asked Dante. Rhett shook his head, which seemed to relax Taryn slightly.

Roni frowned as Marcus draped an arm over the back of her chair and loomed over her shoulder as she studied the photograph of Sergio. The close proximity had her senses going haywire, particularly as his mouth was near the sensitive spot behind her ear, and his hot breath was playing havoc with it.

"Well then, let's go talk to Sergio."

Marcus stiffened. His Alpha had sounded so cool and casual, but there was no way Marcus was buying that act. Trey had a notorious temper and his wolf tended to turn feral during battles. "We can't go in there, all guns blazing."

"I know."

"You're too calm. I don't like it."

Trey's smile was feral. "Of course I am. I'm about to watch the life bleed out of the fucker who's responsible for trying to kidnap Kye."

Now that was the Trey they all knew and loved.

Dante sighed. "We don't know that this guy's responsible. From what we can tell, there's no motive."

"The Alpha sent a request for an alliance via the pack web five months ago," Rhett informed them. Pack webs were social networks. Much like a person's Facebook page might be exclusive to their friends—enabling only them to write on their "wall"— a pack's web page was exclusive to the members of their pack. And just as people could check out the Facebook profiles of others, packs were able to view the profiles of other packs through the webs. "Maybe Sergio wasn't too happy that we turned it down."

Ryan snorted. "Everyone turns down alliances with jackals. Even other jackals don't like to mix with them because they know how untrustworthy their own kind are."

"It seems a little extreme to go after your kid because you didn't agree to an alliance," said Derren.

"My thoughts exactly." Taryn folded her arms across her chest. "Like Ryan said, jackals hardly ever make alliances. They wouldn't have been surprised that we turned it down."

"But they may have felt offended," Nick pointed out. "Alphas have been known to do shocking things when their pride's hurt. Still, I'd have to agree that going after Kye seems extreme in this context."

"Then I guess we need to visit the Glacier Pack and have a *chat*"—Marcus gave Trey a pointed look—"with the Alpha."

Trey rose from his seat, his grin a little . . . well, evil. "No time like the present."

When they pulled up outside Milano's Italian restaurant in the Phoenix Pack's gold, nine-seater Chevrolet Tahoe a few hours later, Roni was beyond irritated. She had spent the entire time crushed between Marcus and the window, and he'd spent the entire time teasing her with subtle touches, sensual smiles, and hot stares— the asshole.

"Smells good." Marcus inhaled the aroma seeping from the restaurant. "Do you think they'll let us eat here afterward? I'm hungry."

Roni snorted. "You're always hungry." She'd never known anyone to eat so much yet look so good.

Marcus smiled as Roni slipped a lollipop into her mouth. It made her look deceptively vulnerable and harmless . . . like a little schoolgirl.

"This could get bad," warned Ryan, indicating the large amount of various breeds of shifters that were hanging around. "Jackals or not, these shifters could decide to involve themselves in any fight that might ensue."

Nick's expression said, "Who gives a fuck?" The guy was out for blood after what happened to his mate, and Marcus didn't blame him. If anyone fucked with his mate, even though he wasn't looking forward to finding her, they'd be dead before they could blink.

It almost looked choreographed the way Nick, Trey, and Taryn entered through the double doors with Derren and Dante closely covering them as Roni, Marcus, and Ryan covered the rear. It was a sight that caught everyone's attention, and every single shifter in the establishment froze.

Nick and Trey both had reputations for being powerful and dangerous. To see both presenting a united front while looking, well, rabid . . . it spelled trouble. The fact that they were accompanied by six very dominant wolves, all of whom looked supremely pissed, made for an extremely intimidating sight that had everyone's "fight or flight" instinct kicking in.

Within seconds, the establishment was empty, apart from several jackals. Marcus immediately spotted Sergio Milano. He was seated at a corner table, surrounded by people who were most likely pack members. The surprisingly slight Alpha looked indifferent, but his amber eyes gleamed with irritation as the wolves came to stand before him. "Do you have any idea who I am?"

Nick smiled. "Of course. That's why we're here."

"Displaying such bold, antagonistic behavior toward an Alpha on their territory isn't a wise move."

Trey arched a brow. "Neither is attempting to kidnap my son." No response. "You don't look surprised."

"It wasn't us."

Taryn's hands fisted. "But you knew about it."

"Every jackal in the shifter community heard about it. Our grapevine works at high speed."

"Then I'm assuming you also know *who* it was."

Sergio stared blankly at Taryn, who let out a low growl. Responding to his mate's anger, Trey slammed his hands on the table, causing Sergio's pack to jump to their feet. But Marcus knew they wouldn't move without a signal from their Alpha.

"This isn't an interrogation, Sergio. If it was, my Beta would be snapping your limbs like twigs while my mate then beat you bloody with them. You tell me straight up who tried to kidnap my son."

Sergio studied his fingernails. "You might remember I proposed an alliance between our packs, Trey. Had you accepted, we could have saved ourselves all this drama."

"You want an alliance in exchange for information?"

Sergio's smile was devious. "It's just business."

Roni sidled up to her brother and pointed her lollipop at Sergio. "You've got to give it to the guy, Nick: he has balls. Of course, we can always fix that by scooping them out with a rusty spoon and shoving them down his throat." She spoke to Sergio then. "I'll bet that'll leave a familiar taste in your mouth."

"Bitch, you—" His words were abruptly cut off as Nick plucked him out of his seat by his throat and slammed him high against the wall while the other jackals yelped and cackled.

Sergio struggled against Nick's hold. "What the fuck!"

"Let me explain something," rumbled Nick, power and rage pouring from him. "We're not here to chat, or negotiate, or interrogate. We're here *to get the facts.* You're going to give us what we want. If you don't, I'll destroy you and every single jackal in this building."

Now Sergio looked suitably afraid. It was impossible not to while Nick was glaring at him with homicidal urges in his eyes.

Taryn squinted up at him. "Glad it's not me up there. I get nosebleeds in high altitudes. Do you?"

"You're still not talking." Trey took one menacing step forward.

"I heard it was the Scorpio Pack," Sergio blurted out.

"Go on," prodded Nick.

"Can you put me down?"

"No."

Sergio sighed in resignation. "I don't know for sure; I'm not in contact with them. They were blacklisted a few years ago."

A pack could be blacklisted for a number of reasons, usually crime-related. They would then be mostly isolated from shifter society, losing their territory and alliances and no longer recognized as a pack by the shifter council.

"You sound disgusted with them," observed Dante.

"I am. They were blacklisted, for God's sake."

Taryn snorted. "It's not like your pack is squeaky-clean."

"But there's not a thing anyone could pin on me. For a pack

to be sloppy enough to have evidence brought against them is worthy of disgust."

"Well, since you have so little respect for them, you won't mind telling me where I can find them." Nick gave Sergio's neck a cautioning squeeze.

"I don't know," he wheezed. "After they were blacklisted, they were forced to go on the road, so they're never in one place for very long."

"Why was the pack blacklisted?" Marcus asked.

"They were running an illegal fighting ring for shifters. It went on for years. At some point, they started including humans. The humans were willing, but they were getting badly hurt. Then some started . . . disappearing. Before it could attract the attention of the extremists, someone tipped off the council, and they blacklisted the pack."

Taryn's brows arched. "Wow, great story. In what chapter do you tell us *where the fuck they are*?"

"I told you, I don't know where they are."

"Then what *do* you know?"

He was silent for a moment. He closed his eyes as he said, "S. N. M."

Dante's brow furrowed. "What?"

Opening his eyes, Sergio elaborated. "It's a website: snm.com. You should find some answers there. But you might not like what you see."

Nick allowed Sergio to slide down the wall. "There. That wasn't so hard, was it?"

Sergio cupped his throat. "All of you get out of here. And don't step a single foot on my territory again."

Nick actually smiled. "Provided you told us the truth, there's nothing for you to worry about. *Except* for the matter of the female trying to creep up on my sister. Unless you want said female to die, call her off."

"Nick," whined Roni, who had easily sensed the jackal trying to blindside her. "Why did you have to tip him off? I was looking forward to having some fun with her."

There was no way Marcus would have allowed the female jackal to touch her, but he knew telling her that he'd planned to intervene and protect her wouldn't have worked out well for him.

Sergio shook his head slightly at the female, and she halted . . . but not before baring her teeth at Roni. His little wolf laughed.

"Aw, isn't she cute?"

Considering she'd used the same tone that one might use when referring to a newborn bunny, it was totally understandable that the jackal jumped at Roni. Marcus had seen it coming, and he was fast as he moved to leap between them. But Roni was faster. Quick as fucking lightning, she grabbed the flailing female by the throat and slammed her onto the floor, pinning her there. And she hadn't even lost her lollipop in the struggle. His wolf growled his approval.

Roni shook her head sadly at the jackal, wagging her lollipop. "My, my, my, we *are* behaving very stupidly today, aren't we?"

One of the male jackals stepped forward. "Let her go!" Marcus blocked his path.

"Well, now, that's up to her." Roni cocked her head at the female. "Are you going to use what few brain cells you have and be a good girl if I let you up?" The jackal nodded, her eyes fearful. "For your sake, you better not be bullshitting me." The female quickly scampered.

As one, the Phoenix and Mercury wolves turned their backs on the jackals—communicating their lack of fear. Sergio's voice stopped them as they reached the door.

"Remember, *don't* come back here."

Taryn shook her head, looking offended. "Ah, now that's just rude."

Roni nodded. "Totally."

Back in the rear seat of the Chevy, Roni once again found herself caught between the window and Marcus, who was currently focused on his cell phone. Frustratingly, she was conscious of every single inch of that solid, supremely masculine body pressed against her side.

She should have felt trapped. He was a very pushy, dominant male who was invading her personal space. And yet, all she felt was the insane urge to turn her head and inhale more of his scent. But could anyone really blame her? The guy oozed sex, power, and danger. It was a lethal cocktail for any dominant female shifter. It made her wolf kind of drunk.

"I can't get onto the website," announced Marcus, returning his cell to his pocket.

"Me neither." Dante twisted slightly in the seat in front of them. Trey and Taryn, who were sitting in the same row as the Beta, mirrored his move. "You need to be a subscribed member."

Taryn shrugged. "So just enter a few fictional details to become a member."

Marcus shook his head. "Can't. The questions are pretty specific, requiring you to state stuff like your pack name, location, and Alpha—things that can be cross-referenced. Whoever created the site, and I'm assuming it was the Scorpio Pack, likes to pre-approve their members. I have to wonder why they're being so careful."

A muscle in Trey's jaw ticked. "Dante, get Rhett on it." Immediately, the Beta took out his cell phone and called Rhett.

"The questions tell us one thing," began Taryn. "It's clearly exclusive to shifters."

"What does 'SNM' stand for?" asked Roni.

"It doesn't say." It was all too mysterious and secretive for Marcus's peace of mind.

Taryn worried her bottom lip. "I don't like this." Trey tugged her closer, and she melted into him.

As the Alpha female took comfort in her mate's touch, Roni watched the scene curiously. She'd been brought up to believe that leaning on others emotionally made a person weak; that it made them vulnerable to that person. Kathy Axton seemed to see weakness all around her—especially in Roni, who she insisted on treating like a helpless kid.

She'd always been emotionally reserved with Roni. In Kathy's opinion, a need for emotional feedback in a female was a weakness, and she did not want her daughter to be weak. So she had withheld physical affection to literally train Roni not to need it, to not even feel the need to give it.

It was the way Kathy herself had been raised, and maybe emotional intimacy was in fact a weakness. But Taryn didn't look weak right then. Just the same, Shaya never appeared weak when taking comfort from Nick. They just looked . . . happy.

A large, warm, calloused hand gently lifted Roni's, taking her from her thoughts. She frowned as Marcus flattened his hand to hers and began examining them from every angle. "What are you doing?" Instead of answering her, he slid his hand down to cuff her wrist, and breezed his thumb over a jagged scar on her palm. There was nothing sexual about it, but her stomach clenched at the skin-to-skin contact.

"How did you get that?"

Roni tried retrieving her hand, but he held tight. "I had a fight with a cougar."

"Shifter?"

"No, a full-blood. I was in my wolf form at the time."

Marcus turned her hand over, exposing a long, thin scar. "What about this one?" He was genuinely curious, but he was also intent on breaking the touch barrier. With Roni, it had to be done slowly and subtly, so subtly that she didn't even realize his intent.

"Eli's ex-girlfriend wouldn't back off and leave him alone. I wasn't okay with that. Things turned a little bloody."

"Did you leave your own marks on her?"

Her smile was a little feral. "Well, of course. I heard that the amnesia's past and her motor skills are back to normal." His laugh was totally wicked. Noticing long claw marks on his forearm, she asked, "Where did you get that?" His entire demeanor suddenly changed. The carefree, playful expression was replaced by a blank mask that was totally in contrast to the dark energy radiating from him.

His gaze turned unfocused, as if he were lost in a memory. His reaction alarmed her, since dominant males were never particularly bothered by scars, seeing them as badges of honor. She kept her voice gentle. "Hey." He double-blinked, his eyes back in focus.

Releasing her hand, Marcus cleared his throat. "Sorry, sweetheart. Woolgathering."

He'd instantly slipped back into his old self, offering her an easy smile, but Roni detected a hint of pain in his voice. Okay, so it wasn't exactly fair that he expected her to answer his questions yet wasn't prepared to answer hers. She might have been pissed if she hadn't seen the look in his eyes. He'd been wrestling with something dark, battling painful memories that had a tight hold on him. She could understand that. Still, she wanted him to know she wasn't fooled. She dug something out of her pocket and held it out to him. "Lollipop?"

Marcus looked from Roni to the candy and started laughing. He got the message: by offering him something she used when she was anxious, she was letting him know that she was very much aware that something troubled him. He took the lollipop with a nod of thanks.

It was then that he noticed Nick eying him suspiciously from the front row. His wolf didn't like it, but Marcus couldn't really blame the guy. If the Alpha had any idea of the fantasies running through Marcus's mind that involved Roni and something else he'd like her to suck, Nick would slash his throat open.

Turning to Roni, Marcus spoke quietly. "Your brother's going to tell you that I'm not good for you."

Taken aback by the comment, she blinked at him. He discreetly nodded toward Nick. If that scowl was anything to go by . . . "Yep."

"He thinks I'm a slut."

"Yep."

"He's going to confront me about it at some point, order me to stay away from you."

"Yep."

"But I won't." Marcus held her gaze, not wanting her to miss the determination in his eyes. "Just thought you should know."

He brushed the pad of his finger over her jaw. This wolf really was smooth, and she . . . wasn't. She pulled back. "Stop, okay. I don't play your kind of games." She didn't know *how* to play his kind of games, wasn't experienced with flirting. It made her feel vulnerable, out of her league.

"What makes you think this is a game to me?"

She snorted. "You flirt with everyone, Marcus. I don't like being played with that way."

"Flirting is supposed to be fun and playful, sweetheart. It doesn't mean I'm not serious." He leaned closer, lowering his voice so only she could hear, making the whole thing painfully intimate. "I want you. I want to make you come so hard that the memory's burned into your brain and you'll never forget the feeling of me deep inside you."

Roni swallowed hard. He'd spoken so directly, without apology, all the while holding her gaze with eyes that had darkened with need. Sexual tension throbbed between them, urging them closer. Her wolf lunged for him.

"Almost hurts, doesn't it?"

It did. The tension was intense, overwhelming, and gripping. It pulled them together, almost like a compulsion.

"I'll have you, Roni," he rumbled. "Even if it kills me, I'll have you." It was a promise.

Once they arrived at Phoenix Pack territory, Nick assured the Phoenix wolves he'd be back the following morning—all the while urging Roni straight to his car. It was obvious that he was putting space between her and Marcus, and she quickly discovered there wasn't anything more embarrassing for a girl than being dragged away from a guy by her brother.

Inside Nick's car, she buckled herself in as she silently cursed her brother. Movement caught her eye, and she looked to see Marcus standing completely still next to his Toyota, staring directly at her. His expression was totally deadpan, but not those watchful, brooding eyes. They were alive with sexual energy and a magnetic intensity that kept her gaze trapped by his, making her unable to break the eye contact until Derren began a slow drive out of the lot.

"Don't fall for his shit, Roni." Nick's voice was like a whip. "Guys like him . . . they know how to suck in and string along a female."

"Are you sure your problem with him isn't just that Shaya considers him a good friend?" Her brother was so possessive he was jealous of Shaya's friendship with other males.

"This is about him, not me. The guy always turns on the charm and uses it as bait—"

"But in your own words, Nick," injected Derren, "Roni's resistant to charm. So you have no need to worry."

"Yeah, but—"

"Give it up, Nick." Roni was rapidly losing her patience. "You wouldn't want to push me into Marcus's arms, would you? You know how dominant females will go against pushy advice just to be contrary."

"I'm just looking out for you. You're my little sister."

"Eli's your little brother, but you don't poke your nose into

every aspect of his life. It's only me you insist on being so patronizing toward."

"Roni, I'm not—"

"No, enough, I'm sick of having the same conversation over
and over." She understood that it was natural for her mother
and older brother to be protective, considering they were both
very dominant wolves. But, dammit, she was a very dominant
wolf too. Would they always look at her and see nothing but a
frightened twelve-year-old? Maybe she was partly at fault, since
she'd never really taken them to task over their behavior. But how
could she, when she owed them so much? The whole situation
sucked big-time.

When she was lying in bed alone watching a movie a few
hours later, she received a message on her cell. Retrieving the
phone from the bedside table, she frowned at the unfamiliar
number. Opening the text, she almost smiled.

I'm horny and it's all your fault—M

How Marcus got her number, she wasn't sure. Probably from
Taryn, she thought. Strangely finding that she wanted to answer
this clear invitation to play, Roni typed:

Explain how I'm at fault

His reply was instant.

All I can think about is sliding my cock inside you

And now she was thinking about it too. A part of her wanted
to keep playing—though it felt odd, she was also enjoying it—
but another part of her wanted to draw back in self-preservation.
Nick was right: she *was* resistant to charm. But as that charm was
tangled with raw sexuality, the spice of danger, and an aura of

power, Roni wasn't so resistant to Marcus Fuller at all. Keeping him at a distance would be best.

Or would it? Should she just take what he offered? After all, she liked sex, and he was apparently very good at it.

The problem was that her wolf felt a little possessive of Marcus. The few times she'd seen him with his ex, Zara, her wolf had wanted to rip the bitch apart. The animal also strongly disliked Trick, since he and Marcus had occasionally shook the sheets in the past. To take what Marcus offered could make that possessiveness worse. As such, Roni wasn't sure what to do. In any case, playing like this wouldn't cause any *real* harm. Right?

Shrugging aside her mixed thoughts, she finally typed:

So take a cold shower and stop bothering me

Within seconds, he responded:

You text slow!

Rather than explaining her little moment of uncertainty, she decided to type something a little wicked instead. Hey, if she were going to play, she'd do it right.

Sorry about that, I'm texting one-handed. The other hand is a little . . . pre-occupied

The phone immediately started ringing, and she couldn't help laughing aloud. Swallowing back the sound, Roni answered, "Yes?"

He didn't even bother with a hello. "And what exactly is that hand doing?"

She cleared her throat, trying to hide the smile from her voice. "Nothing. It's just . . . busy right now. Can you call back later?"

He groaned. "This is cruel, sweetheart. I'm hard as a fucking rock here."

"I didn't do anything."

"You never have to do anything. I think about you, and I'm hard. It's that basic." His voice dropped an octave as he added, "I was working at Dante's desk earlier, and all I could think about was slamming you on top of it and fucking you raw." Damn, that voice was like liquid seduction. And it was certainly doing its job. "Now . . . at the risk of sounding clichéd, what are you wearing?"

She rolled her eyes. "Guess."

"Hmmm. Boy shorts and a tank top."

Her body jackknifed into an upright position. "Where the fuck are you?" Was the little shit spying on her?

He was now laughing hysterically. "In my bed, wishing you were with me."

"Then how do you know what I'm wearing?"

"I know *you*. But I won't know all of you unless you share a little more, sweetheart. Can you do that for me?"

"Since when are guys so interested in a girl's personality?"

"Knowledge is power, my pretty little wolf. And I need every bit of help I can get if I'm going to make myself a part of your little circle. Now, I'm going to let you get some sleep while I take a cold shower. Dream of me."

Considering he'd been the main feature of her dreams for some time, that shouldn't be a problem. She wasn't sure if that were a good thing or a bad thing.

CHAPTER FİVE

The next morning went pretty much the same for Roni: she argued with her mother, aunt, and Eliza at breakfast, she played a prank on Eli, and she was unexpectedly joined by Marcus, who then gave her a ride to Phoenix Pack territory and quizzed her the entire journey.

Soon enough, they were seated at the kitchen table with the rest of the hunting party and Trick and Dominic. Two things were bugging her: One, Trick was watching her very closely; there was no animosity there, but it made her uncomfortable. Two, Marcus wouldn't stop touching her. Okay, fine, it wasn't the touching part that bugged her, it was the fact that it *didn't* bother her. For God's sake, he was practically glued to her side while playing with her hair, and she wasn't even bristling.

"What do you mean you couldn't hack into it?" Trey growled.

Rhett looked more annoyed about it than Trey did. "What I do isn't as easy as it looks, okay? This website, whatever it is, has encryptions I've never come across before. I'm doing my best, but it's going to take a few more hours."

Trey relaxed a little. "Fine. What do you have on the jackals?"

Rhett's smile was smug. "People, meet the Alpha of the Scorpio Pack." He passed a photo to Dante, who took a hard look at it before passing it on. "Right here is Lyle Browne. The pack was based in San Diego until their territory was stripped from them. Before being blacklisted, Browne did business with a lot of packs and had a good number of alliances with powerful Alphas." Suddenly looking awkward, Rhett turned to Taryn. "He . . . did a lot of business with your dad, Taryn. I'm sorry."

Taryn clenched her fist tight, though her expression remained blank. To say that she had a strained relationship with her father would be an understatement. Taryn had been latent—unable to shift—until getting pregnant with Kye, and her father, Lance, had been ashamed of her for most of her life. Worse, he'd tried to force her into an arranged mating, which Trey had thankfully sabotaged.

"There's nothing to indicate Lance is still doing business with them," Rhett quickly added. "But it seems like the jackals still do business with some of their old alliances: Samuel Redford, Morgan Johnson, Jackson Griffiths, and Quinn McGee. All four of them are Alpha wolves."

"We need to question all of them," said Dante.

Nick looked at Trey. "It's time we split up. I know Johnson pretty well; he's allied with my old pack. He'll be more likely to talk to me than to you, if there's anything he can tell us."

"Then it makes sense for you to pay him a visit." Trey leaned forward. "I know McGee, but I know Griffiths much better—his mother and my mother were close friends; we played together as kids."

Roni noticed how Marcus tensed at the mention of Trey's mother, and she wondered at the cause.

"You think Griffiths will talk to you?" Nick asked him. Trey nodded.

"My brother's allied with Redford," said Dante. "I've met his Beta a few times. I could go with Ryan to speak to him, since I'm guessing there's no way you'll part from Taryn."

Trey snorted. "Damn right."

Taryn smiled. "Okay then. Flintstone and I will go see Griffiths. Nick and Derren can talk to Johnson. Dante and Ryan will speak to Redford. Marcus and Roni can visit McGee." Quinn was loosely allied with the Phoenix Pack and had fought alongside them during a pack war with Trey's now deceased uncle.

"Just remember that Quinn can be cagey," Trey told Marcus, "and he likes games. But you've got a gift for getting people to talk—use it."

Roni snickered. "You want him to flirt with the guy?"

Trey appeared confused, but it was Trick who elaborated. "People tend to like Marcus, so they tend to talk to him. But when they don't talk . . . well, Marcus quickly changes their minds."

Ignoring Roni's curious gaze, Marcus turned to Rhett. "What type of business did Browne and McGee do together?"

Rhett glanced at his papers again. "They dabbled in illegal activities such as forgery, stealing antiques, selling stolen and counterfeit paintings—" He paused as the sounds of approaching voices caught everyone's attention.

"I'll never know what my Dante sees in you," Greta was growling in the tunnels.

Jaime made a contemplative sound. "Class. Curves. Sparkling wit. A mouth he swears is perfect for s—"

"Enough!"

"I was just going to say 'smiling.' Really, Greta, you should just build a cabin in the gutter—your mind is permanently there." Jaime entered the kitchen with a bright smile while Greta trailed behind her, glowering—a glower that deepened when she saw that Dominic was laughing his ass off.

Greta paused near Marcus. "Make a better choice for a mate than these two idiots." She gestured at Trey and Dante. It was only then that she noticed Marcus playing with Roni's hair. And she didn't appear to like it.

Jaime, now lounging in the lap of a clearly contented Dante, who was nuzzling her neck, looked at Greta. "You can whine all you want, old woman, but I know you secretly adore me."

Greta humphed, taking a seat beside Tao. "You're not good

enough for my Dante. Just like that hussy's not good enough for my Trey."

Taryn tilted her head, regarding Greta with mock pity. "I can't work out what's wrong with you. But I'm sure it's not something that swallowing the chemicals under the sink can't fix. Want to try it?"

"How about we postpone the conversation of how best to poison my grandmother until later?" suggested Trey with a tired sigh. "We need to get going."

Serious now, Taryn pushed out of her chair. "Yes. Somebody knows something about what happened to my son, and I want to know what it is."

Standing upright, Nick turned to Roni. "Be careful."

"Roni's always careful."

Marcus's words—confident, supportive, and defensive—took Roni by complete surprise. He didn't appear to be any happier about Nick's insistence on coddling her than she was. In fact, Marcus seemed offended on her behalf.

Grinding his teeth, Nick went nose to nose with Marcus. "You'd better not touch my sister, Fuller." That easily, the Phoenix wolves were at Marcus's back.

"Nick," Roni drawled warningly.

"I've seen the way you look at her, and I don't like it. Keep this professional."

Marcus's smile was a pure taunt. "Since you don't seem to have noticed, I'll point out that Roni's a big girl." If the Alpha had some strange idea that Marcus would submit to him, he had to be smoking crack.

"She's still my baby sister, and you're not good enough for her."

"Nick, stop it," Roni bit out, kind of shocked that Trey wasn't intervening to defend his enforcer and friend. But Trey didn't seem the least bit worried for Marcus, and that was when she realized that Marcus was easily holding Nick's gaze. Despite having a powerful Alpha threatening him, he didn't look in the least bit rattled. There was even a little amusement there.

"There's nothing babyish about Roni. All you're doing by coddling her is undermining her strength. Is that really what you want to do? I have a feeling she won't thank you for it."

After a short, tense silence, Nick took a step back. "Remember what I said, Fuller. Keep your cock in your pants, understand?"

"I don't know. Sounds complicated." Marcus almost laughed at Nick's thunderous expression, but then Roni jammed her elbow into his ribs.

"Stop making it worse," she hissed at Marcus. "Nick, just go."

The Alpha shot Marcus a menacing glance before spinning on his heel and marching out of the room with an amused Derren at his side.

Only then did the Phoenix wolves relax. Seeing that they were all gazing with interest at her and Marcus, she had the urge to leave the room and escape their scrutiny. So she did.

"Hey, wait." She didn't, but Marcus ate up the space between them in three strides. Up ahead, Nick glanced over his shoulder and slung Marcus a sneer. His wolf returned the sneer—he wasn't a fan of the Alpha who was trying to come between him and the object of his fascination. Marcus just smiled.

In the parking area, Marcus led her over to his car and chuckled as Nick sped past them in his SUV with a glower on his face. "Personally, I think he's warming up to me."

Grinding her teeth, she hopped into the passenger seat. "Stop winding up my brother."

Inside the car, he said, "I smiled at him, what's wrong with that?"

Like she'd buy the innocent act. "He stood there threatening you, and you made it worse by poking at him."

"I wasn't poking at him . . . much. I was defending you."

Yes, he had defended her. For the third time. Although Roni didn't need anyone to speak for her, it was kind of nice that someone actually had. Kathy and Nick ganged up on her pretty often; she was used to fighting her battles alone. "I know his overprotectiveness is unnecessary and irritating, but he means well."

"Does he?" In Marcus's opinion, Nick's behavior wasn't about Roni at all.

Hearing the skepticism in his tone, she was about to question him. But then she shook her head, not wanting to get involved in male shifter games. "Look, it doesn't matter what you think. Just stop—" She quieted when he placed a finger against her mouth.

"I'm not the enemy, Roni." His voice was low, soft, and soothing. "Hearing people dismiss your strength pisses me off."

"Why?"

"It hurts you. I don't like it." He also didn't like that she let Nick and Kathy get away with it. She had an annoying habit of biting back what she wanted to say, and each time he saw the strain around her eyes, it made his blood boil. Hearing the crinkle of a wrapper, he *tsk*ed. "Oh no, sweetheart. Not with me, remember."

Roni huffed and put the candy in her mouth. The asshole took it back out and dumped it in the cup holder. "Hey, stop that!"

"What do you like to do on weekends?"

The casual question made her huff again. "What does that have to do with anything?"

"Come on, Roni, what's the harm in answering my question?" His tone was coaxing.

Exasperated, she spoke in a rush. "Nick has a huge game room with a bar, La-Z-Boys, and an Xbox. I meet the guys there most Saturday nights. On Sundays, I go for a run in my wolf form. There. Are you happy now?"

He smiled. "Ecstatic." When they stopped at a red light, he looked at her. "Did you know we're throwing a birthday party for Grace on Saturday night?"

"Shaya mentioned it."

"You're coming, right? There'll be plenty of beer. Chicken wings. Pizza. Cake." All things he knew Roni loved.

"I don't like parties." Too many people, too much pressure to seem sociable.

"But you do like chocolate fudge cake."

There would be chocolate fudge cake? "Why didn't you say so before?"

He chuckled, but that chuckle quickly faded because all this talking about food had created a problem. "I'm hungry."

She snickered. "What else is new?"

Seeing a McDonald's sign up ahead, he said, "I could really go for a burger right now."

"We'll eat after we've spoken to McGee."

"It's a two-hour journey. I can't wait that long." He pulled into the drive-through lane and came to a stop near the menu boards. "What do you want?"

She shrugged. "I'll just have a bit of what you're having."

He blinked. "Um, sweetheart . . . I don't share food." She rolled her eyes, clearly missing how serious he was. "No, really, I don't share food."

Amused despite herself, Roni asked, "Not even a few fries?"

"No."

"Not even an onion ring?"

"No." Marcus watched as impatience flickered across her face, like she thought he was being unreasonable—now that was just unfair. "Order a meal."

"But I'm not that hungry."

"So order a snack."

"Why can't I just share with you?"

"Because I'm territorial when it comes to my food."

She arched a brow. "Territorial, or greedy?"

"Both." And he was totally unapologetic about it.

"Fine. I'll have a cheeseburger."

Marcus placed their orders and turned back to find Roni gawking at him. "What?"

"You practically ordered an entire cow. You couldn't have shared just a little of that with me?"

With all honesty, he replied, "No." Once in possession of their orders, Marcus parked in the lot and immediately dug in.

He was halfway through his meal when Roni had finished, and he sensed her watching his fries with a covetous gaze. When her hand reached for them, he quickly positioned the box between his spread legs. "Not on your life, gorgeous." Her eyes narrowed, calculating, but she said nothing. Then, when he was down to his last fry, she snatched it out of his box. "Hey!"

Roni quickly stuffed it in her mouth, close to laughing at his horrified expression.

"Give it back." Instead, she quickly chewed it. Then she opened her mouth, showing him she'd swallowed it down. And the sight of that tongue . . .

Roni gasped as his mouth suddenly locked on hers. As if to ensure she couldn't pull away, he cupped her chin as he traced the edge of her bottom lip with his tongue . . . and the sensuous swipe made her wonder how that tongue would feel on other parts of her body.

She should push him away, right? Of course she should. But she didn't, because that soft, carnal mouth pushed all other thoughts from her mind as his tongue shot inside, tangling with hers. The kiss was wet, languid, and hotly sensual. And it made her body jump to life.

Marcus groaned as her hands knotted in his hair, claws raking his scalp. He gripped her hip and jerked her toward him as his entire body hardened. Need, possessiveness, and a crushing drive to *take* rushed through him—all of it was so primitive, it shook him. The scent of her arousal slammed into his system, acting as fuel to those primal instincts.

Ordinarily, Marcus didn't rush; he took his time with a female—seduced and teased. That patience to take things slow wasn't there with Roni. He roughly shoved his hand under her T-shirt, fingers splaying across her abdomen like a brand. Her eyes snapped open at the possessive move, but she didn't flinch away. Nor did she protest when his hand slid up and closed around her breast in an equally possessive move. He wouldn't take her in a car, he wouldn't, but *fuck,* the scent of her need was driving him out of his mind.

"Are you ready to stop fighting this, Roni?" He pinched her nipple through her bra, pleased when she moaned. "Will you make that sound when I'm inside you?" Her eyes were dazed, heated, but also wary. It was clear that the intensity between them unnerved her. Hell, it unnerved him too. But it changed nothing. "Our first time is not going to be in a McDonald's parking lot. But it will happen, Roni. And soon." He thumbed her nipple as he released her breast.

Her wolf growled in objection when Marcus pulled back, but Roni was glad for the reprieve. Her reaction to him unbalanced her. "Cocky asshole."

"Not cocky," he told her as he piled their waste into the brown paper bag. "Just determined to get what I want."

"A fuck."

"You," he corrected. As they drove out of the lot, he paused the car to wind down the window and throw the bag into the large garbage container. "I've wanted you since the second I laid eyes on you, sweetheart, and that's not going to change."

"Has it occurred to you that maybe you only want me because I didn't throw myself at you?"

"I don't like it when females throw themselves at me."

She barked a disbelieving laugh. "Yeah, right."

"I'm not saying I didn't once-upon-a-time, but not anymore."

"You prefer the chase?"

"A chase can be fun"—he was certainly enjoying this chase—"but no, I just got sick of being around shallow, superficial people who only wanted me because they liked how I look. I mean, what you see here can be injured, scarred, or disfigured. Underneath the skin, I look pretty much the same as every other guy."

There he went again, surprising her. Okay, maybe he *wasn't* cocky, but . . . "You're still an asshole."

"So my sister often tells me. Although that's usually only when I refuse to babysit. Don't get me wrong, I love my nieces . . . I just prefer them in small doses."

"Are you close to your sister?"

Pleased that she'd asked him a personal question, Marcus replied, "I'm pretty close to all three of them." Going through a bad experience had a way of bonding people.

"So you have a close-knit family?" Her hackles raised when his smile faded and his body stiffened. All trace of his usual playfulness had gone. "Now that's a story right there."

"A twisted story, sweetheart. One you'd be better off not hearing."

Okay, if he were going to repeatedly dodge her questions, it could get annoying. But, really, what right did she have to know his secrets? Plus, in all fairness, he'd never asked her a deeply personal question, never pushed her to confide in him about a wound that would clearly be painful to open.

The rest of the journey was spent in silence, but it wasn't awkward or tense. The presence of the male beside her seemed to smooth over her ragged nerves. Though her attraction to Marcus made her edgy, the guy himself had a way of putting her at ease.

As they stopped at the border of Quinn McGee's territory, Roni saw that it wasn't much different from most wolf-shifter territories—lots of land with log cabins scattered all over it. Two enforcers escorted them to the center of the wide territory where they came to a large log cabin. In the living area, Quinn sat on a long sofa at the far end of the room with a platinum blonde and a dark-skinned female who bore a striking resemblance to the dark-skinned male standing beside the sofa.

Quinn got to his feet, smiling, as they came to a stop in front of the sofa. The smile was genuine . . . yet there was a nervous twitch to it. "Marcus, good to see you, it's been a long time."

"It has. This is Roni; she's a Mercury Pack enforcer."

Quinn nodded at them both, worry apparent on his face. He gestured to the blonde. "This is my mate, Lola. Beside her is one of my female enforcers, and over there is my Beta."

The Beta's eyes lingered on Roni in a way that Marcus did *not* like. He arched a brow at the male, who simply smiled unrepentantly. Obviously, he wanted his ass kicked.

Quinn returned to his seat and gestured to the sofa opposite him. Neither Marcus nor Roni sat, and the tension in the room rose. "Okay, what can I do for you?"

Marcus's voice was quiet but grave. "You know why we're here."

An incline of the head. "You're seeking those responsible for attempting to abduct your Alpha pair's son, and the trail has led you here."

"I want to keep this civil, Quinn. You want that too, I'm sure. After all, there's really no need for this to get unfriendly. All you have to do is cooperate and answer our questions. Simple."

Roni hadn't heard Marcus use that tone before—it was dark, menacing, and held a promise of reprisal if he didn't get exactly what he wanted. In fact, she'd never seen him *look* like that before either; there was such energy, intensity, and darkness there. It made Quinn straighten in his seat.

"We know that the Scorpio Pack was responsible," continued Marcus. "We know you have an alliance with them, despite that they were blacklisted."

Quinn shrugged, as if the matter was nothing. "Business is business. Whether or not they're blacklisted is no concern of mine, providing they keep up their end of the bargain."

"Where are they, Quinn?"

"If I tell you that, Trey will kill them."

Well, duh. Roni leaned against Marcus slightly, speaking in a theatrical whisper. "I'm not comfortable around this wolf; he sees the future."

In spite of everything, Marcus found himself amused. "What would you do in Trey's position, Quinn?"

"I'm nothing if not loyal, and the Scorpio Pack is under my protection."

"It won't save them. They crossed a very big line, and there's no going back from that. Choose a side, and choose wisely."

Quinn sighed. "I haven't seen or spoken to the jackals in over three months. I don't know their exact location at this moment—"

"I call bullshit on that," Roni said ever so pleasantly.

He growled, clearly offended. "You doubt my word?"

"You might not be interested in protecting their lives, but you're interested in protecting your business—that means concealing them from us."

"And that would be very bad, Quinn." Marcus tilted his head. "Very bad and very stupid."

"I joined your pack in a war. Trey's son might never have been born without the backup you had that day."

"You didn't do that for my pack. You wanted a shot at Trey's uncle, and he gave it to you."

Quinn's nostrils flared. "You're asking me to condemn the jackals to death. This isn't about me or them. This is about honor and—What's she doing?" He glanced curiously at Roni.

Yes, what *was* Roni doing? Marcus frowned, watching as she slowly paced in a circle on the other side of the room.

Abruptly, Roni stopped and growled at Quinn. "They've been here. I can smell them."

The Beta suddenly dove at Marcus, his claws unleashed, just as the female enforcer launched herself at Roni. It wasn't an attack, but an attempt to subdue them—Marcus saw that right away. But *no one* was subduing either of them.

Confident Roni could take care of herself, Marcus concentrated on the Beta. He gripped the wrist of the arm reaching for him and sharply bent it sideways; a growl of pain mingled with the sound of a bone cracking. Marcus pinned the arm behind the Beta's back and head-butted him hard enough to make him sway on his feet. Then he shoved the male backward, who landed on the sofa. Quinn sprang from his seat, heading for Marcus, and—

"I'll snap her neck, I swear to God."

Everyone froze at Roni's words, surprised to find Quinn's enforcer whining on the floor and Lola in a headlock. Hands raised in surrender, Quinn immediately backed off. Taking his cue, the Beta and the enforcer also submitted, but Roni didn't release Lola.

Marcus smiled. "Now, maybe we can actually—"

The door burst open and two male wolves darted into the room. Quinn's "No!" had one of them skidding to a halt. The other, however, made a grab for Roni. Totally unruffled, the pretty little wolf used her free arm to deal the male a fast, hard blow to the jaw that sent him sprawling on the floor, out cold. Calm as you please, she then turned back to Quinn.

Marcus and his wolf loved her viciousness, and Marcus had to admit to being totally turned on. He sighed sadly at Quinn. "I was hoping it wouldn't come to this."

"Let her go. Just let her go." When Roni didn't loosen her hold on Lola, Quinn moved toward her.

Marcus quickly blocked his path. "You don't touch her. *Ever.*" Quinn's dominant vibes suddenly slammed into Marcus, smothering him like an oppressive desert heat. It was an attempt to intimidate him, to force him to submit—an insult that could get him killed by Trey. Marcus shrugged off the vibes. Maybe if Quinn were a born alpha, it would have worked. Unfortunately for the Alpha, his level of dominance didn't exceed Marcus's. "Are we done playing?"

Wide-eyed in shock, Quinn stepped back, licking his lips nervously.

"You want to get to your mate. I understand, I do. I know Nick was in the same state when he heard that Shaya was battered and bruised after the crash that I'm sure you heard all about. Roni's also Nick's sister, so you can imagine how she feels about it, particularly since she was also in the crash."

Quinn licked his lips again, his eyes darting from Lola to Marcus, wrestling with the decision of what to do.

"Where are they, McGee?" Marcus demanded.

Quinn's gaze met Marcus's determined one. "Marcus . . ." But he said nothing more.

"You're scared of them," Marcus realized. "Aren't you?" This wasn't about protecting the jackals at all. Quinn didn't answer. Then Lola squealed.

"Oh, I'm sorry," said Roni. "Did that hurt? My bad."

Marcus stepped forward, repeating, "You're scared of them, aren't you?"

The Alpha swallowed hard. "Yes, and you should be too."

"Why?"

He stumbled over his words. "They're not . . . normal, Marcus. They fear nothing. Lives mean nothing to them. They'll hurt, and they'll kill, but they won't care."

"Where. Are. They?"

"You'll find them at snm.com."

As they sat in the Toyota while Marcus reported everything to Trey over his cell phone, Roni found herself unable to stop staring at him. In a word, she was stunned. Totally and utterly stunned. In the short time she'd known Marcus, Roni had sensed three things: he could be playful, he could be charming, and he could be dangerous. But she hadn't guessed just how dangerous he could actually be.

Faced with an Alpha who had attempted to suppress Marcus with his dominant vibes, Marcus hadn't buckled. In fact, he'd withstood the power—which was no little thing. He'd been assertive, forceful, and commanding. And she was totally turned on, to her horrified fascination.

She now understood what Trey had meant when he said that Marcus had a way of getting people to talk. It wasn't how powerful he was that spooked them, it was that he'd originally hidden it. By nature, shifters were brash and bold, particularly dominants. They wore their power like a cloak, warning away any would-be challengers.

As for those who very unnaturally downplayed their dominance like Marcus, the quiet ones . . . everyone knew to be wary of them. They were comfortable being quiet for a reason: they weren't afraid to be challenged and even welcomed it—often because they were a little crazy. As Eli had once said, "*They would soon as cut your throat than look at you.*"

Ending the call, Marcus returned his cell phone to his pocket and started the engine. "It all comes back to that fucking website. Rhett's almost cracked its security, so everyone's going to reunite back at my territory." Frowning at her odd expression, he asked, "What?"

"I just watched you withstand an Alpha's vibes, and it became very clear just how much you downplay your level of dominance." She shook her head, incredulous. "How is it that most of your pack thinks you're so laid-back and mellow? I mean, of course they know you're very dominant, but they don't see all that intensity and power lurking there."

He shrugged, pulling onto the highway. "People have a tendency to label others. When you're labeled the charmer whose main aim in life is to get laid on a regular basis, no one bothers to look deeper because they don't expect to find anything else." Sometimes it bothered him, sometimes it didn't.

Yeah, Roni knew what that was like. People looked at her and saw a quiet, awkward tomboy and thought that was all there was to her. It didn't occur to them that she might have an extremely high IQ, or that she could wipe the floor with their faces. As such, she should have known better than to make assumptions. "I'm sorry."

That had to be the most awkward apology he'd ever heard. "For what?"

She shifted uncomfortably. "I misjudged you when I first met you."

Her apology was unexpected. She looked genuinely upset with herself. "Hey, don't worry about it. It happens all the time. It's worse for Dominic. People think he only operates on one level." There was much more to the enforcer, but people didn't see it . . . because Dominic didn't want them to. "Completely off the subject, it was unbelievably hot when you took on the Alpha female. My wolf loved it."

Roni fought a smile. Ever so casually, she admitted, "It was just as hot when you shrugged off Quinn's vibes." Her wolf had growled with arousal.

He laughed. "One minute you were looking defenseless, and the next you had the Alpha female in a fucking headlock. Cute one second, fierce the next. I love it."

Taking offense, she scowled. "I am *not* cute." What was she, five?

"You are many, many things, Roni. And you are definitely cute—especially when you smile."

"I do *not* smile."

"I've seen you smile." It was a rare sight, but a beautiful one.

"No, you haven't."

"Yes, I have. It's a gorgeous smile—there are even cute little dimples involved." He almost exploded with laughter at the sheer horror on her face.

"I do not have dimples, thank you very much!"

"Oh, here's that prim, schoolteacher voice again. Makes me feel like a bad little boy about to get taught a lesson."

She had to bite the inside of her cheek because, dammit, she would not smile. "I have absolutely no response for that."

"Then kiss me instead."

Seeing the impish, lighthearted expression on his face, she realized something. "You're trying to get me to play." Since she mostly hung out with guys, she was used to joking around. But this was a different kind of play; it was intimate, more personal, yet it was also . . . easy.

"You *did* play." And Marcus was smug about that. He was slowly drawing Roni out, just as she was slowing letting him in.

"You're such a dick, Fuller." Annoyingly, he just laughed.

A few moments later, he sighed. "I'm hungry." She rolled her eyes in exasperation. "What?"

Entering Rhett's room with Roni by his side, Marcus found his Alpha pair, Dante, and Ryan waiting. "Is he almost done?" Marcus asked Trey, referring to Rhett, who was totally engrossed in his computer.

"Almost."

"Did you get any information from Jackson?"

Taryn sighed. "According to Jackson, Lyle Browne is a decent guy. He was actually shocked to hear that Lyle was behind Kye's attempted kidnapping. Although he doesn't know Lyle's location, he admitted to being in regular contact with him."

"Did Jackson have a contact number for Lyle?"

Disappointment clouded Taryn's expression. "Apparently Lyle is a fan of disposable phones, so he doesn't have a fixed number."

Marcus turned to Dante. "What about Redford?"

"He said he stopped doing business with Lyle a year ago."

"Do you believe him?"

"No, so I did what I do best." The Beta's reputation as an interrogator was well known—there wasn't anyone he'd failed to crack.

"What did Redford have to say after that?"

"The same thing that Jackson told Trey—Lyle uses disposable cells, checks in once a month."

"Not uncommon for a person who's involved in plenty of illegal activity." Roni wondered why she wasn't stepping away from

Marcus, who was absentmindedly playing with her hair. She should probably also ask herself why she kind of liked it.

"Jackson promised to speak to Lyle about the incident and convince him to call me," said Trey.

Marcus arched a brow. "And if he can't convince him?"

"Then Jackson will give him up. He has pups himself; he knows how it would feel if the situation was reversed."

Hoping he was right, Marcus continued twirling strands of Roni's hair around his finger. The scent of her vanilla shampoo mingled with her own delicious scent, teasing him and his wolf. The sound of footsteps approaching through the tunnels made everyone swerve to face the door. Moments later, Nick and Derren walked inside. Nick took a moment to snarl at Marcus before addressing Trey, who quickly filled them in on everything that had happened.

"Did Johnson have anything interesting to say?" Taryn asked Nick.

"He didn't want to get involved, but he also didn't want me to smash his face into the wall, so he was quite informative. He said the same thing that Redford and Jackson said. But there was something else."

The Phoenix Alphas moved closer to him as Trey asked, "What?"

"He said it wasn't just jackals involved in whatever they're doing." Nick's face hardened. "He said to look more closely at our own breed of shifter."

Marcus cursed under his breath. Breeds tended to stick together, and it was always a blow to hear a pack of their own breed was working against them.

"Whoever it is," rumbled Trey, "is dead. I'll find them, and I'll kill them." Marcus's wolf backed him up with a growl of his own.

Nick took a deep breath. "I'm going to call Shay, update her on what's happening." He was just about to leave the room when Rhett spoke.

"Guys . . . we're in."

At that, everyone crowded around the computer. Roni read aloud the name of the shifter site. "Show No Mercy." A chill ran through her at the blood-red lettering splattered over a black backdrop.

She shook her head, confused. But that confusion quickly cleared up as she glanced at the various videos that had been uploaded onto the site: "Tiger gets ripped to shreds by two wolves," "Bears use wolf cub as a football," "Two lion prides battle to the death," "Jackals having fun with drugged female cougar"—it went on and on, with one very familiar theme: violence.

Trey's voice came out hoarse with anger. "So the jackals have gone from running an illegal fighting ring to setting up a website where they and their members can upload videos of shifter fights and sexual assaults."

"Read the introduction. They basically see this as porn for shifters," commented a suddenly ill-looking Rhett. "They're saying that violence is a way of life for us, but that we suppress that side of ourselves to fit in with humans. To them, by doing all these things, they're letting out the animal to play."

"This has nothing to do with the animal inside them," objected Dante. "This is just a website for sick sons of bitches to congregate."

Beneath each clip, it stated just how many times the video had been viewed, how highly it had been rated, and showed any comments that had been left by viewers. Disgustingly, these viewers had praised the amount of violence displayed. It seemed that the more violent and bloody it was, the higher the rating. Sexual assault seemed to be a particular favorite among viewers, and even the videos that displayed young shifters being beaten or savaged to death were highly rated.

Rhett double-clicked on a video of two juvenile wolves brutally fighting while their parents, in human form, stood in the background urging them on, telling them what to do. It looked to Roni like the juveniles were being forced to fight for the entertainment of those around them and for the purpose of the video. Nauseous, she put her hand to her stomach.

"That wolf cub used as a football could have just as easily been Kye." Taryn's voice was unsteady. "Do you think that's why they wanted him? To use in one of these videos?"

Growling, Trey held her tight against him.

"We have to go to the council with this," said Rhett.

Derren pursed his lips. "I don't think that would be the best idea." At Rhett's questioning look, he went on, "You tell the council about this, two things will happen: One, they'll take the matter totally out of our hands and order us to allow them to deal with it." Trey growled at that, clearly not liking the idea that he'd miss his chance at revenge. "Two, they'll be obligated to inform the families of any of the victims they recognize. You know what will happen next."

"It will risk a number of packs grouping together, declaring war on the jackals," concluded Dante. "Not only would the jackals then go deeper into hiding, but they would just create another site and the whole thing would start over."

Derren nodded. "And the last thing the shifter community needs is for humans to hear about this. A declaration of war would most certainly draw attention."

Roni knew both Derren and Dante had valid points. The human extremist groups would never stop their campaigns against shifters. The awareness of such a shifter website might certainly be grounds for more appeals to be made—or even worse, it might begin a war between shifters and humans.

"It's no wonder the jackals are in hiding," rumbled Marcus. "Can't run something like this and stay out in the open."

"But you can track the IP address and find out the location of the bastards, right?" Dante asked Rhett.

The guy looked insulted by the question. "Of course. But it's probable that they've taken measures to mask their IP address—having a website like this, they'd be dumb not to. If they haven't, it shouldn't take me more than thirty minutes."

"And if they've masked it?"

"A few days. A week, at most."

"Get on it," said Trey. "Then crash the site."

Nick shook his head. "I don't think we should crash it. Not yet. The bastards who committed all these attacks need to answer for what they've done." He turned to Rhett. "Can you find the IP addresses of all the people who uploaded the vids? I can get Donovan to help lessen the load." Donovan was Nick's main contact.

"I should be able to. But if they've used a proxy to do it anonymously, it will take a little time—even with Donovan's help. And if you're expecting us to trace the IP address of every single person who uploaded something, it could take months. I mean, look, there's a whole library of these clips." Rhett scrolled down a page that listed hundreds of videos. "It might be best to just try to get the list of subscribers and track them down that way."

"Wait," said Nick, "go back up a second. There." He pointed to a certain clip. Curious, Roni leaned forward to get a better look at the freeze-frame image of a video titled "Humans get mauled by wolf." At Rhett's click, it enlarged, clearly showing a young female being restrained by an older human boy. The female looked wild, petrified, and enraged. It was . . . it was Roni.

CHAPTER SIX

H er stomach dropped, and her brain . . . it was like it stopped
working. Roni was conscious that everyone around her was
talking at once, aware that Nick was close to losing his mind and
she should probably calm him down. But Roni couldn't. Rage was
coursing through her, heating her up from the inside, demanding
an outlet.

Her wolf didn't understand what was happening, but she
responded to Roni's anger—lunging for the surface, wanting to
shift and eradicate the threat she couldn't see.

She needed to get out of that room.

Turning on her heel, Roni raced through the tunnels, out of
the caves, and into the surrounding forest. She wasn't sure how
long she ran, but she eventually stopped. Unfortunately, the run
hadn't been an adequate outlet for the rage. It was still there, bub-
bling, wanting out, making her lungs ache and her breath leave
her body in short, anxiety-filled pants. Her wolf was frantic with
the need to act, to protect, to defend—her wild agitation only
served to feed Roni's anger.

She punched the nearest tree over and over until her knuck-
les were bleeding, but the rage still didn't ease. Nor did her wolf's
attempts to shift. Scrunching a hand in her hair, Roni let her
head fall back, sucking in mounds of air in an effort to get her

breathing under control. Roni wasn't quick to anger, but when it happened, she found it extremely hard to calm down, especially with her wolf's emotions mingled so closely with hers.

Roni had known about the video, of course. The recording had been the evidence Nick needed to prove that he attacked the humans in the defense of both him and her as opposed to cold-blooded murder. Having been tagged as evidence, she'd assumed it was locked up somewhere. Apparently someone had found a way to get a hold of it, because now it was up on a website for shifters all over the world to see. As shame and horror added to the rage curdling inside her, she once again punched the tree.

"Roni."

She spun to face Marcus, who stood several feet away. "I want to be alone." The stubborn wolf didn't move. "Go."

"No." As if he'd let her be alone at a time like this. She didn't know it, but she hadn't been alone for even one second. Marcus had followed her through the tunnels and out of the caves, staying a safe distance behind her as she ran—giving her solace, but keeping close. "You might think you want to be alone, but you don't. And that's not a weakness."

A tremor ran through Roni as his smooth tone slid over her, soothing her . . . but it also stirred her senses in a major way. "I'm not a good person to be around right now." Restless with dark energy that had nowhere to go, she began pacing back and forth.

Marcus took slow steps toward her. He could see how close to the edge she was, see brief flashes of her wolf in her eyes—an indication that, at this moment, the animal's emotions were heightening hers. He'd never before met anyone who was so closely gelled to their wolf. He could see now how it would be a curse at times.

His own wolf was pacing in distress, wanting to go to Roni and soothe her. He also wanted to rip apart the fucker who was responsible for her distress—and Marcus knew right then that both he and his wolf would kill for this female. Up close to her now, Marcus gently put his hand on her arm. "Roni? Look at me, sweetheart."

Pausing midstride, she found Marcus standing before her, so masculine and solid and unnerving. *He could help*, she thought as her gaze settled on his unfairly erotic mouth. She had no idea what he was saying; she couldn't concentrate on his words because all she could think about was having that mouth on hers again. Her wolf agreed. Yes, this male would give her what she needed—an outlet, a way to take the edge off her anger. But that would be using him like a human Valium, and Roni wasn't comfortable with that. She forced her eyes away from his mouth and took a single step backward. "You need to go."

Nothing in the world could have made him leave her. Even if Marcus had wanted to, his protective instincts wouldn't have allowed it. What he wanted to do was hold her, but he knew Roni well enough to know that physical affection would simply make her uncomfortable. He didn't know how to help her, and it was making him crazy—every instinct he had told him to do *something*. He covered the distance she'd created between them. "I'm staying, sweetheart."

That slow, languid drawl was unintentionally seductive—he was there to comfort and calm her, Roni knew. But that wasn't what she wanted right then, it wasn't what her wolf wanted. Roni's eyes once again settled on his mouth, remembering how talented and hungry it had been. She gave a quick shake of the head, hoping to shake off those thoughts. "Really, Marcus, you need to go."

"Why?"

The truth burst out of her. "Because I like to fuck when I'm angry!"

Just like that, the atmosphere changed, thickened, and became charged with that same old sexual tension that never seemed far away.

"I know that's not normal," she continued. "I know most people like to be cuddled and all that stuff. Not me. No. I like to fuck—hard, fast, rough, and deep. In which case, *you really need to go*." Or she'd use him, just like so many females had used him before, and then she'd hate herself for doing it because he wasn't the shallow smooth-talker she'd thought he was. He knew he looked good and knew how to use that raw charisma to get what he wanted. But he wasn't vain or arrogant or superficial. He had much more emotional depth than she'd given him credit for. He was . . . good.

He was also exciting her wolf with the hungry look on his face. Roni was no less affected by him; her nerve endings sprung to life as that lazy, hooded, sensual gaze fixed on hers—the hunter was awake again. "Don't."

His mouth curved. "What?"

"Don't look at me like that." She backed away.

"How am I looking at you?" He moved toward her, and she immediately backpedaled. Not wanting her to back away any farther, Marcus halted. So did she. And so they both stood there, caught in the grip of an escalating sexual tension that had them both fairly panting.

"Just go." But he didn't. He stayed totally still, his electric-blue eyes focused completely on her, glittering with a promise of sexual satisfaction she'd never experienced before. She felt her cautiousness slipping away, replaced by a need so fierce and hot it was frightening. It was also beginning to drown out the rage.

"I'm not going anywhere. Not just because I want you so badly I ache with it. But because if this is the only form of comfort you can take from me, that's what I'll give you." A growl rumbled out of him as her tongue flicked out to lick over that bottom lip he wanted to bite. "Come here, Roni."

She wanted to. Really, really wanted to. But using him would be wrong. Besides, the guy was living, breathing junk food—he'd taste good, he'd fill her up and leave her satisfied, but he'd also leave her wanting more, craving him again and again. To go to him now would be stupid and reckless. Still, it was so unbelievably tempting, especially when he was looking at her like that—like he could eat her up and lick every inch of her.

But would he continue looking at her like that if he saw her naked? Probably not. Marcus had been with countless beautiful females; she'd pale in comparison. Her wolf, however, was aloof to Roni's human concerns—she pushed at Roni to go to him, to take what he offered.

"Come here," Marcus repeated, sensing her uncertainty beginning to crumble. "I'll give us both what we've wanted since day one."

"I never said I wanted this. I *don't* want this."

"One thing I really like about you, Roni, is that you don't bullshit. But you're bullshitting me now. Why?"

Pinned in place by the dark heat in his eyes, she couldn't lie. "I don't want to be another female that uses you."

She just about broke his heart with that. "Ah, sweetheart, that's not how I see it."

"My body . . . it's not anything like what you're used to." It wasn't all curves and soft skin. It was all battle scars and smooth muscle. It had never made her feel self-conscious or insecure before—she wasn't vain. But with him . . . it was different somehow.

"You've shifted around me, remember. I've seen your body. And I want it. Now."

Fuck it, she thought. Both moving at once, they collided; their bodies instantly locked together—desperate, frenzied, out of control. His mouth was greedy and demanding as it dominated hers, licking and biting and tasting. His tall, powerful body pressed her back against a tree, crowding her, trapping her. Rather than prickling her dominant instincts, it made her even more frantic for him; so frantic that she ripped at his T-shirt as she yanked it off—revealing a broad, hard chest covered in sleek, tanned skin.

"I have to be inside you." In seconds, Marcus had her completely naked and pinned against the tree with her legs wrapped around his waist. No finesse, no preamble, no smooth words—he was simply too caught up in Roni, in the feel and scent of her. He retained just enough sanity to remember he needed to be sure she was ready for him.

Not the passive type, Roni tackled his fly, wanting him inside her more than she'd wanted anything in a long time. Then his cock was in her hand and he was groaning as she gripped him tight. She would have pumped him, but she couldn't concentrate. The brief sting of his teeth on her nipple, the soothing flick of his tongue, the feel of sure, strong masculine hands roaming over her . . . it was too much sensation, but she wanted more. He gave her more, repeatedly pumping two calloused fingers inside her, sucking on her neglected nipple so hard it hurt, and fluttering his thumb over her clit, making it tingle and—

She exploded. He caught her cry with his mouth, swallowing it down. He only gave her a few seconds reprieve before positioning her to take his cock. She shifted in his arms, trying to impale herself on him. But his teeth locked around her shoulder in warning, and the shock of the dominant move made her freeze. As if to reward her, he thrust hard and she sucked in a breath. He was thick and long and he stretched her, causing the most delicious burn. One more forceful thrust and he was balls deep inside her.

Marcus groaned as her pussy clamped around his cock. "Fuck, you feel good." He'd known she would, had known it would be good between them, but he hadn't expected it to be *this* good, this powerful or primal. She'd have him addicted to her after this; his need for her would get worse, not better.

As he stared into her dazed eyes, Marcus felt a sharp tug in his chest. And he knew, he *knew*, that if he didn't leave right then, there was a strong possibility he would cross that line from "simple, safe, and uncomplicated" and topple right into an emotional pit. It didn't make sense, but there it was.

The smart thing to do would be to walk away—he wasn't good at emotional intimacy, wasn't built for it. But he couldn't walk away from her. Not while this drive to have her, to *take* her so completely that all she'd feel and think of was him, was pumping through his system. "Now I've got you." His wolf growled in satisfaction at that.

"Hard and fast," panted Roni, sliding her hands over the solid bulk of his broad shoulders. "Slow won't do it for me."

"Good, because that's the one thing I can't give you right now." He gripped her ass tight as he powered into her, knowing she could take it, loving the demanding prick of her claws. "That's right, sweetheart, show me how much you want it." Other times, Roni was reserved and distant. But here and now, she was open and honest in her responses; she didn't hold back or hide what she wanted and felt. This was how he wanted her: open to him, accepting and unguarded.

Roni practically melted when his mouth latched onto her neck and suckled as he pounded into her harder, relentlessly, and so damn deep she felt him in her womb. God, no wonder females flocked to him. The guy knew exactly what he was doing, exactly where to touch, exactly how to use his cock. Reminded of how experienced he was, she couldn't stop herself from slicing her claws into his back—leaving a temporary brand there for all the Zaras of the world to see. Oops.

Marcus's gaze snapped to hers. "Marking me, sweetheart?"

Embarrassed by her lapse in control, she scowled. "Fuck you."

He just smiled. "Then you won't mind that I'm going to mark you." When she shook her head in objection, he nodded. "Oh, yes, I am. See, sweetheart, I can bite you, I can spank you, and I can take you however I want you, because when I'm inside this pussy, it's mine."

"You bastard!" She punched his shoulders and beat at his back with her legs, but he just pinned her tighter against the tree as he continued ramming his cock in and out of her.

"I *am* going to mark you, Roni. Once with you isn't going to be enough. I'm going to need this again and again." When she shook her head once more, he growled. She snarled. He bit her lip. She nipped his chin. He squeezed her ass. She pressed her claws deep into his back. "You're close, aren't you, baby? I can feel your pussy getting tighter around me." He shifted, adjusting his angle so that his cock brushed her G-spot with every harsh, merciless stroke.

Roni couldn't take any more; an explosion of pure sensation

shot through her, shattering her, tearing a scream from her throat. That was when he sank his teeth into the crook of her neck—the pleasure-pain drew out her orgasm, sending wave after wave of sheer bliss washing through her.

Marcus rammed into her one final time, and held still as he pulsed deep inside her, filling her with everything he had. "Fuck, Roni." He rested his forehead against hers, breathing as hard as she was. Moments later, when he could finally move again, he slipped out of her and gently set her on her feet.

"You marked me," she croaked.

"And you marked me."

"I didn't mean to."

"Yes, you did."

Yes, she had—and that scared the hell out of her.

Marcus watched her immediately begin rebuilding those walls around her. He gripped her chin. "Oh, no, you don't. No clamming up, Roni. This *will* happen again; don't deny it. You're no coward."

No, she wasn't. There was no point in denying that it would happen again. What female in her right mind wouldn't *want* it to happen again? "Okay. But we need the boundaries to be clear. As you may have noticed, despite being a dominant female, I'm not interested in being the dominant partner in bed. An active partner, yes, but not dominant. However, that doesn't mean I'll let you take the lead in any way, shape, or form outside of the bedroom."

"Stop panicking, Roni," he said gently. He picked up his ripped T-shirt and slid it on before fixing his fly. "I have no inclination to control you. You're your own person, you have a mind—a mind I like—and you're able to make your own decisions." He watched in satisfaction as the tension left her shoulders. He knew his gaze was nothing short of territorial as it roamed over the delectable body she was quickly re-dressing. "You should probably know that I'm going to be pretty possessive with you." It had been bad before, but it was going to be even worse now.

Roni was afraid that might work both ways. "Just remember that there's a difference between being possessive and being controlling." She expected him to bristle, like others had before him, but his expression actually softened as he came toward her.

"I don't want to control you, Roni," he assured her in a low, soothing voice, brushing his fingers through her hair. "But I'll be damned if I'll share you."

"Fine. But the same goes for you."

"I don't want anyone else."

She gave him a curt nod. "Okay." Her voice had turned husky with arousal. Well, it was pretty hard to stay unruffled when she had a tower of raw masculinity looming over her, stealing her breath, and claiming to want no one but her.

A noise suddenly penetrated the silence. Someone was calling her name. Not just anyone: Nick. Each time he called out for her, his voice grew closer. "He's going to shit a brick."

A few moments later, Nick appeared out of the trees with Taryn and Trey. Abruptly her brother froze and his nostrils flared. Then he was charging at Marcus. "You son of a bitch!"

"Nick, no!" Roni and Trey both dove between them, bringing him to a halt mere feet away from the object of his anger. Marcus didn't even flinch. He met Nick's gaze head-on.

"I told you to keep your hands off my sister!"

"True," allowed Marcus. "But I didn't say that I would."

"He's not good for you, Roni," insisted Nick. "You don't want someone like him."

"I don't?"

Nick winced at that dangerously soft tone. Telling a dominant female what she wanted or what she thought was not good. Marcus almost felt bad for the guy. Actually, no, he didn't.

"You might be my Alpha and my brother, but you're not my damn keeper."

Trey shoved Nick just hard enough to get his attention. "Walk away before you say something you can't take back."

Nick didn't listen. "The guy's a total slut!"

Roni's wolf did *not* like anyone insulting Marcus. In fact, neither did Roni. "And you were a virgin when you met Shaya, were you?"

"No, he damn well wasn't," Taryn mumbled with a huff.

"He's not what you need, Roni! For him, you're just a little bit of fun until—"

"Enough," snapped Marcus, stepping around Roni. "Say what you want about me, Axton, but don't make out that I think that little of Roni."

Nick dived at him. Once again, Roni and Trey stepped between them.

"I'm not the easy target you seem to think I am," warned Marcus, his voice silky and menacing. "Push, and I'll push back." And his wolf would enjoy it. Maybe it wasn't good to challenge Roni's brother, but the guy would only respect strength.

"He marked her," Trey pointed out. Nick stopped struggling, his eyes finding the mark at the crook of Roni's neck. Marking was a sign of possessiveness, but it was also a sign that the male respected the female in question enough to leave that brand. "Marcus may have had a lot of sexual partners, but that doesn't mean he's an asshole. He's never mistreated or deliberately hurt the females he's been with; he just hasn't shown them any commitment."

Taryn arched a brow at Nick. "And neither did you, did you?"

"Because I was waiting for my mate." At Taryn's meaningful look, Nick sighed. His eyes once again found Marcus. "Hurt her, and I'll—"

"Have to wait until Roni's done emasculating me before you get your turn."

Looking ever so slightly mollified, Nick turned to Roni. "I'll be waiting in the car. Don't be long." He spun on his heel and disappeared through the trees.

Inhaling deeply, Taryn smiled. "For what it's worth, I think you guys make a cute couple." Then she was gone too, with an amused Trey at her side.

Marcus's wolf finally relaxed. "That went well."

Roni gawked. "Are you kidding me?"

"No blood was shed."

"You would have fought him, wouldn't you?"

"If I had to, yeah. I wouldn't have been happy about it—he's your brother. I don't want to put you in an awkward position. But I don't back down. It's not in my nature." He dabbed a kiss on her way-too-alluring mouth. "Your wolf's calmer. How are you doing?"

She sighed. "Pissed, but I'm no longer interested in punching the shit out of that tree over there."

"Once Rhett and Donovan find out who uploaded that video, I'll hunt them down and I'll deal with them."

"*We'll* hunt them down and deal with them," she corrected. "Promise me something. Promise me you won't watch it." Maybe it was stupid, but she didn't want him to see her that way—helpless, terrified.

Understanding why she'd ask that, Marcus cupped her neck. "Roni, I will never see you as weak." She was far from it.

"Promise me."

A part of him wanted to watch it, wanted to know what she'd been through. But he couldn't deny her this, not when there was so much pain in her eyes. "I promise. And I won't let the others watch it either."

She swallowed hard. "Thank you." His arms engulfed her, and she instinctively tensed, not really sure what to do with the contact. Her wolf settled, satisfied. Roni decided to follow her lead and allowed herself to relax. It strangely felt . . . good.

Marcus kissed the top of her head. "Come on, I'll walk you to the car."

"To flaunt this in front of Nick?"

"To remind him that I'm not going anywhere." Smoothing his thumb over his mark, Marcus felt a sense of self-satisfaction he hadn't experienced before. He held those dusky green eyes that always seemed to be filled with wariness. "And neither are you."

"I should have known to search for you in an obvious place."

Sprawled on the sofa, Roni looked to the doorway where Derren stood and shot him a "fuck off" glare. She'd been hiding in one of the guest lodges for hours, wanting some alone time. That was what Roni did when things went to shit: she looked for space and privacy, explored the matter in her head, got her thoughts straight, and faced the problem head-on. But she'd known it would be hard to do that if she had anxious pack members hovering, wanting to comfort and fuss over her, panicking that seeing the video had "traumatized" her.

Derren closed the front door and sank into one of the armchairs. "Almost the entire pack is searching for you."

"I wanted some privacy. Considering it's what *you* like to do when shit happens, you should be able to appreciate that better than anyone." She and Derren had been good friends since he came out of juvie with Nick. The extremely hot Beta was very perceptive and very serious in some ways, yet he could be relaxed with certain people. Like her, he had dark places inside him that haunted him from time to time—a kinship that had made them "click" on meeting each other. Yet, there had never been anything between them other than friendship.

He allowed that with a nod. "But I wanted to make sure you were okay. Not because I thought you might be huddled in a corner somewhere bawling your eyes out. But because I'm your friend. Isn't that what you do for me when *I'm* having a bad day?"

She huffed. "Point taken. Did Nick tell everyone about the video?"

"He told Shaya, Eli, and the enforcers, but that's all."

"My mother doesn't know?" She sighed in relief when Derren shook his head. "Good. It's bad enough that she mollycoddles me in that patronizing, condescending way of hers. This would make her ten times worse."

"She cares. She just has odd ways of showing that." There was a slight pause as a glint of humor entered his eyes. "So . . . Fuller marked you." She didn't at all appreciate the teasing lilt to his voice. "It's a shock that you didn't rip him a new one for that move."

Yeah, but how could she have vilified Marcus for that when she had marked him first? It would have been pretty hypocritical. Not that she planned on telling Derren that. But something in her expression must have given her away, because a wide smile split his lips.

"Oh . . . you marked him too, didn't you?" He laughed. "This is going to be fun to watch."

She sat up and tucked her legs beneath her. "What will be fun to watch?"

"Marcus trying to handle you. It's what guys have always tried to do, threatened by how dominant you are." He cocked his head, frowning thoughtfully. "Although . . . I have to say, Marcus doesn't seem to do that."

As it sounded more like a question, she confirmed, "No, he doesn't."

"When I see him with you, it reminds me of someone trying to approach a wild animal, to gentle them and get them used to him."

"A wild animal?" She wasn't sure she liked that comparison.

"My point is that he doesn't try to handle you, he tries to understand you and coax you. That's good."

It was true that although he was persistent in his efforts to know her and seduce her, Marcus wasn't extremely pushy in that annoying way that dominant males often were. He focused on her intensely, but he didn't overwhelm her with the full force of his personality—he gave her enough physical and emotional space for her to be relaxed around him . . . as if he *knew* exactly what she needed. He lured, cajoled, and charmed her, wanting her to make her own way to him as opposed to forcing himself on her. She liked that.

What bothered her were the compliments. She didn't need them and didn't see how they could possibly be true—particularly the ones about her supposedly intriguing personality. Hell, if she didn't have chocolate in her diet, she doubted she'd have a personality at all. She cocked her head at Derren. "Do you think I'm intriguing?"

He blinked. "Intriguing?"

"Marcus said I intrigue him."

"Why do you sound so insulted by that?"

She shrugged. "I just don't understand what he could possibly find intriguing." Unless, of course, he found people who had difficulties dealing with their own species rather interesting. "He's super good-looking, he's charming, he's good in the sack . . ." Extremely good in the sack. And she was . . . well, *her.*

"I don't know why you're feeling insecure. You're hot, Roni. The only reason guys don't swarm around you is that you intimidate them. Surely Marcus has earned brownie points for not letting your level of dominance be a factor. From what I can see, he respects it. I have to say, though, I'm not sure if you're more dominant than he is. Fuller's not as harmless as he seems."

That was one of the things she liked about Derren—he never missed anything. "No, he's not. But he doesn't hold it over me. He treats me like an equal." And that was a lot more than her mother and Nick did.

"That's a good thing."

"I know, but I *marked* him, and it's freaking me out." She'd never before marked anyone. "Worse, my wolf is totally smug about it." She narrowed her eyes at Derren's speculative look. "What?"

"Do you think maybe he's your . . . ?" He shook his head. "Never mind. Look, I think you should just let yourself enjoy this. As for marking him . . . it's easy enough to get carried away when the sex is good."

Considering that, she nodded. "Yeah, you're right. I just got carried away, that's all."

"That's all," he echoed, his tone reassuring.

Unfortunately, she wasn't reassured, because she was well aware that it had been possessiveness that caused her to make that mark—it had raced through her mind and body in a way she couldn't explain. She'd wanted to warn off any other female that dared to come near him. That wasn't "getting carried away." It was more. And it scared her.

At that moment, the front door burst open, and Nick, Eli, Jesse, Bracken, and Zander piled in the room. How fabulous was that?

Nick plucked her from the sofa and hugged her tight—like Roni, he wasn't the most affectionate person in the world, so it was always kind of odd when he did that. Pulling back to meet her eyes, he spoke. "Honey, are you okay?"

He'd said it softly and carefully, like she was on the verge of emotionally splintering. She stepped out of his hold. "I'm fine."

"You're not fine," he insisted.

Jesse pointed hard at her. "And no one expects you to be."

"Damn right." Eli patted her shoulder. "It had to have been a shock to see the vid on that fucked-up website."

"We'll find out who uploaded it, and we'll obliterate them—I promise you that." Nick gently pushed her back onto the sofa, like she wouldn't be able to stand on her own steam or something.

Zander came over then, his expression sympathetic—hell, she hadn't been sure the hard enforcer was capable of empathizing with another person. "Can I get you anything? Coffee? Something to eat?"

"No," she gritted out, "I'm fine."

"Stop saying you're fine," ordered Nick, though his voice was gentle. "I saw you when you ran out of the tunnels—you were ready to explode. If I hadn't been on the verge of exploding myself, I'd have gone after you." His expression hardened slightly. "I've got to admit you were a lot calmer when I found you with Fuller."

She shook her head. "Don't."

"Don't what? Warn you that you made a huge mistake? Warn you that Fuller isn't good for you?"

"I've heard it all before—it's getting tedious."

"He marked you, for God's sake." Of course that comment drew everyone's attention to her neck. Then they were all talking at once.

"Whoa, he *branded* you?" Eli gawked.

Jesse whistled. "That's not exactly a discreet one either."

"You let a guy mark you?" Bracken seemed mystified.

"Is he still breathing?" asked a wide-eyed Zander.

"You're making a bigger deal out of this than you need to, Nick." Derren sighed.

Roni closed her eyes for a few seconds, seeking patience. "This is my personal business."

Nick folded his arms. "I did some checking on Fuller."

"You did *what*?" she growled.

"I had Donovan dig up some details for me." And he sounded much too unrepentant for her liking. "I always do checks on any guys who show interest in you."

"Will we ever get to meet this mysterious Donovan?" asked Eli, taking the seat beside her.

"No." There was a short pause. "Don't you want to know what he discovered about Fuller?" Nick asked Roni.

"No, I don't. His business is his business." She was curious, of course—particularly since Marcus had claimed to have a "twisted story" about his family. But unlike Nick, she didn't believe it was fair to invade other people's privacy.

"He ever talk about his father to you?"

"Do you really think I'd break his confidence if he had?"

"Roni, the guy was violent. Used to beat his mate until she was black and blue. People were too scared to confront him about it, and his mate always came up with pretty excuses for her injuries." Every male in the room growled.

She could understand their disgust and outrage. Mates were something to treasure and protect, were considered a gift that was sacred. To abuse that gift, to harm that person in any way, was abhorrent and callous. "And while that's a horrible story, I don't see why this would mean Marcus 'isn't good' for me."

"It doesn't bother you that he hasn't helped her? He could have done something, Roni. As a kid, he was helpless. But later on, he could have stepped in and defended his mother. He could have gotten her away from that bastard. But he didn't. He left her with him. That doesn't bother you?"

Eli spoke then. "Nothing's ever that simple, Nick. There could be more to his story than that. Maybe his mom hadn't wanted help. Maybe his dad had beaten him too."

"According to Donovan, there was never anything to suggest that Marcus or his sisters suffered."

"Doesn't mean it didn't happen," said Roni. "Now do us all a favor and concentrate on your own life instead of busying yourself interfering with mine." She'd known Marcus was a guy with secrets even before he'd mentioned his "twisted story," so finding out he had some skeletons wasn't at all a surprise.

What *was* a surprise was that Marcus hadn't whisked his mother away from his father—that just didn't fit with the protective wolf she knew. Sure, his mother might have refused to leave, might have turned on Marcus for trying to interfere. But Marcus was persistent by nature; he would have pushed and pushed until she agreed to leave, or until his father vowed never to touch her again.

Or maybe Roni was reading him wrong; maybe she didn't know him at all.

In any case, there was always more to every story. Roni knew better than most how people's stories could be distorted the more it traveled through the grapevine.

Besides, what right did she have to judge another? What was so special about her that gave her the right to condemn or pass judgment on what another person did or didn't do?

"How about we move off the subject of Fuller?" proposed Derren. "He's not what's important right now."

"Fine." Nick exhaled heavily. "Listen, Roni, I've been thinking and . . . I think we should tell Mom about the vid being on the website."

"*What?*"

"Hear me out. She can help you with this; she's someone you can talk to about it. You've got Shaya too, obviously, but—"

"No way."

"Telling Kathy won't help anyone," Derren told Nick. "All it will do is make her hysterical and, in turn, make Roni miserable because of the subsequent increase in coddling."

"But she can talk to Roni, be a shoulder for her to—"

Roni jumped to her feet, growling. "You tell Mom, and I'll slit your throat."

Nick raised his hands, palms out. "Calm down, Roni." He said it like she was a psycho who was hanging on the edge. "I know you're upset about the vid—"

Calmly but coldly, she insisted, "Get out."

"But you've got us. We're here for you."

"Get out."

"All we want is to help you, be here for you. Come on, come with us—you don't have to lock yourself away. We won't judge you for crying."

Crying? "Fuck this." And she shifted.

The dark-gray wolf growled, and everybody froze.

CHAPTER SEVEN

Leaning back in his seat, Marcus rubbed at his aching eyes. He'd spent most of the day on Rhett's computer, watching many of the vile videos on snm.com with Ryan and Tao, searching for any familiar faces in the hope that it might speed up the process of identifying the sadistic bastards who'd uploaded them. It had taken everything Marcus had to shut off his emotions and observe each one of the vids with clinical detachment.

Unfortunately the faces had been cleverly concealed. They had come to realize that the jackals' kills all appeared to happen in the same place: a dark, square room that was empty except for a bloodstained mattress. However, they had no idea where it was.

Rhett had quickly discovered that the IP address of the site had in fact been masked—and it had been done exceptionally well. Both he and Donovan were working on it, in addition to attempting to trace the IP addresses of the others—in particular, the person responsible for uploading the video of Roni. Unfortunately, said person had done it anonymously, but it wouldn't keep him hidden forever. They'd track him down somehow.

Marcus was glad Roni wasn't with him. She wouldn't have been able to detach herself from the victims' plight, not when she herself had been through something very similar. However, as much as he was glad she hadn't been around, he'd also sort of . . . missed her.

People who didn't know Roni well would never believe it, but she was good company. She was entertaining, though he was sure she didn't mean to be. She was outspoken and direct, which he liked and could appreciate. And although she was wounded in her own little way, she hadn't let it destroy her confidence or hold her back; she kept on going, and he could respect that. He respected her.

His wolf, too, had missed her company and was pushing at Marcus to find her. Marcus would have been happy to oblige—particularly since he was aching to be inside her again, and particularly since he had a very important question for her regarding the video evidence—but the multiple calls he'd made to her cell phone had all gone straight to voicemail. She hadn't returned his calls or text messages.

He'd considered contacting Shaya to check that Roni was okay, but it seemed wrong to go around Roni like that. She wasn't a child that needed monitoring, and she wouldn't appreciate being treated like one. He was well aware that Roni enjoyed having space, and he'd need to respect that.

"What the fuck is wrong with these people?" Tao was referring to a clip of four jackals physically assaulting a bound and gagged juvenile bear shifter. "How could someone truly be that sick?"

"We're looking at evil—pure and simple." That came from Ryan.

"You need a break?" Tao asked the enforcer. Ryan simply scowled at him before returning his attention to the computer screen. Tao exchanged a worried look with Marcus. Neither of them had wanted Ryan to join them. Their fellow enforcer had once been taken by a rival pack, kept prisoner, and tortured for information on the Phoenix Pack. The kidnappers had learned squat, because Ryan hadn't broke, no matter what they did to him.

Marcus didn't even want to think of the things they'd done to him.

Ryan never talked about it, and nobody ever brought it up. But the wolf had enough scars to hint at some of what had happened. If watching these clips brought back memories, he certainly wasn't showing it. But then, Ryan was pretty detached in many ways.

When the clip ended, Tao turned to Marcus. "I heard you marked Roni."

"Yep."

"I knew you wanted her badly, but I hadn't expected you to mark her. I heard Nick went postal." Tao smiled at the idea.

Marcus returned the smile. "I honestly thought the vein in his temple would pop." He twisted his mouth. "But I can't say I blame him. My rep isn't pretty."

"Yep, it seems it's come back to bite you in the ass. I was a little wary of her in the beginning. She just seems so . . . aloof and standoffish. But then I realized she's only like that with people who don't matter to her. I can relate to that."

True. Tao wasn't interested in expanding his world beyond the people he cared about, but with those people he could be considerate, protective, and loyal. For him, everybody outside of his pack, particularly humans with their ignorance and prejudice, was no concern of his.

"She earned my loyalty when she saved Kye," said Tao, a tinge of self-condemnation in his voice.

"Tao, it wasn't your fault that you passed out. Nobody thinks less of you for it. Hell, Roni and Shaya passed out too. It just took you a little longer to come around."

"It still pisses me off."

Marcus went to say more, but then his cell phone rang. Taking it from his jeans' pocket, he saw that the caller was Shaya. "Hey, what's up?"

"Please tell me you're not busy."

Marcus straightened in his seat. "What's going on?"

"Well, Roni shifted into her wolf form yesterday a few hours after she got home, and . . . well . . . we can't get her to change back."

"I'll be right there." He ended the call.

Tao, obviously having overheard the conversation, said, "We've got this; go see your girl."

A short time later, Marcus was striding through Nick and Shaya's lodge. In the living area, he found the Alpha pair, along with Derren, Eli, and the enforcers, having a tense conversation. "Where is she?"

Nick jumped to his feet. "What are you doing here?"

Shaya quickly explained, "I called him."

Nick spun to face her. "You called him?"

"He might be able to do something."

"How do you figure that?"

Leaving the couple to argue, Marcus turned to Eli. "Why are you all so worried? If you don't trust that Roni's going to shift back any time soon, something must have happened. She was calm when she left me yesterday."

Eli sighed, clearly troubled. "After we got back, she vanished, and we thought she'd disappeared in her wolf form. When it happens, she never goes far, but she mostly avoids people; eventually, she makes her way back, but it can still be months before she shifts again. She hasn't done it since moving here, and we were concerned that seeing the vid—reliving the memories—would act as a trigger. As it turned out, she hadn't shifted. She was just hiding in one of the lodges. We tried assuring her that it was okay to be upset—"

"Did she look upset?"

Eli seemed surprised by the question. "What?"

"Did she look upset? Did she say she was?" Because her family had a nasty habit of "assuming" when it came to Roni—assuming they knew what she was feeling, what was best for her, what her limits were, and what she wanted.

"No, she kept saying she was fine. But there was no way she could possibly be fine. Still, it looked like she might not bolt on us. But then she and Nick clashed over the decision of whether or not to tell Mom everything. I think it acted as the cherry on the cake—she was dealing with enough already—and that just made it worse, so she broke and shifted to escape it all."

Maybe. But none of that added up to Marcus. It didn't fit with the Roni he'd come to know—she didn't "break." In any case . . . "Shaya, you should have called me sooner. Has Kathy been told about the vid being on the website?" Marcus might just have to hurt Axton if he'd done something so fucking idiotic.

Shaya assured him, "I convinced Nick not to say anything."

Good. "I want to see her."

Nick took a step toward him. "Wait a minute—"

Shaya grabbed his arm. "No, *you* wait a minute, Nick. There's a good chance he can do something."

"Like what? He has no significance to Roni's life."

Derren cleared his throat. "She marked him."

The air suddenly chilled. Slowly, Nick turned to face his Beta. "You did not just say that she marked him."

"Look, Nick, we know you want her to be happy," said Shaya. "And that's great and all, but right now, she's far from happy. We haven't been able to help her. What's the harm in letting Marcus try?"

The words "letting Marcus try" made him bristle. This wasn't a negotiation. "I won't leave without seeing her."

Nick snarled at him. "You don't have any authority here, Fuller. This is none of your business; it's a pack matter—"

"This is a Roni matter, which makes it my business. I know you're worried for your sister, and I know it will gall you if another male can help when you couldn't. I get it. But this is about Roni—not you, not me, and not anyone's pride." Marcus returned his attention to Eli. "Where is she?"

Eli glanced from Nick to Marcus, and then sighed. "Follow me." He led Marcus out of the lodge, into the forest, and deep into Mercury Pack territory. Nick and Derren came along, but they remained silent. Eventually, Eli halted near a fallen oak. "If you keep walking straight ahead, you'll come to a clearing. That's where she is. We'll have to stop here or she'll scent us. Her wolf won't let any of us near her—not even Shaya."

Derren scratched his nape. "Her wolf is clearly as pissed off as Roni is. And since Roni's frustration will be feeding hers . . ."

"She has no tolerance right now," finished Marcus.

Eli nodded. "We'll wait here for you, just in case she warns you off."

"She won't."

"What makes you think her wolf will allow you close, when she's keeping everyone else away?" asked Nick. The hostility was gone; it was a genuine question.

"Because as far as the wolf's concerned, I belong to her." The brand might only be temporary, but that wouldn't matter to the animal—their wolves were fiercely possessive.

Leaving the others, Marcus walked on ahead, letting the twigs beneath his feet snap loudly so that she would sense his approach. Startling a wolf was never a good idea. Soon enough, he stepped into the clearing. The dark-gray female was lapping at the small stream there, but her eyes—so alert, intelligent, and watchful—were honed on Marcus with lethal precision.

He'd encountered Roni's wolf during the battle against the extremists. She was even-tempered, but she was also vicious when the situation called for it. And that was the very reason why he had no intention of releasing his own wolf—the male's natural reaction would be to attempt to dominate her into calming. That wouldn't work. The female would sooner fight him than submit.

Marcus took a few steps forward. "Hey, gorgeous." Of course the wolf wouldn't understand the words, but his calm, cajoling tone would assure her that his intention wasn't to throw his dominance around. Also, he knew Roni could hear and understand him.

The female lifted her head, but didn't otherwise react. To his relief, she wasn't warning him to leave. That meant she'd at least accepted his presence, though she might not particularly welcome company right now.

He squatted and tapped the ground with his hand. "Come here, sweetheart." She didn't. She just continued to watch him with that hunter stare that missed nothing. Making his way to her wouldn't earn him any points. To the wolf, he was already invading her private time uninvited. There was no sense in pushing it.

A minute or so later, she finally moved. He remained still as she prowled toward him, looking both graceful and dangerous. She didn't halt until she was up close, eating up his space, clearly believing it was her right.

"Good girl," he said softly. He gently stroked her neck; her dense fur was softer than he'd expected. Marcus rubbed his cheek against hers, and she returned the gesture before delivering a delicate lick to his jaw. "Beautiful, aren't you?" Another lick to his jaw. "Come back, Roni."

Human eyes filled with irritation briefly flashed at him. Sharp teeth then nipped his chin and the wolf pulled back. He got the message—she didn't have any intention of shifting just yet.

"But I want to talk to you." The female kicked dirt at him. "Oh, like that, is it?" he asked with a smile as he stood, wiping the specks of dirt off his clothes. "All right, I guess I'd better make myself comfy then." He sat near a tree and leaned back against it, making a statement that he wasn't going anywhere.

Again irritation-filled human eyes flashed at him as the female curled her upper lip, baring her teeth, a low growl trickling out of her. The warning was coming from Roni, he knew. It was actually fascinating to see how close the line was between the human and the animal.

"You can't get me to leave. I'm staying. I'm not here to crowd you. If you want space, you've got it, but I'll be sticking close."

The wolf cocked her head, reminding him a little of Roni just before she delivered one of her useless facts. Then the wolf dismissed him with a distinctly haughty sniff and trotted off.

For hours, he sat against the tree, watching the wolf as she moved around the clearing, lapped at the stream, bathed in the sun, and occupied herself with batting at fish. The entire time, she pointedly ignored him. But he knew the female was supremely aware of every move he made.

When his ass started to go numb from sitting on the hard ground—at which point it was also beginning to get dark—Marcus moved to lie on his back, his arms crossed beneath his head. He was just about to doze off when he heard rustling in the grass. Then a cold muzzle rubbed against his cheek and a wet tongue lapped at his ear.

"Roni," he griped, shuddering and wiping his ear. "I'm not leaving."

Human eyes flashed at him once more, this time revealing confusion.

He patted the ground beside him in invitation. "Come on, gorgeous." With a put-out growl, the wolf collapsed at his side, leaning into him. Stroking her fur, he said, "I don't buy that you shift out of a need to escape memories or feelings." Her tail swished at him in what he interpreted as a "shut up and sleep" gesture.

It couldn't have been more than a minute later when he dozed off, relaxed and content. He woke to the sound of growling. Surprised to find it was daylight and he'd slept so long, he squinted as he sat upright to stroke the wolf who was standing at his side, staring into the trees and growling. "What's wrong, sweetheart?"

She didn't move her gaze from the trees, but he couldn't sense anyone close. Guessing it was one of her brothers stupidly trying to get near, Marcus got to his feet and did a long, languid stretch to get the kinks out of his back. When he went to move forward, the wolf pushed against him—she wanted him to stay exactly where he was.

"Roni, this is the part where you shift back and tell me what's wrong." But he got his answer when a black female wolf stepped out of the trees. Taking in her scent, he immediately understood. "Eliza, do you have a fucking death wish?"

Taking another step forward, she bared her teeth at the dark-gray wolf, which confirmed that, yep, Eliza had a death wish. Not only had she invaded the wolf's space, but there was nothing friendly about her approach.

Immediately, the dark-gray female curled her lips back, exposing fangs and gums, and released a chilling "back the fuck off" growl that made even Marcus nervous. Her hackles were raised and her ears were upright as her raging eyes drilled into the other female. Everything about her posture warned, "I can take you."

Marcus would bet everything he owned that she could. The two females were matched in size, but he was confident that Roni's wolf could wipe the floor with this potential challenger.

Generally, female wolf shifters gave three warnings before attacking. The black wolf had had her first warning, but she didn't appear to be backing off. If she kept pushing, this could get very bad. And Marcus didn't think Jesse would like finding his girlfriend in bits and pieces.

Fishing his cell out of his pocket, Marcus called Shaya. "You'd better get Jesse here fast, or there's a strong possibility your sister-in-law's going to rip out his girlfriend's throat." With that, he shoved his cell into his pocket and crouched down beside the dark-gray wolf. "Roni, come back now." He wouldn't be able to reason with the animal—she saw a threat that needed to be dealt with.

The black wolf took yet another step forward. His female released yet another chilling growl—warning number two. His inner wolf growled, backing her up, agitated at the sight of his female being provoked this way. And it *was* an attempt to provoke her. The black wolf hadn't laid down a gauntlet, but she was testing the dark-gray female.

He stroked his female's flank. "Roni, shift back."

Instead, she delivered a warning growl as the black wolf stupidly advanced another step into the clearing—warning number three.

"Roni, come back to me."

The black wolf took a threatening step forward, flattening her ears and snapping her teeth . . . and apparently the dark-gray female had had enough of this shit. She lunged.

The black wolf sprang from her position, and their bodies crashed hard. There was growling, snarling, yowling, and yelping as they each fought furiously to make the other submit, biting, clawing, body slamming, side swiping. The scent of blood and rage filled the air, further inciting the animals. It was vicious, it was brutal . . . and there wasn't a damn thing Marcus could do about it.

He had no option but to stand there, hands balled into fists, and watch as his female was attacked. His protective instincts demanded that he intervene, but he knew that he couldn't. Even his wolf, equally protective though he was, understood that there was no interfering in a situation like this—their female had been insulted, and she was justly responding to it.

As such, all Marcus could offer was his support. So he nodded in approval as the dark-gray female took a swipe at her opponent, brutally tearing a strip into her shoulder. In retaliation, the black wolf bit down hard on her ear. Marcus winced while his inner wolf growled in anger, nervously pacing. But then the dark-gray female slashed at her opponent's muzzle, making her yelp and bound away as blood sprayed onto the ground. "That's it. Good girl."

Gazes locked, the two wolves began to circle each other, their upper lips peeled back as growls trickled from their throats. Powerful vibes clogged the air as each shifter made her level of dominance clear. It was perfectly obvious that the black wolf was outmatched in power, dominance, speed, and strength.

But the dumb bitch didn't back down.

Instead, the black wolf snapped her teeth tauntingly. Growling, his female barreled into her hard enough to send her crashing into the ground and rolling onto her side. Smartly, although rather inconveniently, the black wolf righted herself fast. She then bounded at his female, and they again leaped at each other.

The two growled, clawed, and slashed at each other's bodies as they each attempted to take the other down. Twice the black wolf managed to wrap her paws around his female's neck in an effort to wrestle her to the ground, but twice she failed—the dark-gray wolf was simply too strong for her to dominate.

But the bitch still didn't back down.

Even though she was beginning to tire—her sides were heaving, she was panting hard, and her knees kept buckling—the black wolf refused to submit.

Suddenly, Eli came rushing out of the trees and skidded to a halt. "Fuck!" As Derren and the enforcers came up behind him, they all cursed at the sight of the females battling.

Bracken shrugged. "It was only a matter of time. She's been baiting Roni since she first got here."

"Eliza!" shouted Jesse. "Eliza, stop!" The black wolf paid him no attention. "Eliza, stop before she kills you!"

"Not working," Zander unnecessarily pointed out.

"I'll have to shift," said Derren. "I can pull rank, make them stop."

"No need." Marcus had quickly come to realize something—fierce though his female was fighting right now, she wasn't using her full strength. "Roni, stop playing with her!"

"Playing with her?" echoed Jesse.

"He's right." Eli folded his arms. "She's just teaching Eliza a lesson."

"Roni, playtime's over!" When she still didn't stop, Marcus called out, "End it, or rip her throat out! One or the other!"

The dark-gray female rushed at her opponent, wrapped her forepaws around her challenger's neck, and wrestled her to the ground. Straddling the black wolf, his female pinned her flat on her back by pressing her paws down onto her shoulders. At the same time, she clamped her jaws warningly around her throat. The black wolf froze, knowing it would take just one abrupt yank for the other female to rip her throat out.

"Submit, Eliza," ordered Jesse. Instead, she growled.

The dark-gray wolf shook her by the throat—a demand for her submission, a warning of what would happen if she didn't.

"For God's sake, Eliza, submit!"

Seconds later, the black wolf went lax. The other female gave her throat one last warning shake before releasing her. With her eyes still fixed on her challenger, the dark-gray wolf slowly backed off.

It was as the black wolf dragged herself from the ground, chest heaving, that Nick appeared. "What happened?"

"The short version is that Eliza's wolf stupidly tested Roni's wolf," replied Marcus. "As you can see, that didn't work out so well for her."

With a haughty sniff at the black wolf, the dark-gray wolf turned to leave.

"Roni, wait," said Nick. Her head ever so slowly swiveled to face him, and human eyes drilled into Nick, glittering in anger. He raised his hands at her growl. "I get it. You're still pissed." The other males received the same growl, making them back away.

The female turned her head again, this time to find Marcus. Her eyes briefly flashed human, and he saw the invitation there. Kind of smug that she was allowing him close while snubbing the other males, he followed her as she walked through the woods, heading for her lodge.

Once inside, Marcus went in search of the bathroom and found it at the rear of the small building. Sadly, there was no chance they could both fit into that shower stall, but that didn't mean he couldn't help clean her off. As her scent swirled around him, he turned to find Roni back in her human form. She was covered in scratches, bruises, patches of dirt, and streaks of blood. A big clump of blood was in her hair beside her ear—it made him recall Eliza delivering a harsh bite to it. "Hey, gorgeous. How are you feeling?"

"Like shit."

That was Roni—frank as they came. He turned on the shower and then helped her step inside the stall. She hissed through her teeth as the hot water rained over her wounds. His entire body hardened at the sight of hers, but his concern for her outweighed his desire to take her. Squirting some shampoo into his hand, he gently massaged it into her hair.

Roni cast him an odd look. She was pretty sure no one had washed her hair for her since she was five years old—her mother had encouraged independence at a young age. "What are you doing?"

"I would have thought it was obvious," he replied with a smile. "I'm taking care of you."

"Why?"

It was asked with all the innocence of a child, widening Marcus's smile. "Because you're mine. I don't like seeing you hurt." It made him want to punch someone.

"Eliza went too far. I had to take care of it."

"I know." It was only natural for dominant wolves in the same environment to want to set a hierarchy, but if their human sides were friendly—or at least cordial—there were usually no problems.

"She seems to want a place in the pack. I think she thought that if she could take me in a fight, it would make her seem like a strong addition."

"Yes. You're highly respected by your pack. They admire your strength and they make it clear. A guaranteed way of Eliza being noticed would be if she established herself as more dominant than you." Waiting as she rinsed the shampoo out of her hair, Marcus poured some shower gel into his hand. "Are you going to request that she's banned from your territory?" When Roni frowned, as if the idea had never occurred to her, he smiled.

"She's just not important enough for you to care, is she?" He'd quickly learned that Roni wasn't easily affected by things, one way or the other. If Eliza hadn't tested her like that, placing Roni in a position where she had to battle with her, he doubted Roni would have bothered at all.

"No." She had to grit her teeth as Marcus gently rubbed shower gel over her body, skimming over her injuries, while Roni applied conditioner to her hair. The soap stung like a mother-fucker.

"Sorry, gorgeous, but this has to be done." When she stepped directly under the spray a few moments later, allowing the conditioner and soap to slip away, he inspected every inch of her. The wounds were already beginning to heal. "It doesn't look like any of the marks are deep enough to scar." He doubted he could say the same for Eliza.

Turning off the spray, Roni stepped out of the cubicle and allowed Marcus to wrap a huge towel around her. "Off the subject, did anybody scan through the videos on the website?"

"Yes," he replied, gently patting her dry. "Don't worry, no one watched yours. Although, there is something you should know. In the comments section underneath the clip, whoever uploaded it said you deserved worse than what you got."

Surprised, she blinked. "So this was personal, to some degree?"

"I'd say so." He'd be more than happy to get very personal with the son of a bitch when he found him. "Any hunch on who it could have been?"

"No, but I've pissed off plenty of people in my time."

"I'd have wondered if it was the other humans involved in the attack, but the website is exclusive to shifters."

"It couldn't have been them."

The absolute certainty with which she spoke, combined with the odd tone she used, made him frown. "You sound very positive."

She was, but she didn't care to explain why. "It's like you said, the website's exclusive to shifters." His narrow-eyed gaze said he wasn't buying that, but he thankfully didn't push. Instead, he guided her into the bedroom, picked up her brush, sat her between his legs on the bed, and began to tackle the tangles in her hair. "Why did you stay? In the clearing, I mean."

"I wanted you to know that you weren't alone; that if you did want me, I was right there. And I wanted to be sure you were all right. I know your pack is good at driving you crazy."

"I'm surprised Nick let you anywhere near me."

"No one was going to keep me away from you."

The possessiveness in that statement made her wolf growl in contentment.

"Next time you're pissed or have something on your mind, I want you to call me. You don't have to tell me what the problem is. We don't even have to talk about it; I just want you to call me instead of bolting. If you need to get away from here, I'll come get you."

Just then someone started pounding on her front door, and she groaned. No doubt it was Nick, checking on her. Her suspicion was confirmed when seconds later the door opened and he was stalking through the lodge. The wolf behind her didn't tense or even pause in what he was doing, apparently totally unaffected by the agitation radiating from Nick.

"Are you all right?"

"Fine. None of the wounds are deep, so they're healing pretty fast."

"Even though it wasn't an official challenge, you have every right to ask her to be banned from our territory. But I'm guessing you don't really care."

"Not even a little bit," she confirmed. "In fact, let her stick around. She knows a lot about what the extremists are up to. If they're planning anything as a result of the other extremist groups 'mysteriously disappearing' on Phoenix Pack territory, we'll find out through her."

"That's what Derren said." Nick sighed. "Roni, why did you bolt like that? You could have just talked to me. Or spoke to Shaya. Or punched Eli."

"Is that a serious question? Look, let's not talk about it. We tried that already. It never helped."

He was quiet for a moment. "I didn't tell Mom."

"I'd say I appreciate it, but I'm guessing you only refrained from doing it because Shaya told you not to." When the wolf behind her let out a knowing chuckle, she knew she was right.

Nick's gaze shifted to Marcus, though he spoke to Roni. "So your wolf was fine with *his* presence."

Marcus shrugged. "I told you she would be." Done brushing her hair, he placed the brush beside him, and loosely circled her with his arms. "I have to get home and change. Come with me."

"Don't forget the game, Roni," said Nick.

"Game?" repeated Marcus.

"The Arizona Grizzlies are playing against the San Francisco Cougars today." Both were all-shifter football teams. "The pack watches the game together."

Marcus could respect that—traditions were important to packs, and as a newly formed one, it was beneficial for the Mercury wolves to start their own. "Fair enough." That got him suspicious looks from both siblings, who had obliviously expected him to bristle at Nick's interference. Setting Roni on her feet, he stood and kissed the corner of her mouth, not wanting to aggravate the scratch on her bottom lip. "Get some rest, and we'll talk later, okay."

It wasn't a question, but Roni still nodded. Unable to shake off her suspiciousness—Marcus hadn't made a single protest to Nick's smugly delivered announcement, which wasn't like him—she watched with a frown as he skirted around her and smiled at a scowling Nick.

When the front door closed behind him, Nick folded his arms. "Derren told me you marked Fuller."

"Derren's got a big mouth."

"Are you sure he's what you want, Roni? 'Cause I gotta tell ya, a wolf like that isn't going to let you walk all over him. He isn't going to let you shake him off if you get bored or restless. He won't put up with you bolting whenever you feel like it. And he's going to be incredibly possessive."

She cocked her head. "So when I told you to stop interfering in my life, what part of that statement did you find confusing? Should I use smaller words? Simpler vocabulary? Or maybe you need me to emphasize it with a blow to the jaw? That would be fun."

He sighed. "I'm just making the point that he won't be someone you can manage. You need to be prepared for that, because I've come to realize that that guy will push and push until he gets what he wants."

She was quite aware of that, which was why she found it so odd that he'd left without even a scowl at Nick. Of course, her confusion completely disappeared when a knock to the door of Nick's game room later that day preceded the entrance of Marcus, Trey, Dante, Tao, and the other enforcers. They all piled into the room wearing wide smiles and carrying beers and snacks.

Nick gawked. "What are you all doing here?"

"You invited us," replied Marcus.

"No, I didn't."

"Yes, you did. Just before I left, you said, 'Marcus, why don't you and the guys come by later to watch the game with us.'"

"I said no such thing."

"No? Really? That's what I heard. But then, I have been told I have selective hearing. Mmm, pizza." Ignoring Nick's grumbles, Marcus grabbed a slice from the box on the table and made a bee-line for Roni, who was lounging in one of the La-Z-Boys, eating a chicken wing.

Shaking her head, she said, "I should have known you'd do this."

He smiled, leaning down to kiss her soundly. "I did say we'd talk later." Scooping her out of the chair, Marcus sank into it and perched her comfortably on his lap.

"Ah, see, I didn't know that translated to 'I'll crash your pack's get-together.' Silly me." She was amused rather than annoyed.

Oblivious to—or uncaring of—Nick's displeasure, the other Phoenix wolves made themselves comfortable, opening beers and joking with the Mercury wolves . . . as if they hadn't just gate-crashed their gathering. Wearing a petulant scowl, Nick returned to his La-Z-Boy. Since Dominic was on it, he shoved him off—but the enforcer just laughed, which only seemed to aggravate Nick more.

"What happened with Eliza?" Marcus asked Roni.

"She actually apologized. Of course, it was totally forced, but I pretended to buy it."

"Was she badly wounded?" The self-satisfaction glinting in Roni's eyes told him the answer. "Will she have any scars?"

"One or two."

"How did Shaya take it?" He knew the Alpha female adored Roni. As such, although this was the ways of shifters, Shaya wouldn't appreciate Roni being targeted whether it was expected or not.

"She performed her knife trick to make a point that no one tested her wolves." Just as shifters taught their children how to hunt and defend themselves with teeth and claws, Shaya's human father had taught her to defend herself. As a recently retired Navy SEAL, Stone had taught her some interesting things. Roni had walked into the kitchen many times to find Nick plastered against the wall with knives framing his body while an irate Shaya yelled at him.

"I'm staying with you tonight."

She might have bristled at what *should* have been a request, but the desperation in his voice made her smile inwardly. "Oh, you are?"

"Oh, I am." He licked over his mark. "I'm going to do to you what I would have done earlier if you hadn't been hurt."

"I'll leave you to wonder what I'll do to you."

He smiled, liking it when she played with him.

"Now hush, the game's starting."

The gathering was a rowdy affair, and Marcus quickly learned that Roni was one of those people who liked to shout things at the TV as if the players could actually hear her advice. There was a lot of, "Get under center!" and "Focus! Wrap it up!" and "Take it home, take it home!" and "Hit somebody! Just hit *some*body!" Then there were the times she cursed the referee and, honestly, if the guy had been within reach, Marcus would have feared for the ref's life.

When the game ended, he kissed her hair. "I'm sure the Grizzlies are genuinely appreciative of your never-ending guidance." She jammed her elbow into his ribs. "Ow! That was so uncalled for."

CHAPTER EİGHT

Walking into Shaya and Nick's lodge a few days later, Marcus almost laughed as he heard Kathy shout, "Roni! If you don't stop hitting your brother, I'll—" There was a loud smacking sound followed by a deep male grunt. "Don't make me come over there!"

Reaching the kitchen area, he couldn't help but smile at the sight of Roni looking quite comfortable holding Eli in a headlock. Everyone at the table, other than Janice, was watching with amusement. Kathy stood at the stove doing that hands-on-hips thing.

"Oh, yeah, take *his* side," griped Roni. "Why break a habit of a lifetime?"

"Roni, he's turning blue," Shaya pointed out, trembling with laughter. With an extremely put-upon sigh, Roni released Eli with a shove. Choking and laughing at the same time, the guy flipped her the finger.

"I saw that, Eli!" Kathy shook her head.

Janice fussed over a coughing Eli, guiding him to a seat. "Really, Roni, do you have to embarrass your mother all the time?"

Roni pouted. "But it makes me feel so warm inside."

"Good morning, everyone," drawled Marcus as he stepped forward. He smiled widely at Roni. "Hey, gorgeous."

116

Roni met his gaze and instantly the air heated, thickened. As always, his entire focus ate her up, made her feel hunted. Yet, it also steadied her and gave her a strong sense of balance. Her wolf stretched out inside her, happy that he was close; she also wanted to climb all over him and lick him like an ice cream cone. Pathetic.

Marcus took her hand and pulled lightly. Her body fit perfectly against his. It also made him hard as a rock. Needing that mouth more than he needed to breathe, he stole a brief kiss. "Have you had breakfast yet?"

Before she could answer his question, her mother was there. "Marcus, it's always a pleasure to see you. Sit, eat." Kathy ushered him into the chair beside Bracken, laid a plate of food in front of him, and handed him a mug of coffee.

Retaking her seat at the other side of the table, Roni snorted. "You get better treatment than any of us do." Kathy fussed over him as he ate, continually topping off his plate and beaming each time Marcus complimented her cooking.

Caleb leaned into Roni and spoke quietly. "Wow, he's good. Your mom's not easy to win over. Just explain one thing to me, though. If she likes him so much, why didn't she look happy when Marcus kissed you? And why has she sat him so far away from you?"

Full, Roni sank into her chair. "She thinks females should save themselves for their mate."

"Got ya. My aunt's the same. She still thinks my uncle was a virgin when they met."

"What makes you think he wasn't?"

"Well, he once—" Caleb was suddenly plucked from his seat by the back of his T-shirt. Then Marcus sat beside her, wearing a very wolfish smile. She just shook her head.

"I hope you'll look out for my Roni," Kathy told Marcus, briefly running her hand over Roni's hair. But it wasn't an affectionate move—it was patronizing, like Roni was "delicate."

"I will, although I'm pretty sure she can take care of any threat herself." Marcus liked Kathy Axton, but he didn't like the way she treated Roni. And he *really* didn't like the way Roni's face fell each time her mother said or did something that insinuated she was weak.

"Yes, but I need to know my baby girl's safe."

Roni almost growled. The term "baby girl" was said with dismissiveness, as if she were a vulnerable, helpless little girl.

"There are a whole lot of dangers out there. Roni doesn't take them seriously."

Roni released a tired, frustrated sigh. "If you're talking about the stranger who tried to drag me into his car when I was eight, let it go already. I got away, didn't I?"

"Not before stealing the candy he was trying to lure you with!"

"He had my favorite lollipops!"

"For someone so intelligent, you can be very careless with your safety at times." Kathy shook her head. "Is it any wonder that I worry about you? When you have children of your own, you'll understand."

"But that's just it, Mom, I'm *not* a child."

"Says the person who had her brother in a headlock not so long ago," muttered Janice.

Roni snarled at her. "Oh, yeah, bring up old crap."

Kathy clucked. "It's this immaturity that worries me. Going on a hunt is dangerous. I hate to think of you in such a situation. I tried talking some sense into her, Marcus. I tried convincing her to let Eli go in her place, but she wouldn't listen. She never does. I need to know she has someone watching out for her, making sure she doesn't put herself in harm's way."

Enough was enough. Roni slammed her mug on the table. "I think you've delighted us long enough with this whole 'trying to insinuate to Marcus that I'm weak and not worth the effort' thing, don't you?"

Kathy rolled her eyes. "Pay no attention, Marcus. Tantrums are a regular thing with my Roni. She can be very petulant at times."

Okay, that got Marcus's back up. Roni was anything but petulant. Painfully awkward at times, yes. Totally without social skills, yes. Vengeful and vicious, yes. But not childish. And if Roni was right and this was Kathy's way of trying to put him off Roni, he needed to make it clear that it wouldn't work.

Marcus pursed his lips. "Petulant?" He shook his head. "I can't say that's a word I'd associate with Roni. She's an extremely capable person. Excellent in a crisis. Takes her responsibilities very seriously. And she stays calm when faced with a dangerous situation. If it wasn't for her, Kye would have been kidnapped."

Those words got him looks of approval from Eli, Shaya, and Derren. Nick was staring at him with a weird expression on his face, but at least he wasn't scowling.

"I'm ready to leave." Roni wished Marcus would stop defending her. Each time he did it, she liked him that little bit more. That wasn't good. He wouldn't be around for the long haul—he wasn't for her, he belonged to someone else, and no amount of jealous growling from her wolf would make a difference.

It was as they both went to stand that Nick suddenly spoke. "Hold up. There's no need to leave so soon, is there?" It wasn't really a question. Nor was it a friendly invitation to stay. In fact, there was a sly tint to her brother's tone that made her wolf's hackles rise. "Stick around for a while."

She tensed. "Nick, what are you doing?"

He folded his arms across his chest. "Well, it seems to me like you two are *dating*. Am I right, Marcus?"

Marcus narrowed his eyes at the Alpha. It was obvious that Nick had emphasized the word "dating" to communicate that he didn't want his sister being just someone's bed buddy. Nick was trying to force him to publically state his intentions toward his sister right there and then, to either up his game or walk out the door. He clearly thought Marcus would do the latter. It would be the sensible option. To stay when such a dare had been thrown at him would be to take a step toward a relationship that was anything but casual.

Instead of recoiling at the idea, Marcus found himself considering it. In the past, he'd kept things short and simple because females had wanted feelings from him he wasn't sure he was capable of, feelings he wasn't sure he'd even recognize if he *did* feel them. Roni didn't lay demands on him, didn't expect anything of him, and didn't make him feel trapped. She made him feel . . . comfortable. Relaxed. Accepted. He didn't want to give that up, and he knew perfectly well that nothing about what he had with Roni was simple anyway.

"Yes, you are right." Marcus covered Roni's mouth with his hand before she had the chance to object.

Nick's brows rose in surprise. "In that case, I was obviously wrong to assume that you intended to use her and dump her like a secondhand toy, wasn't I?"

"Yes, you were."

"Well then, I'm thinking that it's time you and I spent some time together, Fuller, clear up our 'misunderstandings,' show there are no hard feelings." His smile was deceptively pleasant.

Roni bit hard into Marcus's hand and tugged it away. "Wait a cocking, fucking second!"

"After all, you marked her and now you're staking a temporary claim on her—that practically makes you one of us. Why not spend some time here, get to know us better?"

"Nick, don't you dare!" Her brother had given a similar speech to her first real boyfriend . . . then he'd beat the shit out of him during a "friendly game of softball." Friendly, her ass. The guy had been close to sobbing when it was over.

"Sounds good." Marcus was kind of looking forward to whatever the Alpha had in mind. He had some anger to work off with this male who had repeatedly tried to come between him and Roni.

She gawked at Marcus. "Are you freaking kidding me?"

"Oh, come on, Roni, it's just a bit of male bonding." Eli was grinning from ear to ear.

She snorted. "'Bonding' is the last word to describe—"

Eli raised a hand. "Shh, honey, it's time for the men to talk."

Marcus looped an arm around Roni's waist as she tried to launch herself across the table at Eli. "Nick's right, sweetheart, we need to make it clear there are no hard feelings."

"Why don't you go with Shay to Phoenix Pack territory, Roni?" Nick's eyes didn't move from Marcus. "You can act as an extra bodyguard for Shay. She's helping them get everything ready for Grace's party tonight. I'm sure they'd love to have another set of hands."

Roni snickered. "Leave him at your mercy?" She shot to her feet, pulling Marcus upright. "No, we're leaving now." But no amount of pulling on Marcus's hand made him move.

Sighing, Marcus gently drew her to him and rubbed her nose with his. "It's okay. You can kiss me better later."

"But—"

Shaya appeared and guided Roni away. "Come on, let's just leave them to it. It's a guy thing, sweetie. Don't even try to understand it, you'll just hurt your head." Jesse and Bracken, acting as bodyguards for Shaya, trailed behind the females as they left the lodge.

That was when all eyes honed in on Marcus. "So, how do you 'bond' around here?" In other words, what violent activity did they have in mind that would give them a chance to put him through a world of hurt?

Nick smiled. "Follow me." He stood and left the kitchen, the other males of his pack right behind him.

Eli sidled over to Marcus as they strode after Nick. "Sure you want to do this? I don't mean deal with us. I mean deal with Roni. She's more of a challenge than all of us put together."

Marcus grinned. "That she is. In which case, I have to ask, what did you do that inspired her to trap you in a headlock?"

"Put talcum powder in her hairdryer. But only because she hacked into my Twitter account again."

"What exactly did she Tweet?"

"Word for word? 'Anyone know what it means if you get a thick, yellowish discharge dripping from your dick? It's sometimes crusty, if that helps.'"

Marcus burst out laughing. Damn, that female was entertaining. *His* female.

"So that's something for you to consider: it's really not us you need to worry about if you upset her. Roni always gets even."

Roni checked her phone for about the twelfth time in the last six hours, but there was still nothing from Marcus. Something to indicate he was okay—or, at the very least, conscious—would be great. She'd tried calling others from the pack, but none of them had been of any help. As far as they were concerned, Marcus needed to prove that he not only saw her as more than a bed buddy, but also that he was worthy.

"He'll be fine, honey," Lydia assured her while helping Taryn pin up a huge "Happy Birthday" banner in the living area.

"You don't know my brothers." Roni shoved the ninth lollipop of the day into her mouth.

"We all have to run the family gauntlet. There's really no way of getting around it."

Taryn nodded. "Yup. Trey almost strangled my father to death once. They got past it eventually, but neither likes the other. Greta did her best to scare me off, as you know. Now she just does it for fun."

Jaime blew up yet another balloon. "I don't get along with any of Dante's brothers, so I wouldn't worry that Nick and Marcus aren't friends. Thankfully, Gabe and Dante get along, though. Gabe and I are close, so that's important to me."

Shaya came to aid Roni in wrapping Grace's gifts. "You're surprised that Marcus stayed behind, aren't you?"

Roni snorted. "Aren't you?" she asked around her lollipop, but it was a rhetorical question.

"Sweetie, he walked through the door, made a beeline for you, and kissed you soundly on the mouth in front of your pack and family."

"Really?" Taryn seemed excited.

"That kind of public display coming from a guy like Marcus, who avoids relationships like the plague, says a lot about where his head's at." Shaya stuck a huge bow on the gift Roni had finished wrapping.

"The question is," began Jaime, "where's *your* head at, Roni?"

When Roni didn't answer, Shaya gave her a gentle smile. "Okay, I get that you don't really like to confide in anyone other than Derren . . . but I have to admit, I'm totally jealous you don't talk to me. I can be petty like that."

Roni's mouth twitched into a smile. She took out her lollipop. "It's nothing personal, okay. I'm the type to work things out by myself. I talk to Derren because it's the only way to make sure he comes to me when he needs to talk." The guy had some seriously dark demons.

Shaya nodded in understanding. "All right. So what have you worked out?"

"I've worked out that Marcus annoys me."

Lydia laughed. "In what way?"

"He defends me. And he makes me share stuff. And he respects my strength. And he doesn't make me feel like I need to change."

Jaime made an "ah" sound. "He's making himself important to you, and you're not too happy about that, because losing him would hurt. Yeah, I get it. I was determined not to mate with Dante. But he got through all my defenses, the jerk."

Back then, Jaime had stopped shifting because her wolf was so traumatized, she attacked anyone around—viewing them as a potential threat. But her wolf had been fighting to break free, and Jaime had known that if it happened, her wolf might turn rogue and have to be killed. As such, she hadn't wanted to mate with Dante—not even when she'd discovered they were true mates—for fear that if she were killed, he wouldn't survive the breaking of the mating bond.

"I did my best to keep Nick at a distance," said Shaya. "I was just so mad at him, so hurt. But he smashed down every wall I had up. Dominant males are good at that. It's not possible to catch them; they're too elusive for that. But when they decide a female is going to be theirs, they won't stop until they have her."

Roni rocked back on her heels. "Whoa, it's really not that serious between me and Marcus."

Lydia gave her a wan smile. "I know you probably won't want to hear about his sexual history, but let me just say I've known Marcus a *long* time, and he has never been so totally into a female before."

"When he does that thing where he focuses all that charm and dominant male energy on you, Roni . . ." Taryn fanned her face. "Yowza."

Jaime laughed. "May I just say we've loved that you haven't made it easy for him."

Lydia nodded. "It's about time he had to work for something. And he has worked for you, hasn't he?"

Roni couldn't deny that he had. She was private, unsociable, and awkward, but he hadn't let her keep him away. He'd persevered, practically hunted her down. And now he'd publically staked a temporary claim on her. But she wasn't going to make the mistake of thinking he was around for good. "He's going to want his mate."

"Dante didn't," said Jaime, tying ribbons on the ends of the balloons. "He thought she'd be someone who couldn't accept that he was Beta, who'd want him to choose between her and his position. One of the reasons he decided he wanted to imprint with me was that he realized I'd never make him choose. It turned out imprinting wasn't necessary, but you get my point."

Taryn spoke then. "Not all shifters are set on finding their mates. Some don't like the idea that they're not in charge of their own path. Some have a preconceived notion of what their mate will be like, and they reject it. And some choose to imprint, aware that there's a possibility they'll never find their true mate anyway."

"You have to consider that Marcus has been circling you since you guys first met," said Shaya. "It's clearly more than casual sex to him. That's not something you can blow off."

Roni got what Shaya was saying: if things continued to be so intense, the next step would be imprinting—and it could even happen without Roni or Marcus consciously causing it. How had they gone from discussing Marcus's safety to the subject of mating? Uncomfortable with the direction the conversation had headed, Roni shoved her lollipop back into her mouth.

Shaya sighed, her smile affectionate. "Okay, I can take a hint. But let me just say that I know letting yourself care for someone is majorly scary, and I know it's appealing to throw up some barriers, but it truly isn't worth it—he'll just knock them down."

"One last thing." Jaime's expression was serious. "There was something Dante once said to me before we realized we were mates, when he knew I was contemplating ending the whole thing before I got hurt. He said, 'Maybe it's fucking doomed, I don't know. But don't you want to know?' That was when I realized I *had* to know. So I guess you have to decide what your answer is to that question."

Roni said nothing, honestly unsure. But she needed to find the answer, because Marcus would expect her to make the same temporary claim on him, particularly considering how bold and assertive dominant females were. His wolf would expect it too—hell, *her* wolf was expecting it—and dominant males never settled for anything less than what they wanted.

The trouble was that, as she'd told him, she was truly bad at relationships. Roni wasn't good at expressing how she felt or giving emotional feedback. Wasn't what anyone would call cuddly or affectionate. Shifter males were protective, liked to take care of their females, liked to feel needed. Roni was self-reliant, fiercely independent, and had been raised to never need a male for anything. As such, she tended to clash badly with her partners.

It had never mattered much to her before—beyond general annoyance anyway—because she'd never really cared for any of them. But Marcus . . . it would matter with him. She didn't want to hurt him and didn't want him to look at her the way her mother looked at her—like she lacked, like she wasn't good enough. Even the idea of it made her want to hold back.

But to do that to protect herself would be cowardly, wouldn't it? Cowardly and selfish, and she'd like to think she was neither of those things.

It would be unfair to him, because he'd never given her any reason to believe that he thought that about her. He never seemed to be judging her or laughing at her. Her quirks didn't seem to bother him, nor did the fact that she wasn't girly. And although he defended her, he didn't do it in a way that suggested he was "the boss" or that he didn't see her as his equal. In fact, it actually annoyed him when people dismissed her strength.

Damn the asshole for making himself matter to her. But did he matter enough to publicly stake a temporary claim on him in return? Matter enough that she *had* to know if a relationship between them would be doomed or not?

She feared that, yeah, he actually might.

Getting to his feet, Nick spat blood on the ground. "You'll pay for that, Fuller."

"You ran face-first into my elbow—what did you think would happen?" Marcus's wolf bared his teeth in a feral grin, liking the sight of the Alpha hurt. He also liked the sight of Zander's broken nose—super fast or not, the guy couldn't escape a male wolf who suspected he had a thing for his female.

It had quickly become apparent that the "friendly game of football" had merely been an excuse to launch balls at Marcus's head, constantly tackle him to the ground, and for every male there to pile on top of him in what appeared to be an effort to crush him to death.

He was covered in bruises and bumps and gashes, had pain radiating from the shoulder that he'd minutes ago popped back into place, and was pretty sure some of his ribs were broken. Also, he'd almost passed out twice. Clearly they were hoping he'd have "special needs" by the time this was over.

Nick arched a brow. "You sure you don't want to run along home?"

"You sure you don't want to accept my place in your sister's life?"

"Roni can do better."

"So can Shaya."

Nick actually smiled. "You're right, she can. But she's mine."

"And Roni's mine." Marcus briefly slid his gaze to Zander as he said it, who raised a brow, seemingly amused.

"I'll admit you have balls—there aren't many guys who'd willingly take on my sister."

Panting and using the back of his hand to wipe away the blood dripping from a huge gash above his brow, Derren nodded. "But he's clearly tougher than we gave him credit for. You've got a skull like granite, Fuller." Well, he'd know, since he tried to head-butt Marcus and it kind of backfired—the idiot almost knocked himself out.

Flexing and cradling his jaw, Eli nodded his agreement. "He's got a fist like granite too."

"I'll bet everything I own that Roni's right hook is better," said Marcus.

Eli laughed. "I can assure you from past experience, it is."

"He's starting to come around!" shouted a badly bruised Kent from where he squatted beside a moaning Caleb. The guy had been out cold since the ball collided with his head, thanks to a solid throw from Marcus.

Zander popped his nose back into place. "I say we call it quits. Roni will kill us if we rough him up any more than this."

"Yeah. I'd rather not have salt in my coffee again." Eli shuddered.

Derren looked at Nick. "What do you say? Truce?"

All the Mercury wolves turned to their Alpha. Nick was staring at Marcus studiously. "If you hurt even a single hair on her head—"

"Haven't we been over this already?" Marcus sighed. "You'd have to get through Roni to get to me, and I'm pretty sure I'd be dead by that point. At best, you can hope to play football with my severed head."

A smile curved Nick's mouth. "I can work with that."

CHAPTER NINE

Should he have found it kind of endearing that Roni seemed caught in her worst nightmare simply because a stranger was talking to her? Probably not, but Marcus did.

He'd arrived home twenty minutes ago to find that the party was in full swing—a mix of the Phoenix wolves, the Mercury wolves, and some of Grace's relations from her childhood pack.

After taking a shower to wash off the mud, blood, and grime from the "friendly game of football," he'd pulled on some clothes and headed to the living area. Now he was leaning against the doorway, smiling to himself as one of Grace's relations chatted on and on about designer shoes to a clearly uncomfortable Roni.

He was just about to go and rescue her when Trick appeared at his side, wearing the oddest expression. Marcus had no idea what was going on in that mind. Trick seemed like an open book, but in reality, he wasn't easy to read.

Trick took a swig of his beer. "I saw you and Roni the other night."

It was obvious what Trick meant, and it rubbed Marcus the wrong way. "Really?" he drawled, his voice a little menacing.

Trick smirked slightly. "You don't like that I know what she looks like when she comes, do you?"

"No, I don't." His wolf was particularly pissed about it, which was unexpected, given that his wolf liked and trusted Trick. He and Marcus had scratched each other's itch from time to time and even shared females. But if Trick were hinting at sharing Roni, it wouldn't happen. Possessiveness roared through him at the very idea of it, almost making his claws slice out.

Trick casually leaned against the wall. "She marked you."

"Yep."

"And you marked her."

"Yep." When Trick just looked at him, Marcus sighed. "Trick, if you've got something to say, say it. But if you're about to suggest sharing her—"

"That's not what this is about."

"Then, what? Do you have a problem with Roni or something?"

"Not at all. I like her. Tough, shrewd, fast—just my kind of girl. But she's not your kind of girl. She's very different from your usual type."

"What does that matter?"

His expression completely serious now, he asked, "Have you considered that she might be your mate?"

Okay, that wasn't what Marcus had expected him to say.

"You like her, Marcus. I mean *like* her, like her. You've never been so hot for anyone before, never been possessive or jealous. But your wolf wants to take a swipe at me right now because I've seen her naked, doesn't he?"

No, he didn't want to take a swipe at Trick. He wanted to gut him.

"If you were anyone else, I'd let you work it out by yourself. But you've got more issues than Playboy—without a kick in the right direction, you could head down the wrong one. I wouldn't like to see that happen."

"But—"

"Just hear me out. Roni doesn't bristle when you invade her personal space. She doesn't seem to welcome touch, but she allows it from you. Whether she realizes it or not, she's much more comfortable with you than she is with most people. And *fuck,* when you two are together, sexual energy practically pours off both of you."

There was no denying that Trick was right about all of that. And yes, she and Marcus being mates would explain a lot—particularly his reaction to her, and her reaction to him. "It's not her. The Seer I told you about described someone totally different."

Trick snorted. "So?"

"What do you mean, 'so'?"

"Seers can be wrong."

"Yeah, well, her vision was very specific."

Trick pursed his lips. "Okay, let's say the Seer's right. Let's say Roni's not your mate. Let's say this other female the Seer described is the one for you, and she's out there somewhere. That would mean Roni has a mate out there somewhere too, waiting to claim her."

A growl of objection rumbled out of Marcus before he could stop it—it was a growl that came from both him and his wolf.

Trick grinned. "That's what I thought."

"Just because I don't want to give her up yet doesn't make her my mate."

"All I'm asking is that you keep an open mind about it. Look at Dante and Trey—it took them both months to figure out they had their own mate right under their noses, and that's just plain pathetic. They should have listened to their wolves, but they didn't, because they were too wrapped up in their human issues."

"Sometimes our animals have strong reactions to certain females and it doesn't mean anything."

"Yeah, but sometimes it does. You can at least admit it's a possibility that she's your mate."

Marcus opened his mouth, but no words came out. Was it a possibility? He did feel incredibly possessive of Roni, so much so that he would happily slash the throat of any male who tried to take her from him. And he did *like* her, like her. She made him laugh, and she fascinated him with her complex character. She was also so damn tough it was admirable. Any dominant male would be proud to have a mate as strong as Roni. But to admit that it was a possibility would be to hope that just maybe he wasn't destined to have the miserable fate he'd been warned of, and hope could massively backfire on him.

Trick sighed. "If you don't want to admit it, fine, but don't shove what I'm saying to the back of your mind so that you don't have to process it. Don't rule it out as a possibility simply because some Seer described a totally different female to you. Okay?"

"Okay," replied Marcus, but he said it more to placate Trick than anything else. And his friend's agitated expression said he knew it.

"Don't be an ass, Marcus. Look outside the box, and you'll see that you've been subconsciously building something with her."

"What are you talking about?"

Trick rolled his eyes. "You're not the type of guy who feels the need to run to ground any female who doesn't respond to him. It's never bothered you before, but it bothered you this time. You didn't come on strong, though. You stood back, observed her closely, looked for weaknesses in her defenses—circled her like a predator circles prey. You took it slow, got to know her better, did what you could to make her feel comfortable around you, and tried to seduce her on every level. You don't do that with someone unless you're trying to lay a foundation for something *more*.

"You've never in your life pursued a female before, Marcus; you see women as threats." When he went to speak, Trick quickly continued. "Don't try and bullshit me; I *know* you. Women eventually want more than sex from you, and that scares you. For you, love is all mingled up with pain and rejection and anger, thanks to your upbringing. But you pursued Roni because she doesn't make you feel threatened."

"Threatened? I don't even understand what that means."

"You knew she wouldn't get attached to you, wouldn't demand anything from you that you couldn't give, and wouldn't push herself on you or make you feel pressured. It left you in control of where this is going and allowed you to move at a pace you felt comfortable with. And look what you did with that power—you subconsciously laid the foundation for something more."

Was Trick right? Was that what he'd done? Sure, Marcus had circled her and searched for weaknesses in her shields in an effort to seduce her mentally. But that was only so that he might have a shot at seducing her sexually. Wasn't it? And, yes, he had felt comfortable pursuing Roni. The more he'd pursued her, the more he'd come to like her and the more possessive he'd become.

"I know you're scared of finding the mate the Seer told you about; you don't want history to repeat itself, and no one who knows about your upbringing could blame you for that. But considering you don't want that female, is there really any harm in seeing where this could go with Roni, of being open to imprinting? For the record, I honestly believe she could be your true mate."

"The Seer's visions are usually accurate."

"Yeah, *usually*," scoffed Trick. "Not always. Think about that before you walk away from something that could be really yours to keep."

Then he strolled off, leaving Marcus alone with his thoughts. Although many of the things his friend had said made sense, Marcus wasn't sure about the theory that Roni was his mate—not given how specific the Seer's vision had been. But he knew that he wanted a place in Roni's life; he wanted to see where this thing between them could go.

It probably made him a cruel bastard to even consider it. Sure, lots of shifters got into deep relationships with people who weren't their true mates, since they were fully aware that there was a possibility they would never find them anyway. Gabe and Hope were an example of that. But Marcus knew from the Seer that he would in fact find his mate, and that made this situation very different.

If he were honest, though, he didn't believe he could make his mate happy. He wouldn't have children with her, because he refused to let them see the same things he had, day after day, growing up. Considering how miserable they were bound to make each other, he doubted the mating bond would ever fully click into place. That would have eaten at what they'd had and caused resentment to build. No, neither one of them could truly make the other happy.

Roni, on the other hand . . . she made him happy—quirks, lollipops, and all. Everything in him, everything he was, told him not to walk away from her; that if he did, it would be a mistake he would forever regret. His wolf didn't object to Marcus's decision, which was pretty shocking, given that this would take him closer to Roni and further away from his true mate. His wolf, with his elemental nature, wouldn't have Marcus's human concerns about the mate the Seer had described. Yet, he had his wolf's support to remain with Roni, because she made his wolf happy too.

Returning his gaze to Roni, he saw that Grace's relation was still chatting away to her. He couldn't help but smile—his pretty little wolf had the look of a trapped wild animal and appeared to be grinding her teeth around her lollipop. Apparently she'd had enough. He knew what she'd do, knew it was coming any minute now . . .

Finally, she removed the lollipop from her mouth and cocked her head. "Did you know that if your stomach doesn't produce a new layer of mucus every two weeks, it'll digest itself?"

And there it was.

Taken aback, the female opened and closed her mouth repeatedly. "Um . . . no, I didn't know that. How . . . interesting."

"I know, right?"

"I, um, I should probably go and check on my mate."

When she was alone once again, Roni's body seemed to sag with relief. Marcus quietly sidled up to her. "Now that wasn't very nice."

Twisting to face him, Roni blinked innocently. "What? What did I say?" Of course she'd sensed Marcus there, watching her. She always sensed when his gaze was on her, and it always made her body feel restless.

He pulled Roni flush against him and pressed a somewhat possessive kiss to her throat, taking a moment to swim in her scent. "You made her feel uncomfortable so that she'd walk away." He snatched her lollipop and tossed it into the trash can, earning himself a huff.

Roni wasn't surprised that he'd guessed her game; he was too observant. "She was talking about fashion, Marcus. *Fashion*." Roni gestured to her own outfit: combat pants, Converse trainers, and a T-shirt that read, "I'm not a people person—you've been warned." "Do I *look* like someone who reads *Vogue*?" She could take down an Alpha, whether in human or wolf form, whether they were male or female. But have a conversation about stilettos? That was out of her comfort zone.

He raked his gaze over every edible inch of her. "I like your look. It works for you."

That slow, languid smile worked for her. And when that sensual mouth came down on hers, delivered the most devastating kiss, and then followed it up with a bite to her bottom lip—oh, yeah, that worked for her too.

Roni cleared her throat as she snapped out of her daze and took a moment to examine him. There were faint impressions of bruises and scratches here and there, but they were fading fast. Still, neither she nor her wolf liked seeing him hurt. If he hadn't been on his way to being fully healed, she would have clawed her brothers. "It's good to know you're alive. And that you have all your teeth. Any broken bones?"

"Depends whose bones you're referring to."

She opened her mouth to ask, but then shook her head. "You know what, I don't want to know."

Marcus nuzzled her neck, inhaling deeply. "Your scent drives me insane." Drawn to the mark on her neck, he swiped his tongue across it, enjoying the way she shuddered.

When he lowered his tone like that, it did all sorts of interesting things to Roni's body. "Good insane or bad insane?"

Marcus knew his smile was wicked. "Oh, very, very good insane." He nipped her earlobe, just because. Of course, he almost jumped out of his skin when her arm slid around him and her fingers drummed down his spine. One, because it felt amazingly good. Two, because Roni wasn't a touchy-feely person, particularly in public. To touch him like that, and in front of others—it meant something. It was an acceptance and a claim. "I wasn't sure if you'd return the claim."

"Well, I thought hard on it. I figured you could serve some purposes."

He smiled. "Serve some purposes?"

"You can deal with small talk. I don't like small talk. You can change tires. When there are lines, you can stand in them. I hate them. You can also bring me chocolate fudge cake."

"Anything else?"

"Yes. Never neglect the G-spot. That would turn out badly for you."

He laughed. "Duly noted."

"Ro!"

Roni peered down to find Kye grinning at her, a cookie in either hand. "Hey, little man. What you got there?"

Pulling a face, he held both cookies against his chest. "Mine."

"Well, of course."

"Mar!"

Marcus smiled. "Hey, kid, have you showed Roni your Alpha snarl?" Kye's expression instantly turned fierce as he bared his little teeth.

"Wow, scary." Roni frowned as Kye suddenly started spinning in a circle. "What's he doing?"

Marcus sighed. "He farts and then looks for it."

Tao, Dominic, and Ryan made their way over. Dominic was grimacing and rubbing his knee. "Do you have a Band-Aid?" he asked Roni.

Her brow puckered. "No, why?"

"I just scraped my knee falling for you." Laughing, he barely dodged Marcus's fist.

Tao shook his head at Dominic, handing both Marcus and Roni a beer. "I honestly fear for your life sometimes, Dom." Ryan grunted, as if to second that.

"Ry! Ry! Ry!" Kye tugged hard on the enforcer's jeans. The toddler had a soft spot for Ryan, which was odd, considering the guy barely spoke and wasn't the least bit playful.

Looking somewhat pained and uncomfortable, Ryan reached down and grabbed Kye by the back of his shirt. He then lifted him high, letting him dangle in the air. Kye laughed in delight, striving to pinch Ryan's nose.

Taryn came to the enforcer's rescue, taking her son into her arms. "Are you tormenting Uncle Ryan again?" The kid kissed her smack on the mouth in response.

Standing beside his mate, Trey studied Marcus. "Either Roni's brothers took it easy on you, or you didn't hold back. I'm hoping it was the latter."

"What do you mean?" asked Dominic.

"Marcus did some male bonding with the Mercury Pack," explained Grace as she made her way to Roni, giving her a huge hug that took Roni by surprise. "I was told you helped get the party organized, so thank you."

Roni nodded. "No problem. Happy birthday."

"Thanks. I did tell Taryn to cancel the party, what with everything that's been going on and—"

"No, we planned it months ago," interrupted Taryn. "*No way* were we going to let anything mess it up for you, Grace. You do a lot for the pack, always take care of everyone. Now it's our turn to take care of you, because if anyone deserves some pampering and attention, it's you." Marcus had to agree with that.

As Dominic cupped Roni's elbow and tried to move her arm, she slapped at his hand. Dominic held his hands up. "I'm just trying to see what your T-shirt says. No need to get testy. It's hard to tell, though. Can I read it in braille?" If Dante and Jaime hadn't appeared at that moment and pulled Dominic back, Marcus would have knocked him clean out.

Roni simply smiled at the pervert. "Your body is like a wonderland, Dominic . . . can I be Alice?"

Jaime laughed. "Good one."

Dominic, however, wasn't so amused. "Stop that!" he whined.

Eli appeared then, his face a little marked up with lacerations and bruises. Taking in Dominic's expression, he arched a brow at his sister. "You throwing cheesy lines at him again?"

"The dumbass thinks he can take me. Still getting advice about STDs on Twitter?"

The amusement on Eli's face died a quick death. "I'll get you back, sis. Trust me on that." He turned his attention to Jaime. "Oh, and thanks for making it worse by recommending antibiotic creams and wishing me a quick recovery."

The Beta female shrugged innocently. "I didn't know it was just a joke. I was trying to be helpful and supportive."

Dante wrapped an arm around his mate's shoulders. "Baby, you're so good, I could almost believe that."

"Believe what?" asked Trick, coming up behind Trey. Marcus was surprised when Roni stiffened; he might not have noticed if he hadn't been touching her. When Trick came to Marcus's other side, she went totally rigid. There was the smallest flash of her wolf's eyes, revealing the animal's agitation. Well, now, that was interesting.

It hadn't occurred to him that either Roni or her wolf might feel uncomfortable or jealous around Trick, despite that Marcus would have felt the same if the situation had been reversed. Maybe other guys might like that their female was jealous, but Marcus had never cared for jealousy. He didn't want Roni or her wolf feeling uncomfortable or insecure.

"Roni's playing pranks on Eli again," Marcus told Trick, sliding his hand up to rest firmly in the crook of her neck so he could soothingly draw circles on her nape with his thumb. It was an attentive, possessive move that he knew would relax her wolf and hopefully appease Roni. She would get the message that *she* was his choice.

Tao gently nudged Roni. "Why is your mom glaring at you?"

Following Tao's gaze, she found her mother stood at the other side of the room, glowering. "As far as she's concerned, I'm living in sin. She thinks all females should wait for their mate." Roni jerked when Marcus tightened his hold on her neck. "Did she continue making her 'Roni's weak' case to you while I was gone?"

"No, she didn't. She hasn't said a single word to me since I spoke up for you earlier. She did grunt at me when I said goodbye, though."

Eli grinned. "Mom's not used to people questioning her. She wouldn't have expected it. Nick definitely hadn't. Speaking of Nick, have you seen the look on his face?"

Roni almost laughed at his sulky expression. Nick was no more a fan of parties than she was, purely because people in general tended to annoy him. He even found being around his own pack a trial at times. Shaya was the only person whose company he sought out and truly enjoyed.

"He probably wouldn't have come if Shaya wasn't pregnant; he hates being away from her," continued Eli. "By the looks of it, he's trying to get her to abandon her cake and leave."

"Ah, that would explain why she's just whacked his nose with her spoon," said Jaime.

Marcus arched a brow. "There's still cake?"

"Last time I looked," said Dante, "there was one slice left."

Marcus knew exactly who loved cake as much as he did. He met Roni's challenging look. "Not on your life, gorgeous." He rushed out of the room and into the tunnels, but she dived on his back, did some fancy-ass move, and took him down. *Bitch.* She sprung over him, intending to make a run for it, but he grabbed her ankle. The sneaky little minx easily managed to get free of his grip, but by that point he was on his feet. Before she could move, he clamped his arms around her, wrestled her to the ground, and pinned her beneath him on her stomach. Another fancy-ass move later from Roni, and he was on his back and she was straddling him.

"What are you doing?"

They looked up to see Cam standing over them, eating . . . cake.

"Oh, you bastard," said Roni.

Marcus shook his head. "How could you, Cam?"

The guy double-blinked, seemingly baffled. "Do what?"

"Satan's helper—that's all I'm saying." Roni stood and held out a hand to Marcus, but he jumped to his feet. Snarling at Cam, they both shrugged past him.

"What?" Cam sighed. "You guys are weird."

In the kitchen, Roni and Marcus fought over what food was left—to the extreme amusement of those around them—but he didn't mind, because it meant he'd got her to play with him. Later, after she'd annoyed Eli a little more and Marcus had taken about as much as he could of Dominic hitting on her with cheesy lines, Marcus tugged on her hand. "Come with me."

"Huh?"

"Come with me." He led her through the labyrinth of tunnels, straight to his room. The second the door closed behind them, he was on her. Molten need flared through him as his mouth found hers, feasting on her. Pulling the tie from her hair, he buried his hands in the silky tresses—an image of her hair draped over his thighs as she sucked him off flashed through his mind, and a growl rumbled out of him. "I've been thinking about this all fucking day."

The harsh words spoken against her mouth made her gasp. She would have admitted to feeling the same torture, but then he was sucking on her tongue. She fisted her hands in his T-shirt as his hands roamed over her body like he owned her, possessively cupping her ass. Then he froze as one hand skimmed over her hip.

"What's this? Have you brought a weapon on my territory, Roni? Because, you know, as an enforcer, I'd have to deal with that kind of insult."

Breathless and kind of confused, she double-blinked. "What? It's just my cell phone." And why was he talking?

"Hmm. You understand I have to be sure." He spun her to face the wall and placed her hands firmly on it. "Arms and legs spread wide apart."

Okay, now she was *really* confused. And she didn't appreciate his tone. "What's that now?"

"You heard me. Now do as you're told."

"Oh, you motherfucker!" She struggled to move out of his hold, but a sharp bite to her nape had her freezing in shock. Her wolf urged her to be still rather than fight him, to play, which was surprising enough to make her quiet.

"No respect for authority, have you?" He ground himself against her, letting her feel just how hard he was. "I'll say it one more time: spread your arms and legs wide apart."

Curious, Roni did as he asked—well, ordered.

"That's it. Is there anything you want to tell me? You can make this much easier on yourself if you just tell me the truth."

His breath on her neck made her shudder. She would have expected to find role-play kind of amusing, but the sexual hunger creeping over her left her incapable of humor. "No. I have nothing to tell you."

"Fine, we'll do this my way." His body throbbing with a savage, carnal need that would have left him shaken if his brain had room for thought, Marcus kicked her legs wider apart.

"What are you doing?"

"A body search, of course. This will go much easier if you just keep nice and still. No struggling." His tone was uncompromising, implacable.

Starting at Roni's shoulders, he began to slowly but firmly pat down her upper body. His confident, knowing hands were anything but cool and detached, making her tremble and squirm. She gave a low moan as his hands briefly skated over her breasts.

"I have to be certain you're not concealing anything here." Marcus gathered the bottom of her T-shirt and slowly slid it over her head, tossing it on the floor. Her bra quickly joined it. Then he pressed his body against hers as his hands slid to her breasts—they were the perfect handful. He kneaded and squeezed them, pausing occasionally to pinch and tweak her nipples with just the right amount of pressure to make her arch against him while moaning and grinding against his cock.

Nibbling on the back of her shoulder, Marcus snaked a hand down her flat, taut stomach, inching farther and farther toward what he wanted most. "Is there anything hiding in here I should know about?"

Before Roni could say a word, he'd unzipped her pants and thrust his hand inside and past the barrier of her boy shorts to cup her hard. His hand lingered there, unmoving, driving her insane with anticipation. Restless, she twisted her hips, trying to find some relief. The cruel bastard withdrew his hand a little.

"Oh, no, sweetheart. Be nice and still for me." When she stilled, he slid his hand farther down and flicked her clit with his finger. She moaned loudly, but she didn't move. He slipped a finger through her folds, growling at how slick she was. "There doesn't seem to be anything here. But I have to be sure." He squatted on the ground, removed her shoes, and then peeled down her pants. The boy shorts were hot as fuck, giving him sneak peeks of that perfect little ass, but they had to go too. He tapped her lightly on her leg. "Step out of the pants and shorts."

Roni did as he asked and kicked them aside. On one level, it galled her to follow his every order without question. But pride wouldn't make her come, would it? And there was a very big difference in the way that Marcus treated her and the way that guys had acted before. Marcus dominated her during sex, but he didn't try to do it outside of the bedroom. For that reason, it didn't make her bristle. Still, if he didn't hurry and make her come, she'd lose her damn patience.

Marcus shackled her ankles with his hands and slowly slid them up her toned legs. "Hmm. All clear. But what about . . . here?" Canting her hips slightly, he treated himself to a fantastic view of her pussy—her folds were swollen and glistening, making his wolf growl with hunger. "You can't have any idea how good you smell to me."

Roni gasped as he abruptly plunged a finger inside her. He wasn't gentle—each thrust was hard, sure, and bold. Then he found her G-spot at the exact same time that his tongue joined the fray, and she almost crumpled to the floor. Damn, the guy knew his way around the female body.

"You taste good." Without removing his finger, Marcus delivered a sharp bite to her ass before standing upright again and whipping off his T-shirt one-handed. "I'm going to shove my cock in your pussy, Roni." He nipped her nape, making her jolt. "I'm going to fuck you fast and deep."

The feel of hard muscle against her bare back sent a tremor running through her, just as the feel of denim against the backs of her thighs made her moan. Her knees almost buckled when his teeth grazed over the mark on her neck. He licked and sucked, as if fascinated with it. At this point, she was frantic to have him inside her . . . *and he was prolonging the fucking agony.*

"Marcus, now," she gritted out. The asshole spanked her ass instead. "Oh, you son of a—" He did it again. Roni sharply jammed her elbow into his ribs. His response? He drove another finger deep inside her and swirled them both around.

With his free hand, he fisted her hair and snatched her head back. "Striking an enforcer on his own territory is a punishable offense."

Panting with want, she licked her lips. "No more playing." Clearly he needed reminding that he was dealing with a dominant female. Curling an arm around his nape, she scratched hard enough to draw blood—his growl vibrated through his chest, sending a shiver down her back. "I need to come."

Withdrawing his fingers, Marcus curled her hips slightly, positioning her to take him. "Me, Roni, you need *me*," he corrected. Then he rammed every inch of himself inside her.

Roni felt her muscles contract around him as an orgasm tore through her, taking her by complete surprise with its ferocity. He didn't wait for the aftershocks to subside, didn't give her a reprieve. He pumped in and out of her, his hands clamped possessively on her hips, his fingers biting into the skin.

"Yes, this is what I want." He had the feeling it was something he'd always want. With both hands now once again braced against the wall, she tried pushing back to counter his thrusts. Oh, no, he wasn't having that. Marcus slapped her ass with the flat of his hand. "No, sweetheart, *I'll* fuck *you*. All I want you to do is take it." Her warning growl made him smile.

She glared at him over her shoulder. "I'm not submissive."

"I didn't say you're submissive. I said I do the fucking, and you do the taking. It's like I told you last time: when I'm inside this pussy, it's mine. And right now, I want to fuck it."

She might have met that statement with a string of profanities, but then he was pounding into her harder, faster, and deeper—giving her exactly what she needed.

"I'm going to come, sweetheart. I want you to come with me. Now."

His teeth sinking into her shoulder was like a trigger; she threw her head back and screamed as wave after wave of ecstasy racked her body almost violently. He cursed against her neck as he slammed deep one final time and exploded inside her. That was when all her strength seemed to leave her body in a rush. If he hadn't slipped an arm around her waist, she'd have crashed to the floor.

To her appreciation, he very carefully carried her limp body to the en suite bathroom, cleaned them both up, and then just as carefully carried her to the bed. Removing the rest of his clothes, he then lay beside her, lightly tracing the new mark on her shoulder while self-satisfaction glinted in his eyes. "Very pleased with that, aren't you?"

"Yes." So was his wolf.

Hearing her cell phone ringing, she groaned. She'd assigned that ringtone to a person who she didn't want to speak to right then.

"Aren't you going to answer it?"

"No. It's my mother. She's probably having a hernia because she suspects I'm exactly where I am right now. Annoying me is her favorite hobby."

"You know why she does it, don't you? Why she's interfering and overprotective?"

"Because she's convinced that I can't take care of myself after what happened when I was a juvenile."

"No, sweetheart, that's not it at all. That's not why Nick does it either."

Her brows knitted together. "What do you mean?"

Although Marcus didn't know all the details of the attempted rape, he was very sure of one thing: "Nick feels guilty because he's convinced he traumatized you when he attacked those humans to save you."

Yeah, Shaya had said as much to Roni.

"In his mind, he needs to make it up to you. So he tries to protect you from everything bad in the world. It's not because he thinks you're incapable of taking care of yourself—it's his way of trying to ease his own burden." Which was selfish, in Marcus's opinion. But it was possible that it was all subconscious on Nick's part. The guy cared about his sister.

Roni puffed out a long breath, never having thought of it that way before. "Okay, I guess that makes sense. But why do you think my mother does it?"

"Simple: she knows you're more dominant than she is." He lightly circled her belly button with his finger, liking the way her abdomen clenched at his touch. "I'm sure your wolf feels uncomfortable around females more dominant than she is and her instinct is to slap them down, make sure they understand the hierarchy, so they're no threat to you. It's the same for every dominant female. Kathy won't want to go down a step in the hierarchy. It's about pride."

Well, hell. "Why did I not see any of this before?" She considered herself an intelligent, observant person.

"Because they're your family—you don't expect that shit from family. But the fact is that, first and foremost, they're people, and people can be dicks."

There was an edge to his tone that told her he was talking from experience. She didn't want to probe into his "twisted story," but she figured her question wasn't too invasive. "You have the same problem with one of your parents?"

"Yes. My dad." He didn't elaborate, and he felt Roni tense. "Something wrong?"

"I don't like double standards."

"There aren't any double standards with us."

"You repeatedly ask me to share, but then you're all cagey about your own business. I'm not saying you need to tell me everything—I get that there are some things you won't want to talk about. That's fine. But if you're going to be cagey about every little thing, stop asking me to share my own shit."

"All you have to do is ask me, Roni. Like I told you, there are some things you're better off not knowing. As for the rest, I'll tell you whatever you want to know. But you have to ask."

Okay, now she understood what he was doing—pulling her fully into the conversation, making her take an active part in it rather than just answering his questions. Sneaky bastard. "Fine. Has your dad always been that way?"

"It started around the time I had my first shift. But we didn't really clash over it until I was fifteen." In actuality, though, they'd never gotten along.

"Why did you clash?" she gritted out when he purposely didn't elaborate.

"I'd decided to leave the pack with Trey." The pack's decision to ostracize Trey was made after he defeated his father in a duel, and it had caused a divide in the pack. Many had then left with Trey to form their own pack—thus, the Phoenix Pack was born.

"Your dad wanted you to stay?"

"Actually, no. The plan had been for me and my parents to move to my aunt's pack. But when all that shit happened with Trey, I chose to leave with him. My dad didn't like it, and he tried to dominate me into doing what he wanted. But it didn't work, and he realized I was more dominant than him." In Marcus's opinion, getting away from them had saved his sanity.

"He didn't take it too well?" she assumed.

"No. I'd known it for years, and I think he suspected it, but that day confirmed it."

"You said you have sisters. They didn't leave with your parents either?"

"I have three sisters. They're all older, and they'd mated into different packs by then."

"Are things okay with your dad now?" She wanted to ask if he was the violent asshole Nick had described, but that kind of story should be given willingly, not dragged out of someone.

"No." Even if his father had been able to cope well with it, things would never have been okay between them. "We were never close. He's a hard man. He's also an extremely proud dominant male who was Head Enforcer for most of his life. To know that his son was more dominant than him hurt his pride."

"Ah, well, that explains it." She nodded, totally getting this wolf now.

Marcus frowned. "What?"

"Why you downplay your dominance. You've been doing it for so long to placate your dad and protect his pride that it became part of your personality. Add in the fact that you simply have no fear of being challenged, and it's no wonder that you are the way you are."

Marcus thought about that for a minute. "You might be right."

She snorted. "Of course I'm right." He chuckled against her shoulder before kissing it lightly.

As her hand drew patterns down his arm, Marcus closed his eyes in contentment. Her touch was rarely given, so it meant more. When those fingers skimmed over the claw marks on his arm, her hand froze, and she quickly snatched it back—like a kid caught with their hand in a cookie jar.

"Sorry."

"You don't have to be sorry. I'm not going to break down because you touched a scar." And he wanted her hand back on him, but she didn't look convinced. "Will it help if I tell you how I got it?" Before she could answer, he began, "When our old pack split and we left with Trey, there was another among us. His mom, Louisa. She left her mate behind to stay with Trey. Some can handle that type of distance from their mate, but she . . . Some people just aren't strong. The separation was too much for her and her wolf. Eventually, she turned rogue. She targeted me . . . Trey snapped her neck."

Fuck, Roni truly hadn't seen that coming. She'd assumed it was a souvenir from one of his father's beatings—if such a thing had even happened.

"Don't think I wallow or dwell. I don't. She was rogue; there was no coming back from that. But I hate that I'd hesitated and placed Trey in a position where he had to step in, even though Trey's told me over and over that he gets it." He nipped her earlobe, craving some physical contact. As if she sensed that, she smoothed her hand over his shoulder. "I never wanted to be an enforcer, you know. Like you, I don't like to follow or lead. But I took the position because he asked." He tucked her hair behind her ear. "So you see, we're similar in that way, you and me. We're both trying to make up for something that really wasn't our fault."

"I guess we are."

He licked over his new mark, drawn to it in a way he couldn't explain. "I can sense how relaxed your wolf is right now. My wolf wants to play with her." The animal sensed that her wolf would be an interesting playmate.

"Don't you mean 'mount'?" Roni snickered.

He smiled impishly. "That too."

Her wolf had no objections to that. In fact, she was pushing for it, and that was a real worry. "I'm wary about allowing the two of them to run together."

"Why?"

"My wolf *can* be playful. But she's very aggressive when going after what she wants."

Marcus easily read between the lines. "You think she'd brand my wolf?"

"I *know* she'll leave him all marked up." When it came to marking a shifter while they were in their human form, it wasn't so serious; the human half could be okay with it, and the inner wolf might even approve. But when in their animal form, most shifters didn't like being marked by any other than its mate. And Roni's wolf had a very big thing for Marcus Fuller.

"As long as she's okay with my wolf doing the same to her, we won't have a problem."

That sure shocked her. "What's that now?"

Marcus shook his head at Roni's flabbergasted expression. "You have absolutely no idea what you do to my wolf, do you?

He wants you as much as I do. He likes the look of my mark on your skin."

"Just how many females—or males, for that matter—have you branded in your time?"

That made Marcus tense. "You really want to know?"

Did she, even though what suspiciously felt like jealously threatened to surface? "Yes."

"Are you sure?"

"Yes." With more conviction, she added, "I want to know, other than me, how many have you marked?"

He placed his face close to hers. "None."

Her brows flew up. Quietly, she echoed, "None?"

"None." He tapped her nose lightly. "So think about that if you ever get the urge to bolt, pretty baby. I'll just come right after you."

CHAPTER TEN

Whoever was knocking on his bedroom door this early was going to get his fist in their face. "Go. Away."

Marcus tightened his hold on the female he was spooning, burying his face in her hair. Roni hadn't even slightly stirred, which was probably because he'd woken her at least three times through the night. Her body was fast becoming an addiction, and he wanted it again.

Moving her hair aside to lick at the fresh mark on her nape, he cupped her breast and squeezed, smiling at the low moan that escaped her.

More knocking.

He growled. "*What?*"

"It's me. Open up." Dante was using his Beta tone, which meant this had to be important.

Slipping out of bed, Marcus pulled on a pair of jeans as he headed for the door. Opening it wide, he tensed at Dante's serious expression. "What is it?"

Dante shoved a mug of coffee into his hand. "I know it's early, but we can't wait around. Rhett and Donovan managed to track the IP address. We have a location on the jackals."

Five minutes later, Roni and Marcus joined Rhett and the Phoenix half of the hunting party at the kitchen table.

"So . . . where are the fuckers hiding?" asked Roni before shoving a vanilla lollipop into her mouth.

"Seattle." Rhett scratched his nape. "But I have to warn you, this could be a completely unproductive day."

Marcus frowned and paused chewing. Taryn, bless her soul, had placed a large plate of toast on the table. Swallowing it down, he asked, "Why?"

"The problem with tracing IP addresses is that it doesn't necessarily mean the owner is situated there."

Taryn arched a brow. "So it could just be an empty building?"

"Well, from the searches I've done on the house, it belongs to a human family."

The Alpha female pursed her lips. "I doubt the jackals will have help from humans."

"Exactly," said Rhett. "In the beginning, I'd expected it to be a simple case of finding the physical location of the IP address. But considering all the tricks the jackals are using, I'd say they have a hacker working for them. If that's the case, it's possible that they've used a computer virus to place the IP address on some totally oblivious random person's computer."

Trey released a frustrated growl. "In other words, it's not likely they'll be there, whatever the case."

Rhett shrugged helplessly.

"Then do we really *all* need to go?" asked Ryan. "It might be better if me and Dante go and check it out."

"No, we should all go," began Trey, "because there's a possibility that the jackals *are* there. The human family might not truly exist."

Dante took a sip of his coffee before turning to Rhett. "Could someone have faked something like that?"

"A family with a history, complete with photos and everything? Yeah, depending on how good they are." Rhett looked at Roni. "I still haven't managed to trace the IP address of whoever uploaded your video evidence. I'm sorry."

"It's okay," she said quietly.

"No, it's not. But I will find them."

"Do you have any suspicions at all about who it could be?" Taryn asked Roni. "It would help Rhett with the search."

Roni shook her head. "Like I told Marcus, I've pissed off plenty of people."

Dante spoke then. "But for them to do and say something so vindictive, it has to be substantial."

Roni looked at him. "Only to them." He tilted his head, conceding her point.

"Has anyone called my brother or Derren?"

Trey nodded. "Nick's arranging for one of his contacts to lone us a private jet." Nick was in touch with many of the shifters he'd met in juvie, and they all did each other favors from time to time. "As soon as he calls with directions for the jet, we'll head out."

"Does this mean we have time to make more food?" Marcus put his hand to his stomach. "I'm still hungry." Everyone rolled their eyes. "What?"

A few hours later, they were all piling into what Roni thought was a pretty sleek private jet. With the cream leather furnishings, the gleaming marble tables, the mirrored ceiling, and the soft carpeting, the spacious cabin looked more like the reception area of a swanky hotel. Hell, it even had an aquarium.

She found herself stuck between Marcus and a window—which was starting to become a regular thing whenever they traveled. Nick and Derren were sitting opposite them, while the four other Phoenix wolves took the seating area adjacent to theirs.

Dante reclined his seat until he was lounging comfortably. "Now this is nice." Nodding, Ryan grunted. "Nick, there are indeed perks to being so closely allied with your pack."

Eyes closed and arms crossed behind his head, Nick said, "Wish I could say the same. But you all still annoy the shit out of me."

Laughing, Derren took out his iPod and earphones and stuck the buds in his ears.

Dante rolled his eyes at Nick. "You're just pissy because you couldn't keep Marcus away from your sister."

"I do *not* get pissy. Fuller and I have come to an understanding: if he hurts Roni, I get to play with the body parts that she slices off."

Trey spoke to Nick. "Any other Alpha might have been ready to feed you your own kidneys for making their friend's life as difficult as you set out to make Marcus's, but I actually felt sorry for you the whole time."

Nick opened his eyes. "Felt sorry for me?"

"You really believed you could scare him away. It was kind of fun to watch you try."

Dante chuckled. "Marcus is a born hunter; when he truly wants something, he will run down his prey with a patience that not many dominant males possess—obstacles be damned. You were fighting a losing battle from the start."

Damn right, thought Marcus.

Nick growled at Dante, "Fuck you, Garcea." Ignoring the Beta's chuckle, Nick closed his eyes again, dismissing him.

Turning back to his pack, Dante smiled. "Jaime's going to be so jealous she didn't come."

Taryn snorted, cuddling into Trey. "You're not smug that she's missing this, you're disappointed that she's not with us. You hate leaving her."

"Of course I hate leaving her. She's my mate."

"You have to admit to being a little more overprotective than most," said Ryan.

"I have no choice—the female has no flight instinct."

Taryn smiled. "What a pretty excuse for trying to control her."

Dante returned her smile. "It is, isn't it?"

Roni was just thinking how fortunate she was that Marcus didn't attempt to control her, but then it occurred to her that, hey, why would he? He had no reason at all to feel inclined to do so. He'd staked a temporary claim on her, but that was nowhere near the same as being mated.

A mating bond was a metaphysical connection that amplified every emotion. Mates were often possessive and overprotective to the point of being controlling and domineering. It was part of the package, part of how fiercely mates felt for each other. Although it sometimes meant that the couples clashed a lot, it didn't subtract from their feelings for each other.

Having watched the pain her mother went through when Roni's father died, she'd often wondered if the mating link was such a good thing at all. Kathy might still be alive, but it wasn't a full life without her mate. But Kathy had told Roni that she had no regrets, that if she had to do it all over again, she'd still complete the mating, even knowing her mate would die and that she would spend most of her life without him.

She'd told Roni that if she found her mate, she should grab on tight, that the bond was something sacred and special. But, honestly, Roni wasn't sure she'd ever know the intensity of emotion that came with a mating link. Roni was so messed up, she probably wouldn't sense the guy even if she tripped over him in the street.

The best chance she had at mating was through imprinting, though she would bet it would be hard to find a male who would happily take on her and her irritating family. Although Shaya seemed sure that Roni and Marcus would imprint, Roni wasn't convinced. Despite that she had made the decision to explore this thing she had with Marcus, she found it hard to believe that anything would truly come of it.

For one thing, she had more flaws and baggage than even *she* knew how to deal with. For another, Marcus was incredibly loyal. Surely for him, taking what they had any further would feel like he was betraying his true mate. She wanted to ask how far he was willing to allow things to go, but she wasn't sure she wanted to know the answer. It would hurt to hear that she was basically just a way to pass the time until his mate came along. In fact, it would place him in serious danger with her naturally jealous wolf if that were the case.

"You're thinking very hard about something."

Pulled from her thoughts, Roni double-blinked at Marcus, who then picked up her hand and began massaging her palm. Like him, she kept her voice quiet to keep the conversation private. "Just wondering what we'll do if we find nothing in Seattle."

"You do know you can go to hell for that, right?" Marcus nipped the heel of her hand punishingly and then licked over it to soothe the sting. "If you don't want to tell me what's got you so tense, fine. But don't lie to me."

"It's fine if I don't want to tell you?" Doubtful. He was a nosy, pushy bastard.

"Okay, it's not 'fine,'" he admitted with a smile. "I don't like the idea that something's bothering you. I want to fix it."

"I'm not much for sharing stuff."

"I know. But I'd like it if you'd talk to me when something is eating at you."

At that moment, a human female appeared, lathered in makeup and practically marinated in perfume. "Hi, I'm Hazel. I'm your flight attendant for today. Can I get you anything?" Her eyes were solely on Marcus as she gestured to the selection of foods on the menu she handed him. Her eyes were also shining with lust and, therefore, at serious risk of being gouged out by Roni.

"I'm good for now, thanks," he replied with a polite smile. He'd stuffed his face only moments before boarding. "Want anything, sweetheart?" Roni simply shook her head, so he handed the menu back to the attendant. "We're both good."

Hazel blushed at his attention, but Roni couldn't be annoyed with Marcus for that—he wasn't being in the least bit flirtatious. Still smiling, the human continued. "If you change your mind, just press the call button, and I'll be right with you." Again, her words were only for him. "Before I leave, I just have to ask, have we met before? You seem so familiar."

Roni rolled her eyes. Hazel clearly didn't want to walk away from Marcus just yet and was coming up with a bullshit excuse to hang around.

Marcus shook his head. "You must have me confused with someone else."

"Are you sure? Because I never forget a face. Are you a model or something?"

"*Oh my God.*"

Barely refraining from laughing at her outburst, Marcus turned to Roni. "You called?" Her scowl made his chuckle break free. He kissed the scowl away, and by the time he pulled back, the human had gone. "Still mad at me?"

She blinked. "Why would I be mad at you? You didn't do anything wrong. *She* was the one flirting."

That surprised him. In the past, women had snapped at him if another female flirted with him, which had always irritated Marcus. Hey, he was the first to admit that he liked flirting, but he didn't do it when he was involved with someone. Flirting when you were in a relationship was plain disrespectful to your partner. As such, he hadn't thought it was fair that his partners took it out on him if another female tried to flirt with him, even though he could understand why they didn't like it. The fact that Roni hadn't done that pleased him.

"Of course, if you *had* flirted back, I would have smashed your face into the marble table."

That made him smile. "So vicious. And I wouldn't blame you. Nor do I blame you for being annoyed with the human. I feel the same way about Zander."

Confused, she frowned. "Zander?"

Massaging her hand again, he said, "He has a thing for you."

"No, he doesn't."

"Oh, yes he does, pretty baby. But I've made it clear that you're mine."

"You confronted him?"

"No. I broke his nose." At her gape, he shrugged. "I told you I'd be possessive with you. Learn to like it, sweetheart, because it's not going to stop. And neither is my attempt to get you to talk to me about what's bothering you."

"Nothing's bothering me. I was just thinking."

"About . . . ?"

Tingles shot up her arm as he pressed a kiss to her inner wrist. "Lots of things."

"Like . . . ?"

Persistent motherfucker. Fine, she'd let him have it. "Like . . . just how far can things get between us before we're betraying our mates? Would I even recognize my mate for who he was? Is there any way to stop my wolf from ripping your throat out when you leave me for your mate?" He said nothing. She arched a brow tauntingly. "Sorry you asked?"

Leaning closer, Marcus cupped her chin. "Let me make one thing very clear," he rumbled. "As far as I'm concerned, you're mine. I marked you and I staked a claim on you, and I wouldn't do either of those things lightly. If you do come across your mate and recognize him, you'd better hope to God for his sake that he's stronger than me, sweetheart, or he's dead. I'll kill him before I let him take you." She gaped again. "Sorry you asked?"

Roni swallowed hard, totally stunned by the vehemence in his tone. "I should have known better."

He grazed his teeth down her palm to nip the heel of her hand once again. "Better than what?"

"Better than to get involved with one of the 'quiet ones.' Irrational, every one of you."

"You think it's irrational that I'd kill to keep you? Now you're just being judgmental."

She snorted. "And if I said I'd kill *your* mate if she came along to claim you . . . ?"

"I'd ask you to at least make it quick. As I saw from your fight with Eliza, you like to toy with your prey, and I'd be an unfeeling bastard if I didn't prefer for my mate to have a swift execution."

She didn't believe one word of that matter-of-factly delivered statement, but still . . . "You're insane."

He smiled. "I love it when you try to flatter your way into my pants."

Roni hadn't been positive that it would happen, but she managed to get off the jet without mutilating the flight attendant—the slut hadn't stopped flirting with Marcus. Well, not until Roni helpfully pointed out that whale vomit was an ingredient of many perfumes and cosmetics. Hey, the girl had a right to know.

Now Roni and her fellow wolves were parked in a rented SUV across the street from the house that the jackals might potentially be hiding in. It was a decent house, in a pleasant enough neighborhood, suggesting that it had been an expensive buy. For that reason, Roni couldn't imagine the jackals using the place as a front. They could have gotten something much cheaper elsewhere.

"By the looks of things, nobody's home," said Dante. They had been parked there for a few minutes, but there didn't seem to be any activity going on, and there was no car in the driveway.

"Best to be sure," said Marcus, absentmindedly tracing the mark he'd left on Roni's nape. "They could be at the back of the house, in the backyard—even in the basement."

"Ryan, take a closer look." At Trey's order, the enforcer exited the SUV and melted away, utterly silent. The guy was like a ghost the way he moved.

"He's so good," began Nick, "I'm considering offering him a place in my pack."

Trey didn't stiffen or growl, as Roni might have expected. "Go ahead . . . if you want your mate's shotgun permanently lodged up your ass."

After a minute or so of silence, Taryn spoke. "We can't sit out here for long. You know how small neighborhoods can be—everyone knows everybody, and they're suspicious of strange people hanging around."

Roni nodded. "You boys aren't exactly inconspicuous." Trey looked like a damn highlander, Dante's powerful build was intimidating, and Marcus's tall, solid body—not to mention his pretty face—easily attracted attention.

Trey squeezed his mate's shoulder. "As soon as Ryan calls, we'll make a move."

Ryan called a few minutes later, and Trey put him on speakerphone. "What did you see?"

"Nothing and no one. I did a check of the perimeter of the house, but I couldn't see a single person. I haven't picked up any noises coming from inside either."

"Okay, then we go investigate. Hang tight. We'll be right there." Trey ended the call.

"If all eight of us go over there at once, it's going to draw attention," said Roni.

Marcus nodded. "She's right."

"It'll be best if we leave the SUV a few at a time, and then enter through the back door," Dante told them.

So that was what they did.

The side windows didn't stand a chance against shifter strength, which meant all of the wolves were able to enter the house without breaking a single pane of glass. Roni, Marcus, Dante, and Ryan checked the bottom half of the house while the others checked upstairs.

It was apparent to Roni as she and Marcus wandered through the living room, dining area, and kitchen that the place was a family home—photographs were everywhere, drawings were stuck to the refrigerator, and there was a pile of children's DVDs beside the TV.

In the hallway, Roni peered down at the different pairs of shoes. "If this is all a stage to fool people, it's a damn good one."

Marcus had to agree. "The appliances are all plugged in, and the food in the refrigerator is fresh and half-eaten. Somebody uses the place, so either the human family is real, or the jackals spend time here."

Dante and Ryan appeared then. "We checked the basement. There's a wine rack, and the rest is just storage space. No one's down there."

"I don't smell anything here other than human. You?" Ryan asked Roni and Marcus, who both shook their heads.

Dante sighed. "Me neither."

"Hey, guys," Taryn quietly called from upstairs. "We found the computer."

With the males behind her, Roni ascended the stairs and followed the Alpha female's scent. It led her to a boy's bedroom, where the other four wolves were waiting. The computer was placed in a little nook under a cabin bed.

"There's no way the jackals are running things from this house," said Trey, shaking his head.

Dante regarded the computer. "I think Rhett was right; they've used a virus to place the IP address on a random computer."

"Poor kid," muttered Derren. Yeah, the human had no idea what sadistic shit could be traced back to his home.

"Do you think this computer was selected totally at random, or is it possible that this family is connected to the jackals somehow?" Derren asked Nick, who shrugged.

"I'd say it's random," said Roni.

Derren cocked his head. "Why?"

"If they're going to go through this much trouble to conceal their location, it seems odd to then place the IP address on the computer of someone who could be traced back to them."

Marcus twirled strands of her hair around his finger. "She's got a point."

Taryn released a heavy sigh. "Well, it wasn't a completely wasted journey."

Nick frowned. "How do you figure that?"

"It answers one question for us: it tells us how they're running the website, that they have a hacker, and that we're not going to track them electronically. Up until now, that's mainly what we've relied on."

"If we want to hunt them down," said Trey, "we'll have to hunt them old style."

"But we don't have a clue where to start," Dante pointed out.

Derren folded his arms. "Do you think they could be in Seattle?"

"It's possible," replied Nick. "But as Roni said, they've gone through a lot of trouble to avoid being traced. I doubt they'd want to be close to this place in case anyone traced the IP address here. They'll want any potential hunters to be far away from them. I would, anyway."

Taryn's expression was resigned. "So, this leaves us at a dead end."

Trey draped an arm around her. "For now. But not for good."

No, definitely not for good, thought Marcus. There was no way he would allow these sick bastards to get away with the things they had done, attempting to kidnap Kye and hurting Roni in the process. For that alone, he'd happily slaughter every one of them—along with whoever uploaded the video evidence onto the website. Neither he nor Roni would allow them to get away with it. His female was delightfully vengeful. She didn't take anyone's shit, didn't let anyone hurt or victimize her, or . . .

"Roni always gets even."

Eli's words suddenly rang in his mind, seemingly from nowhere. It was true, Roni always got even. And that was when a thought snuck into his mind. But it wasn't until that night, when they were alone in his bed, that he was able to address it. Keeping his voice casual, he asked, "What happened to the other humans who attacked you?" She tensed against him, and he brushed the tips of his fingers up and down her arm reassuringly. "After they served their sentences, I mean."

Without lifting her head from his shoulder, she replied, "As far as I know, they and their families were given new identities." She hoped he'd let it go, but of course he didn't.

"You tracked them down, didn't you?" She went to move, and he tightened his arm around her, keeping her nestled in the cradle of his shoulder. "Shh, I'm not going to judge you, sweetheart. Fuck, if it had been me, I'd have done the exact same thing." She didn't relax, but she did stop struggling. "What happened to the other attackers, Roni?" he asked gently. Marcus cupped her face and lifted it, wanting to meet her eyes. "Like I said, I'm not going to judge you. I just want to know."

He wanted to know what the person he was holding was capable of? Fine. "When I was eighteen, I tracked them down . . . to make them pay. To kill them." Startling her, he pressed a soft kiss to her hair. It wasn't until she was confident that he wasn't about to push her away that she continued. "They were already dead; they'd been dead for three years."

"You think Nick arranged it from juvie?"

"At first, I thought so. But Nick wouldn't have had the resources to track them down. Not then."

"Eli."

"Eli said he didn't, but he can be a ruthless motherfucker. He knows a million ways to kill. Can do it without hesitation. And he doesn't like anyone messing with his family."

Marcus kissed her forehead. "In his position, it's what I would have done. If they were alive right now, I'd hunt them down." She didn't need to know what else he'd do to them.

"That's why I'm confident it wasn't the humans who uploaded the video. I know who it *wasn't*, but I don't know who it was."

"We'll find them, Roni. We'll find them."

CHAPTER ELEVEN

She was an idiot. Everyone knew that going to a donut shop at lunchtime was a mistake unless standing in eternally long lines sounded like fun. But Roni had wanted to pick up some caramel donuts for Shaya. Usually, Roni came early in the morning, but she'd only left Phoenix Pack territory half an hour ago. Marcus had . . . delayed her. She would have thought their night of endless hot sex would have satisfied his libido. But no, Marcus had reached for her the second he woke, just as he had several times through the night—just as he had every night over the past couple of weeks.

For once, Roni didn't get taunting looks from the pack when she walked into the kitchen that morning with Marcus, despite his leaving a brand-new mark on the soft flesh of her neck—nice and visible for all to see. Bastard. But no one had batted an eyelid. Apparently the extent of his possessiveness was old news.

It had been obvious that Greta, however, had wanted to comment on the brand. She'd skimmed her hostile gaze over Roni, and there had been a dark glint in her eyes that Roni had seen a thousand times before—seen it appear each time Greta attempted to rile Taryn or Jaime.

She had felt Marcus tense beside her, known he'd planned to smoothly step in if Greta said even a cross word to Roni. But as usual, it had been Trey who had warned the woman off. He'd insisted that since Roni had saved his son, he wouldn't have her treated with anything but respect. As always, he'd turned Greta's words on her, claiming that they were all in Roni's debt.

All the other Phoenix wolves had worn expressions of total agreement. Although Greta hadn't said a word, she'd stared hard at Roni, and Roni had stared right back. If the old heifer thought she could toy with Roni, she was out of her damn mind.

Finally in possession of her order, Roni made her way to the parking lot across the road. It was as she approached her car that it happened: the unmistakable feeling that someone was behind her crawled up her spine. She waited until she knew they were up close before acting. In a swift, fluid movement, Roni swerved on the spot, grabbed a hand holding a syringe, and forced the strange female to stab herself in the neck. Within seconds, the dumb bitch was out cold. Huh. A sedative.

Roni locked her gaze on another female, who was staring at her wide-eyed and looking terribly amused. Even, strangely, a little excited.

"Oh, you *are* good." She'd said it like Roni had come recommended or something. "You will be lots of fun for us."

Roni didn't recognize either of the females, but she'd smelled scents similar to theirs before, so she knew one thing: these were jackals. That made both Roni and her wolf growl. "I'm tired, I'm pissed, and I'm seriously unhappy that the donuts I waited half an hour for are now splattered on the ground. So make this really, really quick, and really, really sweet."

"We're going to need you to come with us." The jackal gestured to a waiting car that contained two other females, both of who were watching in morbid fascination. They were trying to drug and kidnap Roni in a public area in broad daylight? Really? Quinn was right: the sick freaks just didn't care.

"And why would I do that?"

"Let's see . . . there's four of us, and one of you."

"*Three* of you, actually." She toed the unconscious body at her feet. "This one's not going to be much use to you for a while."

"Those still aren't good odds for you. So be a smart little girl and get in the car."

Roni pursed her lips. "Nah, I don't think I'm going to do that."

The jackal's face hardened. "It wouldn't be wise to try to fight us off, wolf."

"You're right: willingly getting into a vehicle with a bunch of shifters who intend to kill me makes a lot more sense."

"Last chance. Get. In. The. Fucking. Car."

"You can call that 'Plan B,' okay?" Roni didn't wait for the jackal to make the first move—she needed to get this over with quickly and quietly. This wasn't the time for fancy moves or toying with the bitches' spleens. So Roni did what she always did when having a good, long fight wasn't an option. She dealt her opponent a hard blow to the temple. And, yep, down the bitch went.

Cursing, a dark-haired jackal jumped out of the passenger seat. At the same time, a guy came running over, shouting. It was clear by the way he moved that he was no shifter. *Shit.* Roni turned wide eyes on the human male. "Help! They're trying to rob us, and they've hurt my friend!" Roni squatted down and put a protective hand on the stomach of the drugged jackal. This bitch was going nowhere.

Thinking on her feet, the dark-haired jackal dragged the other unconscious female into the car, and then the three shifters hightailed it out of there without even a second look at their drugged friend. No loyalty among . . . sick freaks.

"Hey, are you girls okay?" asked the human, panting. "Do you need me to call the cops?"

Now how to get rid of this guy.

"I'll file a report later. Right now, I have to get my friend to a doctor. My other friend's in the bakery. Could you please go over there and tell her I need her right away? Her name's . . . Sheridan."

Like the good citizen he was, the human sprinted over to the bakery. By the time he came back, Roni would be long gone.

"Um, Roni, could you please tell me why there's an unconscious female in the trunk of your car?" Rubbing at his nape, Eli frowned down at the blonde. "When you said, 'Come see what I've got,' I thought you meant new sneakers or something."

He'd made his way to Roni the second she pulled up on their territory to warn her that Kathy was looking for her. Although it was fair to say they took sibling rivalry to a whole new level, they always stood united against a common foe—particularly their mother.

Roni removed the lollipop from her mouth to answer. "She's not just any unconscious female. She's an unconscious female jackal."

"Jackal?" he growled. "I wondered what that smell was."

"Blondie here and three of her friends tried to jump me in the parking lot when I went to pick up some donuts for Shaya. They wanted to whisk me away in their car."

He spat out a stream of curses. "You all right?"

"Fine. But we need to tie her up and put her somewhere to question her. The drug should wear off soon."

"You drugged her?"

"It was only fair, since she tried to drug me."

He exhaled a long breath, shaking his head. "Marcus is going to lose his shit."

"I'm fine."

"It doesn't matter. He isn't going to like that someone tried to harm you. Call him, tell him to pass on the story to his Alphas. The Phoenix wolves will want to be here when she wakes up; they should hear what she has to say."

She walked a little distance away so she could talk to Marcus privately.

"Hey there, pretty baby. How's my favorite wolf in the world?" Marcus's smile was obvious in his voice.

"I, um, I'm fine. Good. I, um . . ."

"Roni, what's wrong?" he asked cautiously.

"Nothing's wrong. Look, don't panic, don't go postal. Everything's fine, but—"

"Roni, tell me what the fuck's going on." So she told him. As Eli predicted, Marcus exploded. *"What?"*

"Really, Marcus, I'm fine. It's okay."

"They tried to drug and kidnap you! No part of that is 'okay' to me! Wait there; I'll be five minutes."

She refrained from pointing out that he couldn't possibly complete the journey in five minutes. "Make sure you bring the others with you. I brought one of the jackals home for a chat." She ended the call before he could lecture her on bringing home strange shifters that had tried to hurt her.

"See, told you he'd lose his shit." Eli, who'd crept up behind her to eavesdrop, didn't bother hiding his smirk. So she punched him in the gut.

"Now I have to tell the other overprotective male in my life. Won't this be fun." After binding the jackal and dumping her in the tool shed, she and Eli locked the door securely behind them and sought out their brother.

They found Nick sitting with Shaya on the porch swing at the rear of their lodge; he was having a beer while Shaya was drinking a bottle of water. Maybe it was Shaya's presence, or maybe it was simply that Roni didn't have a scratch on her, but he seemed to take the whole thing pretty well. He didn't interrupt her even once. Didn't say a word. To add to that, his cool expression didn't alter.

Once she was finished, he leaned forward. "Let me get this straight." Damn, that dark rumble meant bad things, which was most likely why Shaya winced. Clearly he wasn't so cool and collected after all. "And tell me if I've left anything out. You were almost drugged, abducted, and got into a fight with two jackals—"

"I wouldn't call it a fight. More like a scuffle."

"—in full view of any humans who might happen upon you—"

"Only one actually saw something."

"—and then you decided that, hey, you'd bring home the crazy bitch who tried to stab you with a syringe."

"We have questions, she has answers; it makes sense."

Shaya shrugged at her mate. "She's right, it does."

"Why didn't you call me, Roni? I would have come to you!"

"I didn't need you to," Roni stated. "I took care of it."

"What about afterward? You don't think I'd want to know someone just tried to take you?"

"I'm telling you now."

Nick gaped at her. "How can you be so fucking calm? It's obvious why they wanted you, Roni! You were supposed to star in one of their special vids!"

"Well . . . yeah. But it backfired on them, and now we have one of their people. So it's all worked out quite well for us, don't you think?"

"Worked out quite well," he echoed quietly before turning to Eli. "Is she fucking kidding me?"

"She was actually whistling a merry tune when she pulled up outside," Eli ever so helpfully chipped in, chuckling.

"Sorry about the donuts, Shaya," said Roni. "I'll get you some more tomorrow."

"*Donuts?*" bellowed Nick. "*Who cares about fucking donuts? You were almost taken!*"

"I know."

"*Stop being so damn calm!*"

"You want me to shout and scream, or something?"

"I want you to be normal! And I want you to contact me from

now on whenever there's a problem! Not come to me afterward with an, '*Oh, by the way*' story!"

"You know, all this tension can't be good for the baby—apparently they can hear things from the womb. You should try to calm down." Roni's words seemed to actually make him worse.

He pointed his finger hard at her. "You just can't—"

"There'd better be a damn good reason why you're roaring at her, Axton."

That smooth, male voice never failed to send a shiver of excitement through Roni. Turning, she watched as Marcus rounded the lodge and prowled toward her. "Wow, you were fast."

As Marcus finally saw for himself that she was unharmed, the knot of anxiety in his chest began to unravel. He went straight to her, uncaring of their audience, and brought his mouth down hard on hers as his hands slid into her hair. Her taste and scent flooded his senses, soothing the frays in his control and calming his wolf. "I swear, I'm going to find that pack and destroy every fucking one of them. You should have called me immediately."

"No, she should have called *me* straight away. I'm her Alpha, and her brother."

Marcus glanced at Nick curiously. "You say that like you're more important than me. I'm confused."

Roni bit the inside of her cheek to stop herself from laughing. "I didn't need to call either of you. I was fine."

"I didn't say you *needed* to call me, sweetheart. I said you should have." Marcus smoothed his hands up and down her arms. "If something had happened to me, even if I was unharmed, wouldn't you have wanted to know?"

"Point taken," she mumbled. "Next time, I'll call you."

Nick gaped at her again. "Why is it that you promise to call *him* but not me?"

"You didn't ask me to promise to call you. You just kind of yelled at me. And then there was the snarling."

Marcus shook his head at him. "If you don't know how to talk to a dominant female by now, you're never going to learn."

Smiling at Nick, Shaya idly swished her water bottle from side to side. "It's at times like this I understand why fate gave you a submissive female as a mate. A dominant female would have surely slit your throat by now. I have more patience."

He snorted. "*You're* patient?" At her growl, he quickly said, in a tone of total agreement, "You're patient."

"Okay, so, where's the jackal?" At the sound of Taryn's voice, they all turned to see the Phoenix Alpha pair approaching with Dante and Jaime.

"In the tool shed," replied Eli. "Where's Ryan?"

"Jaime's come in his place," explained Dante. "She insisted on coming here to, and I quote, 'smack the shit out of the bitch who tried to drug Roni.' As you can tell, my mate's painfully shy and has trouble expressing herself." Jaime just snorted at him.

Taryn smiled sweetly at Roni, but her rage was so profound it was almost tangible. "Well then, lead us to the tool shed."

Inside the wooden building that was roughly the side of a small barn, the peroxide-blonde jackal was struggling against her binds. She froze when all nine of them entered. Oddly, though, she didn't seem scared. Roni would be happy to change that.

"You're awake. Good." She slowly strolled toward the little bitch with Taryn, Jaime, and Shaya at her heels.

When the males attempted to follow, Taryn raised a hand. "Hold it, boys. This one's ours."

Dante gaped at her. "This is what I do, Taryn."

"It would trouble you to hurt a female, Popeye, and you know it," said Jaime. "It would trouble all of you. But it won't bother me or my girls here. Besides, you get to have your fun all the time. Don't be so selfish."

Marcus shrugged at the other males and went to lean against the wall a little behind Roni, needing to be close to her. Jaime was right: it would trouble them to interrogate a female, might even make them go easy on her. She didn't deserve "easy." As long as he had Roni in his sights, he could deal with staying in the background. The guys must have reached the same conclusion, because they joined him.

Pleased, Taryn smiled. "Good. Watch and learn, boys."

Roni cocked her head at the jackal. There was still no fear in her eyes or her scent, but there was wariness. "You can sense my wolf, can't you? You can sense how much she wants to rip out your throat."

"Am I supposed to shiver in fear?" The blonde snorted, tossing her long, silky mane over her shoulder.

Taryn smiled. "Yes, you should. You know who I am, don't you?"

"I know it's pointless that you wear a bra. I mean, if you didn't have ears, you wouldn't wear earrings, would you?"

"Your pack tried to take my son. Why?"

"I won't tell you shit."

"No?" Jaime sighed. "That's too bad, 'cause we have a lot of questions."

"What's 'too bad' is that you have curves like a racetrack."

Roni frowned at her fellow interrogators. "She seems to think her opinion matters to us. Weird, huh?"

"*You're* calling *me* weird? That's rich. I mean, *look* at you. You don't wear even a scrap of makeup. You dress like a boy. And haven't you heard of a hair straightener?"

Shaya looked at the jackal curiously. "You're right, Roni. She thinks we care."

The jackal sneered at Shaya. "Oh, we have a ginger in the house."

"How many times must people be told it's red?"

"And why are you so pale? Tanning lotion is your friend."

"I think she's entertained us long enough," declared Taryn. "Let's get started. We want to know more about snm.com. Did your pack create it?"

The jackal looked surprised, which meant that Quinn clearly hadn't admitted to her pack that he'd mentioned the website to Marcus and Roni. "You don't like it?" she asked with a smirk.

"It's sick, and you know it."

"It's just shifters acting according to their true animal nature."

"But even animals don't do what those bastards did."

"Except dolphins," interjected Roni. "They're a race of violent predators who kill their own babies for fun and who have a predilection to gang rape."

"Dolphins, really?" Shaya pouted. "But they seem so sweet. Guess you never can tell."

"What had you planned to do with my son?" demanded Taryn.

"Let's just say he wouldn't have survived it." The blonde shrugged. "But I'm glad we didn't get him. Kids annoy the hell out of me—crying over and over for their mommy and daddy, begging to go home, when no one's coming to save them."

Oh, the twisted bitch.

It was no surprise when Taryn slapped her hard across the face. "Where's your pack?" But the jackal didn't answer. In fact, she was smiling. "Where. Is. Your. Pack?"

"Do you really think I'd ever tell you that?"

"One can but hope."

The odds of the jackal answering that question were nonexistent. For a shifter to give up their pack to another was the ultimate betrayal, totally taboo. It would stain their family's name, possibly lead to the entire family being ostracized from the pack simply because of what that one shifter did. By keeping that information to herself, the jackal was protecting her pack and her family.

"I'm not answering any of your questions. There's nothing in it for me—you'll kill me anyway."

Jaime tilted her head, conceding that. "But we can do it swiftly and cleanly if you cooperate. If you don't . . . well, that would be a bad decision."

"I've known pain. There's nothing you can do to me that hasn't already been done."

"I wouldn't be too sure about that," growled Taryn, taking a step forward.

Roni touched Taryn's arm to stay her, taking a moment to study their prisoner closely. The jackal had four females in front of her who would happily put her through a world of pain before finally killing her. She should have been terrified, sweating nervously. But no. She just looked resigned. This was someone who'd known a lot of violence, who'd gotten used to it and knew how to shut out the pain. She wasn't scared, wasn't on the verge of talking. And that presented them with a problem.

A tap, tap, tapping sound made Roni glance down. The jackal was moving her foot impatiently, making those clearly expensive stilettos tap on the floor. They were most likely just as expensive as the indecently short skirt and the strapless top, though probably not as expensive as the jewelry decorating her body. With her perfect hair, perfect makeup, and perfect appearance, she made Roni think of Eliza, Janice, Zara, and all of Marcus's other exes: shallow, superficial people obsessed with their looks.

And that gave Roni an idea.

"Just give me a sec," she told the girls. Then she walked to the wall on their right where a selection of tools was hanging. Grabbing the shears, she made her way over to the jackal.

The bitch curled her upper lip. "Pain doesn't scare me."

"Oh, I believe you," said Roni, selecting a few strands of that peroxide blonde hair and holding them out straight. Fear of pain definitely wasn't the jackal's weak spot. But something else was.

The jackal tensed. "What are you doing?"

Snip. "I figured I'd put some layers in your hair." Roni let the strands fall to the floor, and the jackal screeched. So Roni did it again. And again. And again.

"*Stop it, you bitch!*"

"I think that makeup might need removing," said Roni. Instantly, Shaya opened her bottle of water and splashed it all over the screaming jackal, paying particular attention to her face. Then she scrubbed at it with a dirty cloth she found on the tool bench.

"Those shoes look kind of uncomfortable, don't they?" Taryn and Jaime each took a stiletto and slammed them against the wall, breaking the heels and totally wrecking them. "Her clothes look a little tight too." They then slashed at the top and skirt over and over with their claws.

Shaya fingered the Pandora bracelet. "Maybe we should take this off so it get doesn't scratched or anything." Using her shifter strength, she snapped it off and trampled all over it before making her way over to Roni. "Let me have a turn. I am a hairstylist, after all." Looking the ultimate professional as she worked, Shaya did some snipping of her own before handing the shears to a very eager Taryn.

The Alpha female hummed a song as she moved, looking like a kid at Christmas. All the while, the jackal cursed and screeched. "Take it like a woman." Snip, snip, snip, snip.

"Ooh, can I have a turn? That looks fun." Happily taking the shears, Jaime then proceeded to cut even bigger chunks from the jackal's hair. "This is kind of therapeutic."

As the males all watched in morbid fascination, Trey quietly spoke. "I have to say, I did not see this coming."

"I don't think I've ever seen so much glee on Jaime's face." Dante shook his head in both wonder and amusement.

Eli chuckled. "As unbelievable as it seems, it looks like what they're doing is working; the jackal's close to breaking."

Marcus nodded. "They found her weak spot, and they pounced on it."

"Do you think we should hide those shears when they're done?" asked Nick. "They seem a little too fond of them."

Trey thought about it for a moment, then nodded. "Probably for the best."

"Yep," agreed Dante. "One thing we can learn from this is to never underestimate our females."

"You know, looking at them right now," began Marcus, "it's safe to say they're all a little crazy and vicious." Nick, Trey, and Dante all nodded in agreement, looking proud.

"Yeah," said Trey. "We lucked out."

The four females stood back and took a long look at their handiwork. The jackal's makeup was smudged all over her face, making her look like the masked figure from *Sinister*. Her expensive clothes were now so stained and tattered she resembled a hurricane survivor. In addition, her hair looked like it had been attacked by a lawn mower. She was actually sobbing.

Taryn tilted her head. "Looks kind of pitiful, doesn't she?"

Jaime nodded. "Bless her little black heart."

"Heart?" snorted Shaya.

"Well, the hole where her heart *should* be."

Taryn stepped forward. "Who created snm.com?"

The jackal didn't lift her head as she sniffled, "My pack did."

"Be more specific."

Her shoulders shook with her sobs. "My Alpha, Lyle Browne."

"Anyone else involved?"

"No." Her voice was low, sad, and sluggish—she sounded defeated. "Sometimes people hire him to get rid of someone, and he uses them for the vids. But the website is his. It's his baby."

"Speaking of babies, why did you go after my son?"

The jackal shrugged, like it was simple. "The more notorious the pack, the more credit people receive if they manage to get their hands on one of them."

"Is that why you went after Roni?"

"One of the reasons. I mean, she's an enforcer, a powerful Alpha's sister, and she's fucking a Phoenix enforcer."

"And the second reason?"

"She pissed someone off."

Roni snorted. "That's a regular occurrence. Who was it this time?"

"Lola McGee."

Jaime frowned. "Quinn's mate?"

"Motherfucker," Roni bit out as all the wolves growled.

Marcus came forward then, equally enraged. "How involved is Quinn? Does he know Lola sent you after Roni?"

"I don't know. She spoke to Lyle when he made his monthly call. I don't know exactly what she said."

Marcus turned to Dante, his voice like ice. "Quinn had to have known."

"Not necessarily," said the Beta male. "Lola didn't go through Quinn; she spoke directly to Lyle—that might mean that she knew Quinn wouldn't allow it so she went around him."

Nick came to stand beside Roni. "Where's your pack?"

The jackal looked up then. "Would *you* give up *your* pack? Nothing's worth that kind of betrayal."

"They left you behind," Roni pointed out. "When they saw a human was coming, they scampered. They didn't try to fight me to get to you. They must know I've got you and that I brought you here, but they haven't come for you. What does that say about them?"

Taryn squatted in front of the jackal. "It says they have no loyalty to you. So why should you have any loyalty to them?"

"Why should I have any loyalty to you?" the blonde retorted. "You're going to kill me. You want to do it so badly, don't you? I can see it in your eyes. You want to give in to the basic urges we all have. You're like me. We're the same."

"I'd never hurt a child. That makes us very, very different."

The jackal gestured at Roni. "*She's* not different. I saw you in one of the videos. You were terrified, weren't you? But I've got to give you points for one thing: you didn't beg. No matter how much he threatened you, how much he screamed at you and ordered you to beg him to let you go, you just wouldn't. You even spat in his face. I enjoyed that part."

Roni didn't give the bitch the reaction she wanted. "So glad I entertained you."

"Your pack has a kill site," rumbled Marcus. "Where is it?"

"Ooh, well done. Lyle would be pissed if he knew you'd figured out that our attacks happen in one spot."

"The site. Where is it?" repeated Marcus.

"I told you, I won't betray my pack."

"For you to say that, the kill site must also be where your pack is hiding out," concluded Jaime.

"Maybe you should leave my pack alone and take a closer look at your own breed."

Knowing that statement echoed something that Johnson had told Nick, Roni exchanged a worried look with her brother. She didn't want it to be true.

Nick took another step forward. "Are you saying a wolf shifter is involved in this?" She nodded, her smile taunting. "But just a few minutes ago, you said this was Lyle's baby."

"The idea is, yeah. But he needed someone to help him set up the website."

"Why would a wolf help out a bunch of jackals with something like this?"

"Because he gets off on watching. Sometimes, he kidnaps young females and takes them to the site. Then he watches while my pack tortures, rapes, and kills them."

Sick piece of shit.

"Who is he?" demanded Taryn.

"I don't know his name." When Nick's claws sliced out, the jackal shouted, "I don't, I swear! Lyle just called him 'the tech guy,' or 'the wolf.'"

"What does he look like?" asked Shaya.

"Tall, gangly, dark eyes, and he has a tattoo on his arm. They're Chinese symbols, but I don't know what they mean."

Marcus recalled seeing a tall male lurking in the background of the vids with such a tattoo on his arm, but none of the footage showed a clear image of him or the tattoo. They'd all assumed he was part of the jackal pack.

"That's all I can tell you without betraying my pack and endangering my family."

"Good enough." Without warning, Taryn shoved her claws into the female's stomach and twisted her hand sharply, slitting the jackal open. "That's how it felt when I realized my son might have been taken from me. And that's what every other parent will have felt when you took their child. You deserve exactly what you got."

CHAPTER TWELVE

How did one go about calming a six-foot, brooding, pissed-the-fuck-off, dominant male wolf? Roni didn't know.

She had soothed her brothers' anger many times, but her techniques were having no effect whatsoever on Marcus at the moment. He was pacing outside the barn, refusing to go inside the lodge with the others while he was in that state. His protective instincts were going crazy, feeding his rage, feeding his desire to invade McGee's territory and, as he'd so eloquently put it, "tear his fucking head off his shoulders and feed it to his bitch of a mate."

Being the voice of reason was hard when she kind of liked that idea too. "Marcus, we don't know that he had anything to do with Lola's plan."

He didn't pause in his pacing. "She's his mate. He had to have known."

"You know it's not that simple."

"I think the bastard knew all about it. I think he played a part in it." And Marcus would make him pay for it.

"No, you *want* him to have known and played a part in it, because then you would have someone to take out all this rage on—you can't hurt Lola because you wouldn't hurt a female; it's not in you."

He was aware that his smile wasn't at all nice. "I'm tempted to make an exception after what she did."

"It's hardly surprising that she retaliated in some way. I humiliated her—I'm a mere enforcer, she's an Alpha female, and I overpowered her. It would have made her pack question her strength and suitability as their leader."

"So she should have challenged you, one on one. But oh, no, she plotted to have you killed—and then have the footage uploaded onto the net."

"Are you really saying you would have been happier if she had challenged me instead of doing this?"

No, he wouldn't have been happier. Roni was his. He didn't want anyone or anything to hurt her in any way, shape, or form. "That's not the point."

"I hurt her pride, Marcus. An Alpha's pride is a big thing."

He slid his hands into her hair and pressed his forehead to hers. "That doesn't matter to me. She doesn't matter to me. *You* matter to me. And absolutely nobody gets to harm you. Not because I don't think you can take care of yourself, but because the very idea of anyone targeting you offends me and pisses me the hell off. If anyone touches you, they die."

His wolf was so close to the surface, it was worrying her. "Okay, but just . . . calm down." Unfortunately, the soothing tone wasn't working. Remembering how Shaya, Taryn, and Jaime calmed down their males, Roni slid her hands under his T-shirt and smoothed them up and down his chest—occasionally dragging her nails along his skin. Eventually, a contented growl rumbled out of him, and she sensed his wolf drawing back.

"I'm not letting this lie, Roni."

"Neither am I, but I'm not going to march onto their territory and risk starting a war between the packs either." If Lola hadn't been Alpha female, Roni would have challenged her immediately. But to challenge an Alpha female was to challenge the entire pack. "Shaya's pregnant—the last thing I want is for her to be in any form of danger, particularly in the middle of a pack war."

Okay, he could concede that she had a point there.

"Besides, right now we've got bigger things to worry about than some spineless bitch." Her wolf was certainly pissed about it, but as she already knew she could overpower the Alpha female, she wasn't particularly excited about dealing with her. It could wait.

"So what are you suggesting we do? Because if I don't do *something,* I'm going to fucking lose it."

"Well . . . this is what I had in mind."

Half an hour later, they dumped the female jackal's dead body over the border of Quinn's territory with a sheet of paper taped to her chest that said, "You bring shit to my door, and I'll bring shit to yours."

Marcus had to admit that Roni's idea was a good one. If Quinn weren't involved in the attempt to kidnap her, he would certainly be confused by the message and would undoubtedly call Marcus to ask what was going on. If he were involved, he'd now be very much aware that they knew, and he would sit and sweat about what they would do to retaliate and when exactly they would do it. Lola would do a lot of sweating too. In addition, it would mean that Lyle would definitely see the body at some point, because the Alphas were bound to tell him. "Smart little shit, aren't you?"

"So my mother tells me. Come on, let's go."

"Yeah, I'm hungry."

She rolled her eyes. "Only you would have an appetite after dumping a corpse."

Once inside the Toyota, he said, "You do know that the interrogation I just witnessed was the most hilarious one I've seen, right?"

"It wasn't funny. It was imaginative. Creative. Brilliant."

"It was hilarious, freaky, and shocked the shit out of me when it worked."

She sniffed. "You're just jealous because you didn't get to join in."

"Maybe a little."

After a short journey, they arrived at a diner that Roni thought would look right at home on the *Grease* movie set. It was kind of charming, and the most delicious smells were wafting from it.

"You ever been here before?" asked Marcus as they made their way toward it.

She shook her head, wondering at the strange twinkle in his eyes. "You?"

He smiled. "You could say that." His smile disappeared at the long appreciative whistle that split the air. A guy who was leaning against a motorcycle was eying Roni from head to toe. Marcus growled warningly, making the human pale and turn away. He noticed Roni staring impatiently at him. "I don't like it when people want what's mine." Her little huff made him grin.

Possessiveness usually irritated Roni, but she actually found it kind of amusing—even a little satisfying, if she were being honest—when it came from Marcus. Her amusement didn't last long, since they hadn't been inside the building for more than five seconds when someone squealed excitedly, "Marcus!" Then a dark-haired female was circling the counter and hugging him tightly—and he was hugging her back. Huh. Roni wouldn't have thought that Marcus was curious about having his balls sliced off and dumped in a blender, but apparently so.

Marcus held his hand out to Roni. "Come here, gorgeous. I want you to meet my sister."

Oh. Taking his hand, Roni stepped forward and offered the female an awkward smile.

"Roni, this is Teagan—she's the oldest. Teagan, this is Roni. She's mine." That, he knew, would say all there was to say. He didn't claim females, and Teagan knew that.

Eyes wide in pleasant surprise, Teagan nodded at Roni. "Very nice to meet you. Come. Sit." She ushered them over to a corner booth.

Marcus slid in beside Roni, which she was glad of since she felt weird while his sister stared at her in open fascination. There were two more squeals, and then two identical dark-haired females were racing toward them. Marcus stood and hugged them both as they nattered to him. When they finally noticed Roni, they both froze and looked at her in pure amazement. Great, more attention.

Marcus returned to his seat and took Roni's hand. "This is Deana and Trish—my other sisters. Girls, this is Roni."

Deana gasped and put a hand over her heart. "You've brought a girl. I'm so proud."

Trish nodded. "Never thought I'd see the day." Then all three sisters grabbed chairs and gathered around them. Worse, they started launching questions at Roni.

"So, Roni, are you a Phoenix wolf too?"

"Do you have a role within the pack?"

"How old are you?"

"How long have you been dating Marcus?"

"Where did you get that T-shirt? I love it."

"What's your last name?"

"Can you cook? Because Marcus needs constant feeding."

"Are you open to imprinting?"

Overwhelmed and out of her element, Roni did what she always did when that happened. She cocked her head. "Did you know that—?"

"Roni." It was supposed to be an admonishment, but he knew it was filled with too much amusement and affection to be even close to stern. Of course she was the personification of innocence when she looked at him.

"What? What did I say?"

Marcus just shook his head. Then out came a lollipop. Typical. It made him realize how long it had been since she'd pulled the lollipop or useless fact stunt on him. That sure made him smug. He turned to his sisters. "Her name is Roni Axton. She's not from my pack, she's from the Mercury Pack. She's an enforcer. Now could you stop interrogating her?"

"I'm sorry, Roni," said Teagan. "It's just that he's never brought a female to meet us before." At that moment, some customers arrived.

"We'll be back in a few minutes." Deana and Trish scuttled off to take their orders.

At the same time, Teagan jumped up from her seat. "Time to feed you. Marcus, I take it you want the usual?" He nodded. "Roni, what will you have?" Teagan wrote down her order and then disappeared.

"I'll bet it works out nicely for you that your sisters work in a diner. Lots of free food."

Chuckling, Marcus threaded his fingers through hers and nuzzled her neck. "The diner's theirs. Although they live in different packs, they run the business together. And I do admit to taking advantage of the free food." Seeing his sisters exchanging knowing smiles, he said, "They like you." That was important to him, because it was mostly his sisters who had raised him.

"They don't know me. And if they did, they definitely wouldn't like me."

"You make me happy. They see that. Therefore, they like you."

As she was used to making people feel either uncomfortable or annoyed, she couldn't help frowning doubtfully. "Happy?" His sensual smile made her stomach clench.

"You're hot. Smart. Competent. Funny. Fierce. Lethal. And you rock in bed. Why wouldn't you make me happy?"

That statement had been delivered in such a smooth, languid voice that her wolf growled, as if he'd stroked her. "I never stood a chance, did I?"

"Of what?"

"Holding out against you."

He laughed, pleased. "Nope. I was too determined to have you." And he had every intention of keeping her. She'd never believe it, but Roni Axton was an easy person to care for. Cuddly and fuzzy? No. Outgoing and friendly? No. Polite and open? No. But she wasn't hard or cold, wasn't unkind or selfish, wasn't hateful or vile.

He'd come to learn what Shaya had meant when she said that Roni had a real depth of emotion. She cared deeply and in an almost pure way. And she expressed it in the simplest of ways, like keeping Shaya stocked up on her favorite donuts, like giving her undivided attention to Kye, like letting Marcus share her cake. Those acts might seem like nothing to others, but coming from someone like Roni, who had trouble verbally expressing what she felt, they meant something.

She endeared him with her many quirks. The lollipops, the useless facts, the antisocial T-shirts . . . Maybe another person wouldn't have found it all adorable, but he did. He'd never known anyone to smile so little, which was why it was so satisfying and rewarding when he earned one from her.

She amused him constantly, particularly when people fruitlessly tried to rile her. She rarely cared enough about people's opinions to actually participate in conflict, so she'd simply ignore them, tell them to go away, or hit them with a useless fact that would shut them up. And when she *did* participate in conflict, she was so damn vicious it made him hard every time.

Hearing her phone ring, Roni groaned. "My mother."

"You're not going to answer it, then?"

"It will just be another lecture about how I'm betraying my intended mate by being with you. Then, of course, she'll top it off with some insults to remind me I'm not the little girl she wanted. I'll pass."

He kissed the palm of her hand. "She does love you. She just doesn't understand you."

"And you think you do, don't you?"

"I know I do. Just like you understand me." She saw past the charm to the person beneath when few others did; she saw the parts of him that weren't so smooth, but she was there with him anyway. "Don't let it worry you, Roni. Isn't it good to be really known by at least one person?"

Oddly, it did feel good. For as long as she could remember, she'd felt like she didn't fit. People didn't always like "different," and Roni was different in many ways. She flitted around, bonding with very few people. But with Marcus . . . it was like he gave her somewhere to fit, if that even made any sense. Still . . . "Trick knows you better." That bothered her, though it was probably stupid.

He nipped her bottom lip and then licked it soothingly. "No, he doesn't. Not because he doesn't know me well—he does. But you see more." And she expected him to *be* more than a pretty face. He liked that.

"Oh my God, Marcus, what are you doing here?" An Amazon practically flew toward them, her face a picture of total delight. "How are you? I haven't seen you since—" She stopped dead, right smack in the middle of the diner, upon spotting Roni. Her eyes widened, her face paled, and her jaw dropped.

"What's her problem?" Roni couldn't work out whether the female was shocked or horrified. Maybe a little of both. She was pretty sure she didn't know the Amazon, but the woman sure seemed to think she knew Roni.

Marcus frowned. "I don't know."

After a moment, the female seemed to recover. "I'm sorry, I thought you were someone else for a second there," she said to Roni.

That explained it. So why did Roni have the feeling the woman was lying her ass off?

"I'm Kerrie. I'm from Teagan's pack. That's how I met Marcus. He and I are, um, *were*, um . . . well, you know."

Oh, Roni did know. She also knew that Kerrie was trying to rub it in her face. Bitch. So she didn't bother introducing herself. If that seemed rude, good.

"This is Roni," said Marcus, breaking the tense silence.

"Nice to meet you, Roni." Nice? She didn't seem to find it "nice" at all. Kerrie switched her focus to Marcus then, her smile bright and huge. "How are you? You look great. Better than when I last saw you, which was . . ." Her eyes briefly slid to Roni. "Anyway, how are things going for the Phoenix Pack?"

Marcus had been around females long enough to know when they were making subtle "I once slept with him" statements that would provoke another female. He wouldn't have expected it of Kerrie. She'd never struck him as petty or bitchy. But right now, he was seeing her in a new light.

Delivering a clear message to both Roni and Kerrie, he kissed the palm of Roni's hand again and then began massaging her inner wrist with his thumb. "Everything's fine, thanks."

As she stared at the Amazon, Roni realized she'd never experienced jealousy before. Not the kind of jealousy that made someone want to jump across the table and rip out some bitch's spinal cord. Right then, though, that seemed like a sound plan. Her wolf was sure up for it, despite being slightly placated by Marcus's possessive gesture. Roni wasn't so placated, but she *was* rather enjoying the bitter gleam in Kerrie's eyes. The bitch was envious to the point of being bitter? What fun.

Kerrie grabbed a chair. "You don't mind if I eat with you, do you?"

"Yeah, I do," said Roni. If Marcus didn't back her up on this, she was *so* out of there.

"Excuse me?"

"Did I stutter?"

Kerrie's mouth bobbed open and closed. "Have I upset you in some way?"

"Upset me?" Roni snorted. "You're on solid food, aren't you?" The female simply wasn't important enough to affect her that deeply.

"Look, I'm sorry if I've offended you or something, but—"

"You can't eyeball someone's male and expect her to eat with you. It's really that simple." Kerrie looked to Marcus for some backup, but he wisely said nothing. "You can go now."

Wearing a wounded look that was totally fake, Kerrie walked to the counter and began talking to Deana.

Only then did Roni turn to Marcus, who was surprisingly quiet. "You're not going to lecture me about being rude to your friend?"

"Sweetheart, you really have no idea how hard it makes me to see you get all possessive like that." It made him want to fuck her within an inch of her life.

Typical male. "I'm not dumb, I know you've got a past. But that doesn't mean I have to be okay with it being flaunted in my face."

"You're right, she was being a bitch. You handled it well." Just then, Teagan brought out their orders, and Kerrie was forgotten. Roni really enjoyed the food, which pleased Marcus and his sisters. He wasn't impressed that she wanted to share with him again—or that she snatched some of his fries.

Unsurprisingly, his sisters dragged him into the kitchen for a "chat" before he left, which was basically an interrogation about how he felt about Roni and what he intended to do about those feelings. He managed to artfully blow off most of the questions.

When he exited the kitchen, he saw that Kerrie was talking to Roni, who looked ready to slap her. Protectiveness made him want to barge over there and bare his teeth at Kerrie, but he knew Roni would be pissed by that, so he stood back to allow her to take care of the matter herself.

"He must like you a lot to bring you to meet his sisters," said Kerrie. "I'm sure you know what I told him, that he's spoken of me."

"Nope. Never heard about you before." It was clear to Marcus that Roni meant it as an insult, and it clearly hit home.

"I'm a Seer. I had a vision of Marcus with his mate; I saw her. You're not her." Kerrie seemed to take delight in saying that. "She's bruised deep inside, and she needs him. Don't get in the way of that."

Shit. Marcus hadn't wanted to bring this up to Roni, worried she'd do something stupid like make the way clear for this female he didn't even want.

"She needs him," continued Kerrie. "His path is to find her, to save her—only he can."

Roni's expression was deadpan. "Well then, she'd better come fight for him." Her unexpected words made him smile.

Kerrie gaped. "You'd really stay with him? You'd really get in the way of that?"

"I spoke to a Seer once. She told me my father would be Alpha of the pack one day. He was already dead at the time."

"My vision was—"

"Just a vision. I don't place much faith in them. But if Marcus's path truly is so set in stone, he'll find her without trying, won't he? So don't worry your bitter little head."

Marcus chose that moment to approach. "Ready, gorgeous?"

Roni nodded. "Definitely. There's a weird smell in here." She then cast Kerrie a withering look and strolled out of the diner, knowing Marcus would follow. She'd sensed him behind her and Kerrie, knew he'd been listening, and she appreciated that he let her deal with the bitch herself. It wasn't until they were both in the car and leaving the parking lot that she spoke again. "So . . . Kerrie's a Seer."

He smoothed his hand along her thigh. "I didn't tell you about the vision for three reasons: One, I was worried it would make you walk away. Two, I don't want the vision to come true— the future she described isn't one I'd want. Three, I'm not sure I believe the vision means anything anymore. In any case, I couldn't make the female the Seer described happy, and she couldn't make me happy either."

That made Roni frown. "Mates make each other happy."

"That's the theory."

"Your parents weren't happy at all, were they?" she guessed.

"No, they weren't," he admitted.

So maybe Nick's suppositions were right after all. "Were they true mates, or had they imprinted?"

"They were true mates. And yet, they were never happy. In fact, they were miserable. But you don't look very surprised by that."

She thought about denying it, but not only would it be unfair, he'd most likely know she was lying. "It's just that Nick . . . he had his friend do a check on you, on your past."

"Did he now?" he drawled, his tone deadly.

"He had no right to do that; it was an invasion of your privacy, and I'm sorry."

"Well, what did he find out?" But Marcus was afraid he already knew.

"You once told me your dad was hard. Did he ever . . . ?" It was difficult to ask, felt wrong when she could sense his pain.

"Was he abusive? No, he wasn't."

"But your mom . . ."

"He never laid a single finger on her."

Roni's brows drew together in confusion. "Nick's friend said she was always badly bruised."

"She was."

"Marcus, I don't understand."

Pulling up at the side of the road, he killed the engine—resigned to the fact that he'd need to tell Roni this twisted tale. "She used to disappear for days at a time. When she'd come back, she'd be battered and bruised. Not because she'd been attacked, but because she'd wanted it." Seeing Roni's perplexed look, he smiled weakly. "I don't really understand it myself. I've heard about sexual masochism, but most people involved in that lifestyle are totally normal people with a kink that others might not understand. But my mother . . . it's not sexual for her, she just likes to suffer. And in being the way she is, she makes everyone around her suffer."

Wow. Nothing he said could have stunned Roni more.

"When we were in our old pack, she knew everyone thought my dad was abusing her, knew about the whispers and rumors, but she didn't care. He tried to help her, but he couldn't, because she didn't want help—she still doesn't. I think she does love me and my sisters, but she doesn't seem to want us to love her. If I tried to hug her, she'd push me away. She needs to be a constant victim."

The pain of that rejection was in his voice, and it made Roni's wolf whine. Wanting to comfort him but not really sure what to do, Roni simply laid a supportive hand over his. He threaded his fingers through hers and squeezed gently.

"When she'd vanish for a few days, I was glad. I used to dread her coming home because I knew what state she'd be in: covered in whip marks, bruises, cuff marks, burns. I don't know where she used to go—I know there are clubs that cater to that kind of thing. Or maybe she had an arrangement with someone who got off on beating the crap out of women."

"It must have been hard." She almost groaned at herself for the clichéd comment, but she didn't know what to say. What did a person say to someone who grew up with that shit?

"Confining her to the house didn't work because she'd resort to self-harm. I once found her in her bedroom with a plastic bag around her head." He'd thought he was saving her when he freed her, but she'd been angry at him. It hadn't been the last time something like that happened.

"Was it an attention-seeking thing?"

He shook his head. "She didn't do any of it for attention—she just liked it, liked the pain, liked the humiliation, both physical and emotional. My dad tried everything to help her. He stood by her through it all. He never told anyone; he let everyone believe he was abusing her. My sisters and I were sworn to secrecy."

"Did anyone find out?" Surely something like that couldn't be kept totally buried.

"Trick knew. He was with me one day when I found her slicing her arms with her own claws. But he didn't betray the secret. I wanted to tell people, but I knew my dad would have made us switch packs to protect her from their disgust—he always put her first. Other than my sisters, who were the ones who really took care of me, my friends were all I had."

"Are you in contact with your parents?"

"No. I tried to have a relationship with them, but I can't. What my mother does . . . it's like an addiction. Whether my dad realizes it or not, he's her enabler. He's emotionally distant, which helps her since she recoils from affection. But he can't give her the physical pain she needs. So he takes her to these clubs, lets someone beat the living shit out of her, and then he takes her home."

What a total mind fuck. Following her wolf's instinct, Roni rubbed her jaw against his shoulder. It seemed to soothe him, because he took a deep breath and then kissed her hair. She knew now why he hid behind a carefree mask. He didn't *want* to care, because then he wouldn't hurt anymore. Not only had his mother rejected him, but his father had rejected him too when Marcus's strength became apparent. If someone was carefree and happy on their own, they didn't need anyone else, they didn't need love, and then they couldn't be rejected, could they?

"Maybe it's unfair, but I can't go there to visit them, Roni. I can't look at them and pretend I'm okay with it. I get that, in their own way, they're both trapped. And I get that my dad thinks he's making the best out of a bad situation. But I can't be part of it. If that makes me a shit son . . . well, then, I'm a shit son. I just can't be part of the lies anymore."

She leaned into him, feeling helpless. "It doesn't make you a bad son."

"On my dad's birthday last year, he asked us all to get together for a family meal. I didn't want to go, but my sisters convinced me to give it a try. My mother was sitting there, black and fucking blue with rope burns around her neck and wrists, and we all had to pretend it was fine. I couldn't do it. I walked out, and I haven't seen either of them since. Teagan doesn't visit them either, but she talks to Dad over the phone sometimes."

Understanding now the source of all that anger trapped in ice, Roni felt like shit. He'd grown up watching his mother hurt herself over and over again, had been forced to let his father bear unwarranted shame, and she'd just made him talk about it. "Marcus, I'm really sorry I dredged this up. I really—"

He put a finger to her lips. "I would have told you at some point.

It's just not an easy thing to talk about. But now that you know, maybe you can understand what I've been saying to you. My mother doesn't want love or affection, but she's still needy and clingy in her own way. You worry that I want to control you. You don't get that your independent streak is one of the things I like most about you. You're not needy. You're not weak. You're not self-centered. You're self-reliant, strong, protective, and good to those who matter to you."

She gave a soft snort. "That's quite a glossy picture you painted there. I have my flaws."

"We all have our flaws, sweetheart. If we were perfect, we'd be boring and predictable. You are *never* boring."

"The Seer said your mate would be like your mother, didn't she?" Roni guessed. It would explain why he believed he couldn't make his mate happy and vice versa.

He nodded. "Teagan confides in Kerrie, so she knows about my mother. She said she thought it was fair to warn me that my mate was the same." He raked a hand into her hair. "But I'm not interested in visions or spiritual bullshit. *This*—you and me, here and now—is real. You're what matters, Roni. I want *you*. You said back there to Kerrie that you wouldn't walk away because of some vision. But did you really mean it? Do you really want me the way I want you?"

Surprisingly, the answer to that was easy. "I do." If he'd tried to steamroll his way into her life, Roni could have fought that. But he'd done it so sneakily, so subtly, that she initially hadn't even realized it was happening. And then it was too late; he was inside her now, embedded deep, and there was no pushing him out.

It was her own fault, really. In the very beginning, she'd branded him a smooth-talking player who could never truly interest her, thus deciding he was of no threat to her defenses. She hadn't been on her guard, and he'd taken advantage of that, slipped through the cracks of her shields and began to worm his way in, little by little.

The guy was so different from her, it was laughable. He was charming, very likeable, at ease dealing with people, and easily accepted by those around him. But he was also similar to her in some ways. He was loyal, perceptive, protective, and he took care of those who mattered to him; he knew what was important.

Honestly, he could do so much better than her, but she'd be dumb to push him away. She didn't want to. Being the focus of such a strong, solid, dominant wolf . . . it wasn't just thrilling and flattering. It made her feel safe, secure, respected . . . even cherished. He defended her, but he didn't do it in a way that disrespected or undermined her. Although he worked hard to get his own way, he didn't try to manage her or dictate to her. What's more, he made her feel like she was fine just the way she was. Nobody had ever done that before.

"Be certain, Roni. Be absolutely positive that you want this, because there'll be no backing out." If she were his mate—which he was afraid to hope for—then great. But if she wasn't, he was still going to keep her. He wasn't kidding when he'd told her that he'd kill her mate before he let him take her.

"I'm sure. But are *you*? Is this going to be something you can handle if we do take things another step further? Everything you saw growing up has made you confused about what it means to care. You've never seen it as a positive thing. To you, it was toxic: misery, suffering, and pain."

"But not with you."

"How do you know that, when you've never really let yourself care about me? You wanted to own me, because you thought that if you did, I couldn't reject you and leave," she now realized. "That's different. To take things further is to take a step that would most likely lead to imprinting. You have to be sure you want that."

Thinking on that, Marcus realized she was right. From the beginning, he'd wanted to possess her, own her—but that wasn't "caring" about her. The fact was, though, that he *did* care about her. He hadn't expected it, hadn't seen it coming. But then, he hadn't expected Roni. "I'm positive. This, *you*, is what I want."

Assured by the conviction in his tone, she nodded. "Good."

"Then it's done." The words were final, a vow. There was no going back now, not for either of them. Pulling her closer by her hair, he kissed her hard, needing her taste in his mouth. "Mine. All mine." She actually rolled her eyes at him. He smiled. "You can be just as possessive, Roni. Gets me hard every time."

She snorted. "A burger gets you hard."

"But it doesn't taste as good as you do." He licked along her bottom lip. "When we get back, I'm going to bite my way down your body, marking every bit, until I get to your—"

"Enough." Seeing that his smile had grown to epic proportions, she asked, "What?"

"You just smiled."

"I did not."

"I saw it."

"You were hallucinating."

He shook his head, chuckling. "Nope, I saw you smile. I saw those pretty little dimples."

"I do not have dimples, Fuller!" She had to resist the urge to immaturely stomp her foot.

"Here comes that schoolteacher tone again. Will I have to stay behind after class? I'll do whatever it takes to get an A."

How was she supposed to keep a straight face when he said stuff like that?

"You're smiling again."

"Fuck. Off."

"Now that's just mean."

CHAPTER THIRTEEN

Having finished drying her hair in Marcus's room, Roni began making her way through the tunnels en route to the kitchen. She'd sent Marcus ahead of her, tired of listening to him whining that he was "wasting away" and needed breakfast. She honestly didn't know how his system coped with the amount of food he consumed on a daily basis, honestly couldn't believe that—

She halted at a junction as she came almost face-to-face with none other than Greta. Marcus had repeatedly asked Roni to avoid being alone with the old woman, suspecting that Greta would ignore Trey's warnings and set out to aggravate her. *Well, duh.* Over the past two months, Roni had done just that in order to keep the peace.

It was kind of sweet that Marcus was so protective of Roni that even the thought of a senile old heifer giving her shit bugged him. But it was also amusing that he thought she needed his help, because if there was one thing Roni knew how to deal with, it was an interfering relative.

Greta started to speak, and Roni raised a hand. "I know what you're going to say. You don't think I'm good enough for Marcus." She sighed, being sure to look sad and insecure. "Honestly, I'd have to agree with you. I mean, I'm not pretty like the other females he dated. I'm not warm and caring like he is. I'm not the least bit likeable. God, even my own mother doesn't like me."

Greta's scowl eased the tiniest bit. "I'm sure she does."

Roni shook her head. "No, she loves me because I'm her daughter, but she doesn't *like* me." Roni let some fake tears surface and then acted as if she were discreetly wiping them away. "She says I need to change. She says I should be more girly and wear makeup and stuff. She wants me to be like Eliza."

"The attorney?" Greta curled her upper lip in distaste. "I don't like her. She flirted shamelessly with my boys, tried seducing them all."

"She flirts like that with everyone, even Marcus." Which was why the bitch had ended up with salt in her coffee. "I don't want to be like that."

"You don't have to be."

"My mom says I'll have to if I want to keep Marcus's interest. But he's not shallow. Whatever others may think, that male is far from shallow. It makes me mad that they don't see it. But you see it, don't you? You know him better than most."

Greta's chest almost seemed to puff up slightly. "Yes, I do. That boy is special."

"I agree. And I appreciate you being so protective of him. He's like a son to you, so it's only natural that you would be. It's clear that you had a hand in raising him, Ms. Tyler." Roni forced an admiring smile. "You did good with him. Really good."

Hearing footsteps heading through the tunnels and suspecting it was Roni, Marcus turned his head to greet her. Seconds later, she entered the room . . . with Greta's arm linked through hers. Equally astonishing, Greta actually led Roni to the seat beside him.

Trey's grandmother then gave him a stern look. "You look after Roni, Marcus. You hear me?"

He wasn't sure if he *had* heard her, because those words sounded a little surreal. "W-what?"

Greta actually pointed her finger at him. "I won't have her treated by you the way her mother treats her. I like Kathy, I do, but I don't agree with cold parenting." She gave Roni an affectionate pat on the hand. "If it ever gets too bad at home, sweetheart, you come stay with us for a while."

Roni smiled softly. "Thanks, Ms. Tyler."

"None of that—I told you, call me Greta." She found a seat farther along the table as Roni sat next to Marcus.

He could only stare open-mouthed at his pretty little wolf. "Good God, Roni, how did you do it?"

Roni gave him a "seriously?" look. "I was raised by Kathy Axton. You don't survive that without learning how to cope with fierce, interfering, old females."

Opposite Roni, Taryn shook her head incredulously. "I don't know what you did, or how you did it, but I'm in total awe of you."

"What are you whispering, hussy?" snarled Greta.

"If I wanted you to know, I'd have said it loudly."

The old woman humphed. "It's rude to whisper. But I wouldn't expect anything different from you—no manners."

"Are we back to this again? As you can see, your complaints are very important to us here at 'Still Not Giving a Fuck World.'"

"You should take a leaf out of Roni's book. She knows how to speak to her elders." Greta gave Roni a smile of approval. The entire table looked at Roni in wonder and respect.

At that moment, Dominic entered the room, took the seat on Roni's other side, and smiled at her. "Well, I'm here. What are your other two wishes?"

Jaime laughed, the others groaned, Marcus slapped Dominic over the back of the head, and Roni hit Dominic with another cheesy line. All in all, a normal morning at Phoenix Pack territory.

After breakfast, Roni insisted on going to check on Shaya, since Roni hadn't been home for a few days. She had begun to spend more and more time at Phoenix Pack territory—so much so that some of her things had made their way into Marcus's room. Likewise, some of Marcus's belongings had found a home in her lodge. They rarely spent a night apart, which she would have expected to find irritating, since Roni liked her space. But she never felt like Marcus was eating up that space. It was more like he was fitting into it.

Considering they had decided to make their relationship permanent, Roni had expected imprinting to start. But it hadn't. And she didn't know what that meant. Didn't understand it. She'd made the decision to stay with him, just as he had her. She cared about him more than she was comfortable with, and she believed that he cared for her. Yet, nothing.

Of course it could mean that she was simply too messed up to really accept another person that fully into her life. Maybe Marcus hadn't begun imprinting on her for the same reason. In any case, it hurt.

Halfway home, she asked, "Has McGee sent any more messages to Trey through the pack web? I'm pretty sure Nick's still getting them." The first apologetic messages had been sent just a few hours after the jackal's corpse had been dumped on Quinn's land. Quinn claimed to have been oblivious to Lola's plan, but no one was convinced of that, and no one had responded to his messages.

Just thinking about Quinn made Marcus growl. "Yes. He keeps apologizing for his mate's behavior and promising that he's dealt with the matter himself. Basically, he wants reassurance that our packs won't retaliate. That's something we can't give him." Marcus had every intention of confronting the bastard.

"We can't afford to act on it right now. We've got more important things to do." Like track down the wolf hacker.

"I know." His hands tightened around the steering wheel. "Doesn't mean I don't often imagine ripping Quinn's throat out."

Yeah, Roni had a similar fantasy. Something caught her eye in the wing mirror, and she frowned. "What is that?"

"What?"

"Something's hanging on the end of the tailpipe." To get a better look, she squeezed through the seats and onto the back row. "Oh, the little shit."

"What? What is it?"

"It's a fucking condom."

Marcus double-blinked. "A condom?"

"Eli must have put it on the end of the tailpipe, or had some-one else do it"—most likely Dominic—"and now it's totally inflated and dragging behind us." When Marcus stopped the car, she removed the condom, feeling equally irritated and amused.

Marcus had quickly come to learn that Kathy hadn't been exaggerating when she told him the pranks were an ongoing thing. Pulling off the road, Marcus turned to Roni, who was focused on her cell phone. "So, basically, you and Eli have an inherent natural drive to win and prevail, and you exercise that drive on each other?"

"Don't try to understand or rationalize our sibling bond, Marcus. I'm not sure it's possible." Roni had planned to avoid her mother, but Kathy was waiting—arms folded—at the front of the main lodge when they arrived. "Great," she mumbled as they exited the car. "I get to have another lecture about living in sin."

"I don't know . . . I'm pretty sure a scenario of a pure little virgin being corrupted is a fantasy we could work with. If you think it'll hurt too much, I could just put the head in."

"Perve."

"Ha, you smiled!"

"I do *not* smile."

"Sure you don't, Dimples." He grinned at her low growl.

As Roni neared, Kathy said, "You haven't been answering my calls."

Roni expertly dodged her mother and walked straight into the lodge. "Because I only like intelligent conversation. Besides, Marcus and I have been . . . busy."

Kathy followed her into the relatively empty living area. "Females should save themselves for their mate." From her seat on the sofa, Janice nodded her agreement. Eli just snickered.

"Mom, I wasn't a virgin before Marcus, so I hardly think it matters."

Janice sneered. "You're a constant embarrassment to your mother."

"Well, I do try." As Marcus came up behind Roni, her aunt immediately perked up and flashed him a flirtatious smile. Typical. And creepy. Ignoring Eli's smug grin, Roni gave him a nod of greeting.

He arched a brow. "What, no scowl? No outburst? No attempt to get me in a headlock?"

Studying an imaginary speck of dirt on her T-shirt, she asked, "Have you checked your Facebook profile recently?"

He stiffened. "My Facebook profile?"

Roni shrugged. "I could be wrong, but you might find that your inbox is pretty full." Eli immediately dug his phone out of his pocket.

Slipping an arm around her, Marcus splayed a possessive hand on her stomach. "What did you do?" He remembered her using her cell in the car, but he hadn't thought she was hacking into Eli's Facebook account.

She shrugged again. "Not much. I just sent out a little message."

Eli's face turned a worrying shade of red. *"Oh my God! I can't believe you did that!"*

"Did what?" asked Marcus.

"You sent this to every single person on my friends list?"

His pretty little wolf somehow looked the image of innocence. "What did she do?"

Outraged, Eli explained, "She sent this out to every single one of my Facebook friends: 'MALE SUB SEEKS MALE DOM. MUST ENJOY ANAL SEX AND BE WILLING TO EXPERIMENT. NO EXPERIENCE REQUIRED.'"

Marcus couldn't help it—the laughter simply exploded out of him.

"Sis, you're evil! Everyone now thinks I'm gay, submissive, *and* into kinky shit!"

"How many responses have you gotten so far?" chuckled Marcus.

"A shocking amount. I wouldn't have even suspected these people were into this stuff." Eli looked at Roni like he wanted to strangle her. "I will get you back for this."

"So you always say, little brother."

"Roni, how could you?" Kathy turned to Marcus. "Still think 'petulant' can't be applied to her? Honestly, she's so immature, it's embarrassing."

Sometimes, Marcus really wanted to yell at this woman. "That's not petulant or immature, it's inventive and hilarious. Your daughter never fails to make me smile."

She snickered. "Well, I'm guessing she must be very talented at making you 'smile.'"

Picking up the double meaning, Marcus released Roni and turned to Kathy. "Don't talk about Roni like that."

The dark, menacing tone made Roni tense. Marcus looked just as he had on Quinn's territory—intense, dangerous, and intimidating. Crap. Not that she thought he'd actually attack her mother. No, the problem was that Eli had straightened in his seat, his wolf watchful and weighing whether Marcus was a threat that needed dealing with. This could get bad.

Kathy gasped. "Excuse me? She's my daughter."

"Which is all the more reason why you should talk to her and about her with respect."

Roni tugged on his arm. "Marcus, just leave it."

"No, I won't leave it. All she ever does is put you down, criticize you, and make out like you need to change—and all because she can't handle that you're more dominant than she is." Surprise flashed on Kathy's face. "What, you think no one senses it just because you dictate to her *like* she's less dominant than you?"

Again, Roni pulled on his arm. He didn't budge.

"Do you really think it's fair to do that to save your pride?" continued Marcus. "You treat her like a victim because you think making her look weak will make you look stronger."

Roni yanked his arm this time. He still didn't move. Trying

a new tactic, she proceeded to leave the lodge, hoping he would follow her.

"You think you know my Roni so well, don't you?"

"I know her a lot better than you do. Oh, and she's *my* Roni, just to be clear."

Outside, he trailed after Roni, calling out her name. She didn't even slow down as she stalked to her lodge. Yeah, okay, he knew dominant females liked fighting their own battles. And yeah, okay, arguing with her mother probably hadn't earned him brownie points. But he hated seeing that strained expression on Roni's face, hated seeing the hurt in her eyes.

He found her in the kitchen making coffee. "Why do you let her get away with it?" He hadn't wanted to snap at her, but his anger at Kathy was still fresh in his system.

Avoiding his eyes, she said, "Let it alone."

Cupping her chin, he lifted her head to meet her gaze. "Roni, you don't deserve that. Why do you take it? Why do you accept it, day in, day out?"

"She's my mother. I'm *supposed* to take whatever she does." As pain briefly flickered in his expression, she sighed. "That's not what I meant. Or, at least, that's not how I meant it." It was a completely different situation with his own mother.

"I know."

"Kathy . . . She's had a bad time of it. When my dad died, she sort of . . . latched onto Nick, Eli, and me like we were a lifeline. She could have let go and died with my father, but she didn't. She fought to live *for us*."

"That's not a reason for you to take her shit. There's no reason for you to take Nick's either."

"You don't know what they went through because of me."

He framed her face with his hands. "Roni, none of what happened was your fault."

"I know. The blame belongs to those fuckers who tried to rape me—I know that. But the aftermath . . . it was bad, okay?"

"Tell me." He could see the struggle on her face. "It's not weak to lean on someone, Roni. It doesn't make you helpless; it makes you normal. In fact, it requires strength to let someone else take some of the weight." He guided her into the living area and over to the sofa. Sitting down, he then positioned her between his legs, and began massaging her shoulders. "Let me take some of the weight, sweetheart."

"I'm not good at confiding in people."

"Then think of it as telling me the story."

Relaxing slightly under his touch—damn, the guy was good with those hands—she spoke. "People think that if you've been attacked, those around you will give you the support you need. It doesn't always work that way. The court case put our pack under the spotlight—no one liked that, and it bred resentment. I was basically alienated."

"Alienated how?" he asked softly, hiding his anger.

"Some of the kids used to torment me about what happened, claimed I really had been raped, used to laugh that I'd probably lost my virginity to a human rapist. The worst was the Alpha's son, Nolan. The extremists had poked into his father's background, revealing that the Alpha had actually been banished from his old pack when he came "under suspicion" of laundering drug money—it caused a lot of conflict within the pack, and some wanted him to step down from Alpha.

"Nolan blamed me for that. He made up different versions of the assault, spread them around. He even managed to get hold of the photos that were taken of my injuries—he made copies and posted them all over our territory." She rubbed Marcus's thigh when a chilling growl rumbled out of him. "I lost my friends. As for Nick's friends . . . they hated me because he'd been sent to juvie, so they made my life as miserable as they possibly could."

When she remained silent, Marcus prompted, "I take it things didn't get better?"

"No, they got worse. So bad that my mother transferred us to another pack. Things were okay until the Alpha we had was replaced. The new one was an absolute bastard, ruled by intimidation and fear. He made Eli, along with many others, fight in an illegal fighting ring, threatening to add me to his little harem if Eli refused. The Alpha used to keep me in the main house as insurance. He did the same with siblings of the other fighters. He was just evil. When Nick got out of juvie, he took over."

"But your family's grip on you tightened," he guessed.

"Like you wouldn't believe. You think they're bad now. Back then, it was worse; it went beyond protection. Even though we were all safe, my mother tried to control my every move, Nick scared off any male who showed interest in me, and he used his position as Alpha to tighten the reins on me until it was suffocating."

As he began to work his hands down her back in a kneading motion, Marcus kissed her shoulder. "You must have come very close to leaving." For a dominant female, that type of treatment would be unbearable—enough to make her wolf snap.

"I did. I couldn't breathe, couldn't have a life, but I couldn't desert them either."

It all suddenly fell into place. "Ah, that's why you do it." That was why she disappeared in her wolf form—it was her only escape that didn't involve abandoning her family. He pulled her back to lean into him and nuzzled her neck. "I've never bought that you spent a lot of time in your wolf form to escape the memories and guilt. You let other people believe that it is, because you want to protect your family's feelings." He grazed his cheek against hers. "You know you can't do it anymore, don't you?"

"Huh?"

"You can't disappear on me, Roni. I won't let you."

She glared at him over her shoulder. "Won't *let* me?"

Turning her to face him, Marcus brought her to straddle him, and wrapped his arms around her. "If you still don't feel you can tell your mother to butt the hell out, fine. But you don't get to run. If you shift and bolt on me, sweetheart, I will track you down. You're mine." She simply rolled her eyes, and he realized that to her, those words were nothing more than a possessive statement. She didn't see how much she mattered to him, because not only did Roni not see herself clearly, but also he hadn't told her how much he cared.

Marcus had never been much good at expressing how he felt. He could give smooth compliments, but voicing serious feelings was something totally different. He had a tendency to keep things inside, but this wasn't a time when he could afford to do that. Roni needed the words, needed the truth in its entirety. And what was the truth? Something he'd known on one level from the very beginning. "I had a conversation with Trick once. He told me to ignore what the Seer told me . . . because he thinks you're my mate. And so do I."

Roni tensed, sure she'd misheard him. "What?"

"I think you're my mate." No, he knew it.

She practically scrambled from his lap. "We'd have sensed it."

"Really? How?" He kept his voice calm and even. He understood why she was scared. He'd had a similar reaction when Trick had suggested it to him—it was the fear that came with "hoping" and knowing how much it would hurt to be wrong. "We're both guarded. How would we have easily sensed it?"

Roni knew he had a valid point. It was no secret that she had a protective wall built around her. Marcus seemed so open and straightforward, but he wasn't. He didn't let people get close to the real him. He hid himself, his feelings, his secrets, and his anger behind the smooth-talker mask. In that sense, he was as much of a loner as Roni was. But the possibility that he might be her mate . . . Roni didn't have that kind of luck.

"We haven't imprinted, Roni. Despite how intense this is, despite how much we care about each other—and don't dare say you don't care for me—we haven't imprinted. You don't think that's strange?"

"Maybe you just don't care as much as you think you do."

"That's bullshit, and you know it. What's between us isn't normal, Roni." Marcus had enough experience to know that. His hunger for her, his wolf's responses to her, the crushing drive to possess and to keep her that had been there from the very beginning . . . It just wasn't normal. "You're comfortable with me. You let me in when you let very few people close. Doesn't that tell you anything?" Slowly, he stood, but she backed away. "Don't hold yourself back from me. It won't work anyway. I know how that complex mind of yours works. And I know that it isn't just me you're holding yourself back from—it's the idea of being happy."

"What are you talking about?"

"I know what it's like to carry the guilt that someone killed for you, to feel like you owe a person more than you know how to repay. That kind of guilt . . . it weighs you down, tempts you to keep people away because being happy doesn't seem right." He approached her slowly and cautiously, like he would a wild animal. "But don't you want to be happy, Roni?"

He was right: being saddled by guilt did have a way of making a person feel like it wasn't fair for them to be happy. But she'd never been a martyr. "Yes, I want to be happy, but—"

"Then let yourself be happy with me." Stopping in front of her, Marcus slid his hands into her hair. "Drop that shield. Let's see if I'm right." He knew he was asking a lot: Roni kept a part of herself locked away, where no one could hurt her. He was asking her to expose herself completely, and that wasn't easy for someone who had known a lot of hurt and rejection. He knew that better than anyone.

"And what if you're wrong, huh?"

She tried to shove him back, but Marcus stood firm. She looked more vulnerable than he'd ever seen her, and it made his wolf want to nuzzle her.

"What if I drop it, and then you realize I'm not her? That she's still somewhere waiting for you? Where does that leave me?"

"The same place you are now." She shook her head. "Yes. Whether you're my mate or not won't make any difference to how I feel or what I want." He scrunched her hair in his hands, bringing his forehead to rest against hers. "But we have to know."

Roni shook her head again, not even sure what it was she was protesting. Being his mate? Him wanting her, no matter what? Letting herself hope? She couldn't think, couldn't reason, and felt totally off balance.

"All the signs are there: the possessiveness, the protectiveness, the jealousy, the intensity, the attraction between our wolves." That gave him an idea. "Listen to your wolf, sweetheart." His Roni wasn't good with complex emotions; she applied reason and logic to everything, tried to measure her feelings and break them down like math problems. But her wolf's elemental nature would be far from technical. Their wolves felt deeply, intensely, fiercely. "What does she want right now?"

Considering how close she and her wolf were, it wasn't hard to push aside her jumbled human concerns and concentrate on her wolf. There was no confusion there, no muddled emotions. For the wolf, it was all very straightforward and uncomplicated. "To brand you."

Thank God. "Why?"

"She sees you as hers."

"Hers to mark, or hers to claim and keep?" There was a big difference.

"Hers to claim and keep."

"Why does she want to claim me, Roni? Because she's possessive, or is it more than that?"

After a long pause she said, "She thinks you belong to her, that you're hers to claim. She thinks . . ." She paused again, swallowing hard.

"What, sweetheart, what does she think?"

To Roni's surprise . . . "She thinks you're her mate."

He released a heavy breath. "And what about you?" He tapped her temple as he said, "I'm not talking about up here." He placed his hand on her stomach. "I'm talking about in here. What does your gut tell you?"

She swallowed hard again. "That you're mine. My mate."

Groaning, Marcus brought his mouth down hard on hers. He poured every ounce of his hunger into the kiss, every bit of his need, and every bit of the vicious urge to brand her irrevocably as his. A claiming between mates was always rough and fierce—even violent. Now he understood why: the mating urge was driven by the need to take, to own, to keep this one thing that would always mean more to him than anything else. He needed to bind her to him, to be sure he couldn't lose her.

Roni almost squeaked in surprise as she was suddenly thrown over Marcus's shoulder and carried through the lodge. She delivered a hard smack to his ass. "Hey!" Her indignation didn't appear to bother him, because he just as roughly dumped her on the bed. Then he was clawing at her clothes, shredding them to nothing, until she was totally naked. *Little shit.*

The reprimand died on her tongue as she saw the darkly possessive glint in his eyes. It was heady to see him looking at her like that—like he owned her, like he wanted to drive his cock deep inside her and brand her as his. An almost territorial growl escaped him as his wolf looked back at her, so she let her own surface for a moment, let their animals mingle briefly.

Then she pointed at her pussy. "Well, it's not going to lick itself."

A wicked smile curved his mouth as his eyes returned human. "I'll give my pretty baby what she wants." Joining her on the bed and blanketing her body with his, he added, "When I'm ready."

Oh, the motherfucker.

Gently slapping aside the hand that warningly swiped her claws at him, Marcus curled his tongue around her nipple. She moaned, knotting her hands in his hair. He toyed with each of her breasts; molding and squeezing them with his hands while licking, sucking, and biting her nipples.

"Why are you still dressed?" That could easily be changed. Roni destroyed his clothes with her claws, wanting his flesh pressed to hers, wanting her scent all over him and his scent all over her. Each time he marked her, it sent an almost electric jolt to her clit. Her wolf urged her to leave her own brands, so she did—clawing the sleek skin of his back, loving the feel of his powerful muscles bunching beneath her hands.

Unable to resist the lure of her scent, Marcus raked his teeth down her abdomen as he slid down her body, briefly stopping to dip his tongue into her navel. Hands clenched on her thighs, he then swooped down and lightly fluttered his tongue through her slit. "This is mine," he growled against her pussy. "And I'm going to fill it up. Going to fuck it until you scream and this tight pussy comes all over my cock."

Roni moaned, groaned, and whimpered as he sank his tongue inside her, swirling, stabbing, and licking until her legs were trembling and she was writing like crazy. He then licked between her folds and circled her clit before flicking it with the tip of his tongue—knowing exactly how much she liked it. Then he was sucking on her clit, and each tug, tug, tug sent sparks of pleasure lancing through her, but it also worsened the empty ache in her pussy. "Marcus, inside me, now." Instead, he suckled harder on her clit before shoving one finger inside her, curving it just right. Like that, she shattered.

Possessiveness roared through Marcus when she came all over his hand. "Your pussy is dripping for me." As he knelt above her, eyes that briefly flashed wolf roamed down his body and fixed on his cock—he was thick and full and aching. Her covetous gaze almost made him groan. "You look hungry for it, sweetheart." She hadn't sucked him off yet; dominant females always did oral sex on their own terms.

Her eyes flicked up to his. "I want to taste you."

Anticipation thrummed through him. "It's all yours." Sitting up, she fisted him, leaned over and delivered an almost catlike lick to the tip of the head. "Fuck." She licked his cock like it was a fucking ice-cream cone, doing some clever swirly thing with her tongue. Bunching her hair in his hand, he growled. That was when she finally took him into her mouth, sucking so hard her cheeks hollowed. "That's it, sweetheart, suck it." Her mouth was heaven, and it was his. She was his. This body was his. The sex-crazed look in her eyes—that was his. He had to have her.

Roni gasped as she suddenly found herself pinned to the bed with such strength that a jolt of excitement sizzled through her. Just for the hell of it, she struggled against his hold, but he didn't loosen his grip on her wrists. In fact, he pressed more of his weight on her, crushing her breasts against his solid chest, and sinking her into the mattress. She couldn't move, yet she liked it. Just as she liked the look on his face right then—it was a look that promised her she was about to be ruthlessly fucked, but she'd have to submit. Finally, she went pliant beneath him.

"Good girl." Releasing one of her wrists, he slipped a hand under her ass and tilted her hips. "I think my pretty little wolf is ready for me." Knowing he was about to claim Roni as his mate . . . it was like a narcotic.

Locking her legs around his waist, Roni bit his bottom lip hard. "Then make me take it."

He slammed into her, groaning as her muscles clamped around him. Her back arched as a gasp flew out of her. "Feel me," he whispered harshly, flexing his cock. "You're mine, Roni." He possessively fisted a hand in her hair and tugged. "All mine." His jaw clenched as he powered into her, so deep he knew he was in her womb. His pounding was ruthless, and his pace was relentless as he claimed her with every stroke.

Clinging to him, Roni met every demanding thrust—taking what he gave her, wanting more. His mouth landed on hers, thrusting his tongue inside; they shared breaths, moans, pants, and gasps. Meanwhile, sensation and friction built, winding her tighter and tighter. "I'm close." His response was to reach a hand between their bodies and circle her clit with his thumb—that was when her climax crept up on her.

As he felt her pussy begin to flutter around him, Marcus

groaned. "Yes, sweetheart, come hard for me." He dug his teeth into her throat, tasting blood, licking and sucking to ensure that his brand could never be mistaken for anything else. At the same time, her body contracted around him as she screamed his name and her claws pierced the flesh of his back. Then her teeth locked on his shoulder and sank deep. The pleasure-pain shoved him over the edge and he exploded deep inside her, coming harder than he'd ever come before in his life.

Roni's breath trapped in her throat as her back bowed. A brief flash of pain sliced through her head, but it was quickly soothed away by the warm feelings that washed through her—feelings of home and safety and rightness. They were soppy and weird and unfamiliar, but they also settled her in a way she couldn't quite explain.

More important than that, she could *feel* Marcus. Feel him in her, over her, all around her . . . almost as if they shared the same skin—a sensation she knew she'd feel even when they were apart. She couldn't see the bond, but she could feel it as surely as she could feel her connection to her arm. She could sense what Marcus was feeling as it hummed through the bond: pure masculine satisfaction. Although not yet fully developed, the bond was stable and vibrant. "Can you feel what I'm feeling?"

Marcus nodded, licking over his claiming mark. He'd felt everything she'd felt—experienced every single flicker of emotion, every sensation, every bit of wonder. "Balanced."

She pursed her lips. "I don't trust it."

He laughed, liking the mischief in her eyes. "Why shouldn't you feel balanced, sweetheart? You're anchored now."

"It doesn't mean I'll start smiling or anything."

"Of course not, Dimples." That got him a whack over the head. Laughing again, he rolled them over so she was straddling him, and shaped her waist with his hands. "Now that wasn't nice. You're supposed to treasure and worship me." She just rolled her eyes.

Marcus couldn't help marveling at how much more centered he felt, at how the feel of her inside him steadied him. Not that the anger was gone. It was still there, always would be. But Roni's presence smoothed over the jagged edges inside him, so they were no longer sharp and cutting—healing him without changing him. "You really can't bolt now."

"I wouldn't have anyway," she answered honestly. That got her a wide smile. When that smile turned impish, she arched a brow questioningly.

"You know, a petty thought just crept into my brain."

She sighed. "You like that Nick's going to freak, don't you?" Her brother had come to tolerate Marcus, but that was as good as it got—for the simple reason that she was his sister, and he liked to think of her as a sweet, innocent virgin.

"Do you think he'll cry? I hope so."

"On another note, aren't you a little . . . I don't know . . . disappointed?" Like that, his amusement vanished and he bolted upright.

Wrapping his arms around her, Marcus held her eyes with a serious gaze. "I need you to listen up, sweetheart. Hear me when I say that you are more important to me than any goddamn thing in this world. I'm proud to have you as a mate. Everything about you appeals to me—your strength, your intelligence, your complexity, your frankness, and the fact that you use pointless facts as social repellents. And let's not forget your ass. I love your addictively supple body, sweetheart, but *especially* that phenomenal ass."

It was impossible not to believe him when she could *feel* his sincerity. She could feel something else from him too—a flash of insecurity. "You don't honestly worry that I might be disappointed, do you? Because that means I'll have to dish out some compliments to assure you I'm perfectly happy, and I won't be good at that."

"You're perfectly happy?" Smiling, Marcus lifted her by her waist, aligned his hard cock to her pussy, and impaled her on him. "That tells me all I need to know."

CHAPTER FOURTEEN

H e's your mate?"
Smiling at Nick, Marcus slid an arm around Roni to cup her hip possessively. "I knew you'd be happy for us."

From his seat on the sofa, Nick gaped at his sister. "Seriously? *He's* your mate?"

Looking delighted, Shaya came over and kissed both Roni and Marcus on the cheek. "Congratulations!" Then she was crying and fanning her face. "It's the hormones."

"*I* suspected it," said Eli, "but I wasn't totally sure." He kissed Roni on the cheek, and shook Marcus's hand. One by one, Caleb, Kent, and the enforcers rose from various seats around the living area of the main lodge and congratulated them—careful not to get too close to Roni. While the mating bond was incomplete, the possessiveness would be worse than ever. Nick seemed too shocked to move.

Roni raised her brows at her uncharacteristically quiet mother. "Happy to hear I'm not living in sin after all?" Kathy didn't answer. And, yeah, that kind of hurt. Similarly, neither Janice nor Eliza offered their congratulations, but whatever.

"Oh, come on! *He's* your mate?"

Roni rolled her eyes. "For God's sake, Nick! Can't you be happy for me?"

"I am happy that you've found your mate; I was hoping you would." Nick shrugged, practically pouting. "I was just hoping it wasn't him."

"I thought you liked Marcus," said a clearly amused Eli.

"Like? No. Prepared to tolerate? Yes."

Shaya patted her mate's thigh. "Do you think, maybe, it's not that you truly have a problem with Marcus, it's that you're just a little bummed that you have to let your sister go now? You've been used to being the main man in her life, and now that's changed."

Nick folded his arms across his chest. "Maybe."

"I wouldn't take it personally that he's not warm to you," Eli said to Marcus. "According to Mom, Nick's been alienating people since he was two years old."

"When will you have the mating ceremony?" Shaya did a little clap. "Ooh, can I plan it, *please*?"

It was tradition for the other females of the pack to plan the event, and since Roni wouldn't have a clue where to start, she nodded. "Sure. Just no fairy-tale theme."

Shaya nodded. "Got it. How about on Saturday evening?"

"Can you have it planned and sorted in just two days?" asked Marcus.

"Of course. Taryn and Jaime will help me anyway."

Marcus squeezed Roni's hip. "Okay then, Saturday it is."

"Great!" Then Shaya was crying again. "They're good tears."

"I've just had a thought." Jesse leaned forward. "Where are you guys going to live?"

"One of you will have to switch packs," said Zander.

"I'm not," both Roni and Marcus said in unison. Wincing, they turned to face each other.

"This is probably something we need to discuss in private," suggested Marcus.

"You can't leave me, Roni," whined Shaya. "I'll be the only female."

Kathy arched a brow. "What am I, chopped liver?"

"And what about me?" moaned Janice.

"You've got me, Shaya," said Eliza.

Shaya rolled her eyes. "Kathy, I think of you as more of a force of nature than a person. Janice, I don't like you, and I'll never like you. Eliza, you have no chance in hell of transferring to this pack, so crawl back out of my ass." Sweet though Shaya was, she could be pretty outspoken at times.

An outraged Janice marched out of the lodge, and a concerned Kathy trailed after her.

"What if Jesse and I imprint?" Eliza's glare switched to Jesse when he snorted. Chin up high, she huffed. "Fine. I don't believe in staying where I'm not welcome." She jumped up so abruptly that she tipped over the satchel by her foot. A case file slid out, and papers spilled along the floor. Cursing, Eliza bent down and began gathering the sheets together—snarling at Jesse when he tried to help. Just as she went to grab a particular sheet, Marcus picked it up and studied it closely.

Curious, Roni glanced at it; her eyes were immediately drawn to the photograph that was clipped to the paper. *Holy fuck.* It clearly fit the description of the wolf shifter who the jackal mentioned, tattoo included. And according to the personal details provided, Noah Brunt was in fact a wolf shifter.

"That is confidential information," growled Eliza, snatching back the paper. She turned to Roni. "I'd say congratulations on the mating, but I find it much too hard to believe that *you* could possibly be the mate of someone like Marcus."

"Well, considering we're wearing each other's scent, and you can see our claiming marks easily enough, I'm confused by your disbelief. But I also don't care." Roni raised a hand when Eliza went to speak. "No, really, don't bother answering—I've already lost interest."

"Seriously, Marcus, she's a—"

"Think very carefully before you continue that sentence," he rumbled.

Eliza snickered. "You wouldn't hurt me."

"No, but my mate would. And we all know she can take you—she already did."

"Maybe. But I could take her in a courtroom. She'd be sorry she touched me again."

"Hey, I know plenty about law," claimed Roni. "For instance, I know that in Baldwin Park, no one's allowed to ride a bicycle in a swimming pool. And I know that it's illegal to hunt whales in Oklahoma. Oh, and in Singapore, it's illegal to buy or sell gum—you can only have it prescribed by a doctor." Everyone just stared at her. "What?"

Marcus pulled her closer. "I love how that brain absorbs everything."

"If you don't find that irritating, you really must be mates," mumbled Nick.

"*These* people might buy that you're mates, but I don't." Pivoting on the spot, Eliza stormed out of the lodge, slamming the door closed behind her.

"You have a pen and a piece of paper, gorgeous?" Marcus asked Roni. Once he had them, he scribbled down Brunt's address, then turned to Nick. "I have to speak to my pack. You have Skype, right?"

Sensing the urgency in Marcus's manner, Nick leaned forward. "What's going on?"

"The photo of Eliza's client, Noah Brunt, matched the description of the jackals' tech guy. If it's him, we now know his name and where he lives. But we've had plenty of false alarms since trying to hunt down this wolf, so we'll need Rhett to do a check on Brunt."

Nodding, Nick stood. "I'll have Donovan see what he can find out about Brunt too. Wait here, I'll get my laptop." Pretty soon they were connected to Rhett's computer, and a number of Phoenix wolves were gathered around him. Immediately, they noticed Marcus's and Roni's claiming marks.

"You're true mates?" asked a smiling Taryn.

"Yes," replied Marcus. With that, his pack began exchanging

money. Un-freaking-believable. "You bet on whether or not we're mates?"

Counting the wad of dollars in his hands, Trick spoke. "We were all sure you would both end up together, but we took bets on whether you were true mates. Oh, and on how long it would take for you guys to claim each other."

"You're not in a position to judge, since you bet on whether Taryn would stay for good when I brought her home," said Trey.

Jaime smiled brightly. "Forget all that! Congratulations!" The other Phoenix wolves followed her lead, passing on their best wishes . . . other than the blond pervert.

Dominic pouted. "I'm so bummed. I can't believe you would do this to me, Roni."

"*Dominic,*" Marcus gritted out.

"We could have been so happy together. I feel so betrayed."

"*Dominic.*"

"But even though you've smashed my heart into pieces, I don't regret loving you. If I had to choose between loving you or being able to breathe, I'd tell you I loved you with my last breath."

As Jaime laughed and everyone else groaned, Marcus exchanged a look with Ryan. The enforcer nodded and then smacked Dominic over the back of the head.

"Hey, that hurt!" But the pervert was laughing his ass off.

Roni sighed. "You know, Dominic, I think it's about time I tell you what everyone says about you behind your back." A brief pause. "Nice ass." A large hand suddenly wrapped around her throat and shook her playfully.

"You're not allowed to do that anymore, sweetheart," Marcus told her, chuckling. "Not if you want the perve to live, anyway."

Smug, Dominic pointed at Roni. "Ha! You can't do it anymore!"

Shoving the idiot aside, Trick grinned at Marcus. "I told you to ignore the Seer, didn't I?"

"You did. And you were right. I'm not saying Kerrie lied, but—" Marcus paused when Roni snorted. "You think she lied?"

"Totally. When she saw us together at the diner, she was jealous, Marcus. I don't think it's too much of a stretch to conclude that she'd wanted some commitment from you and was bitter that she didn't get it. Maybe she wanted to get back at you."

"You're saying she fabricated that vision, knowing it would make me dread finding my mate, make me opposed to mating?"

"I'd say so. I do think she had a vision of you and me together, because she went pale when she saw me. But by giving you a false description of your mate, it made you expect someone very specific; that was guaranteed to make it harder for you to recognize me as your true mate when we met."

"That makes sense," said Trick. "Maybe the Seer had even hoped that if the future she described was really so repugnant to you, you'd give *her* commitment."

"But I never made her any promises," Marcus told him, "I never led her on. I don't do that."

"Some females get the idea that they can change 'the player,'" explained Jaime, "and make them settle down. Maybe that's what she did."

"Maybe," Marcus allowed. The more he thought about it, the more it *did* make sense that Kerrie had lied. And that made him want to slit her throat—he might have walked away from Roni, thanks to her "vision" of his supposed future.

Taryn spoke then. "Okay, so where is this bitch, and when can we smack her down? Roni, don't forget to bring the shears."

Trey shook his head. "No, no shears. You girls are lethal with those things."

"I heard about your interrogation," said Ryan. Although his usual scowl was firmly in place, humor was glinting from his eyes. "I'm disappointed I wasn't there to see it." Tao and Trick nodded their agreement.

Eli smiled. "It was honestly the best entertainment I've had in a while."

"On to the subject of the interrogation," began Marcus. "I might know who the tech guy is." The Phoenix wolves tensed. "I got a brief look at a photo of one of Eliza's clients. He fits the description, and he sure looks like the guy I've occasionally glimpsed on the vids."

"Did you manage to get any personal details?" asked Rhett. "I can look him up."

"His name is Noah Brunt. I have his address here." Marcus held up the slip of paper on which he'd written it. Having read it aloud, he then continued. "According to Eliza's paperwork, he's been accused of trying to kidnap a fourteen-year-old human girl."

Jaime chewed on her bottom lip. "The jackal did say that the wolf hacker liked to kidnap females and then take them to her pack's kill site. It could be him."

"I've never heard of him before," said Trey. He ran a questioning gaze along the others, but they all shook their heads. He turned back to Marcus. "Rhett will see what he can dig up about him. I'll get back to you later."

"So," drawled Taryn. "You're moving to our pack, Roni, right?" Shaya gasped in outrage, and the two best friends began squabbling. Nick was no happier with Taryn's question, so he then proceeded to argue with Trey about it. Dante and Jaime both joined in, claiming it was only practical that Roni join their pack. Then Eli jumped in . . . but his words were totally unexpected.

"I don't like to get involved in other people's business, but I think Roni should move to the Phoenix Pack." Everyone gaped at Eli.

Shaya put her hand to her mouth, horrified. "Why would you even say such an evil thing?"

"Because even though she's mated, Nick and Mom will still do their best to interfere in Roni's life. That means Marcus will clash with Nick all the time, and Mom and Roni will argue even more than they already do." He looked at Roni. "I don't want you to go, sis. Everyone else here is unbelievably boring. But I want you to be happy. And I don't want you to rip Nick's throat out or poison Mom."

The mention of Kathy had Marcus wondering where she was.

It had pissed him off that she hadn't congratulated Roni—he'd sensed her hurt and disappointment. Really, he didn't understand Kathy's problem, didn't understand why she wouldn't be pleased that her daughter had found her mate.

While Roni was busy trying to placate a crying Shaya, Marcus discreetly left the lodge in search of her mother. He found her on the porch swing, staring off into the distance. She didn't appear to have sensed him, but her words proved him wrong.

"You think I'm harsh on Roni."

Coming to stand next to the swing, he looked down at Kathy. "I think you do your best to undermine her just to make yourself look better. I think you're hard on her and try to keep her constantly off-balance, and it pisses me the hell off."

"I used to feel the same way about my mother; she did the same things to me."

Baffled, he shook his head. "So, why do you do it to Roni?"

Kathy inhaled deeply. "When I lost my mate . . . I've never felt that kind of pain before or after. It was like someone had ripped me open and the bleeding wouldn't stop. I suppose that's sort of what it's like, only it's your soul that bleeds, not your body."

Now that he was mated to Roni, now that his soul was knitted with hers, he could imagine exactly what it would be like if she were taken from him—a never-ending agony, a wound that would never, ever close.

"My mother brought me up to not need a male for anything, to be emotionally and physically independent. That was the only thing that made me strong enough to fight the need to slip away when my mate died. I didn't want to live anymore, but I was strong enough to fight the temptation to let go, and to live for my kids."

Kathy met his eyes. "I hope and pray that Roni never experiences what I went through. But I was going to make damn sure that if it did happen, she got through it. And if that meant raising her the same way I was raised, if it meant we had a strained relationship, so be it."

Now he understood. Kathy truly did love Roni—he could see it right there in her eyes. She'd wanted what was best for Roni, and she'd done exactly what she thought was best. It was a messed-up kind of loving gesture, but it was still done out of love.

"So hate me if you want to, Marcus Fuller. Judge me for how I've raised my daughter. But I'll never be sorry. My girl . . . she's strong, resilient. Tougher than I ever was—not a thing in this world could break her." It was said with utter pride. "I pray she never loses you, but if she does, she'll keep on going. She won't leave children behind who'd otherwise suddenly find themselves with no parents."

She was right, Roni would have the strength to keep going. And that was what Marcus would want if the unthinkable happened.

Sighing, Kathy returned her gaze to the view in front of her. "Maybe I *am* a little guilty of putting her down because she's more dominant than I am. But you're wrong if you think I don't love my baby girl. I adore her. I'm proud of her. Not that she'd ever believe that, but it's true."

There was a long pause before Marcus spoke again. "I get why you've raised her the way you have. I get why you think it was the right thing to do. But I'll never like it. I'll never like how it makes her feel. And I'll never stop defending her if she won't defend herself."

Kathy gave him a measuring look. "Good."

"The least you can do is congratulate her on the mating. She'd want that."

"I'm shocked at how long it took you both to see you were true mates."

"You suspected it?" His brows drew together. "But . . . you were always lecturing Roni about being with me."

She looked at him with what could only be described as pity. "Really, Marcus, it's good that you have such a pretty face. You're not too bright."

"Lecturing her served a purpose?"

"The more I lectured her, the more she . . ." Kathy trailed off, prompting him to fill in the blanks.

"Spent time with me," he finished.

She grinned. "Exactly. She spent more time with you to get away from me *and* to be contrary. If I'd tried to push her to spend some time with you, she'd have done the opposite."

"No, but she'd have tried. I wouldn't have let her run."

Kathy chuckled. "I like you, Marcus Fuller. You'll be good for my Roni."

At that moment, the door opened and Roni stepped out onto the porch. "Hey, gorgeous." Marcus held out a hand to her. Eyes dancing from him to Kathy, she slowly walked to him and slipped her hand in his.

Kathy rose to her feet and sniffed at her daughter. "I suppose this is the part where I congratulate you."

Roni snorted. "Don't be too happy for me. Really. Calm down."

"I'm glad you've found your mate. I'm not saying you'll manage to keep him, but . . ." Kathy turned and went back inside.

Growling, Roni shook her head. "She was sent to test me. And I'm failing miserably."

Marcus curled his arms around her and indulged in a long, thorough taste of that luscious mouth. "Let's go for a run. My wolf badly wants to play with yours. He wants his mate."

Her wolf liked that idea too, wanted to finally brand her male. Despite Marcus's assurances that her wolf was free to mark his wolf as much as she wanted, Roni hadn't let them run together before. Quite frankly, she'd worried that her wolf would claim Marcus fully as her own, and Roni hadn't wanted to do that until imprinting started. Only then would she have felt confident that the relationship had progressed far enough to do that.

Now that Roni knew he was hers on every level, she had absolutely no problem with answering her wolf's desire to run with and brand Marcus's wolf. So, after dumping their clothes in Roni's lodge, they shifted forms.

The female dark-gray wolf and the male, whose fur was a mix

of gray, brown, and yellow, licked and nipped at each other's muzzle in greeting. Then the female delivered a sharp nip to the male's ear and bounded away. He followed her, and together they loped through the woods of Mercury Pack territory. They spent hours mock fighting, ambushing, pouncing, shouldering one another, and jaw wrestling before finally claiming and branding each other.

It was dark when they returned to the lodge. In the living area, Marcus shifted forms first and collapsed on his back. The long day had left him sapped of strength. A dark-gray female wolf stood over him, sniffing behind his ear and then licking at his chin. He smoothed his hands down her graceful neck. "Come back to me, Roni." Seconds later, he had a gorgeous, naked woman sprawled on top of him.

"Your wolf is as insatiable as you are," Roni mumbled against his chest, exhausted. She came close to purring when his fingertips traced the length of her spine.

"You weren't kidding when you said your wolf is aggressive when going after what she wants." Not that his own wolf had any complaints about the multiple brands.

"Your wolf isn't exactly shy." The bite on her nape had hurt like a motherfucker, but it had only served to further incite her wolf. Yep, their animals were well matched.

Rolling her onto her back, Marcus lapped at his claiming mark. "I love looking at this." He wouldn't have thought he could be this possessive. He hadn't imagined it would be like this—so consuming, so fucking intense that it stole his breath. He wanted to keep her locked away, so he wouldn't have to share her. Wanted to gouge out the eyes of any male who dared ogle her. Wanted to know her better than anybody else did, to be vital to her. He wanted to own her—body, mind, and soul.

At the same time, though, it wasn't a destructive possessiveness like he would have imagined. It wasn't a sinister greed that would grow into something unhealthy. It wouldn't suffocate or hinder or hurt her. Not this. He didn't look at Roni and see an object, he saw some*one* whose happiness meant more to him than anything. And, yes, jealousy came with it. But not out of insecurity or distrust. It came from a soul-deep need to protect and keep this person who mattered most to him, to safeguard their bond from any external threat.

"I want you to remember something. No matter how possessive or protective I am, don't ever see me as not respecting you or believing you can't defend or think for yourself. Don't ever think I want to squash your independence." He licked along her collarbone, pausing to swirl his tongue in the hollow of her throat. "You're perfect to me exactly as you are."

"I'll remember. It doesn't mean I won't push back."

He smiled. "I wouldn't expect anything different." Supporting himself using his elbow, he propped his head on his hand. "So, which one of us is switching packs?" When she didn't say anything, he continued. "I'm going to be honest with you. I don't want to switch for two reasons: One, I'm close to the people in my pack; they're all family to me. Two, I agree with Eli: Nick and your mom will make themselves a problem for us—they truly can't help themselves. *But* if you really want to stay here, I'll switch."

"Why would you do that?"

"Because you matter more than any of that." With his free hand, he doodled patterns on her flat stomach, liking how it quivered beneath his touch. "I want you to be happy."

"Which is great and all, but I want *you* to be happy. So we can't try to make this decision based on happiness or we'll just go around in circles. Let's look at it practically instead." At his nod, she went on. "It would be practical for me to stay here. My pack is smaller than yours. If I leave, the pack gets smaller and it loses an enforcer. Your pack doesn't need me. It doesn't need another enforcer."

"Trey won't object to having another enforcer, but I see your point." He took a moment to nuzzle her neck. "If I was to join your pack, you'd gain another member. But I strongly doubt your brother will want me as an enforcer—no Alpha wants their sister's mate directly under their rule like that in case they give an order that results in a tragedy. That means I'd have no role here. *But* I never wanted the position anyway, so I guess I could live with that."

Roni narrowed her eyes at him. "You're being too agreeable."

"You're complaining?"

"Yes, because switching isn't what you truly want; you're badly opposed to the idea. I can *feel* it. You're just saying what you think will make me 'happy' again."

"What I've said is true. Me moving here is more practical than you switching packs."

"But something is holding you back. What is it?" Realization hit her, and her exasperation faded. "You feel disloyal leaving Trey. You feel like you owe him for what happened with his mom."

"And *you* feel disloyal at the idea of leaving your family," he pointed out, nipping her bottom lip. She retaliated with a nip of her own.

"Yeah, I guess I do. I really have no idea how we're going to work this out."

"Then we put a pin in it for now." Draping himself over her again, he softly brought his mouth down on hers. The kiss was slow, wet, and languid. "I thought I was happy before you came along. I wasn't at all." How could someone be happy when they weren't whole?

"Give it time and I'll annoy you, like I do everybody else. It's a talent."

"Oh, you annoy me sometimes. Like when you steal my fries, or when you eat the last piece of cake, or when you threaten to withhold sex if I don't let you have a tiny taste of what I'm eating."

"So, basically, I just annoy you when I come between you and food?"

"Exactly." She rolled her eyes at him. "I'll have to call my sisters and tell them about the mating. They'll be thrilled."

"I sure do hope they pass along the news to Kerrie. When I think of how she used the knowledge of your childhood to torture you like that, I want to kill her."

She'd said it so matter-of-factly that he had to smile. "When I think of how her 'vision' stopped me from recognizing who you are to me, *I* want to kill her."

"You said Trick told you to ignore the vision." It was half question, half statement.

Marcus slid down her body so that he could trace the wolf tattoo on her abdomen with his tongue. "He figured out we were mates pretty much straight away. He made me think about it."

"I wouldn't have expected that from him, considering you've been, you know, friends with benefits."

"You thought he'd be jealous?" He shook his head. "We enjoyed the 'benefits' of being close friends, but there wasn't anything more than that."

Combing his hair with her fingers, she said, "I didn't think he liked me."

Marcus snorted. "If he could, he'd whisk you away. You're exactly his type. But no one will take you from me." He'd kill anyone who tried—no questions asked.

"I'm pretty sure no one will be tempted to try. I'm not exactly a catch."

He bit her hard. Right on the edge of her navel. "Don't talk about my pretty baby like that," he warned, swirling his tongue inside her belly button to soothe the sting before trailing his fingers up her inner thigh. "I'd hate to have to keep you hanging on the edge until you beg me to let you come."

Asshole. Roni cocked her head. "Did you know that thousands of different types of bacteria can be found in a person's belly button?"

"*Roni.*"

"What? What did I say?"

CHAPTER FİFTEEN

Too damn fucking early.

Swinging open Roni's front door, Marcus glared at Dante. "You know, this new 'getting woken up at the crack of dawn' thing isn't working out so well for me." It was still freaking dark outside.

Like last time, the Beta pushed a mug of coffee into his hand. "Get ready and come to the main lodge. We need to talk about Brunt."

Closing the door, Marcus turned to find Roni doing an almost feline stretch, dressed in only his T-shirt. "Did you hear that?"

"Yep. It's obviously important. Doesn't mean I won't put salt in the bastard's coffee."

When Marcus and Roni entered the main lodge a short while later, they found Shaya, Taryn, and Jaime huddled at one end of the table while Nick, Derren, Trey, Dante, and Ryan were seated at the other end. The females didn't even look up from whatever notes they were making, and Roni guessed it was most likely something to do with the plans for the mating ceremony tomorrow night.

Once Marcus and Roni both poured themselves a cup of coffee and helped themselves to some cereal, they took a seat at the table.

"So, what warranted the early wake-up call?" asked Marcus before scooping a spoonful of Cheerios into his mouth.

"The fact that I have a feeling it's going to be a long-ass day," replied Trey. "As I've already explained to Nick and Derren . . . there's a problem."

Roni frowned. "What?"

"We can't get to Brunt."

"He's well protected?"

"No, he's in jail."

Marcus paused with the spoon halfway to his mouth. "Jail?"

Trey nodded. "He didn't make bail."

Marcus shrugged. "So, then, we go to his apartment, take a look around."

"We can't risk it," Nick told him. "As you know, a lot of accused shifters are 'named and shamed'—their personal details are leaked to the extremists, who not only expose those details on their website, but hang around their addresses, holding billboards and marching. Right now, Brunt's place is surrounded by them."

"Shit," hissed Roni. "Did Rhett find anything on him?"

Dante answered, "He managed to get ahold of his criminal records and basic details such as where he works and his date of birth, but that's all. Brunt's a hacker; he was able to delete his proverbial paper trail."

"We know that he's a lone shifter." Trey drummed his fingers on the table. "He was banished from his pack when he was twenty-three. No reason was given publicly."

Marcus took a sip of his coffee. "What's his criminal history?"

"Short. There were accusations of stalking young girls when he was a juvenile, but nothing ever went to court. I'm assuming his pack somehow covered it up. But when he was twenty-four, he was accused of harassing a human female. Same thing again a couple of years later. Then a year after that, his human ex-girlfriend got a restraining order against him, but it's not clear why. One thing we're quite sure of is that he's the jackals' 'tech guy.'"

Marcus cocked his head. "What makes you so sure?"

"When Rhett hacked into his criminal files, he was able to see a clear picture of Brunt—including the Chinese symbols on his arms. He managed to translate them. They're three letters."

"Let me guess," drawled Marcus. "S, N, M?" At Trey's nod, he growled.

"At least we know who the motherfucker is." Roni briefly stroked Marcus's thigh, still not feeling good at the whole soothing thing. Before she could pull her hand back, he gripped it tight.

"Brunt's court date is in a few days' time." Trey folded his arms over his chest. "If the case is thrown out of court, we can get our hands on him—though we'll have to be careful, since the extremists will most likely be waiting outside the courthouse. If he isn't released, there's no way of us getting to him—at least, not for a long time."

Derren twisted his mouth. "Let's hope Eliza's as good as she claims to be, or we won't get our answers from Brunt."

Ryan leaned back in his seat. "In the meantime, we could talk to people who know him—friends, colleagues. They might know about his habits, might have heard about some place he likes to go."

"No." Roni shook her head. "If there's one thing I've learned from all this, it's that talking to 'friends' and 'associates' doesn't help much. We need to speak to someone he pissed off. They'll be willing to talk." Ryan's brows raised slightly, and he nodded his approval.

"We could speak to the ex-girlfriend who got a restraining order against him," suggested Dante. "From what Rhett discovered, she lives in New York now."

Nick smiled. "That's when private jets come in handy."

Dante balked and then spat a mouthful of coffee on the kitchen floor. "Roni," he whined. She shrugged innocently while the others laughed.

It turned out that Brunt's human ex-girlfriend, Margo Lincoln, was a librarian. Apparently he went for the quiet, timid, academic type. She was also pretty unfriendly and amazingly observant. She'd taken one look at Roni and Taryn as they approached her in one of the aisles of the library, and said, "You're shifters."

Taryn smiled. "And you're smart, Margo Lincoln."

"It's the way you all move—controlled, graceful, stealthily." Her tone held a tint of bitterness.

"You seem to know a lot about shifters." The human said nothing. "I'm Taryn. This is Roni." As Roni was busy sucking on a lollipop, she simply gave Margo a short nod.

Turning away, Margo inserted one of the many books she was holding onto a shelf. "If you're here about Noah Brunt, I have nothing to say."

Roni felt Marcus's surprise. All the males were spread out but within hearing range—something that was made easier by the fact that this part of the building was mostly empty and exceptionally quiet. They had figured that Margo might be less inclined to talk about her issues with Brunt if six large shifter males were surrounding her.

Taryn tilted her head. "Why would you think we were here to talk about that asshole? I mean, we *are*. But why would you immediately assume that?"

Apparently the fact that Taryn had called him an asshole went a long way with Margo, because her expression lost some of its anger. "You're not from his pack?"

"If he'd been a member of my pack, I'd have put him down like a rabid dog."

Margo narrowed her eyes, studying Taryn. "An Alpha female," she concluded. She then turned that studious gaze on

Roni. "And you . . . you *could* be one, if it was what you wanted. Not quite as harmless as you appear."

Taryn's smile widened as she looked at Roni. "I like her. Back to the subject matter, though, Margo. What makes you assume we're here about Brunt?"

Margo glanced around. "This isn't the time or the place for such a conversation. People come to libraries for peace and quiet."

Taryn, too, glanced around. "But as you can see, no one's close-by. Please, Margo."

Margo gave a frustrated sigh. "When I got the restraining order, the extremists somehow heard about it, and they tried pressuring me to go public with my experience."

"Yeah, it's not uncommon for them to harass victims."

"Lately, that pressure has greatly increased, and I wondered if someone from Noah's pack would visit me to insist that I keep my mouth shut."

Frowning, Roni removed the lollipop from her mouth. "Brunt was banished from his pack. He didn't tell you that?"

Margo's expression hardened. "No, he didn't."

"I'm guessing the reason the extremists are putting more pressure on you to talk about him is because of the latest accusation made against him," mused Taryn.

Margo stiffened. "What accusation is that?"

"He's been accused of trying to kidnap a human female—a teenager. Margo, we have reason to believe he's involved in far worse than that."

"How so?" When Taryn hesitated, Margo lifted her chin. "If you want me to answer your questions, you can at least have the courtesy to answer mine."

"Fair enough. We have reason to believe he's kidnapped many humans in the past, that he's working with people who are dangerous and, quite frankly, evil. But we don't know where to find these people. We need to know as much as we can about Brunt. Maybe it can help us track down those assholes."

She sighed. "You want to know about Noah? He's a very pleasant, gentle, caring man. He has impeccable manners—even while he has one of his friends beat you, he's polite and soft-spoken. Tells you how well you're doing. How proud he is of you. How beautiful you are."

Like that, Roni felt sick. "Did he hurt you himself?"

"No. He just liked to watch." A bitter, humorless chuckle. "He had me totally fooled."

Taryn bit her bottom lip. "I'm sorry to ask you these questions, I know this has to be hard, but can you tell me where this happened?"

Margo turned her eyes back to the shelves. "I'm not sure. He came here to give me a ride home, just as he did most nights. The second we got in the car, he drugged me. When I woke up, I was bound and gagged in an empty room with bloodstained walls."

She stopping speaking, and Roni assured her, "You don't have to tell us what they did. But I would like to know how you got out of there alive."

"I didn't think I would. I knew I had to be smart. So when he told me how proud he was of me, I pretended to be glad. Pretended to be happy that I had pleased him so much. I wasn't sure if it would work—especially since his friends didn't think he should let me go—but it did. He drove me back to his house, wearing this beaming smile. I'll never forget that smile. After what felt like a few hours, when we stopped at a red light near his neighborhood, I took the pepper spray out of my bag."

Roni inwardly winced. Pepper spray on shifter eyes would hurt like a son of a bitch.

"While he was busy screaming, I got out of the car and ran to the nearest house. The couple there called the police. Noah was gone by the time they arrived, but they found him at his home and arrested him."

Taryn's brows knitted together. "So, wait . . . You'd been drugged, taken somewhere against your will, and beaten . . . and he wasn't prosecuted for those things?"

"It didn't even go to court." Another bitter chuckle. "Some members of his pack—or his old pack, whichever—got involved, discredited my accusations, and promised to keep Noah out of my life if I promised to not go public with the story."

Roni just bet they did. His pack might not want him, but they wouldn't want him drawing attention to them either.

"I'm a librarian, I don't have more than three figures in my bank account; I had no way of fighting him legally. All I really wanted was to know he couldn't hurt me again. He hasn't."

"But you live in fear that he will one day, don't you?" Roni understood that, because for a long time, she'd feared the other humans involved in her attack would come back for her.

"He's sick and cruel, and he doesn't deserve to live." She looked from Taryn to Roni. "Will you kill him?"

"That's the plan," replied Roni.

"Good. Make it excruciatingly painful."

Taryn's mouth curved. "I think we can manage that."

"And his friends?"

"Once we find them, they'll wish they hadn't been born. But we have no idea where to look for them. Is there anything at all you remember about the place? Maybe something Brunt once said about a certain place he liked to go?"

She thought for a minute. "I remember the smell. Death. Blood. It was everywhere." So it was safe to say Brunt had taken her to the jackals' kill site. "That's all, I'm sorry."

Taryn nodded. "Thanks for speaking with us, Margo. Take care."

Rounding the aisle, they advanced through the building toward the exit. The males slid out of their hiding places, and Marcus immediately went to Roni, just as Trey went to Taryn. It wasn't until they were outside that anyone spoke.

"Well, that was a wasted journey," grumbled Dante.

Taryn held up a finger. "Not necessarily. Margo said it was a few hours before she got near Brunt's home, so that would help pin down the location."

"She'd been drugged and beaten, Taryn," Ryan reminded her. "Being trapped with Brunt while she was so afraid . . . the journey could have seemed a lot longer than it was." Taryn inclined her head, conceding that.

Roni slipped the lollipop out of her mouth—only to have it snatched from her hand by Marcus. Casting a brief scowl his way, she said, "One thing we have learned is that Brunt is being monitored by his pack. They might know something."

Reaching the SUV they'd rented, Trey unlocked it and they all piled into the vehicle. "I doubt it. They'd have killed him to protect the pack's reputation if they knew just how bad things are. But it's safe to say they'll try to get him off again. Not sure it will work this time, though."

"We'll get to him," said Nick. "Even if he is imprisoned. No one's untouchable. I know that very well." In juvenile prisons, the human guards were often paid to target the prisoners.

At that moment, Trey's cell phone started ringing. Putting it on speakerphone, he answered, "Hello."

"Trey, I'm not sure you're going to like this," said Rhett. "Well, actually, you might. I think Marcus will. Or maybe not, since he now can't get his hands on them."

"Rhett," interrupted Taryn, "make sense."

"Sorry. It's just that, um, I was checking the new vids on snm.com. Quinn and Lola McGee are dead."

"Dead?" repeated Dante, leaning forward in his seat.

"There's a clip of them being savaged while in their human forms by several jackals—all of whom were in their furry form. They also destroyed McGee's pack."

Marcus turned to Roni. "They might have found out that Quinn told us about the website."

"Or they were a little pissed at finding the female jackal dead and decided to take it out on them," said Taryn.

"Damn," muttered Marcus. "I wanted to kill them myself."

Roni wanted to laugh at the petulant pout on Marcus's face.

"It's okay. You can take it out on the jackals when we find them."
She fully intended to.

"You can bet your phenomenal ass I will." But the idea didn't
improve his mood. In fact, he wasn't too proud to admit that he
more or less sulked over the next few hours. Even later on, when
Marcus and Roni took his Toyota from her pack's parking lot and
he drove to his territory, he remained pissed.

Roni snorted. "You sure know how to brood."

"I'm not brooding, I'm—" Marcus halted midsentence as he
approached the large security gates of his territory and noticed a
familiar vehicle parked outside. *Son of a bitch.*

Feeling the anger that surged through Marcus, she looked at
him. "What's wrong?"

He pulled up outside the gates. "Wait here for me, sweetheart."

"You have trouble of some kind, and you expect me to wait
here?"

"It's not trouble. There's just someone I need to have a little
talk with." Without another word, he hopped out of the Toyota
and made his way over to the vehicle. He didn't halt until a dark,
middle-aged man exited the driver's side. "Dad." The word was
clipped, toneless.

"Son." His response was just as flat.

"What are you doing here?"

Jonas Fuller's expression hardened. "Kerrie told me what's
going on."

Confused, Marcus arched a brow. "What is it, exactly, that's
going on?"

"You're forsaking your mate. Yes, Kerrie told me all about her
vision, all about this female you've been dating. Even though you
know how much your mate needs you, you're forsaking her. How
could you? From what Kerrie's told me, she's like your mother. She
needs someone to take care of her, to save her, she needs her mate—"

"And you need someone who depends on you, don't you?" That
stopped his father mid-rant. "It didn't occur to me at first. I always

felt bad for you, figured you were trapped, that you stood by Mom because she was your mate. But it wasn't that at all, was it?"

His father lifted his chin, but he said nothing.

"You need someone who can't take care of themselves. It makes you feel good to be so indispensable to someone, doesn't it? Makes you feel good to take care of someone so broken, to have someone whose happiness depends totally on you—even to the point where you would happily enable a sickening addiction."

"We're talking about you," said Jonas. "About your mate and your future."

The passenger door of his father's car opened, and Kerrie exited. This wasn't going to go well.

"Marcus, please don't be mad at me for going to your dad. I needed to do something. I needed to make sure you didn't ruin your life." She moved toward him, but his growl stopped her short.

"How would I have ruined my life?"

"By getting serious with that Roni girl," replied Kerrie. "She's not the one for you."

"Says who?"

"My vision."

"I don't place much faith in visions," he said, repeating something Roni had once said. "Not anymore."

Kerrie's nostrils flared. "Has she convinced you not to listen to me? To ignore what I told you?" Marcus looked at her blankly. "She's turned you against me, hasn't she?"

"Don't do something stupid, Marcus," barked Jonas. "To forsake your mate would be the height of stupidity. You'll spend your life wondering what could have been. You'll abandon someone who needs you."

The sound of a car door slamming shut had his father and Kerrie looking at the Toyota. Marcus could feel Roni's annoyance. Not only that, he could feel her wolf's annoyance.

Roni came to stand at his side. "Everything all right, Marcus?"

"That's her, Jonas!" exclaimed Kerrie, pointing. "That's the one who won't clear the path for his mate!"

Jonas sneered at Roni. "So not only are you willing to forsake your own mate, you're willing to make Marcus forsake his?"

She cocked her head. "I could almost believe you care."

He reared back. "Of course I care! He's my son!"

"You care? Really? So what did you do when his mother rejected him and pushed him away? What did you do to make him feel safe and happy at home? Oh, yeah, nothing."

Marcus watched as his father clenched his fists. The old man had never liked being questioned or criticized.

"He didn't have a real mother—she was a selfish child who only saw her own needs," continued Roni. "Did you give him affection and the assurance that he was loved to make up for that? No, you were hard with him. You forced him to lie for her and for you; you made him feel alone. He grew up feeling guilty because he couldn't save her, couldn't make her happy."

Jonas growled. "That's not—"

"Together, you both made him believe he wasn't loveable, worthy, or accepted—that he wasn't important to either of you. In doing that, you made him live a life where he didn't give enough of himself to let people see the real him, because to do that would be to give them a chance to reject him. Instead, he rejected them first. So you tell me how, exactly, you 'care,' *because I just can't see it.*"

Marcus curled his arm around her, and whispered in her ear, "Shh, it's okay, sweetheart." Hearing her defend him like that put a lump in his throat.

"Marcus, you can't possibly want her!" whined Kerrie. "She's plain and boyish and foulmouthed and selfish!"

Roni waved a hand, finding the woman nothing but pitiful at that moment. "Really, Kerrie, there's no need to put me on a pedestal."

The Seer actually stamped her foot. "If you really cared about him, you wouldn't ruin his life this way."

"It both astonishes and irritates me that you think your opinion matters."

"There, son," began Jonas, "she doesn't even care enough to stand aside for your mate!"

"She *is* my mate." He looked at Kerrie then. "But you know that, don't you? You had a vision of me with Roni. You lied in the hope that I wouldn't recognize her."

"No!" Kerrie shook her head madly. "Marcus, I would never do something like that. You have to believe me."

"I don't believe you. Roni and I have mated—it's done."

"You're true mates?" said Jonas, losing his bluster.

"Yes. And it wasn't until I mated with Roni that I realized something—joining with your mate makes you whole. They suit you on every level, make everything right and balanced. So Mom had to suit you then, didn't she? In a sense, you're just the same as her—you want to suffer. It's the whole martyr complex, isn't it?" Jonas said nothing. Kerrie, on the other hand . . .

"You can't possibly believe she's your true mate! She tricked you or something, she—"

Roni growled. "Kerrie, you need to shut the fuck up or I *will* make you." The female gulped.

"Are you done?" Marcus asked his dad.

Jonas straightened his shoulders, his expression softening. "So . . . you're happy?"

"I am. Roni makes me happy. But you sure never cared if I was happy before, so why now?"

"He wants something," Roni suspected.

"I wanted to find out if we could bury the hatchet, so to speak." As if the whole thing had been a minor argument.

"Why would you want to?" asked Marcus, because there was always a reason when it came to Jonas Fuller.

"Your mother . . . she misses you. We both regret that we didn't leave with you when Trey was banished from our old pack. We've often wondered if things could have been much better if we hadn't parted ways. You're our son—we love you, we're proud of you, and we want to be part of your life. Especially now that you've mated. It can only be good for both of you to have additional people around you, supporting you."

"You want to switch to the Phoenix Pack," guessed Roni. She'd seen this with Eliza and Janice—the emotional manipulation, the flattery, and the implication that they could be useful.

Marcus narrowed his eyes at Jonas. "Roni's right, isn't she?"

"If it would help reunite the family, your mother and I would consider it." Like he'd be doing Marcus a favor.

"Outstayed her welcome, has she?" Marcus smiled, but there was no warmth in it. "Did someone find out what she's been doing to herself?"

"No, she misses you. We both do. You're our son."

Marcus was quiet for a moment as he stared at the hard man in front of him. "I don't wish you unhappiness. I don't hate you. You see, I don't care at all—and you did that. I watched the shit that goes on between you and Mom when I was growing up because I had no choice. Now I do. And I won't expose Roni to it. I won't expose myself to it." He kissed Roni's hair. "Come on, sweetheart."

Allowing Marcus to lead her back to the Toyota, she glanced over her shoulder at Kerrie. "You—if you come near us again, I'll make you choke on your own ovaries. And I'll enjoy it. What's more, I'll make *you* enjoy it. Just sayin'."

CHAPTER SIXTEEN

Roni could describe the mating ceremony with three words: Awkward. As. Shit.

She wasn't the romantic type, never had been. Lovey-dovey stuff had always made her uncomfortable. In fact, it confused her. For instance, she didn't see the logic behind buying a girl flowers. Why buy a person something so that they could watch it wither and die? That was like giving someone a sick puppy. How could it possibly amount to a romantic gesture?

Nope, Roni didn't get it. Nor did she get why she had to wear a dress. Nor did she get why Shaya, Taryn, and Jaime had insisted on applying makeup to her face, or why she couldn't wear sneakers. Shouldn't she at least be allowed to feel a *tiny* bit comfortable? Apparently not. So, yeah, that had pissed her off. But Roni had agreed to everything. Why? Because she cared about Marcus enough to make the effort.

So, primped and barefoot, she had advanced from her lodge through the forest on Nick's arm, following Shaya's fairy lights. He'd escorted her to the center of a huge circle of people—all the Mercury and Phoenix wolves bundled together, in addition to Marcus's sisters, their mates, and children. The massive amount of attention made her heart race in the worst way, had made her want to turn back, but she hadn't. Why? Because she cared about Marcus enough to brave it.

As Trey had performed the ceremony, she'd kept her eyes on Marcus the entire time. Just as he always did, her mate managed to put her at ease . . . despite looking at her with that piercing gaze that told her she was getting fucked within an inch of her life as soon as they were alone. And when Trey had asked them to make their vows, she'd done it, even though she saw absolutely no sense in it. After all, the ceremonial words had no power. It was all simply a way to celebrate a mating: "an excuse for a party," her mother had called it. Still, Roni had dutifully repeated the words. Why? Because she cared about Marcus enough to do so.

What's more, she'd smiled, she'd danced, and she'd resisted pulling out her lollipops. She'd pushed past all of the awkwardness for Marcus, particularly as he'd promised not to leave her on her own—knowing how she didn't like parties, attention, and mingling. That was why she found herself *seriously* pissed a few hours later.

Marching up to Dante, Jaime, and Derren, she asked, "Where's Marcus?"

A frowning Dante glanced around. "I thought he was with you."

"He went missing about twenty minutes ago. He said he was going to the tent to get a beer, and I haven't seen him since."

Derren smiled. "He probably got distracted by all the food."

That had been her first thought. "I already checked. He's not there. He's not with his sisters either." Marcus's sisters had tried interrogating Roni again, so she'd offered them a few random facts and, basically, ran away.

Smiling, Jaime touched her arm. "Off the subject, did you see Greta crying at the ceremony? They were tears of joy. She's been singing your praises throughout the entire party, which is weirdly annoying your mother." She gestured to where the two women stood having a heated discussion while Grace, Rhett, Lydia, and

Cam looked on in amusement. Roni couldn't hear the words over Lilah's baby babbling. "Where's your aunt?"

"She left yesterday—to our utter delight." Blowing out a frustrated breath, Roni scanned the surroundings for any sign of her mate.

"It's okay, sweetie, he's probably just talking to the other enforcers."

Figuring Jaime might be right, Roni made her way to where the Phoenix and the Mercury enforcers were grouped together. "Anyone seen Marcus?"

"I saw him about half an hour ago," said Trick.

Tao nodded, smiling at Roni. "He was with you at the time. You were fighting over a chicken wing." She'd done it purely to irritate him.

"You don't need to worry." Bracken gave her a manly pat on the back. "He'll be here somewhere." Ryan grunted.

She arched a brow and pointed at her face. "Do I look worried?"

It was Zander who answered. "No. You look . . . pissed."

"Maybe he's with his Alphas," suggested Jesse.

Hopefully he was right, or Roni might just have to seriously hurt her mate. The Alphas were comfortably situated in a seating area with Kye, Shaya, Caleb, and Kent. But there was no sign of Marcus.

"Ro!" called Kye the second he saw her.

Shaya laughed when the kid tried to jump out of her hold and over to Roni. "I'm jealous that he likes you more than me."

"Sometimes I think he likes her more than me too," muttered Taryn playfully, leaning her head on Trey's shoulder.

Cradling Kye against her—who then preceded to sloppily blow raspberries on her cheek—Roni announced, "I can't find Marcus anywhere."

"He's not with his sisters?" asked Caleb. "I thought I saw him with them earlier."

Roni exhaled heavily. "They haven't seen him for a while."

Kent cocked his head, a pensive look on his face. "Have you spoken to Grace or anyone from her little group over there?"

"No, actually, I haven't. Thanks, Kent."

Taryn clapped her hands at Kye and then opened them wide in invitation. "Come on, baby. Ro has to go now."

Scowling at his mother, he curled his arms around Roni's neck. "Mine."

"Yes, of course," chuckled Taryn. "But she still has to go."

"Mine, mine, mi—ooh, cookie." He practically flung himself at Shaya, who teasingly waved a cookie at him.

"Oh, while you're over there," began Shaya, placing Kye in her lap, "ask them if they've seen Nick."

Roni's brow furrowed. "Nick's not around?"

"I haven't seen him for half an hour or so."

Trey exchanged a look with Taryn. "Come to think of it, I haven't seen Eli for a while."

"Oh, I'll kill them." She knew her brothers well enough to know they would take utter joy in pulling some kind of stunt. "I can only imagine what they've done to Marcus."

"Who? Your brothers?" Kent shook his head. "They wouldn't do anything to your mate."

Roni arched a brow, disbelieving.

"Okay, they *would* do something to your mate, since they appear to like torturing him. But Marcus would be alert for that kind of stuff."

"Yeah," agreed Shaya. "He won't let them spoil the night of your mating ceremony. No way."

Oh, but it turned out that that was exactly what her mate had done. Later that evening, after the party was over, Dante and Ryan had appeared at her lodge, holding a singing Marcus. A singing Marcus who'd also had his face painted like a tiger and was naked . . . apart from a sparkling thong.

They dragged him into the living area as Dante spoke. "It wasn't us, it was your brothers. They got him drunk and then tied him to a tree, looking like this."

"Those motherfuckers. I'll kill them."

"Something tells me you won't have to. At this moment in time, Kathy's ripping Eli a new asshole, and Shaya's chasing Nick with her shotgun—and I'm not even kidding. I believe the last words she said to him before we left were, 'Run, Alpha-boy.'"

"Where shall we put him?" asked Ryan.

She sighed. "On the bed."

Dante raised a brow. "You sure?"

She knew what he was thinking: Why didn't she want Marcus to suffer for choosing to get drunk with her devious brothers over spending the night with his mate? What Dante didn't understand was that she had every intention of ensuring Marcus suffered. "Oh, yeah. I'm sure."

It was the bright light that woke Marcus the next morning. Or was it the pounding ache in his head? Or was it that irritating noise? The sound of his own breathing, he realized. He wasn't sure. He went to pull the covers over his head to block out the light. Weirdly, he couldn't move his arm. He tried again. Nope, it still didn't budge. Even more strange, neither did the other one.

Forcing his eyes open, he winced as the sunlight practically blinded him. Blinking a few times, he turned his head and, yep, his wrist was tied to the headboard. He looked at the other wrist to find that, yep, rope was binding that one too. Moreover, his ankles were secured to the foot of the bed with the same rope. He was spread eagle, totally naked.

This was so *not* funny.

Lifting his head, he called, "Roni?" He winced—even the sound of his own voice hurt.

Fighting through the cobwebs clouding his mind, he recalled

the previous night. Recalled how gorgeous Roni had looked as Trey performed the ceremony. Recalled how adorable it had been that she couldn't have been more awkward. Recalled how she hadn't run off somewhere and hid from the party, which had made him proud. Recalled how her brothers had . . . oh shit.

"Roni!" Nothing. He fought the bonds hard, but they didn't give an inch. It seemed his mate was very good with knots. Why wasn't he surprised? No matter. Unsheathing his claws, Marcus angled his wrist just enough to slice at the rope. All he'd need to do was weaken the material and it would snap right off.

But it didn't. The rope didn't even slightly give.

"Keep slicing if you want. It won't work. Shifter-resistant rope."

His head snapped up to find his mate leaning against the doorjamb, arms folded, in the same black dress she'd worn at the ceremony. And she did *not* look happy. It was fair to say he had some apologizing to do. He really didn't think the excuse, "Your brothers said I couldn't handle tequila better than them and macho-man pride dictates I can't ignore that challenge" would help his cause. "Gorgeous . . ."

Roni pushed off the doorjamb, fixing her eyes on his—letting him see every bit of her exasperation. She kept her voice even, flat. "Yes?"

Marcus blew out a breath. "You're pissed."

"Pissed? Why would I be pissed? All you did was let my brothers get you blind drunk, *knowing* how their cunning minds operate. All you did was choose to spend time with them over having time with me. Any other night, I wouldn't have cared. But the night of our mating ceremony . . . yeah, that's a problem for me."

Feeling like shit—and, admittedly, a little nervous considering his mate was pretty vicious when crossed—he said solemnly, "I'm sorry."

She came to stand at the foot of the bed. "It was our mating ceremony. It was, in your words, 'one of the most special evenings we'll ever have as a couple' . . . And you're sorry?" That was the best he could do? Hell, she should have left the thong and face paint on.

Wolf eyes flashed at him, and he glimpsed her animal's righteous anger. "Gorgeous, I'll make it up to you."

"I know you will." Roni peeled her dress up and over her body, watching as his eyes flared with hunger as they roamed over every inch of her. "You'll give me exactly what I want."

"I will," he promised with a low growl. "Just untie me, and I'll—"

She laughed. "Untie you? Why would I do that?"

She had to be kidding. Right? "Sweetheart, I'm sorry. Really."

"You know, topping someone never really appealed to me before. But now, looking at you all tied up, mine to play with . . . the idea has its merits."

He tensed. "Roni . . ."

"What, you don't like the idea that you're not in control? That you can't 'take' what you want? That you'll only get what I give you?"

No, he didn't. But he still couldn't help moaning when she fluttered her fingers up one thigh. Clearing his suddenly dry throat, he rasped, "What do you want?"

"What I wanted last night." She dragged her nails down his other thigh, making him growl, as she flicked her gaze to his cock. "Hmmm. Uncomfortable with the situation, yet hard as a rock."

"Because you're standing naked in front of me and I can smell your arousal." If he were being honest, this whole thing was revving his engines a little bit; he was curious as to what his pretty little wolf would do. But, dammit, he *shouldn't* be curious because dominant males did *not* submit. He'd never submitted in his life in any form. Not even to Trey—it was what made Marcus a good enforcer; his Alpha didn't want obedient pets, he wanted people who would think for themselves.

"That's all it is?" she asked doubtfully.

"That's all it is."

"I see." Roni crawled on top of him and licked a path from his navel to one taut nipple. She flicked it with the tip of her tongue, and he hissed through his teeth. Lowering herself, she rubbed her body over his, grazing her cheek on his chest.

He groaned, loving the feel of her skin on his, and arched just enough to grind his cock against her. Wanting her mouth, he lifted his head and ordered, "Come here."

She flicked the other nipple with her tongue. "No."

"*Roni.*" He jolted as she bit his pectoral hard. "Fuck."

"Maybe. But not yet." She licked and bit her way around his upper body, intending to deliver some sensual torture until he was desperate and on the verge of losing control. Between groaning and growling and making efforts to placate her, he struggled against the bonds.

"Roni, let me up, and I promise I'll make it up to you."

"But this is fun." She raked her teeth over her claiming mark, eliciting a low growl from him. Crawling a little farther up the bed, she dangled her breasts over his face. He latched on tight to a nipple, sucking hard enough to make her pussy clench. Then he held it firmly between his teeth while flicking it with his tongue.

"Untie me so I can play with them."

She sat upright. "No."

He growled warningly. "Come here. I want to touch you." It wasn't a request. It was an order. She was *his* to touch. Neither Marcus nor his wolf liked being denied access to what was his.

"And *I* wanted my mate last night." She lightly scraped her nails over his nipples, making him jerk.

"I said I was sorry."

"Oh, well, if you said you're sorry . . ." she snorted.

"Free my hands. I want to touch you." He needed it. Needed to feel her. Needed to feel that smooth, toned skin, needed to feel her breasts filling his hands, needed to palm that ass he was obsessed with. His cock was heavy and pulsing and felt ready to burst.

"Apparently, the strongest muscle in the body . . . is the tongue." Shuffling forward, she knelt over his face and lowered herself. "Prove it."

Gladly. He swiped his tongue through her folds, groaning as her taste exploded in his mouth. Fuck, nothing tasted better than his mate when she was slick and ready. Again and again he licked through her folds, pausing to lash at her clit or circle it with the tip of his tongue. When she squirmed and let out one of those frustrated moans that always made his cock twitch, he speared his tongue inside her.

Marcus swirled it around before sinking his tongue into her over and over. Her thighs were shaking and she was writhing restlessly. Knowing she needed to come, he briefly suckled on her clit before thrusting his tongue back inside her pussy. At that, she arched her back and came. He lapped up every drop, growling in objection when she moved away. "Get back here."

"I was going to reward you." Straddling one of his thighs, she clamped her hand around his cock, and pumped him once before sweeping her thumb over the head. "Don't you want a reward?"

Helplessly, he arched into her fist. "Again." She pumped him hard and fast, doing some twisting motion that almost made him lose his fucking mind. "That's it. Harder." Christ, he was so close . . . almost there—

The little vixen stopped. He bucked against the restraints. "Let me up!"

She folded her arms over her chest. "Now I don't really think you're in a position to order me around, do you?"

He growled. She was so close yet so far, and it was driving him insane. What's more, she knew it. "When I get free, I'm going to fuck you so hard—and I won't give a shit if you like it!"

She laughed. "Fascinating."

Fascinating? "Either let me up or put me inside you."

Cocking her head, she pursed her lips. "Nah."

Nah? Oh, he was going to kill her. Really, once he got his hands on her . . . after he'd fucked her . . . he was going to kill her.

"We'll get to the fucking, but not yet." She leaned over and licked his cock from base to tip. "I need you nice and wet . . . so I can ride you."

He groaned as she curled her soft hand around the base of his cock and took him inside her mouth. She sucked him hard, taking him deeper with each pass and stroking the underside of his cock with the flat of her tongue. "Fuck, yeah. You have the best mouth." And with her soft hair trailing over his thighs and her moaning around his cock, he was in absolute heaven. Pausing, she danced her tongue around him before lightly grazing the head with her teeth. "That's it. Make me come." Instead, she stopped and bit down hard on his inner thigh, marking him. "Untie one hand. One hand." He wanted to touch her so badly, it was an ache in his gut. He didn't think he'd been this desperate for anything in his life. Only Roni could do this to him.

Straddling his cock, she shook her head. "No. I'm going to ride you while you're all tied up. And there's nothing you can do about it." She slammed down on him, impaling herself fully.

Her muscles clasped him tight. "*Fuck*, Roni." Slowly she raised herself until only the head was inside her, and then she slowly impaled herself again. A few more times she did that before he rumbled, "Faster."

Paraphrasing something he'd once said, she replied, "No, because when I have this cock inside me, it's mine. And right now, I want to ride it nice and slow."

He snarled. "You don't like 'nice and slow.' This is killing you as much as it's killing me. Let me up, sweetheart, and I swear I'll take care of you." She swiveled her hips. "Do that again." She did, and he groaned. "Roni, I need it harder. You need it. Come on, give us both what we need."

"You need it?"

"Yes," he gritted out.

"Bad?"

"Yes. Fucking do it, Roni!" Nails digging into his waist, she rode him hard. He arched into each of her downward thrusts, needing to be as deep as he could possibly go. He wanted to grab a fistful of her hair, wanted to yank her close and bite down on her neck. Bound, all he could do was watch as she fucked herself on his cock, slamming up and down. It was a sight that would be burned into his memory. "Untie me so I can touch you."

"Not a chance. You'll get what I give you." She paused to rotate her hips. "Understand?"

Marcus was ready to tell her he'd never submitted in his life, and he wouldn't start now. But this wasn't "anyone." It was his mate. In that sense, it didn't really matter who was in control right then, because she owned him anyway. It didn't mean it wouldn't gall him to verbally agree to submit, though—or that she wouldn't pay for torturing him. "Fine. I'll take what you give."

"Yes, you will." Again, she began impaling herself over and over, grinding her clit into his pelvis. The friction kept building, the sensations kept drowning her, and the tension kept intensifying until finally a climax swept over her. It seemed to ripple up her spine, bowing her body, and Roni threw her head back and screamed.

Her muscles tightened and contracted around him, milking his cock. "*Son of a bitch.*" Marcus thrust up one last time and exploded inside her—it went on, and on, and on. Then she collapsed on top of him, panting. Since his mate had a way of scrambling his brain, it was a good few minutes before he could speak. "You okay, gorgeous?"

"Hmmm."

"I really am sorry for last night."

She snickered. "You'd better be."

"It was shitty of me, and you didn't deserve it." A brief pause. "You going to untie me now?"

"Well . . ."

"*Roni.*"

"It's just that you made quite a few threats." And her mate always made good on his threats.

"It was driving me insane that I couldn't touch you, that's all," he assured her. "Come on, untie me. My arms are starting to hurt."

She hadn't thought of that. Sitting up, she shuffled forward and leaned over to free one wrist. That done, she freed the other before reaching back and releasing his ankles. She was just about to massage his arms when she was abruptly flipped onto her back. Electric-blue eyes filled with resolve and hunger stared down at her. "Now, Marcus . . ."

He nipped her bottom lip hard. "You denied me what's mine."

"Not exactly."

"Yes, you did." He swirled his tongue in the hollow of her throat. "See, this body belongs to me. I wanted to touch it"—he smoothed a hand down her side—"lick it"—he delivered a long, sensual lick to her neck—"bite it"—he sank his teeth into her throat—"and fuck it." He ground his reviving cock against her clit.

"It's not like I left you high and dry."

"That's not the point now, is it?" He breezed the pad of his thumb over her bottom lip. "It's one thing to ask me to submit, but you wouldn't even give me your mouth. That was cruel."

"You can have it now."

"Yes, I can. And I will." He slammed his mouth on hers, sweeping his tongue inside, dominating the kiss. He lashed her tongue with his, demanding a response. She gave it, twining her tongue with his. Like always, his mate gave as good as she got. But she didn't try to make the kiss her own, didn't try to dominate it. Placating him, he knew.

Marcus wasn't in the mood to be placated. Hard again, he quickly flipped her onto her hands and knees and teased her entrance with the tip of his cock. "You stopped me from taking what was mine. So I'm going to take it now." He rammed into her.

Her muscles clasped him tight as her back arched. He pulled out of her in one long, drawn-out slide, making her feel every inch. Then he plunged back inside. He kept his strokes sluggish, gentle. When she tried pushing back to meet him, he slapped one ass cheek. "No. We're doing it nice and slow."

Understanding that he was torturing her for using those exact words on him, Roni glared at him over her shoulder. "What, you can't spank me harder than that?"

Oh, the little witch. He brought his hand down hard on one ass cheek, and then the other. "Does that answer your question?" Placing his hand between her shoulder blades, he pushed down hard. Before she could lash out at him for the extremely dominant move, he gripped both of her shoulders and started lunging in and out of her.

Trapped beneath him, she growled. "Let me up!"

"Why? *You* didn't let *me* up when I asked." He knew Roni could get up using one of her fancy moves if she really wanted. No, being pinned down wasn't the source of her frustration. His little mate liked a struggle. What she *didn't* like was that he wasn't fucking her as hard as she wanted. "You need it harder, sweetheart, don't you?"

"Yes," she ground out.

"Tough."

"*What?*"

"I warned you I wouldn't give a shit if you liked it." Oh, that seemed to piss her off. Growling, she unsheathed her claws and reached back to slash at him. Fortunately for him, the angle was too awkward for her to do any damage. That just pissed her off even more. She writhed and struggled, cursing him. "That's it, fight me." She did. But the fighting stopped when he started slamming into her, giving it to her as hard and fast as she liked it.

Startling Roni, he suddenly withdrew his cock. "What the—" She gasped as two long fingers pushed inside her. "What're you doing?" Then one of those fingers slid to the puckered hole at the back, circling it teasingly.

"Has anyone taken you here?"

"No. And neither will you."

He chuckled. "Oh, yes I will." He gently pushed his finger inside, and she bucked, hissing. "Don't pretend you don't want it. You've thought about it, imagined it." His pretty little wolf was too inquisitive to *not* wonder about it. He pulled his finger out of her ass and slowly thrust it back inside.

Okay, she could concede that she was curious. And she could concede that, surprisingly, the sensation was . . . nice. It hurt, but there was a bite of pleasure to it. After a few more thrusts, she started to relax around his finger. But then a second finger probed, and she tensed.

"Ssh, it's okay. You can't take my cock there just yet. We need to stretch you first."

"You're too big." How lucky was she to be able to say those words and mean them?

"You're my mate. You were made to take me—anywhere and everywhere." He repeatedly thrust two fingers in and out of her ass while licking over his claiming mark. She was soon moaning and squirming, so he added a third finger. He'd expected her to tense again, but she didn't. "That's it, sweetheart." He gently slid three fingers in and out, until she began pushing back to meet them. "I think you're ready for me."

As Roni felt the thick, round head of his cock press against her ass, she did her best not to tense. Instead, she pushed out as he began to very slowly sink inside her. It felt like . . . she couldn't describe it. It was a combination of pleasure, pain, and pressure as he fed her inch after inch of his cock, stretching and filling her. "It hurts," she rasped, though she wasn't complaining.

Marcus paused and kissed her shoulder. "Shh, you're doing so well." Again, he pushed forward. Fuck, the feel of her, the sight of his cock disappearing into her ass, those frustrated moans she made . . . it was a shock that he hadn't come already. Once he was finally fully sheathed, Marcus groaned. "Fuck, you're tight." Blanketing her back, he spoke into her ear. "You okay?" Through their link, he could feel that she was fine, but he wanted the words.

She nodded once, panting. "I'm okay."

Cupping her ass, Marcus slowly withdrew until just the head was inside her. Then he smoothly drove back in, seating himself to the balls. "You know I love your ass. It's the tightest, sweetest ass. And it's all mine." Again and again, he slowly thrust in and out. "Feel good? More?" At her moan of assent, he upped his pace a little and hardened his thrusts. She reared back to counter each one. "That's it, take it."

"Harder."

Growling, Marcus locked his teeth on her nape and began punching his cock in and out of her, giving her exactly what she wanted. Every whimper and moan spurred him on, drove him further and further to the edge of his control until he was slamming into her. She groaned his name—it was a sound of total frustration, and he knew she was close.

Sliding one hand underneath her, he pumped two fingers into her pussy. "Give it to me, Roni. Come." He sank his teeth into her nape deep enough to draw blood and growled as her ass tightened around him. He drove himself inside one last time and held still, pulsing deep inside his mate—claiming her all over again.

Feeling the force of both her climax and his, Roni screamed. Tremors shook her entire body as pure and utter bliss whipped through her. It was so good, it almost hurt. When her climax finally eased off, she slumped onto the mattress, and a big, solid body folded over hers. Minutes or hours later, he disappeared from the bed and came back with a wet cloth. Without moving her, he cleaned her up and then blanketed her body once again, pressing kisses to her spine.

It was then, while she was still happily floating on that post-climax cloud, that her wolf snapped her teeth at her. Not in anger. The wolf wanted her attention. She was . . . gloating, and she was annoyed with Roni for missing what she had so easily sensed. "Our scents have mixed."

"I know." He'd noticed it the second his brain had switched back on . . . which had been somewhere between rising from the bed and cleaning himself up in the bathroom. Like his wolf, he was reveling in the whole thing. It meant that their mating bond was advancing, which was amazing in and of itself. It also meant that shifters would know Roni was mated the very second they scented her. It massively appealed to the possessive streak in him.

"What caused it?" From what she knew, it took certain steps to make the bond advance.

"Do you see any sense whatsoever in mating ceremonies?"

"None at all."

"But you went through with ours. Why?" He already knew the answer.

A small shrug. "Because I thought it was important to you."

"It was very important to me. For you, parties and being the center of attention is a nightmare. But you did it for me." If she understood why, he wasn't sure. Marcus kissed the back of her shoulder. "I've never submitted to anything or anyone in my life. But I did it for you." He hadn't done it quietly or easily, but he'd done it. Because it was Roni. There wasn't anything—big or small—that he wouldn't do for her.

"I love you, Roni. I know you'll find it hard to believe, because you have this stupid idea that there isn't anything about you worth loving, that you're nothing but annoying and awkward. You don't see what you mean to the people who really know you. You don't see what you mean to me. So I'm telling you. Because to hold the words in . . . it's just stupid and unfair."

He pressed a long kiss between her shoulder blades before

continuing. "I don't think I'll ever be someone who's upfront about what I'm really feeling. But I don't want to be that way with you. I don't want you to ever wonder how much you matter to me. That place where you wonder if someone who you love loves you back . . . it's not a nice place to be. It would be selfish and gutless to let the feelings that run up and down the mating link do all the talking for me." He rested his forehead on her back. "Aren't you going to say anything?"

There was a pause before she spoke. "Did you know that—"

"*Roni.*"

"Okay, okay. It's just . . . I'm not good with feelings." Maybe it was because she overthought things. Or maybe it was because she was more practical than emotional. "But I do know that I love you. No other reason would have made me go through with that nightmare." His chuckle made her smile. "Sorry if you were hoping for some soppy words. I'm not expressive. At least not with words, anyway." Fists, claws, teeth, and shears—that was how Roni got her emotions across.

Gently turning her onto her back, Marcus kissed her hard. "Thank you for telling me."

"You were right. It's senseless and unfair to hold back. Just . . . don't be offended if I don't say it a lot."

"I'm not expecting you to change. I'd just like you to give me the words from time to time."

"I can do that." What she couldn't do was work out what it would take for the mating bond to *fully* form. Considering Marcus's twisted experiences with loving relationships and Roni's difficulty in recognizing loving emotions, she would have thought coming to the realization of how they felt for each other—particularly since they had openly admitted it—would be enough. But no. And she didn't understand why.

Marcus kissed her again, taking his time exploring her mouth. She squirmed and then winced. "Sore?"

"A little." She frowned at him. "You're more smug than concerned."

"I kind of like the idea that every time you move today, you'll remember how it felt when I took your ass." She just sniffed. Noticing a piece of rope still hanging from the headboard, he gave her a faint smile. "I have a question. Why didn't you just yell at me?"

She shrugged one shoulder. "Arguing is a waste of time and energy."

"We'll never really have super big arguments, will we," he then understood. Neither of them liked rowing or drama, and they both preferred action to words. Besides, Roni rarely allowed herself to get angry enough to engage in conflict. But when she *was* angry, she would never let him get away with any stunt he pulled. She would never take his shit. No. His vengeful little wolf would always dish it back, but in her own special way. Like tying him up and sexually torturing him, for instance.

"I doubt it." Hearing his stomach grumble, she rolled her eyes.

"Hey, I'm a growing boy."

"Fine. Let's go eat. I'd like to see my brothers anyway."

"What are you going to do?" He couldn't help smirking. Roni's brand of vengeance was always entertaining.

"Oh, I've already had my revenge, silly." She'd taken care of that while Marcus had been in dreamland. "I just want to see the damage for myself."

"What did you do?"

CHAPTER SEVENTEEN

Oh, his mate was cold. Marcus smiled at the human sitting beside Shaya on the porch swing. "Hey, Stone." Though Shaya's father was tall and burly, he reminded Marcus a lot of Jack Nicholson—a slow-dawning Cheshire Cat smile, a gravelly drawl, and an easy, confident posture. A person only had to take one look at Stone Critchley's neat, smart appearance to know that he valued precision and control.

"Marcus, good to see you." Standing, Stone clasped his hand. "Always a pleasure to see you, Roni. I hear that you've mated. Congratulations. It's good to see a couple that actually suit."

Shaya winced at the sharp dig, though she looked amused. "Dad . . ."

Tone indulgent, he asked, "Yes, baby girl?" She just shook her head.

Nick, from where he was leaning against the wall, scowled at Roni. "You invited him, didn't you?"

Roni shrugged innocently. In the beginning, she hadn't been too sure about Stone, since he hadn't been very pleasant to Nick. But then Roni had come to learn a few things about Stone: One, he absolutely adored his daughter, and Roni could like anyone who loved Shaya. Two, he was a tough motherfucker with the soul of a predator, and Roni could respect that. Three, he actually liked Nick . . . he just also liked fucking with him.

Basically, Stone's problem was that Nick hadn't immediately claimed Shaya. And Nick's problem was that Stone was . . . well, Stone. The human was an alpha in his own way, and he liked to think of himself as the "main man" in Shaya's life. Of course, Nick was very much opposed to that idea, so he didn't like Stone being around. But since Nick always found the time to irritate her, Roni wasn't above getting a little payback. Pranks didn't work on Nick, but a condescending father-in-law who believed himself to be the most important figure in Shaya's life and persisted in calling Nick "kid"? He certainly pushed Nick's Alpha buttons.

In response to Nick's question, she replied, "I thought it would be good if Shaya had someone tough with her when we invaded the site. If Brunt gets out on bail later and gives us the info we need, we could actually need to leave tonight."

"You thought I planned to leave her unprotected?"

"No, but I figured it would be nice for her to have her dad around anyway, so I thought Stone could stay for a few days."

"*A few days?*"

Stone sank into the porch swing, arms draping over the back. "You don't mind, do you, kid?"

"Of course not," Nick replied through his teeth. His eyes flared with the promise of retribution as they settled on Roni.

Sliding his hand around to rest in the crook of Roni's neck so he could massage her nape with his thumb, Marcus asked Stone, "How's your mate?"

"Dying. That was her diagnosis this morning, anyhow."

Shaya rolled her eyes, groaning. Gabrielle Critchley was quite the hypochondriac.

"She also informed me that she doesn't want a big funeral. She's picked out a dress, wrote down what flowers she wants, and even made a CD of the music she'd like to have playing." He shrugged. "She's nothing if not organized. So, Marcus, I hear my daughter's mate put up a bit of resistance when you pursued Roni."

"Just a little," said Marcus.

"But you didn't let it stop you, I see."

"Not once I'd made up my mind to have her."

"That's good. *Some* males don't hesitate in going after what they want."

Shaya closed her eyes. "Dad . . ."

"Yes, baby girl?" Again, she just shook her head.

Suddenly the back door flew open, and Eli stepped outside holding up his cell phone. He pointed at Roni. "You! That's was evil, Roni!"

She double-blinked. "I'm not sure I know what you mean."

"Does your cruelty know no boundaries?"

"What did she do?" chuckled Marcus.

"Take a look. Take a long look at who you've mated." Eli tossed his cell to Marcus. "Total. Fucking. Bitch."

As his mate continued to brush off her brother's insults, Marcus found himself looking at Eli's Facebook profile while Nick, Shaya, and Stone peeked at it over his shoulder. Eli—or Roni pretending to be Eli—had posted on his wall at four-thirty in the morning: "I've got an announcement to make. I've found my true mate. Yep, turns out my mate was under my nose the whole time." Under the post was a photo of a naked Eli curled up in bed . . . with a grinning Kent spooning him.

Shaya clapped a hand over her mouth, but she couldn't hold in the laughter. "Oh, Roni, you didn't!"

Nick gawked at Roni, his eyes glinting with humor. That humor disappeared when a laughing Stone slapped him—a little too hard—on the back. "Your sister's ruthless. I like that."

Shoulders shaking, Marcus threw the phone back to Eli and snuggled tighter into his mate, pressing a kiss to her temple. "I see now that I got off lightly."

His expression pained, Eli continued ranting at Roni, "Do

you know how hard it's been, thanks to the last stunt you pulled, for me to convince people that I'm not actually gay, and it's just you messing around?"

"Calm down, Eli," interjected Shaya. "I'll bet half those 'friends' aren't really your friends anyway."

Eli looked at her like she was dumb. "You think this is just about my friends list? Did you not notice how many times that announcement has been shared on Facebook?" He turned his glare on Roni. "I'm now known on a global scale as a gay, submissive, kinky, mated male recovering from an STD!"

Roni tilted her head. "If you're looking for remorse, you can find it in the dictionary somewhere between rectum and runt."

Throwing his hands up, Eli made a sound of exasperation. "Don't think I won't kill Kent for this when I find him," he threw over his shoulder before marching back into the lodge.

Lounging back on the swing, Stone sighed. "Glad I came here today." He flashed a shark grin at his daughter's mate. "Aren't you, kid?" Then he chuckled.

Nick snorted. "Keep laughing, old man. Just don't forget who chooses your nursing home."

After breakfast, Derren proposed they all go on a pack run. Roni could understand why: restlessness was wafting from all of them as they hoped for the call to say that Brunt had been released on bail. The one thing guaranteed to calm them was the touch and support of their pack.

Roni was one of the first to shift back to her human form, wanting to spend a little time with Shaya—who had opted out of the pack run due to being tired. Then, leaving the Alpha female to have some quality time with her father, Roni went to sit on a fallen tree, watching as the other wolves played. Although . . . she wasn't sure if Marcus's wolf was necessarily "playing" when he leaped hard enough at Zander's wolf to knock him into the stream. That might have been why Jesse's and Bracken's wolves dived on him.

A jet-black male wolf and gray-white male—Derren and Eli—joined the fray. It was hard to tell whether they were helping anyone or just plain wanted to play. Caleb and Kent's wolves were sprawled on the grass, resting, apparently uninterested in the others.

Footsteps coming from behind Roni preceded Nick's scent. Having shifted back into his human form and redressed, her brother sat beside her on the oak. "Okay, so my own medicine doesn't taste good. You wanted to give me a little reminder of what it's like to have family meddle and play games."

"Yes, and you need to stop," she said firmly. "Whether you consider him a 'man-slut' or not, Marcus is my mate, which means you have to let it go."

Nick sighed. "I know. At first, I thought I was looking out for you by trying to keep him away. I wanted to keep you happy and safe and—"

"You wanted to relieve your burden of guilt." He went silent, looking confused and a little off balance. "Nick, whatever you may think, you didn't traumatize me that day in the woods. I've never been anything but grateful to you for what you did. In fact, I've felt indebted to you my whole life."

He reared back. "What? That's stupid."

"Then we're both stupid. Everything that happened . . . it was awful. But it wasn't my fault, and it wasn't your fault. Stop trying to make up for something that's all in your head. All the overprotectiveness ever did was make me feel suffocated, like you didn't recognize my strength."

He gave her a pointed look. "I've never seen you as weak. Never." Inhaling deeply, he kind of slumped. "I'll stop the coddling."

"And you'll stop toying with Marcus."

"He's my sister's mate—it's my right to irritate him. It's what we males do."

That was the thing about shifter males: no logic was required.

"Then I guess you won't mind Stone spending much more time around here."

A huge sigh of frustration. "I'll ease up on your mate."

"Thank you." At that moment, Marcus's wolf came loping toward her, panting. Reaching her, he stood between her legs and nuzzled her breasts. "Typical." He then licked at her jaw happily as she stroked his flank before delivering a warning growl to Nick.

Disgruntled, Nick raised his hands. "All right, I'm going." As he stood, his cell phone rang, and everyone froze. Digging it out of his pocket, he answered, "Hello." By the time he'd ended the short call, all the shifters were back in their human form. "That was Trey. Brunt made bail. As planned, Ryan and Dante are covering the exits of the courthouse, ready to follow him wherever he goes. Once they grab him, they'll take him to their territory." He danced his gaze along Derren, Roni, and Marcus as he tipped his head and said, "Let's get going."

Dante blocked the doorway of the hut with his arm as Roni and Taryn went to walk inside. "Sorry, this one's for the boys." The hut, which had been rebuilt after being set on fire by the extremists that invaded pack territory, was where interrogations took place. Dante and Ryan had snatched Noah Brunt from the motel room he was hiding in after he exited the courthouse using the back entrance to avoid the extremists.

Roni removed her black-currant-flavored lollipop from her mouth. "I've no intention of interfering. But I want to hear what he has to say."

"*We* let *you* watch when we had our fun with the female jackal," griped Taryn, "so step aside, Barney Rubble."

Dante sighed. "Taryn, honey, we both know there is no chance in hell you'll be able to stand back and just watch."

"You say that like I have no self-control."

Nick snorted. "Do you?"

Taryn just huffed at him, like he wasn't worth explaining herself to. "Dante, just get the fuck out of our way. I'm talking to you as your Alpha female—*move*."

Dante appealed to her with a look. "Yeah, but—"

Behind Roni, Marcus spoke to Dante. "I'm really not sure why you're wasting time out of your life having this conversation. Surely experience has taught you that nothing can stop these two females from doing what they want to do."

Trey shrugged one shoulder. "He's right, D."

"I'm sure the girls promise not to interfere, right?" Derren looked pointedly at both Roni and Taryn.

The Phoenix Alpha female rolled her eyes. "We know the plan, we like the plan, and we have no intention of interfering with the plan."

Nodding, Dante dropped his arm and stepped aside. One by one, they entered. In the center of the small, empty building was a dark, gangly, male wolf. He was blindfolded, gagged, and bound to a chair.

Once Dante closed the door, he slowly moved toward the wolf. The Beta removed the gag and blindfold, revealing a pair of freakishly dark eyes. "Noah Brunt. You're not an easy person to find."

His gloating expression said he knew it. "Who are you?"

"You know."

Brunt's eyes skimmed everyone in the room, coming to settle on Trey. "I had nothing to do with what happened with your pup. Or with the attack on your enforcer's female." It wasn't said defensively. It was simply a statement of fact.

Marcus stepped forward. "Would that be *my* female you're talking about? She's actually my mate." That made things very different, which Brunt would know. A shifter wouldn't hesitate to kill anyone they suspected of meaning any harm to their mate. Marcus would destroy anyone who so much as threatened Roni, and he wouldn't miss a minute's sleep over it.

"I had nothing to do with it," stated Brunt, looking bored.

Nick snorted. "So you say."

Brunt's attention moved to him. "You're Alpha of the Mercury Pack."

"If you know that, then you know my pregnant mate *and* my sister were in the car crash that was nicely orchestrated by your jackal friends."

"I had nothing to do with the crash. I wasn't behind it." Again, it wasn't said in his defense; he was just stating a fact.

"Then who was?" asked Dante.

A brief pause. "I don't know."

Dante folded his arms across his broad chest. "Do you want to know one of the reasons my mate suits me so well? She's honest. I don't like it when people lie to me. Why would you want to lie to me, Noah?" The wolf didn't respond. Dante began to circle him. "We know about snm.com. We know about the Scorpio Pack's involvement. We know about *your* involvement. Your technical skills sure are good. But not good enough to save you from shifters whose pups and mates were threatened. They're a force like no other."

"We also know you like to watch," said Nick. "I'm a merciless bastard, and I know it. But I'd never hurt a female. I'd never get off on watching someone else doing it either. In fact, just the idea of it makes me want to . . . kill."

"Same here. I have to say, though," began Trey, "I think I might actually enjoy watching my Beta hurt you."

Brunt's eyes widened as Dante's claws sliced out. "Wait—"

Dante cocked his head. "Oh, I'm sorry, you have a few last words?"

Brunt licked his lips, seeming to realize this wasn't an interrogation that would allow him to play mind games. He'd been brought here to be tortured and killed, nothing more—or so he thought, thanks to Dante's plan.

It was a fucking good plan, in Roni's opinion. Dante had pointed out that interrogating didn't always involve threats. Noah Brunt was very intelligent, and he liked control. He would have stupidly thought he could control the interrogation—that he could play them all like they were puppets because he was too important for them to simply kill him, considering what information he had. Dante had known that the only way he would volunteer that information was if it was on his own terms, if he was trying to prove himself valuable.

"You don't want to kill me," Brunt croaked.

"Really?" drawled Dante. "Why is that?"

"I know things."

"We know things too."

The wolf laughed. "There's so much you don't know. You think it's simply a website for people to share their vids. It's not." He paused, shaking his head. "The jackals' victims aren't always random."

"We know." Marcus ensured he sounded bored and unimpressed. "Lyle Browne's often paid to target certain people."

"But you don't know *who* hires him often," said Brunt, gloating again.

"Someone from the council." That came from Ryan. "It's the perfect way to dispose of shifters or packs that draw too much attention."

Stunned, Brunt stared at Ryan. "How do you know? Only Lyle and I knew that. Not even the rest of the council knows."

"Wild guess."

Roni cursed herself for not thinking of it. The council wanted peace above all else—particularly to avoid the attention of humans—so it would make sense for one of them to utilize Lyle's talents. Well, it was a good thing they hadn't gone to the council with what they'd found. It would have made them next on their hit list.

Again, Brunt's eyes glanced at the faces surrounding him, as if searching for a potential ally. They stopped on Roni. "I saw your vid. Did you trace who uploaded it?" A wide smile spread across his face when she didn't answer—it made her wolf growl. "You didn't, did you?"

Roni gave a dismissive shrug. "There are far bigger things going on than who managed to illegally get ahold of logged evidence."

"I know who it was. I could tell you. Just like I could tell you where the Scorpio Pack is."

"In exchange for what, exactly?" asked Dante.

Suddenly, Brunt's expression hardened. "I want them dead. The jackals. I want them all dead."

Trey frowned. "Why would you want them dead?"

"Does it matter?"

"It does if you expect us to believe you. It makes no sense for you to betray them—they've been feeding your sick little kink."

"They killed Margo."

Playing dumb, Dante said, "Who's Margo?"

Brunt's gaze seemed far away. "She was different. She loved me."

No, thought Roni, the human had cared for who she thought Brunt was.

"They tortured and murdered her just last night—even sent me a picture." His upper lip curled back in anger and distaste.

Marcus spoke then. "Why would they go after this Margo person?"

"She talked to the extremists about me, about our relationship. She was safe until she did that. They punished her. I want them dead."

"You always want someone else to do your dirty work," muttered Derren.

Ignoring him, Brunt concentrated on Dante. "I'm not stupid, and I'm not delusional. You're not going to free me. You want me as dead as I want the jackals. But I want this over with quickly and cleanly. Agree to make my death quick, and I'll tell you where the Scorpio Pack is *and* who uploaded the video evidence."

Marcus smiled. Yes, Noah Brunt was indeed smart. He knew he'd have to make his offer damn attractive if he wanted a swift death from a bunch of wolves eager to make him pay for targeting pups and mates.

Dante exchanged a look with Trey and Nick before nodding. "Done."

Brunt nodded. "They're two hours away from here, by the old fairground exclusive to shifters—the one a pride of lions destroyed in a war with the owners."

"And the shifter who uploaded the vid?" prompted Marcus.

It was Roni he looked at when he revealed, "Nolan Richards."

Nick looked at her. "That's our old Alpha's son. The asshole who practically led the campaign to alienate you from our old pack."

Yep, and Roni was totally and utterly fucking pissed. Hadn't he caused her and her family enough damn problems? Any other time, she might have ranted and raved. Not now, though. Because while she had a true monster like Noah Brunt before her, it made Nolan seem like a cute, fuzzy kitten that shot golden nuggets out of his ass. She'd save the ranting for when it was all over. Then she'd get even, like she always did.

"So," said Dante, glancing at the wolves around him. "Who goes first?"

Taryn spoke for the first time. "Before you boys get started, I'd like a few minutes with this piece of shit."

As the female unleashed her claws and prowled toward him, Brunt struggled against the bonds. "Now wait a minute. You agreed to make this quick."

Dante puffed out a long breath. "Make it quick . . . that's such a loose term. I mean, 'quick' could mean anything really. Relative to whatever time frame a person has in mind, it could be seconds, minutes, hours, days—even weeks."

Nick's smile was dark. "We intend to give you exactly what you deserve."

"And since we won't be attacking the jackals until tonight," began Marcus, "that gives us all day to play with you."

Brunt moved his gaze to Roni, as if expecting her to speak up on his behalf since he'd revealed Nolan's name, but she shrugged at him. "You can't expect mercy from shifters whose pups and mates were endangered. But I'm sure you can understand that. After all, that's your motto, isn't it? Show no mercy."

CHAPTER EİGHTEEN

F*unny how torturing a sociopath could ease tension,* mused Roni.

Both packs had been restless since the car crash a few months ago, desperate to get their hands on those responsible. Dealing with Brunt had taken the edge off everyone's anger, honing it into a lethal blade.

Having had their fun at the hut, Roni, Marcus, Nick, and Derren had returned to their territory to collect Eli, Zander, and Bracken. The plan was to meet the Phoenix wolves a short distance away from the jackals' location, leaving Shaya with Jesse, Stone, and Kathy while Kent and Caleb monitored the border of their territory.

As everyone said their good-byes in the kitchen, Roni looked up at the male who'd tucked her into the cradle of his shoulder. "Was it hard?"

Marcus rubbed her lower back. "What?"

"Coming here with me instead of going home to your pack?" His instincts had to have balked at it. Had the situation been reversed, she'd certainly have found it difficult.

Framing her face with his hands, Marcus kissed her softly. "*You* are home to me." She was everything to him. A small part of him feared that, feared the power she had over him. "I admit, the enforcer in me feels like I'm abandoning them. But it's not like there's a war between our packs. We're fighting as one."

"Yeah, I know. But you're a very loyal person—"

"Yes, and my loyalty lies with you, first and foremost. Always will."

"Stop hogging my sister-in-law," griped Shaya, pulling Roni to her and then hugging her tightly. "You make sure you come back," she sniffled. Behind the Alpha female, both Nick and Eli practically melted at her anxiety. It was impossible not to adore Shaya.

"I will," Roni promised. "Keep this bunch calm—especially Jesse. It's galling him that he's been told to stay behind."

Releasing her, Shaya nodded. "Don't forget: jackal shifters are bigger and stronger than full-blooded jackals, so be ready. And they always go for the legs and the throat when fighting. And they're sly little scrappers—they don't fight fair, so make sure you don't fight fair either." She slapped her hands to her cheeks. "I hate that I can't come with you."

Nick stroked his mate's red corkscrew curls. "You know why you can't, baby."

Shaya snorted at him. "And you know that you'd have tried to keep me home even if I weren't pregnant." Nick just shrugged—totally unrepentant about his overprotectiveness.

That got Roni thinking. She turned to the three men in her life. "I don't want any of you trying to protect me tonight." Marcus, Nick, and Eli frowned. "I mean it. I'll be nothing but a distraction if all you're thinking about is my safety. Besides, if you really want me safe, the way to do it is to rip apart any jackal you see—you concentrate on what's in front of you. Got me?" Her brothers nodded with an unhappy sigh.

Marcus rubbed his nose against hers. "I got you, sweetheart. But that works both ways." He almost smiled at her rebellious expression. He and his wolf liked that she was so protective. "Don't worry about me. You just worry about this." He lightly tapped her ass. "It's mine, and I want it safe."

"We good to go?" Derren asked Nick as he, Zander, and Bracken approached.

When Nick flicked a worried look at Shaya, clearly hating the idea of leaving her, Stone came to her side and vowed, "Nothing will happen to her while I'm here."

Nick opened his mouth to speak, but then his cell started ringing. Digging it out of his pocket, he answered, "Hello. You're kidding me. Are you sure? I'll be right there." Ending the call, he swallowed. "That was Kent. He and Caleb found a corpse dumped just over the border of our land, near the edge of the cliff."

"Corpse?" Bracken gaped.

"They think it might be Eliza, but they're not sure."

Everyone glimpsed at Jesse to find that his expression was as blank as usual.

"It's got to be the jackals paying us back for killing one of their own," said Shaya, who had gone from being a bag of nerves to a fierce Alpha ready to burn shit down.

Zander nodded. "They must have thought Eliza was still Jesse's girlfriend."

Marcus spoke then. "We should check it out before we leave."

"I'm coming," announced Jesse.

Shaking his head, Nick told him, "I need you to stay with—"

"While you launch the attack on the jackals, I will remain here to guard Shaya. But I need to see for myself if this is Eliza. I might not have cared about her, and I know she was a pain in everybody's ass, but . . ."

But it would feel disrespectful to not identify the body in case it *was* Eliza, Roni understood. "I'll stay here so that Jesse can go with you," she said to Nick.

Jesse nodded at her. "Thank you."

"Let's move." Nick turned to leave. Obediently, the males of the pack followed.

Marcus kissed Roni gently. "I'll be back soon." He ran with the Mercury male wolves to the opposite side of their territory.

Kent and Caleb waved them over before standing back to give them room. Staring down at the brutalized corpse, Marcus felt bile rise in his throat. He hadn't liked Eliza in the slightest. The fact that she'd provoked Roni into a fight and actually injured her—shallow wounds or not—meant he'd had no respect for her. But surely no one deserved to die like that.

She'd been stabbed, beaten, burned, and quite possibly raped. On top of that, "SNM" had been carved into her stomach. Her bruised, swollen face had been mercilessly slashed until skin actually peeled away in some places. If he hadn't recognized her scent, Marcus wouldn't have been convinced it was her.

He slid his gaze to Jesse. There was no grief or devastation in his expression, but there was anger. As the guy had pointed out, Eliza had been a pain in everyone's ass. But she hadn't deserved that.

Zander was the first to speak. "It was ballsy of the jackals to come here."

"But they weren't that ballsy," began Jesse, "or they would have picked a spot that wasn't so secluded. They would have chanced getting nearer to the main lodge."

"It just doesn't fit that they would do this to get at you," Marcus said to Nick. "I can understand them wanting to get even for what we did to their pack member. But as retaliations go, this isn't exactly tit-for-tat, is it? I mean, Eliza might have been"—he struggled for a way to put it politely, not wanting to disrespect the dead—"an acquaintance . . . but she wasn't a member of your pack."

"But she was Brunt's lawyer," Derren pointed out.

Eli turned to the Beta. "You're thinking they killed her because they were worried Brunt might have told her about the website."

"It makes sense. Then they dumped the body here to taunt us."

"And now we have to decide what to do with the body." Nick sighed. "Her family deserves to know what happened to her, but we can't trust the council with any of this. Not if one of them is involved."

"Maybe we could leave her body in a place it will likely be found," suggested Bracken.

Nick was quiet for a moment. "This isn't something we can act on right now. We need to leave; we'll discuss it when we get back. Kent, Caleb, transfer her body to one of the empty lodges so the wildlife won't savage it any worse than it already is."

"I'll call Trey, tell him we're on our . . ." Marcus trailed off as a sense of wrongness suddenly slithered over him.

Nick stiffened. "What is it?"

"Something's not right."

An abrupt yelp was quickly followed by a succession of shorter yelps that seemed to come from every direction.

Zander growled. "Jackals. The bastards have crossed the border."

"They've surrounded us," rumbled Marcus. They'd surrounded them in a loose circle, and then slowly closed in, little by little. He'd scented them, but as Eliza's body reeked of them, it hadn't raised any alarms. Marcus could now scent something else too. "And they've brought some friends."

A siren-like howl was answered by a hollow cackle. Suddenly jackals and hyenas were charging at them from every angle. Without the slightest hesitation, Marcus shifted, along with the others. Seeing a black-backed jackal leaping at him, the wolf slammed into the animal and clamped his jaws around his throat.

As Kathy handed a mug of tea to Shaya, the Alpha female sighed. "I miss coffee. And runny eggs. And tuna."

Returning to her seat beside Shaya, Kathy smiled fondly at her. "Not long to go now before the baby's born."

"I honestly don't know how humans cope with being pregnant for nine months, I really don't. Five months will be enough for me." She squirmed, her expression pained. "My back is killing me."

"When you have your baby in your arms, it will all be worth

it." Kathy cast Roni a look of displeasure. "I doubt I'll get any grandchildren from Roni."

"Probably not," allowed Roni, slowly pacing. Her wolf didn't like being left behind and away from any action. Roni didn't much like it either; she wanted to remain with her mate and see the corpse for herself. It gave her an idea of how Shaya was feeling. "Kids hate me."

Shaya laughed softly. "No, they don't. Kye adores you, and you adore him. Admit it."

Roni shrugged. "Everyone loves Kye—it's impossible not to."

"I'm going to do a circle of the lodge," Stone announced, pulling out his Glock.

Shaya frowned. "The body was dumped on the other side of our territory. The jackals are too cowardly to come anywhere close to the main lodge."

"Still, it's always best to be safe. Here." He handed Shaya her shotgun. "Kathy, lock the door behind me. Just to be safe," he quickly added when Shaya went to object. Once he headed out the back door and was swallowed up by the darkness, Kathy closed and locked it.

Sighing, Shaya leaned forward to prop her elbows up on the table and rest her face between her hands. "I feel so helpless. I wish I could come along tonight. Don't get me wrong, I would never put the baby in danger. Not in a million years. But it will still be hard to sit here, twiddling my thumbs, while my pack puts themselves in jeopardy. Especially Nick. He runs straight into the thick of things."

"He'll be fine, honey." Kathy lightly squeezed her hand.

"I hope you're right, because if I have to—" Shaya's breath seemed to suddenly get trapped in her throat.

At the same time, Marcus's rage slammed into Roni as his wolf shifted and faced the threat in front of him. The impact made Roni stumble. "Fuck."

Kathy tensed. "What's the matter? What is it?"

"The jackals have crossed over the border, and they're attacking," replied Shaya, breathing heavily.

"Call Taryn," Roni told her, enraged and fearful for her mate and pack. Nodding, Shaya did just that. Roni glimpsed out the window; the urge to dash outside and join the fight was strong. So damn strong. Every instinct Roni had screamed at her to go to Marcus, to fight at his side and help protect her pack. But she couldn't leave Shaya with only Kathy and Stone—wherever the hell he was—for protection.

"The Phoenix wolves are on their way." Shaya returned her phone to her pocket. "Roni, if you need to go to Marcus, I understand."

"I'm not leaving you."

"It's fine. I'd go to Nick if I could." Shaya's hands clenched tightly around her shotgun, and Roni had a feeling she was imagining shooting every bastard jackal out there. "I hate being helpless, Roni. Hate it. Hate it."

Roni crouched down in front of a rapidly breathing Shaya. "I need you to stay calm for me, Shaya. Okay? It's important for you and for the baby that you're calm. Breathe with me, all right? In and out."

Nodding, Shaya did as Roni asked. "The body was bait, wasn't it? The whole thing was a trap."

"It's going to be fine, Shaya, we're—" A noise coming from upstairs made the hair on Roni's nape stand up. She placed a finger to her mouth, and both Shaya and Kathy immediately froze. Another noise: a slight scuffle. "Someone's inside," she whispered, suspecting they had entered through the balcony. Which meant the body hadn't been bait at all. It had been a diversion, a way of separating the pack to make them weaker—possibly even a way to get to Shaya.

"It could just be my dad," Shaya said quietly.

"Your dad wouldn't creep around." More noise: the padding of paws on the wooden floor above them. "We have to move."

"Move where?" asked Shaya as Roni took her arm and urged her to stand.

"We can't go outside." Kathy got to her feet, her eyes narrowed as she glanced around. "There could be more out there."

"The basement," said Roni after a brief pause. "It has a security steel door, and the emergency exit isn't easily visible from outside. It's the only exit they won't have covered." For once, she was thankful for Nick's overprotectiveness.

"Wait, what about my dad?"

"He's probably out there hunting them," replied Roni. "He knows I'd hide you at the first sign of trouble."

Silently, they hurried through the kitchen and dining area with Roni in the lead and Kathy covering the rear. As they reached the archway that led into the living area, Roni held her hand up for them to stop. Popping her head around the arch, Roni searched for any sign of an intruder. Satisfied no one was in sight, she continued onward, not stopping until they reached the doorway. They all pressed up against the wall as Roni poked her head out to glance up and down the hall, satisfied to find it empty.

"Almost there," she reminded a panting Shaya.

The three of them kept one shoulder near the wall as they quietly scurried down the hallway, stopping at the T-junction. Roni quickly peered around the corner, confirming the small hallway that led to the basement was clear. "Go, go, go." She ushered Shaya and Kathy to precede her around the corner, along the hallway, and down the small flight of stairs at the end.

Roni went inside first. On their left was a bar and seating area while an indoor pool was on their right. Once she was satisfied that the basement was empty, she urged Shaya and Kathy inside. "Keep this locked."

Eyes wide, Shaya gripped her arm tight. "Wait, Roni, you can't leave us."

"I have to fight them off."

The Alpha female shook her head madly. "No, there could

be lots of them. You're tough, but you're not invincible. I know it grates on your pride to stay. But you're not hiding, you're protecting me. Please, Roni. *Please*."

How could she resist that watery plea? She couldn't. Sighing, Roni nodded and secured the door. "Call Taryn again. Warn her that jackals are inside the lodge."

While Shaya quickly updated her friend on what was happening, Kathy spoke to Roni. "Even a safety door won't stand up to shifter strength."

"No, but it will hold them back for a while and give the Phoenix wolves time to get here."

"Well, that's good, because the only things we can barricade the door with are those sun loungers."

"Moving things around will do nothing other than make enough noise to give away our location."

"Taryn says they're almost here," said Shaya, tucking the phone in her jeans' pocket. "A few of them plan to search the lodge while the others join the fight. We just have to hang on." She ran her hands through her hair. "Nick's in so much pain. He's tiring, but he won't take any energy from me through our bond."

Mates were able to boost each other's strength using their mating link, but only if it was fully developed. Since Roni and Marcus's bond hadn't yet fully formed, she didn't have the ability to add her strength to his—and it was pissing her off, because he was tiring too. "How do you complete a mating bond?"

Shaya blinked. "Mates have to be one hundred percent open to each other. You have to face whatever holds you back from him."

"Nothing holds me back."

"Are you sure about that?"

"Yes." She'd admitted she loved Marcus, both to him and to herself. She'd confided in him, had come to trust him, and even to lean on him in some ways. She had accepted that it didn't undermine her level of independence or strength to do so. Had realized that it was possible to be too self-reliant. In fact, it could even be viewed as selfish, because it was a form of rejection. Helping others could make a person feel good, and this "give and take" could help toward developing their connection. To deprive Marcus of that, to deprive their mating of that, wasn't fair.

"Maybe the problem's him, not me." Marcus had held back from people his entire life. It wouldn't be easy to snap out of something like that, no matter how much a person wanted to. It was possible that he didn't even realize he was still doing it.

Shaya shrugged helplessly. "If that's the case, this is out of your hands. He needs to come to that realization on his own." Her eyes shot to the door, wide and wary, as an animalistic yap sounded in the near distance. Another yap, this one closer. "They're coming."

Moments later, paws padded along the hallway toward the basement and then down the steps. There was sniffing and panting at the door, and then claws were raking the floor as if trying to dig a hole. *Shit.* A loud and urgent yelp split the air, and it earned several yelps of response as what sounded like a small stampede headed toward them.

"They've found us," whispered Kathy.

As if to confirm that, something charged at the steel door. Then there was yelping and barking as the animals repeatedly slammed their bodies against it, leaving dents and impressions. It instantly became clear that the door wouldn't hold for long.

"We need to use the emergency exit." They sprinted for the door. Roni pulled up the blackout blind and jumped back in surprise at the male standing just outside the glass. Realizing it was Stone, she sagged in relief and unlocked the door.

He pushed his way inside, Glock in hand. "Goddamn hyenas are patrolling the area." Noticing that the steel door was being attacked, he cursed.

"Hyenas?" Kathy shuddered.

"I managed to take out a few of them, but when I realized the jackals had broken into the lodge, I came to get you out. We've got a better chance of protecting Shaya as a team."

In agreement, Roni nodded. Conscious that the door would cave in any second now, she placed a hand on Shaya's back and urged her forward. "Let's get to one of the SUVs and drive Shaya out of here."

Eyes on the steel door, Stone took Shaya's hand and led her outside. Kathy quickly followed. That was when Roni slammed the door closed and locked herself inside the basement.

"Roni, what are you doing?" Kathy demanded—the words were barely audible through the glass.

"Protect Shaya. Get her away from here." Roni pulled down the blackout blind, shutting out a grim-faced Stone and two very outraged females. Then she turned, claws out, and took up position in the center of the room just as the door gave way, leaving her no time to shift. She'd expected to find herself instantly swarmed by jackals. Instead, several of them slowly slinked into the room—their eyes fixed on her and glinting with malicious intent.

Her pulse quickened, her heart raced, and her muscles tightened as they circled her, trapping her, and making her wolf fight to surface. But Roni couldn't take a moment to shift, couldn't leave herself vulnerable for even a second.

Two more jackals entered then, both in human form. One was Lyle Browne. And the other . . . she had no idea who he was, but the object in his hand made her blood boil and her wolf snap her teeth.

"Meet Dave, my cameraman." Lyle smirked. "I bet this must bring back some memories for you."

It did. And with those flashbacks came feelings of helplessness, terror, humiliation, and pain. "You won't get to her."

"You thought it was the Alpha female I was after, didn't you?" Laughing quietly, Lyle shook his head. "I knew you'd protect her like the good enforcer that you are. I knew you'd hold us back while she had the chance to slip away. And now here you are . . . alone. Mine." Smiling, he cocked his head. "Scared? I do hope so. Working out someone's worst fear and then subjecting them to it . . . now that's power. That's real entertainment."

His pack, all now back in their human form, chuckled—including the three female jackals who had tried to kidnap her.

"You cost me the Phoenix rug rat. You cost me one of my pack members and had a lot of fun with her before you killed her. Now it's time for me to have some fun with you. And from what I've heard, you'll be quite entertaining. It's time for you to face your worst fear."

As three jackals took a single step toward her, Roni instantly understood. Lyle intended to make her relive what had happened twelve years ago. His pack members intended to hold her down while he raped her—maybe they would even take turns. Her stomach rolled and her heart slammed inside her chest. Not again. Not. Fucking. Again.

She'd always promised herself that if she were ever placed in that situation again, she would fight until someone was dead—even if that someone was her. Death would have been preferable now too if it weren't for a very important fact: if she died, there was a possibility that Marcus would die also.

The fact that their bond was only partially formed could mean that he would survive the breaking of it, but she wasn't prepared to take that for granted, because Lyle was wrong. Reliving her nightmare wasn't her worst fear. Not anymore. Her worst fear was that something would happen to Marcus. She loved the smooth fucker. Loved his playfulness. Loved his hyperactive metabolism. Loved that he defended and protected her.

Now it was time that she did the same in return. But that didn't just mean surviving. No. If she let these bastards harm her, Marcus would *feel* what they were doing to her through their link. He would experience the violation, the fear, the powerlessness, and the pain along with her. She could no easier handle that than she could handle him dying.

That meant she had to fight. Unfortunately, she was at a total disadvantage. She was outnumbered, without allies, and couldn't shift. Her best chance of survival would be to run and fight another day. There was no shame in that. But there was nowhere to go. She was trapped. Surrounded by people who were apparently eager to watch her be raped—she could sense their anticipation and excitement. It was sickening, and it made her wolf growl in distaste.

"Don't think your mate will save you," said Lyle. "Oh, I've no doubt that he'll come for you, no matter how hurt he is. That's why I have the place surrounded. If he does get to you, it won't be in time to help. You're on your own."

No, she wasn't. Underestimating Marcus was a definite mistake on Lyle's part. Her mate would do whatever it took to reach her. A muscular arm suddenly wrapped around her neck from behind and pulled her against a hard chest. Dark memories flashed through her mind, making her stomach churn and her wolf buck to be freed. Roni could practically taste her fear.

"Who knows?" Lyle shrugged. "You might even enjoy it."

The cameraman chuckled, momentarily catching her attention. A memory of another cameraman, another time and place, slapped her hard. She recalled how the bastard had laughed at Nick's rage as he was held back; how he'd taunted her brother with what they would do to her as he was forced to watch; how he'd egged on the others.

In that moment, as those flashbacks overtook her mind, Roni's fear faded and was replaced by raw anger. A taut knot of rage formed in her throat, making her face heat and her heart thunder inside her chest. But that wasn't good, she knew. To fight in anger was to lose before the battle even began. The rage would cloud her thoughts, mess with her head. When Roni lost it, she always found it a trial to calm down, especially while her wolf's anger fed her own.

Instead of focusing on the past, Roni focused on the present—kept her attention on Lyle, reminded herself and her wolf of what was truly important. Not the past. Not the sense of powerlessness that threatened to overwhelm her mind and body. Marcus—he was what mattered. And he needed her to be clear-headed right now. So she fought to maintain her composure and keep her expression entirely neutral as Lyle—who apparently loved the sound of his own voice—began to talk smack about her brothers, her mate, and her pack.

She ignored the words, refusing to engage with him or be baited. Instead, she watched him carefully. Searched for weaknesses. Watched how he carried himself, what side he favored. Registered how much taller he was than her. How much heavier he was. Estimated his physical strength and agility. Sadly, there was no denying that he outmatched her. But there were ways to use his strength against him.

As the jackal holding her let out a malicious chuckle and licked her cheek, she barely resisted shuddering in revulsion. Only once since the attack had she been in a chokehold. She and Eli had been practicing combat moves, and she'd asked him to restrain her this way until the panic abated and she could learn exactly how to get out of the hold if it ever happened again.

Eli had learned a lot from being forced to participate in the illegal fighting arena, and he had passed on all those teachings to her. He hadn't taught her how to better defend herself. He'd taught her how to kill without blinking. How to fight dirty and brutally without conscience. Ordered her to "go bat-shit crazy on the ass of any attacker because there is no such thing as a fair fight in the real world."

Lyle came to stand in front of her and skimmed his finger over her chin. She forced herself not to flinch. "Unlike those humans, I'll make you beg for mercy."

Not fucking likely. Just the idea had adrenalin pumping through her veins, sending a surge of energy and enhanced awareness rushing through her. Roni looked over his shoulder and let her eyes widen slightly before quickly returning her gaze to his. She watched as his eyes narrowed suspiciously. The moment he glanced behind him in shear paranoia, she struck, delivering a hard blow to the side of his neck that made him stumble backward.

Without pause, she let herself go limp in her restrainer's grip; her weight made him stagger and bend over slightly, which allowed her to drop down just enough to sharply dig her elbow into the bastard's groin. With a grunt of pain, he released her and folded over, cursing a blue streak.

Holding Lyle's stunned gaze, she shifted away from the restrainer and stated, "I challenge you."

If Lyle had been human, the strike to his neck might have been enough to make him pass out. But shifters were made of sterner stuff. "Excuse me?" he croaked.

"I challenge you, Lyle Browne, to a duel." Because that was the only way to ensure that they couldn't attack her as a group. A one-to-one duel would at least make the odds more even. To turn down the challenge would make him look weak to his pack and to anyone who watched the video. Not that she intended for there to be a video, but Lyle was certainly confident that there would be.

After a beat, Lyle threw back his head and laughed—well, gurgled, "You're shitting me."

She offered him an evil grin. "You're not scared of a girl, are you?"

"You know what this means, don't you, sweetheart?"

Her wolf growled at that; she didn't like him using Marcus's endearment.

"It means that by the time I'm done with you, you'll be worn out. There'll be no fight left in you. And you won't even be able to attempt to defend yourself against me and my pack when we have our fun. You'll have to lie there and take it, almost as if you accept and want it."

"*Or* it will mean that you die an excruciating death. I kind of like that idea."

CHAPTER NINETEEN

Growling, the male wolf tore out the throat of a hyena and tossed it aside. He hadn't even lifted his head before a jackal latched onto his leg while another bit into his already injured throat—giving him no reprieve, no moment to catch his breath. The wolf slammed his body against a tree, cramming the jackal between him and the tall oak, dislodging his grip. Then the wolf clamped his jaws around the jackal's throat, tasting blood. Death. Victory.

As teeth dug harder into his leg, the wolf reached back and bit hard into the second jackal's ear, ripping it off. The animal made a sound of agonizing pain, bounding away. The wolf didn't intend to let his prey flee. He crashed into the shifter, trapping him on the ground, and moved to deliver the killing bite. But then a heavy weight landed on his back. Another jackal.

The wolf yowled as the animal's teeth sank into his shoulder, scraping bone. More blood soaked his fur. He rolled onto his back, crushing the jackal until he yelped in pain and released him. Righting himself, the wolf then sliced open the jackal's stomach and left him to bleed out while he tore out the throat of the other jackal.

Sides heaving, the wolf glanced around, searching for new prey. He was tired. Bleeding. Panting. In much pain. He was covered in bites. Claws had sliced into his sides and muzzle. His badly chewed legs were unsteady. His fur was matted with blood—some his, some not. And he was weakening. But he could not rest. He had to protect his mate. He had to protect her pack.

He charged at a hyena that had pounced on an injured submissive wolf—Kent—and tackled him to the ground. Jackals came at him from both sides. The wolf had been repeatedly attacked by many at one time. He concentrated on the main threat: the hyena. He clawed, bit, maimed, and destroyed his enemy.

The wolf's badly hurt hind leg buckled when sharp teeth pierced through fur and muscle, grazing bone. The Mercury Head Enforcer suddenly slammed into the animal, forcing him to release the leg and—

Several sharp cracks split the air. The wolf froze. *Bullets.* More angry sharp snaps. Coming from the direction of the Alphas' home. The wolf howled, raging that harm might reach his mate.

He rushed through the trees, intent on reaching her. But the breath left his body as jackals barreled into him from either side and leaped on top of him, teeth latching onto painful wounds. The wolf howled again, bucking in an effort to shake off his attackers. They held tight, pulling his legs from under him. One went for his throat but then yelped as another wolf slammed into it. A Phoenix wolf—Trick. More of his pack appeared, joining the fight.

His Alpha female skidded to a stop in front of him and shifted into her human form. "Marcus, you need to shift and let me heal you. Jackals got into the main lodge. You need to get to Roni."

The wolf didn't understand the words, but he felt pressure from Marcus, knew he feared for their mate's safety and that he wanted dominance. Reluctantly, the wolf drew back and allowed his human half to take control.

Marcus fell onto his back, chest heaving as anxiety for Roni rushed through him. "Tell me you didn't say the jackals got into the lodge," he panted. There wasn't a part of his body that didn't hurt. The jackals had repeatedly leaped at him, crawled over him like ants, and attacked every vulnerable area he had. He knew he'd lost a lot of blood, knew he was mostly running on rage.

Taking his eyes briefly from the scene around them, Trick grimaced. "Shit, Marcus, you're in bad shape."

Squatting, Taryn placed her hand on Marcus's forehead, causing all of his injuries to illuminate. She winced as the extent of his wounds became clear. "Shaya called me. Dumping the body here was just a distraction. The jackals wanted you far away from the main lodge. I think they're after Shaya. We sent Dominic and Tao to help so we could join the battle."

"God, the fuckers are everywhere," Trick commented, wrestling a jackal to the ground and stamping his boot against the animal's throat, crushing his windpipe. "Looks like the Scorpio Pack called in a few favors and brought along their business associates—and maybe even the alliances of their business associates."

Marcus suspected that the intruders were acting as a diversion while most, if not all, of the Scorpio Pack was at the lodge. Which meant he had to get to Roni *fast*. "I can feel Roni through the bond. She's pissed and scared. I have to go to her."

"Yes, you do, so stay still." Taryn put her mouth to his and inhaled deeply. She then lifted her head, and blew out a heavy breath. At that, black particles whooshed out of her mouth. Again and again, she did it, but stopped before the luminous patches had completely disappeared. Although the worst of his wounds had closed, they hadn't faded and he was still a mess—covered in bruises, lacerations, teeth marks, and jaggedly healed scratches.

Having stabbed his claws into the throat of a jackal that came too close, Trick asked Taryn, "You okay?" Healing tended to weaken her.

A little pale, she nodded before turning back to Marcus. "I can't afford to fully heal you, I'm sorry—I have to save some strength to help the others."

With a nod of understanding, Marcus shifted once more into his wolf form. The wolf raced through the forest, not slowing until he approached the Alphas' home. Two of his pack members—Dominic and Tao—were wrestling hyenas while his mate's mother—Kathy—fought two jackals.

There was a gunshot, the sound of a hyena whimpering, and then a voice screeching, "Marcus!"

The wolf turned his head to see the Mercury Alpha female leaning out of a car window, gun in hand. Giving his human half control again, the wolf drew back.

"Where is she, Shaya?" demanded Marcus.

"She's in the basement," cried Shaya. "I didn't want to leave her!"

Stone, who was leaning out of the other window with his Glock in hand, shouted, "She locked herself in to keep them from getting to Shaya!"

Typical Roni. She was extremely protective of those she cared for, and her position of enforcer meant protecting her Alpha female was her job. That didn't mean he didn't want to spank her ass. "She's alive," he reassured Shaya, realizing the Alpha female was panicking that Roni was dead. "I'll get her out of there." It was a promise to his wolf as well as to Shaya.

"You can't win this, little wolf."

Roni almost snorted at his use of the word "win." What Lyle clearly didn't realize was that for her, this wasn't a fight. Wasn't a duel. This was life or death. She would kill him. She wouldn't be anybody's victim ever again. But instead of letting him see her resolve and determination, she shrugged. "Maybe. But I'll be the best damn runner up you've ever had."

Seemingly amused, he prowled toward her. "I'm actually looking forward to this."

"Don't forget to watch for her right hook, Lyle!"

Roni recognized the voice as that belonging to the female jackal who'd tried forcing her into the car—the one who had also been knocked out cold.

Holding Roni's gaze, Lyle said, "Oh, yes, Jenna told me all about how you like to go for the temple."

As much as that annoyed Roni, she was also grateful to Jenna at that moment. Neither the bitch nor Lyle had realized it, but they'd actually helped Roni by letting her know he'd be on guard for that move. Now she knew to concentrate on her other moves.

She watched as he clenched his fists, dropped his chin slightly, and shifted one foot in front of him—and she knew he was going to hit her. Roni struck first, and she struck fast and hard, making it count, slamming her fist into his solar plexus, knocking the breath out of him.

Twelve years ago, her instinct had been to go straight for the groin. Now, she knew better. Knew it was a predictable move that was easily countered. Giving him no time to defend himself, she came at Lyle with a quick burst of moves. A hard blow to the ribs. A harsh kick to the kneecap. A palm strike to the face. She didn't let up, keeping the pressure on, being careful not to telegraph her movements.

It was fast, it was brutal, and it was explosive. Lyle jabbed, punched, slapped, and repeatedly attempted to restrain her. She quickly recognized that he was trying to get her on the floor. No way. If he managed to pin her down, it would be very unlikely that she would get back up.

As she aimed for his nose, Lyle blocked the strike and abruptly swung his fist at her head. She jerked away to avoid the hit, but it managed to clip her jaw. The bystanders cheered. *Damn, that hurt.* And it was going to bruise. Marcus would lose his shit. The adrenaline dimmed the pain enough for her to keep moving. But she knew she'd feel the true brunt of it later.

Jenna screeched, "Make the bitch bleed!"

Lyle did just that: clawing her chest, raking over a nipple. *Fuck.* Pain knifed through Roni, making the bud feel like it was on fire. She could feel blood soaking her T-shirt, knew it was bad. But she fought the pull to check the wound. Refused to move her attention from Lyle. The moment she did, he would be on her.

Instead, she did as Eli taught her; she moved like water, flowing with Lyle's moves as opposed to cowering from them. She never stopped. Not even for a moment. She hit, she ducked, she jumped, she dodged—ensuring she was too squirrely for Lyle to get a firm grip on her.

Aiming to obscure his vision, she crossed a little as she slammed her fist hard into his nose. An ominous crack was quickly followed by a roar as blood gushed from his nose and splattered on the ground. The audience booed and cursed.

Growling, Lyle wiped blood from his face and flicked it at her. The distraction cost her. He abruptly swept out his foot, knocking her feet from under her. She hit the tiled floor hard, grunting in pain, and he quickly advanced on her. She rolled before Lyle's boot could connect with her ribs. Jumping to her feet, she parried his next blow. And the next. And the next. Seeing an opening, she rammed her elbow into his throat. He staggered back, cupping his throat.

With a loud cry of outrage, Jenna came charging over like a damn spider monkey. *Oh, for fuck's sake.* Roni punched her breast hard—the bitch might now have an idea of exactly how Roni was feeling; her nipple was still throbbing, felt like it was on fire. Roni grabbed her by the hair and shoved Jenna's head down just as she brought her knee up hard to connect with her nose. Another nauseating crack. Jenna cried out, and again, the crowd booed.

Roni had just shoved the whining jackal aside when Lyle's hand locked around her wrist, squeezing painfully as he dragged her close. Instead of trying to pull free, she clawed his face, catching his eyeball. With a roar of pain, he backpedalled and reflexively retracted his hands to bring them up to shield his face. But he kept his cruel gaze locked on her. And Roni saw something in those eyes that hadn't been there before. It was in his scent too. Behind the coppery tang of blood, the sour stench of sweat, and the burning whiff of anger was the metallic scent of fear. It satisfied her wolf.

With his eye red and watery, he again advanced on her. They went at each other, both merciless and thirsty for vengeance. Punching. Kicking. Slapping. Clawing. She was fast losing her breath, but she didn't let up. Even though her chest heaved, sweat dotted her forehead, and blood was trickling from several wounds on her body, she kept on going. Lyle was in no better shape than she was, which only served to further incite the crowd.

At that moment, she sensed Marcus, knew he was close. Knew he was desperate to get to her, fighting and killing his way through the hyenas and jackals who were surrounding the lodge. But she didn't want him anywhere near Lyle Browne or his pack of sick fucks.

Cupping her hands, she slapped them hard over Lyle's ears. He roared and staggered as his eardrum shattered. She moved to attack him again, but an arm came around her from behind. *Motherfucker.* Using her claws, she sliced the arm from wrist to elbow. It released her. She twisted her hips and delivered a side kick to the bastard's kidneys.

That was when she heard a bellow of rage coming from Lyle. She turned, but she turned too late. His punch caught her ribs, and there was a sickening snap. Ripples of sheer agony rushed through her. *Son of a bitch.* Her hand flew to her body as she sucked in deep mounds of air, trying to catch her breath. The heel of his boot slammed into her shin, and she stumbled, almost losing her footing on the slippery, blood-covered tiles. He took advantage, charging at her. The impact sent her sprawling onto her back.

The bastard straddled her and wrapped his hands around her neck. Instantly, she tucked her chin down to prevent her windpipe from being obstructed. Ignoring the reflex to try to pry his hands from her throat, she punched him in the dick. He made a choking sound as his hand cupped his groin and he curled over her.

Determined to get free, she pulled at his hair, bit into his throat, clawed at his face. Her wolf's panic drove her on, insisted she didn't give up. Sensing that Lyle's friends were about to surround her, Roni stabbed her claws into his inner thigh, targeting the major artery. He roared in pain, and she rolled them, coming to straddle him. But the big bastard rolled them again and again and—

The cold pool water swallowed Roni, almost making her gasp in shock. For a short moment, she didn't move, stunned. Then panic set in, and she freed herself from Lyle's grip and kicked to the surface of the pool. As her head penetrated the surface of the water, relief filled her, and she gulped in huge clumps of air.

She swam for the edge of the pool, but then a hand fisted in her hair and forced her head under the water. *Fuck.* She fought against the panic that threatened to overwhelm her, but as Lyle's hold on her tightened and he pushed her deeper and deeper into the water, all Roni could think about was getting to the surface.

She frantically thrashed and kicked her legs, all the while struggling to hold her breath. At that moment, her wolf's anger was a live thing. It acted as fuel, boosting Roni's strength . . . but it wasn't enough. Roni fought and fought, but she couldn't reach Lyle well enough to hurt him; she couldn't get free.

The chlorine filled and stung her nose and her airways as she helplessly inhaled the water. It felt like something was tearing and burning her throat, like it was shrinking, as the water filled her lungs. At the same time, she began to feel heavy, tired, and weak.

And she had the fleeting thought that she was going to die, that she would never see her mate again.

It should have increased her panic, but suddenly the fear slipped away. A sense of calm and tranquility began to settle in. She felt strangely at peace. Was confident that Marcus—strong, powerful, and resilient—would be fine without her. Her wolf was still frantic, clawing at Roni, fighting to surface and protect them. But her body didn't have enough physical strength to shift. And as she succumbed to the need to sleep, her mind distantly registered the sounds of wolves growling and jackals yelping in pure agony.

Marcus felt it the second Roni lost consciousness. He'd just shifted to his human form, having ripped apart the hyenas who were guarding the emergency exit to the basement. The shock of her blacking out made him stumble as he rushed down the steps toward the basement door. *Fuck.* His wolf howled, terrified for his mate.

Shaking with the need to reach her, Marcus shoved at the door, but it didn't open. He kicked at it, determined to somehow bash his way through the protective glass. Hearing a series of approaching howls, he knew that the battle at the opposite side of the land was over, that his pack and the Mercury wolves were on their way. But it wouldn't be fast enough to help Roni.

Racing back up the steps, Marcus grabbed a rock from beside the lodge and launched it at the door. It chipped the glass slightly, leaving spiderweb cracks. Again and again, he did it, until finally there was a big enough hole for him to squeeze his arm through.

Having unlocked the door, he shoved it open, knocking down the blackout blind as he barged into the basement. His brain noted that three wolves—Kathy, Tao, and Dominic—had entered through the other door and were now fighting the jackals, viciously tearing them apart. But all he gave a shit about was his mate; he could *feel* her organs beginning to shut down, could feel her heartbeat slowing and becoming erratic.

His eyes slammed on Lyle Browne, who was forcing her head beneath the water. And she wasn't moving. Marcus rushed across the room and dived into the pool. Startled, Lyle twisted slightly, releasing a limp Roni to defend himself. But before he could act, Marcus grabbed the fucker by his hair and slammed his head against the side of the pool. Once. Twice. Three times. Until something cracked and Lyle was out cold. Marcus released him, prepared to let the water do its job. Any other time, Marcus might have taken the time to make his death more agonizing. But right now, all he cared about was getting Roni out of the water.

Holding his breath, he let the water envelope him as he abandoned Lyle's unmoving body and swam to Roni. She was halfway to the bottom of the pool, motionless. Wrapping an arm around her, he kicked for the surface and found Eli and Derren hovering there. They took her from him, sliding her onto the tiled floor. She was pale, her lips and fingernail beds were blue, and *shit,* he'd never been more scared in his life. His wolf released a mournful howl.

By the time Marcus was out of the pool, Derren had already started CPR. He immediately took over, shoving Derren out of the way, *needing* to do something. With the fingers of both hands at her jaw just below the ears, he kept her jaw jutted as he pinched her nose shut and sealed his mouth over hers. He blew hard enough to see her chest rise, then did it again two seconds later. His enhanced hearing picked up that she still wasn't breathing.

Hands clasped together, he pushed down to compress the chest, repeating it every few seconds while Derren counted. "Baby, you have to breathe for me." She couldn't die, she just couldn't. "Come on, sweetheart, breathe."

"Please, Roni," begged Eli, kneeling beside Derren. "You have to wake up."

Marcus was distantly aware that the fighting had all stopped and that several wolves were now gathered around them, but he was solely focused on Roni.

"I should have known she'd lock herself inside," sniffled Shaya. "I should have stopped her." Nick murmured comforting words into her ear, assuring her that it wasn't her fault.

Again, Marcus blew air into Roni's mouth. She *would* live, dammit. Compressing her chest again, he ordered, *"Breathe."*

But she wasn't breathing. She was dying. Both he and his wolf could feel it through their link, could feel her slipping away, could feel that bond weakening right along with her. No, this just wasn't happening. "You can't fucking die!"

She couldn't. He loved her. He *needed* her. And it was only then that he realized he'd actually been afraid to let himself need her. What's more, he'd been afraid to let her truly need him. His determination to not be needy like his mother or be mated to anyone like her had held him back from Roni without him even realizing it.

With Roni, it was okay to have her lean on him, because she would never drain him. Just as it was okay for him to lean on her—it didn't make the relationship codependent in any way. There would always be give and take with them. It was a two-way street.

He sucked in a breath at the sudden sensation of a sledge-hammer crashing into his chest and head. But the pain quickly eased, and he realized their mating bond had snapped into place—filling both him and his wolf with relief, triumph, and hope. Instinctively, Marcus pushed strength and energy down the bond, feeding it to Roni. At the same time, he resumed CPR. "Please, baby, please. Brea—"

"We've got a pulse," announced Derren. "It's weak, but it's there."

Marcus felt it through the bond, felt her coming back. His relief was so profound, it took everything he had not to bawl like a fucking baby. He kept on shoving energy through the bond, just as he kept up CPR. Moments later, her body suddenly bowed and a strange sound seemed to rumble up her throat. Realizing what was happening, he tipped her onto her side; water gushed out of her mouth.

"Thank fucking God." Cradling her against him, Marcus buried his face in her hair as she coughed repeatedly, like she was still choking—as if unable to adjust to the air. "It's okay, sweetheart."

He did his best to calm her as he continued giving her strength through the bond, even though it was beginning to tire him. His wolf didn't stop in his pacing, still an emotional wreck, unable to fully shake off the fear.

Roni wanted to speak, wanted to tell Marcus that she was so glad he was okay, wanted to ask about the others in the pack, wanted to check his entire body for wounds, but she couldn't seem to catch her breath. It had felt like only a moment after falling asleep that a painful pressure was pounding on her chest.

"Here." Kathy, tears streaming down her face, handed Marcus a blanket.

Surprised to see her mother crying—*showing emotion*—Roni might have commented if she'd had the strength. Instead, she snuggled into Marcus, pleasing her anxious wolf.

Instantly, Marcus wrapped the blanket around Roni. She wasn't freezing, but she wasn't warm enough for his peace of mind. Noticing that his Alpha pair wasn't around, he turned to Trick. "How many were hurt?" If anyone from his pack had died, Marcus would have felt it through the pack link. And considering the Mercury wolves didn't appear to be interested in anyone other than Roni, he figured they were all alive.

"Dante, Tao, Dominic, Bracken, Kent, and Caleb were in bad shape," replied Trick. "Taryn halfway healed each of them in order to preserve her energy, so they're resting now. But she's about ready to drop, even with Trey lending her his strength."

Feeling Roni shiver in his arms, Marcus cradled her even closer to him. "I need to get these wet clothes off you."

Nick nodded. "Come on. You can both use one of the guest rooms."

Marcus slowly got to his feet with Roni still in his arms. His knees buckled slightly, and Eli was instantly there.

"Let me take her." When Marcus hesitated, Eli added, "I know the last thing you want is to be away from her right now, even for a second, but you're no good to her if you pass out."

And he *was* close to passing out. Lethargy was creeping up on him. He felt a sudden spurt of energy through the bond and realized it was Roni. He gave her a stern look. Her answering expression was pure stubbornness. Reluctantly, he handed her to Eli. Trick and Ryan came up on either side of him. He tried shrugging them off, determined to walk on his own steam.

"Swallow your pride, asshole," growled Trick, irritated and amused.

For no other reason than that he didn't want to lag behind, he allowed Trick and Ryan to support his weight as Nick and Shaya led the way to one of the upstairs bedrooms. Within seconds, both Marcus and Roni were naked and wrapped in a blanket while locked together as they leaned against the headboard. Seeing all her injuries, he might have lost his mind if it hadn't already been in total turmoil. Roni was scowling at the sight of his own wounds, cursing the jackals and hyenas under her breath.

Taryn burst into the room, shrugging past Nick, Shaya, Kathy, Eli, and Derren. "Let me at her."

"Taryn, you're weak right now," said Trey, trailing behind her. She really was. Hell, she was almost as pale and groggy as Roni. "You need to recover. She's alive."

Ignoring him, the Alpha female came to Roni's side. "That doesn't mean she's okay, Flintstone. She could develop pneumonia, an infection, or heart failure. I'm not taking any chances."

When Taryn went to touch her, Roni jerked back, shaking her head. No way was she going to be the cause of Taryn hitting the floor.

"Don't give me any shit, Roni Axton." Taryn pointed hard at her. "You saved my son's life, and I'm going to make damn sure you live too."

Yeah, well, Roni didn't give to receive. She pushed Taryn's hand away, her face mutinous.

"Just let her do it," grumbled Trey. "She's going to drop any minute, whether she heals you or not."

Accepting that, Roni didn't struggle as Taryn did that weird healing thing—even though it freaked her out and fascinated her at the same time. As expected, Taryn's legs gave out once she was done. Trey was there to catch her. Picking her up, he griped at her stubbornness as he began to leave the room. So she slapped him over the head.

Nick came over then, swallowing hard as he looked at Roni. "You risked your own life to keep Shaya safe. I don't know whether to thank you or strangle you for risking yourself that way."

Personally, Marcus was leaning toward the latter. He could understand Nick being torn, but the fact that she had risked her life wasn't at all acceptable to Marcus, no matter who she had been trying to protect.

Nick took her hand in his. "Thank you. But make that the last time you ever do something like that." Then he kissed her forehead. "We'll leave you both to rest." He ushered everyone out of the room.

Once the door closed behind them, Marcus nuzzled her. "Feel better?" He skimmed his hands over her, needing to touch her, to assure himself that she was alive.

Nodding, she cupped her throat. "It's not hurting anymore. And the wooziness has gone."

"Good." Then he spanked her ass hard.

Jerking, she gasped. "Hey!"

"Don't you ever, *ever*, do that again," he growled. "Risking your life is not acceptable to me."

A little startled by the fear emanating from him, she blinked. "I was protecting Shaya."

He cupped her chin firmly, unable to keep his touch gentle while his emotions were so chaotic. "You almost died, Roni. I felt it happening, felt you slipping away. Do you have any idea how terrified I was?"

"I couldn't let them have her."

"And if I'd risked my life to save Taryn?"

She would have been furious and tempted to torture him, despite that she would have understood. "Point taken."

"I understand that being an enforcer means doing what you have to do to protect your Alphas and your pack. I get that. But you're mated now, which means they have to come second. That's how it works."

The hurt in his voice made her frown. "I wasn't putting you second. But Shaya . . . It wasn't about protecting my Alpha female, it was about protecting my pregnant sister-in-law and my niece or nephew. Shaya's one of the very few people I care about. Besides, I knew you'd come. I was one hundred percent confident in you."

Feeling her sincerity through the bond, he relaxed ever so slightly. His wolf curled back his upper lip, nowhere near placated. "Never again." His hand slipped down to collar her neck. "I need you, sweetheart. Do you understand me? There's no point in anything if I don't have you."

She rubbed her nose against his, the way he often did to her. "Never again." His relief ran down the mating link. "Our bond's fully formed now. When did that happen?"

"When I was resuscitating you." He rested his forehead against hers. "I didn't realize I was holding back. It wasn't intentional."

"I know."

"I was scared of needing anyone, scared of having anyone need me."

"I get it."

"No, you don't. You have no concept of how much I need you. It scares me."

"Same here." Needing someone went against every instinct she had developed, but Marcus was essential to her.

"Then don't ever endanger your life like that again. You keep this ass safe for me." He palmed it and gave it a light squeeze. "Okay?"

"Okay." His mouth came down on hers, licking, nipping, and biting. Pulling back, he gave her one of those sensual smiles that did very interesting things to her body.

"I love you, Roni Axton."

"And I love you, Marcus Fuller." Watching as a familiar pained expression suddenly formed on his face, she said, "Seriously? Despite almost dying, you're hungry?"

"I don't know how to answer that question without irritating you." His mate just rolled her eyes, making him smile again.

CHAPTER TWENTY

W hy do you hate me?" griped Marcus.
Roni barely resisted the urge to whack her mate over the head. "I just want a little taste."

"So get your own."

"You took the last slice."

"There are other cakes."

"But I don't like them. I like chocolate cake." When he just stared at her wearing a sulky expression, she sighed. "Let me put this another way. Do you enjoy sex?"

"Yes."

"Then you'll share with me, and you'll *like* it." She stabbed her spoon into the sponge cake and scooped out a piece.

If she'd been anyone else, he'd have gone for her throat. Hearing laughter, Marcus looked up as the newly mated Caleb and Kent dragged Gabe and Hope onto the makeshift dance floor where many were already dancing. Actually, Marcus wasn't sure that what Rhett was doing could be described as dancing—he looked like he needed medical attention, which was most likely why all the enforcers stood to the side, watching in a kind of hor-rified fascination.

"I hadn't expected Caleb and Kent to imprint." Tonight was the couple's mating ceremony, and all the Phoenix wolves had come to join the celebration, since Caleb was a childhood friend of Taryn's.

Following his gaze, Roni nodded. "They look happy." They were also trying to drag Ryan onto the dance floor. He stared at them until they stopped, which had all the other enforcers laughing. She had to admit that his stare was unsettling, but she happened to like the broody male and found him easy to be around. He spoke when he had something to say, which meant there was no small talk. He was very action-orientated and unafraid to get his hands dirty, which she could relate to.

Sliding his arm around her waist, Marcus pulled Roni close. "This makes me think of our mating ceremony. How beautiful you looked." He couldn't help frowning when she ate another spoonful of his cake. "And how you tortured me the next morning."

"You deserved it." Still, she pressed a kiss to his throat—right by a scar he'd gotten from the fight with the jackals. The day after the attack, the Phoenix and Mercury enforcers had driven to the kill site and destroyed everything—cameras, videos, photographs, and motor homes. One particular area of the site was piled with bodies, most of which had been set alight.

They found the laptop computer, which the enforcers brought to Rhett. He then downloaded the membership list and all the e-mails exchanged between Lyle and the council member who had occasionally hired him. Only then had he crashed the website.

After that, they had given both the laptop and Eliza's body to the rest of the council members, leaving them to deal with the issue—but first making sure they had copies of everything, letting the council know they *would* deal with the ugly matter themselves if they decided to "overlook" it.

As for the matter of Nolan Richards, the bastard responsible for uploading the vid of Roni's attack . . . she had done her best to track him down, only to find that he was already dead. Suspecting Marcus, Nick, or Eli had something to do with that, she had confronted them. They had all answered her questions with "No comment"—which meant all three of them had to be responsible.

She'd been pissed that they had robbed her of her revenge by dealing with the matter themselves, but she couldn't really expect different behavior from three extremely dominant, overprotective male shifters. They would be offended and enraged on her behalf, and would have seen such a move as taking care of her.

"Ro!"

Peering down, Roni found Kye chewing on his thumb. "Hey there, little man. Melted anymore hearts today?"

He held up his arms, clenching and unclenching his little fists. "Up!"

Roni picked him up and perched him on her hip. He pointed at Marcus's cake and began smacking his lips together. "Want some?" Scooping a little chocolate sauce on her spoon, she fed it to him—ignoring Marcus's grumbling. Adding to her mate's torture, she then fed herself a little more of the cake.

With Dante at her side, Jaime came over, cradling a baby girl in her arms—Roni's niece. "Wow, you're getting Marcus to share. It really must be love."

Marcus looked at Dante, who grinned at him and mouthed "whipped." *Asshole.*

"Why are you talking so quietly?" Roni asked Jaime.

"I'm hiding from your mother. I promised I'd hand Willow back to her . . . but I don't want to."

Kathy and Nick literally fought over Willow Mika Axton all the time, both equally possessive and protective. Shaya seemed to be enjoying the reprieve from being on the receiving end of such overprotectiveness. The Alpha female had been an absolute trooper throughout labor, while Nick had been white as a sheet and had nearly lost consciousness.

Stroking a hand over the baby's small tuft of blonde hair, Roni said to Kye, "What do you think? Isn't she beautiful?"

Kye's little face scrunched up. "No."

Jaime laughed quietly. "I think she's gorgeous, like her mom. I want to keep her."

At that moment, Taryn and Trey joined them. "Oh, Kye, you can't eat Uncle Marcus's cake," Taryn gently admonished. "He'll sulk for, like, ever."

When his father held out his arms, Kye practically jumped into them. Trey's gaze danced from Roni to Marcus. "Have you decided which one of you is switching packs?"

Sighing, Marcus exchanged a look with Roni before replying, "We can't choose."

Taryn pursed her lips. "Well, we have a suggestion."

Unable to guess where this was going, since he'd considered every possible option, Marcus frowned. "What's that?"

"Instead of switching packs, you could belong to both."

"That won't work," said Roni. "Our wolves would feel confused and unsettled."

"It'll work if Trey and Nick blood. That would join the packs. Not unite them into one, but connect the pack links on a psychic level through the Alphas."

"That would be awesome." Jaime's eyes went wide with excitement. "Please say you will!" Kathy suddenly appeared, scowling, and Jaime laughed a little awkwardly. "Oh, *there* you are."

"Give me back my granddaughter." Kathy reached for the baby, but then Nick was there—an amused Shaya in tow.

"Why does everyone keep disappearing with Willow?" he grumbled, taking the baby into his arms. Shaya placed a soft kiss on the baby's head.

Kathy placed her hands on her hips, complaining, "You're always holding her."

"Of course I am." Nick stroked his finger over her cheek. "She's my baby girl."

"And she's my grandchild. I suspect she'll be my one and only grandchild, unless you and Shaya decide to have more." Kathy cast Roni a meaningful glance.

Instead of being annoyed, Roni was amused. "Be as bitchy as you like, woman, I saw you crying when I nearly drowned." Kathy just huffed.

Brushing his lips over her temple, Marcus said, "Don't remind me of that day." The fear and anxiety hadn't quite left him yet. As if she sensed that, she fleetingly rubbed his lower back. His mate still wasn't a touchy-feely person, and he knew she never would be. But she was slowly becoming more and more tactile with him.

"I was just telling Roni and Marcus our little alternative to them switching packs." Taryn repeated her proposal to Nick and Shaya.

"You would be willing to do that?" Shaya asked Trey.

The Phoenix Alpha male shrugged carelessly. "I don't want to lose Marcus to another pack. He's my friend as well as one of my best enforcers. Besides, Roni would make a valuable addition. That makes this a logical move." And Trey was all about logic. When Kye struggled to get down, Trey placed him on the ground before turning to Nick. "What about you?"

Nick looked like he wanted to stamp his foot. "I don't even like being blooded to my pack members."

Marcus gave Nick a look of mock sympathy. "Need a hug? Bro?" He received a glower.

Stifling a smile, Shaya laid a hand on Nick's shoulder. "I think it's a good idea. We don't want to lose Roni. And if you connect with Trey, Marcus would be ours as much as theirs."

"But which Alpha would they answer to?" asked Dante, sliding his arm around Jaime. "It can't be both."

Trey snorted. "When has Marcus ever answered to anyone for anything?"

Nick sighed. "Yeah, Roni's just the same. You won't get obedience from her."

"No," agreed Taryn, "but we'll get someone who can handle

Greta. That makes your sister worth her weight in gold." Jaime nodded in agreement. "Packs have done it before, including my father's. As you know, Lance collects alliances, and it worked out well for him."

Feeling someone fiddle with the back of her top, Roni twisted to see Dominic reading the label inside her collar. "What are you doing?"

He just nodded. "Made in Heaven. I knew it." Jaime laughed, Marcus growled, and everyone else groaned. "I tell ya, I didn't know angels could fly so low." He chuckled when Marcus took a swing at him.

When Roni went to retaliate with a cheesy line of her own, Marcus clapped his hand over her mouth. "No."

Eli, Tao, and the Phoenix and Mercury enforcers appeared, took in an irritated Marcus covering Roni's mouth while Dominic laughed hysterically, and instantly summed up the situation. Ryan obligingly cuffed Dominic over the head.

"Ry! Ry! Ry!" To everyone's amusement, Kye proceeded to climb the enforcer like he was a fence post. Poor Ryan couldn't have looked more awkward.

Coming to Roni's side carrying Lilah, Greta lightly kissed Roni on the cheek and gave her a winning, affectionate smile. "Hello, sweetheart, how are you feeling?"

"I'm good. You?"

"Oh, I'm fine. Now that one of my boys has found a worthy female, I couldn't be happier."

Taryn leaned toward Roni, her voice quiet. "Roni, I have to know how you do it."

Greta sneered at the Alpha female. "It's rude to whisper."

"And yet, I just don't care."

"So," began Trey, obviously looking to halt the argument, "what do you think, Nick? You willing to blood or not?" As he elaborated on the matter for Greta and the enforcers, Nick thought about it for a moment.

When the Mercury Alpha male finally spoke, it was to Roni and Marcus. "Is it what you guys want?"

Marcus looked at his mate, who was worrying her bottom lip. He could sense through their bond that she was seriously considering it, but something held her back. "What is it?"

"I like the idea of not having to choose between packs, but we'd still have to choose where to live, so I don't see how belonging to both packs would make much difference."

"We could just do what we do now: spend a few days a week here, and spend a few days a week at Phoenix territory." It would mean that Roni had a break from Kathy when she needed it—as Eli predicted, the woman still did her best to taunt Roni and interfere in her life. Nick had eased up a little, but it was still irritating.

"That could work." The arrangement would allow her to break away from her family's hold without actually leaving them.

Nick nodded, handing Willow over to Shaya. "Then that's what we'll do."

"You sure?" Roni didn't want him to do it if he were truly against it.

"I don't want to lose you to another pack, and I don't want Fuller here twenty-four/seven. This works for me."

Marcus chuckled, seeing the humor in Nick's eyes.

Turning to face each other, the two Alphas sliced their palms and then slapped them together. Roni felt it as the links combined. It wasn't like the two were one, but like each was an extension of the other. Everyone on the dance floor immediately sensed it and crowded around them. To Roni's relief, they all seemed happy with the decision. In actuality, though, the only opinion that truly mattered was that of her mate.

Long after the celebrations were over, as she was fixing him a late-night snack in her lodge—*their* lodge—she asked without looking at him, "Are you sure you're okay with being a member of both packs? I mean, you don't feel like you've betrayed Trey?" It would be stupid, but she could understand it.

From his seat at the kitchen table, Marcus replied, "Hmm." He had no idea what she'd asked. Come on, did she really expect him to understand a word she said when she was strolling around in nothing but a tank top and a pair of boy shorts? It was one of the hottest things ever and gave him little peeks of that ass he loved. It didn't matter that he'd been inside her only twenty minutes ago. He could never get enough of her.

Confused by his response, she looked over her shoulder . . . and rolled her eyes. "Could you stop ogling my ass for just one second?"

"Hmm."

Placing his sandwich on the table, she repeated her questions. And he looked at her with pity.

"Of course I'm okay with it." All he'd wanted was a solution that made her happy. She was happy. Problem solved.

Feeling his sincerity through the bond, she relaxed. "Just checking." By the time she'd cleared the countertop, he was done eating. As she went to take his plate, he lifted her and placed her on his lap, straddling him.

He bit her bottom lip. "I'm still hungry." But this was another kind of hunger. "Feed me." The second her mouth opened for him, he thrust his tongue inside. He took what he wanted, gave her what she needed. Fisting a hand in her hair, he yanked her head aside and latched onto her pulse—sucking, nibbling, and marking. Claws pricked into his arms warningly, reminding him he was dealing with a dominant female who would let him lead but wouldn't let him push. So he bit her hard, reminding her she was dealing with a dominant male who couldn't be handled.

She hissed out a breath. "I should claw you for that."

"So vicious." Bunching up her tank top, he peeled it off and flung it aside. "It's one of the things my wolf loves most about you." He growled in approval when she leaned back and draped her arms over the edge of the table, arching her body so that her breasts thrusted upward.

"That's because your wolf is bloodthirsty." The words came out kind of breathy, since he was now suckling her nipple while his skilled hands lightly but possessively skated over her. There was nothing hurried about his movements. This seduction was languorous, almost lazy.

"I love that you're vicious, but I also love that you're soft-hearted with those who matter to you."

Offended, she scowled. "I'm *not* soft." She lost her scowl when he moved onto her neglected nipple. At the same time, one hand gripped her hip and began grinding her against him. She could feel him, hard and hot, through her shorts.

"Don't worry, I won't tell anyone." He punctuated that by biting the peak of her breast. He cupped them both in his hands, marveling at how perfectly they fit there. How perfectly she fit against him. "Mine." He licked his claiming mark. "My Roni."

"Yes," she agreed. And he was hers. Achingly gorgeous, charming as hell, danger prettily dressed—and all hers. Her stomach clenched as his hand slid inside her shorts and smoothly drove a finger inside her.

He groaned. "You're already wet for me." The thought had his cock throbbing, demanding release. Marcus ground the heel of his hand over her clit with each thrust of his finger, all the while kissing and biting her neck. She squirmed and moaned, making it clear exactly what she wanted. Withdrawing his finger, he shoved it inside her mouth. "Suck." Boldly holding his gaze, she sucked and licked.

Roni suddenly found herself sprawled on her back over the kitchen table, her legs hooked over his shoulders, and her boy shorts in shreds. Apparently the unhurried seduction was over. "That was my favorite pair."

Shoving down his jeans, Marcus fisted his cock. He was heavy and aching, and her hungry gaze almost made him come right then. "You want this inside you?"

"Yes."

"Tell me. Tell me you want it."

She licked her lips as she watched him stroke himself. "I want it."

Cupping her ass, Marcus angled her just right and plunged deep inside her, seating himself to the balls. Jaw clenched, he fucked her just the way she liked it—hard, fast, rough, and deep. Seeing her lying there with her hair flowing around her, those breasts bouncing with each thrust, and her pussy stretching over his cock, he knew he wouldn't last long. Her claws shot out, leaving deep grooves in the wood as she arched against him, moaning. "That's right. I want to hear you." Her eyes flashed wolf, making his own wolf lunge toward her.

"Come here. I want to bite you."

It was her wolf's need, he knew. Marcus gave her a wicked smile. "In a minute." As he'd expected, her claws slashed his chest. Not enough to draw blood, just enough to communicate that she didn't like being denied. He growled low in his throat. "Be good."

With her wolf's irritation driving her, Roni sprung up and bit into his pectoral. Instead of fighting her, Marcus pounded into her even harder. Satisfied, Roni slid onto her back, once again arching into his thrusts. That was when a hand snapped around her throat, collaring her. Roni snarled, "Let. Go." But he didn't. Of course he didn't. He bit into the spot behind her ear.

"Say it, Roni."

The order rung with dominance; it was reflexive to ignore it. His hand flexed around her throat. "*Say it.*"

Practically melting as his thumb briefly circled her clit, she relented. "I love you."

His mouth crushed hers, biting and tasting. "I'm going to come. You're going to come with me." He hardened his thrusts as he again circled her clit with his thumb before pressing down hard. A scream seemed to tear from her throat as her pussy contracted around him. Pleasure whipped through him, making him stiffen and slam deep one final time as he emptied himself inside her.

There was an ominous creak, and then the table collapsed beneath them.

"We can't keep breaking furniture."

He nuzzled her throat. "It's worth it every time."

Yeah, it really was.

Carefully scooping her up, he carried her to the bedroom and gently laid her on the bed. Crawling on top of her, he brushed the hair from her face. "I love you, gorgeous."

"Hmm."

"Say it."

"I already did."

"So say it again." But, of course, she didn't. He nipped her earlobe. "Now."

"Okay, okay, I love you." She moaned as his mouth took hers, devastating it, claiming it, reminding her she was his. It was only minutes later of him caressing and sucking on her breasts that she felt something long and thick brush against her thigh. She sighed inwardly. "You can't be ready to go again."

"It's your fault."

"Give me an hour to rest."

Straddling her, he fisted his cock. "No. Now."

Really, he could be such a spoiled little bastard at times. Watching him stroke himself, she cocked her head. "Did you know that if you get caught masturbating in Indonesia, you can be decapitated as punishment?"

"*Roni.*"

"What? What did I say?"

Acknowledgments

I know that it's important to thank those who help with research, so thank you very much to Google. I couldn't have done it without you.

A major thanks to my husband and children, who lovingly overlook how often I zone out to listen to those voices in my head. I have to express my gratitude to Nick Jr. for helping to keep said children entertained so I could finish this book.

Humongous thanks to my editor, JoVon Sotak, and the rest of the Montlake Romance team—particularly Melody Guy and Jessica Poore. All of your help and support have been invaluable.

Last but not least: thank you to all the people who have taken a chance on my book. I really hope you enjoyed it!

About the Author

Author Suzanne Wright, a native of England, can't remember a time when she wasn't creating characters and telling their tales. Even as a child, she loved writing poems, plays, and stories; as an adult, Wright has published eight novels: *From Rags*, three Deep In Your Veins novels, and now four books in the Phoenix Pack series. Wright, who lives in Liverpool with her husband and two children, freely admits that she hates housecleaning and can't cook, but that she always shares chocolate.

Website: www.suzannewright.co.uk

Blog: www.suzannewrightsblog.blogspot.co.uk

Twitter: www.twitter.com/suz_wright

Facebook: www.facebook.com/pages/Suzanne-Wright/1392617144284756

25354161R00190

Printed in Poland
by Amazon Fulfillment
Poland Sp. z o.o., Wrocław